THE NUCLEAR DRUID

EXTINCTION PROTOCOL

BOOK 2

FELIX R. SAVAGE

THE NUCLEAR DRUID
EXTINCTION PROTOCOL, BOOK 2

First published in the United States of America in 2017 by Knights Hill Publishing.

Cover design by Christian Bentulan
Photography by Andrew Dobell
Interior design and layout by Felix R. Savage

ISBN-10: 1-937396-29-0
ISBN-13: **978-1-937396-29-9**

THE NUCLEAR DRUID

EXTINCTION PROTOCOL

BOOK 2

FELIX R. SAVAGE

CHAPTER 1

A covered cart jolted through the forest. It was night, but a pale light seeped through the snowclouds. The wind dislodged snow from overhanging boughs, slopping it on the shoulders of the infantry walking behind the cart, and on the cloaked riders ahead of it.

One of the riders slumped in his saddle. He was tied to the pommel. Another rider led his horse on a short rein. His hands—bound in front of him—looked clumsy, elephantine. They had put high-potential gauntlets on him, rubber on the inside, leather on the outside, stretching up past his elbows, so he couldn't try anything.

His name was Dhjerga Lizp. He had deserted from the Earth front. They had caught him just twenty miles from home. He'd been an idiot to make for home, he knew. At least he hadn't gone *straight* home, so the twins could plausibly claim to know nothing about it.

The horses' harness jingled. For an instant, Dhjerga heard another sound. A high, metallic clattering, keeping time with the jingling of the harness. He glanced up, but saw nothing.

*

Inside the covered cart, a sentry kept watch over the horse-powered generator. This machine consisted of a cast sulphur globe mounted on a horizontal spindle, which was connected to the front axle of the cart. As the cart moved, the globe whirred around. The friction device, a large piece of burnished leather, hung in its mounting at a distance of two feet from the globe. The generator was not presently in operation. The sentry had nothing to do except keep an eye

1

on the storage jar, a six-foot aluminum-coated cylinder decorated with the raised seal of the Magistocracy—a two-headed eagle. A metal sphere stuck up from the jar's lid.

The sentry didn't notice at first that it was getting warmer in the back of the cart. He tugged at the collar of his shapeless khaki uniform, without understanding why. His function was to understand nothing except the orders he had been given. And the Magistrates hadn't said anything about warmth. They wouldn't like it, doubtless; they never liked anyone to be comfortable. The sentry had just enough self-awareness to think—*Screw them*. Seated against the side of the cart, with his rifle beside him, he dozed off.

In the moments after the sentry fell asleep, it got darker and darker inside the cart.

Blue brambles of electricity wriggled from the sides of the storage jar, and from the steel ball on top. They shot off spikes that humped and writhed into the corner behind the device.

In that corner, the shadows clumped as dark and dense as a living thing. They heaved and shimmered and coagulated into a man.

Naked as the day he was born, at first. Six feet, pasty-skinned, broad-shouldered, with the pale trace of a removed tattoo on one bicep—it had depicted a big-bottomed girl wrapped in a Scottish flag—and a ginger buzz-cut.

Half-stunned, he toppled onto his knees. Something fell from his right hand with a clatter.

By the time he hit the floor he was wearing a blue dress uniform. The Navy blue, and his soft-soled gray and orange boots, designed for spaceship decks, clashed with the gentle tones of leather and wood around him. He seemed to give

2

off an unnatural light of his own, actinic, blue-tinted. Within seconds it faded.

The thump woke the sleeping sentry.

The two men stared at each other across the dark interior of the cart.

Colm saw the sentry's khaki uniform.

Oh, Jesus. He's a Ghost—

—and he's got a gun.

As the sentry reached for his rifle, Colm lunged. He grabbed the rifle and wrenched it out of reach, while slamming the heel of his other hand into the sentry's nose. In a panic, he brought the butt of the rifle down on the man's head. The sentry slumped. Blood trickled out of his nose. A loud snore rattled from his mouth. Colm knelt over him, poised to hit him again, until he was sure that the man was still breathing, but wouldn't be waking up for a while.

Colm had killed hundreds of Ghosts over the years, but almost always from the metal cocoon of his cockpit. Now, as the adrenaline wore off, he realized he couldn't kill this one. It was partly a surrender to squeamishness—he was not a man who enjoyed killing, certainly not with his bare hands— and partly doubt. Did the guy deserve to die? Colm didn't know who was an enemy and who was a friend anymore. He didn't even know where he *was*.

The floor jolted rhythmically. He was in a moving vehicle.

He found a chink where the canvas roof met the side wall, and peeked out, gripping the Ghost's rifle in one hand.

It was night, but the snow caking the trees gave an eerie visibility. Cold wind brought tears to his eyes. He saw horses, kitted out with colorful saddle-cloths and tasselled bridles. Their riders sat erect, swathed in black hooded cloaks with a red symbol on the back, which resembled a stylized two-headed eagle.

All except one, who slumped, his hood down around his shoulders, as if he didn't care about the icy wind and the flurrying snow.

Dhjerga!

Dhjerga Lizp was the Ghost who'd helped him liberate Juradis from the sentrienza. Then he'd left. Colm had followed him here—wherever *here* was.

Colm drew breath to shout Dhjerga's name. In the nick of time, he saw that Dhjerga's hands, muffled in huge gloves, were tied together with a chain that looped around the front bit of his saddle.

He was a prisoner.

Colm glanced back at the sentry—still out cold.

Well, it stood to reason, didn't it? Dhjerga had deserted from the Ghost army.

And deserters generally get caught.

As the reality that he was surrounded by enemies sank in, Colm miserably dropped onto his haunches. Five minutes ago he'd been on the weather deck of the *Unsinkable,* the old supercarrier where he had served as a pilot, playing the spoons, while Gilliam Tripsilion Nulth the queazel held the door. Now he was—*where?*

And where were his spoons?

He felt around on the floor until he found them. They were just coffee spoons, borrowed from the office of Admiral Hyland, a.k.a. the Rat, the commander of the *Unsinkable.* Colm's father used to play soup spoons, ugly tarnished things he'd inherited from *his* grandfather. It was a pity the old bastard had never told Colm exactly what the trick was. Colm pocketed the spoons and glanced up at the weird contraption that occupied most of the space inside the cart.

A spinning globe, with a sort of a broom suspended where it would brush one side of the globe. That end of the broom sprouted long wires. The other end terminated in a metal ball, a few inches from a similar ball atop an embossed jar taller than Colm.

The arrangement rang a faint bell, although he couldn't put his finger on it. It looked strikingly old-fashioned. Every component had clearly been made by hand and painstakingly ornamented. The bolt-action rifle in Colm's hand, with its carved wooden stock, exuded the same primitive ethos. This cart was drawn by *horses,* for God's sake.

Feeling desperate, he peered out of the chink again. It was getting on for evening. Snowflakes twirled in the wind. The riders had their heads lowered, their faces muffled. Dhjerga sagged over his horse's neck. The possibility that he was injured struck Colm.

He had to get out of here, and get Dhjerga out of here, too.

With what?

This sodding antique rifle?

Well, Ghosts had used identical rifles to mow down humans across eighteen colony systems. But it only had a 10-cartridge magazine, and there were six riders, which meant he'd have to make every bullet coun. In the snow. With dusk coming on.

He scrambled to the back of the cart and made another chink by working the canvas loose from the tailboard. He immediately binned the idea of opening fire like some sort of berserk commando. A company of Ghost infantry trudged in the cart's ruts, shapeless in sodden cloaks, snow-epauleted. There had to be fifty of them.

He turned back to the contraption in the middle of the cart. He could scarcely see it in the gloom. But he suddenly realized that he could *feel* it.

He had an esthesia implant. It enabled him to fly a spaceship by feel, processing real-time information from the ship's systems in the form of sensory feedback. For example, he would experience the electrical output from a ship's reactor as a sensation of pulsating warmth in his lower belly …

… and that was exactly what he could feel now. A warm throb. Very faint, compared to the output of a typical ship's reactor. But definitely there.

He edged closer to the ornate jar. That's where the warmth was coming from.

The pieces of the device clicked into place in his mind.

Spinning globe.

That leather thing applies friction.

The broom's the collector.

And *this* is …

A freaking Leyden jar.

He reached out a hand towards it—and then drew back.

You can do better than that, Mackenzie.

He dug the spoons out of his pocket and cast around for something to use as a string.

*

The convoy stopped. Colm had finished what he was doing. He knelt at the chink, watching the riders dismount and order the footsoldiers around. Build a fire. Put up the tents. See to the horses. He could understand everything they said, which seemed odd, because wherever this was, it wasn't Earth.

Snow was now falling steadily. The infantry got a fire going in a clearing among the trees. The cart stayed on the road—that is, the unpaved, snow-covered track.

Dhjerga was hauled off his horse and dumped in front of the fire. He sat motionless, his heavy gloves resting on his knees, staring into the flames that licked over the soggy wood.

At last one of the footsoldiers plodded towards the cart. Colm tensed in dismay. It wouldn't do him any good to nail a single grunt! He picked up the rifle and darted to the tailgate. When he heard a bolt being drawn back, he fired a shot through it.

The report deafened him. Wood splinters flew. As his hearing returned, he heard a commotion outside—"What the hell?! Lanke!" That must be the name of the sentry, who Colm had had to knock out for a second time. He probably should've just killed the guy. Scruples wouldn't get him out of here alive.

The tailgate fell open.

Outside, someone held up a lantern.

One of the riders leapt in, pointing a handgun into the gloom.

He didn't see Colm crouching behind the ornate Leyden jar.

He saw the unconscious sentry.

"Lanke's down," he shouted. He had an indefinable foreign accent. "His weapon's missing. Gimme some light in here."

The lantern-bearer climbed into the cart. Several more people pressed into the circle of shuddering yellow light behind him.

One of them saw Colm. He yelled in shock and levelled his gun.

7

CHAPTER 2

Colm swung the sentry's rifle up, holding it awkwardly, because he was wearing his boots on his hands.

He'd picked their velcro loose and used it to fasten the coffee spoons to two of the wires from the collector—three feet long, nice and stiff. He'd used the sentry's belt to tie the wires to the barrel of the rifle.

One of the spoons touched the first rider who'd entered the cart.

The other rider fired at Colm. The round carved a furrow through his hair.

The second spoon touched the ball on top of the Leyden jar.

That's what it was called on Earth, anyway. It had been invented at the University of Leyden in the 18th century. It was probably called something else here. But it worked the same way.

It stored the electricity produced by the electrostatic generator. With an apparatus this big, the charge probably amounted to hundreds of kilovolts.

Colm had improvised a discharge pole.

The spoons and the wire created a path from the jar to the astonished Ghost. A mighty spark leapt along the path, lighting up the inside of the cart like a strobe, emitting a noise like a gunshot.

The rider's scream ripped through Colm's head. The shock threw the man backwards against his companion, who collided with the lantern-bearer and knocked him out of the cart. The lantern went out.

Colm still had the rifle. He flattened himself against the side of the cart and sprayed bullets out of the tailgate, shooting from the hip, not caring if he hit anything or not. When the weapon was empty, he threw it down. He would have liked to take one of the riders' pistols, but it was far too dangerous to touch the bodies. He could smell the porky odor of charring,

Silver conducts electricity nicely.

Sorry about the spoons, Admiral.

The boots on Colm's hands had been extra insurance. Wood is a poor conductor, but the stock of the rifle had felt a bit damp. Had he held it in his bare hands, he could've been electrocuted, too. He was still alive, so it had worked.

Carrying the boots, he circled the bodies, very carefully, in the darkness, and jumped out of the cart. Confused yells and running steps approached. Another lantern bobbled across the snow.

Colm ran headlong towards the fire, in his sock feet, crashing into people running the other way.

Dhjerga was still sitting by the fire. Everyone else had rushed towards the cart, drawn by the havoc Colm had created.

Recognition lit up Dhjerga's eyes. "How the *hell*—?"

Colm hauled him to his feet. "Let's get out of here." His feet were wet and stinging. He hopped on one leg, putting on a velcro-less boot, although there wasn't really time for that.

"Help me get these fucking gloves off," Dhjerga said urgently.

The gloves were joined together by a chain that ran around the back of Dhjerga's neck. Colm yanked it up and over Dhjerga's head, taking off the top layer of his scalp in the process. They stumbled away from the fire. Dhjerga hurled the gloves into the trees. "Next stop, home," he said, grabbing Colm's arm. Then he released it. "No. Wait. I'm going to dead a few of these fuckers first. What'd you *do* to them?"

Colm looked back at the cart. Chaos reigned around it as the riders pushed their minions to tend to the casualties. There probably wasn't any charge left in the bodies, as it would have dissipated when they touched the ground. "Electrocuted them," he said.

"What?" Dhjerga said irritably, as if he didn't understand.

A footsoldier clumped towards them, carrying his rifle.

Dhjerga raised a hand, palm out. "Give me that," he said.

The solder hesitated.

"I command you!"

The soldier mutely handed the weapon over.

"Thanks," Dhjerga said. He shot the soldier.

The soldiers around the cart turned towards the noise.

The lantern light turned them into highly visible targets. Dhjerga fired rapidly and accurately from the shoulder, darting sideways between shots, so that return fire aimed at his muzzle flash went astray. Ghost after Ghost fell. When Dhjerga had emptied the rifle he looked around for Colm. who was crouching in the snow, trying to stay un-shot. "Out of ammo. Well, at least I got a few of them. Let's go."

Colm heaved himself upright. He knew that Ghosts like Dhjerga treated their 'copies' with extreme callousness. The footsoldiers were not men who had once been children: they were some sort of clones, created by an unknown energy-to-mass conversion process, which the Ghosts called magic. But they were made of flesh and blood, and they breathed, and ate and drank, and died. Colm swallowed a cold, queasy knot.

The warmth of esthesia feedback in his stomach had gone. They crashed around the tents to where the horses were tethered under a large tree.

"I hope you can ride," Dhjerga said.

"Where is this place?"

"It's the middle of fucking nowhere, obviously. This forest belongs to my family, although we've got no use for it. I want to stay away from power sources for the moment." Dhjerga shouldered in between the horses. "Don't want them following me home."

The horses stamped their feet and shied. Some looked like pack animals. A few of the larger, shiny-coated mounts still had their saddles and bridles on. Dhjerga pointed at a large gray mare. "You take that one." He clucked and cooed at a sorrel gelding and swung up onto his back.

Colm hadn't ridden a horse since he was seven. He wedged one foot into a stirrup and scrambled into the mare's saddle. "I don't even know what planet I'm on," he grunted.

"Kisperet. My homeworld. It's a nice planet, when people aren't trying to kill you." Dhjerga kicked his own horse. When he realized Colm wasn't following, he circled back and grabbed Colm's bridle.

Gunfire crackled around them. The Ghosts were shooting into the forest, aiming at any shadow that moved. Dhjerga guided the horses away from the fire at a walking pace—all they could manage in the trees.

A cloaked figure rose up almost under their hooves. Moonlight glinted on a pistol barrel.

Dhjerga let out a wild cry and rode the man down. The horses, Colm realized with a feeling of sick recognition, were trained like their riders. Trained for war. Steel-shod hooves trampled the man's flesh. Colm's horse plunged forward of its own accord and bit the poor bastard's upflung arm. Colm dragged on the reins, nearly pulling his arms out.

Dhjerga swivelled all the way out of his saddle and snatched the man's pistol.

The snow had stopped. Moonlight shone between the trees. Blood glistened on the mutilated thing twitching in the snow.

"They're just copies, right?" Colm yelled at Dhjerga. "It doesn't matter about killing them. They're not really people! Right?"

Dhjerga's teeth flashed. "It can be hard to tell the difference!" he said.

The moonlight now shone full on Colm. The man on the ground twitched. His eyes found Colm. "You ... were in the cart."

"Yes," Colm said.

"Where ... do you come from?"

"Earth," Colm said.

"Earth." The man coughed up blood. "Impossible. There are no mages ... on Earth."

"Believe me now, arsewipe?" Dhjerga said. He shot the man in the head.

"Was *he* a copy?" Colm said angrily.

"No," Dhjerga said. He jumped down, ripped the blood-sodden cloak off the corpse, and tossed it at Colm as he clambered back onto his horse. "Hide your hair. None of us have red hair. That's how he knew you weren't from here. Also, your uniform."

Wordlessly, Colm wrapped the cloak around his upper body. It might help to keep out the cold. The wind cut like a knife, although the sky was mostly clear.

Dhjerga led the horses on a circuitous path through the trees. By the time they reached the road again, they had left the campsite far behind.

There was something off about the shadows on the snow. They seemed to be faintly doubled … *tripled.* Colm looked up for the first time—and gasped in astonishment.

Two moons.

One small, green-speckled crescent.

And one bright beige pearl that spanned a full quarter of the sky.

"What the fuck is that?"

"Huh?" Dhjerga looked where he was pointing. "Oh, that's Cerriwan. It's one of those, you know, the big planets that are made of clouds."

"A gas giant," Colm translated.

"If you say so."

"Wait. This planet—Kisperet?—is actually a moon?"

"Well, we have got our own moon. Look, it's right there."

"I can see it."

Colm could also see a very bright star at the horizon. To outshine a moon and a gas giant, it had to be incredibly luminous, or else incredibly close.

"What's *that?*" he asked, without much hope. The Ghosts were so uninterested in astrophysics that it seemed unlikely they bothered to name stars.

But Dhjerga surprised him. "Oh, you can actually see that from the Kuiper Belt." Colm and Dhjerga had met for the second time in the Kuiper Belt, two years ago. "I thought it looked familiar, so I asked your encyclopedia thing."

"The net."

"Yes, the glowy window that you talk into. We call that star the Spearhead, but you call it Rho Cass … something."

"Rho Cassiopeiae."

"That was it."

Rho Cassiopeiae was a hypergiant. This world, Kisperet, must lie very close to it: the goddamn thing was casting *shadows*.

Colm felt dizzy. He clutched his horse's reins in white-knuckled hands.

Rho Cassiopeiae lay 8,000 light years from Earth.

Dhjerga suddenly twisted around in his saddle. "Shit!"

"What?" Colm said dully. He was mentally reeling. He'd come *eight thousand* light years from home. And it had taken him no time at all.

"The bastards are chasing us, aren't they?" Now Colm heard the distant drumming of hooves. "Why couldn't you have brought some of those great rapid-firing weapons you Earth people have? I'd have deaded them all in one go."

"Sorry. I didn't expect to land in the middle of yet another bloody war."

Dhjerga did not notice the irony. "This isn't a war yet. But it *will* be, at this rate." He reached over and slapped Colm's horse on the rump, before kicking his own steed. "Ride for your life!" he shouted over his shoulder.

CHAPTER 3

Colm could not really ride. He'd bumped along a few pony trails as a child. That was more than 99% of human beings had done. So at least he had a dim idea of how not to fall off. But he couldn't ride like Dhjerga—glued in the saddle, moving with the horse as if he were surgically attached to it. He bounced and slid around, while Dhjerga alternately laughed and yelled at him.

Behind them, the thudding hooves drew closer. Dhjerga stopped laughing and pushed his horse into a flat-out gallop. Thankfully, this made Colm's mare think it was a race. She stretched out her neck and thundered after her stablemate. When Dhjerga jerked his horse's head around and careened down a much narrower trail, Colm's mount followed without any input from him.

They half-cantered and half-slid downhill between the snow-laden trees. At this point Colm was merely clinging on, his hands locked on the pommel. The moonlight glimmered between the trees on black water, flowing fast between banks fringed with sheet ice. They turned and rode upstream. Colm sagged over his horse's neck. Dhjerga said, "By Scota's grave, that was close. I *think* we've lost them. There isn't officially a road here at all."

"Won't they see the hoofprints?"

"Not at the speed they were going; and they don't know the area. By the time they turn around and come back, the trail'll be all mucked up with their own prints."

Firelight shone from the windows of a cottage. A man appeared at the door, carrying one of the ubiquitous Ghost rifles.

"It's me!" Dhjerga leapt off his horse and embraced the man. They spoke in low tones. Dhjerga waved at Colm to dismount. "This is Hralf. He' ll look after the horses. Come on."

Colm patted his mare's sweaty neck. "Thanks for the ride," he whispered. Even if she was a vicious brute, she'd saved his life. He wondered what the hell the Ghosts were doing with horses, 8,000 light years from Earth.

"Hurry up!" Dhjerga said.

The cottage looked warm and cozy and safe. But Dhjerga ploughed on past it, past the outbuildings, along a narrow trail shovelled out of the snow. The trees straggled away. On the far side of an open field, a dam blocked the river, walling off the head of the valley. Snow coated brick spillways. The river flowed fast and black out from under a patio covered with a pristine white carpet. On the patio stood a grim blockhouse with unlit windows.

The door of the blockhouse was not locked. Colm followed Dhjerga into a cavernous hall, which nevertheless felt cramped, because most of it was taken up by the massive turbine shaft descending into a pit in the middle of the hall, and the generator mounted above it.

"A hydroelectric plant!" Colm exclaimed. At last, *something* familiar.

*

"I'm going to open the intake gates," Dhjerga called up from the dark, mouldy-smelling shaft.

"Roger," Colm yelled. He leapt up the steps to the catwalk that ran around the room at head height. Leaning over the rail to reach the generator, he threw the lever that released the rotor.

The roar of rushing water echoed up from the pit. Dhjerga clambered out of the shaft, caked with moss and rust.

Colm hurried back along the catwalk to the little black-start generator mounted on the wall. It hummed as water poured through a 2-inch iron feedstock pipe, spinning its rotor. The stator was equipped with permanent magnets. That created enough power to induce an electrical field in the rotor windings of the big generator. The Ghosts knew about electromagnets. But the plant produced only DC current— Colm had had a peek inside the generator housing and seen that there was a commutator on the windings. They hadn't even discovered alternating current. There were pretty pictures of deer and girls enameled on the generator's bell-shaped housing.

"No such thing as a transformer?" he said as he came down off the catwalk. "No regulator? No *wires?*" Actually, he could see some cabling coming out of the top of the generator. It hung in swags between ceiling brackets thick with cobwebs.

"I don't understand half the things you say," Dhjerga said. "Come on, quick." He grabbed the kerosene lantern and hurried along a dark hall, into another large room. Colm followed, stiff and aching, but hopeful. He reckoned that if the hydro plant generated a sufficient load, he could use it to return to the *Unsinkable*. He was done with this miserable, snowbound planet. He would have a talk with Dhjerga, so he could say he'd tried, and then go.

"These are the batteries," Dhjerga said. "They're a bit small, I know. You probably have much bigger ones on Earth."

A row of wooden tubs marched down the center of the hall. Each tub was ten feet long and four feet high, and filled to the brim with water.

"Ah," Colm said. "The type of battery you can take a bath in. Yeah, I've got one of those at home, too." He was starting to wonder if he and Dhjerga were really speaking English. Sometimes he could hear a strange echo behind their voices. And what Dhjerga had just said was complete gibberish. These were not batteries.

"You wouldn't want to have a bath in this stuff," Dhjerga said. "Quick, let's assemble them. The faster we're done, the faster we can get out of here."

A clatter made Colm jump. In the far corner of the room, two small boys, dressed in stiff trousers and hand-knitted sweaters, were lifting a metal disc as wide as they were tall off a stack of identical discs. They staggered with it over to a tub and rolled it into the rack on top of the tub, so the disc sank vertically into the water. Some of it sloshed onto their shoes.

Starting to understand, Colm peered into the tub. Dhjerga shouldered him aside and dumped another two discs into the rack, splashing droplets onto Colm's hands. Wooden spacers separated the discs. Colm sucked a wet knuckle, tasted metal. *Aha.* "What are the discs made of? Lead?"

"Right. One plain, one webbed, one plain," Dhjerga yelled at the children. "Don't get them mixed up." He added to Colm, "It should be one lead, one copper, one lead. But there's a copper shortage. So we web half the cells with copper wire, and let the copper solution do the rest."

Basic electrochemistry. The water wasn't plain old H_2O. It had copper sulfate dissolved in it. When charged with power from the generator, the CuS solution would deposit copper on the webbed discs. Hey presto, one ten-foot battery.

Actually, twenty of them.

"Are you going to help, or just stand there with your thumb up your arse?" Dhjerga said, lugging three discs at once.

Colm looked up at the naked ends of the wires dangling from the ceiling. He looked down at the puddles on the floor. This was about to be the most dangerous place he'd ever been in, including war zones. "Can you not at least send those kids away?"

Dhjerga dumped the discs into the tub. "Why? They work for my family. They're not copies." There was an odd, bitter edge to the last words.

As he spoke, one of the little boys dragged a step-ladder over to the tub and climbed it to grab the end of a wire, leaning dangerously out over the acidic, corrosive solution. Colm shut his mouth. He wasn't here to debate the morality of child labor in alien civilizations.

But *were* the Ghosts an alien civilization? It kept niggling at him. Horses, Leyden jars, hydroelectric plants … 8,000 light years from Earth.

When they had assembled half a dozen batteries. Dhjerga called a halt. The turbine in the other room thundered, shoving current into the cells. Colm estimated the output of the plant at about one megawatt, and the batteries must hold at least a kilovolt, given the size of the things. But he couldn't feel it the way he had felt the esthesia feedback from the Leyden jar. In fact, he had a familiar feeling of lethargy and sadness, although it was hard to disentangle the sensations from saddle-soreness and all-around exhaustion.

"Gods, that feels good," Dhjerga said. "Let's flit." He held out a hand to Colm.

Colm stayed where he was, with his wet, cold feet planted on a dry bit of the floor. Think about Earth, Gilliam

Tripsilion Nulth the queazel had advised him. Think about the places you know, the people you love. He thought about Drumnadrochit. Heather and gorse on the hillsides, rain slapping the windows when you're cozy indoors. The last time he'd seen it, the place was crawling with Ghosts. He thought of his mother and his younger sister Bridget. Not his father, no. *Love* was just another four-letter word where Lloyd Mackenzie was concerned. Colm could see Mam and Bridget's faces in his mind's eye ... but the images were just memories, no more real than the faces of the niece and nephew he'd only ever seen in holos—he even had to struggle to remember their names. Morag and Ivan? No, Ivor. He remembered Mam saying that Bridget had moved up north, but he couldn't remember where ...

Oh, it's no use, is it?

The kerosene lantern reddened his eyelids. He opened his eyes, and found both little boys standing right in front of him, staring curiously, as if wondering what this weirdo was doing.

They looked so damn human.

They scuffled away, giggling in embarrassment. Colm watched them go, not even able to muster a smile.

"Are you ready?" Dhjerga said impatiently. He reached for Colm's right hand and laced his fingers through Colm's. The gesture felt too intimate, and at the same time childish, as if they were little boys about to play a game, instead of grown men in a world rife with murder and magic. "Wait until you see Dam Lizp Hol. I guarantee you'll be impressed."

Sparks twisted around their joined hands. A weak static shock pulsed up Colm's arm. Startled, he tried to pull away.

"Hold on!" Dhjerga's voice already seemed to come from a long way off. His face and body shimmered, and for an instant the darkness in the battery hall seemed to thin into something unbreathable.

Then the taut, stretched feeling in the air faded. Dhjerga dropped Colm's hand.

"What the fuck?" His expression of astonishment would have been comical at any other time. "Why can't you flit? You *are* a mage. You've got to be one, or you couldn't've come here in the first place!"

"I'm not a mage like you're a mage," Colm said. His voice was low. He was furious with himself. "My father's a conjuror who does kids' birthday parties. The old bastard never taught me anything useful, so they supplemented my natural abilities with technology. Without asking first, mind you. But even the fucking technology doesn't work as advertised."

Human DNA is 99.8% identical to Ghost DNA. That's what Gilliam Tripsilion Nulth had said.

The rest is chemical, so Gil and the other geniuses behind the CHEMICAL MAGE project had arranged for a new esthesia implant to be installed, without Colm's knowledge, in his head.

But even with the implant, he still couldn't access his genetic heritage … unless he was also using hard drugs. He just came from a world too hostile to magic, was his theory. He needed to be in an altered state of consciousness to make anything happen. No wonder his father was a hopeless drunk. But alcohol isn't as potent as the compounds magicked up by modern chemistry. When Colm made his 'flit' to Kisperet, 8,000 light years from the *Unsinkable,* he'd been juiced to the gills on tropodolfin, a painkiller commonly used off-label as a stimulant.

But it had been hours since he crashed to the floor of that

cart, and the stuff had completely worn off.

His implant was dead, his stomach hollow, despite the megawatts building up around them.

"So no, I won't be flitting anywhere. Sorry."

"Fuck," Dhjerga said blankly.

"Go without me." Colm made an indifferent gesture. He honestly did not care whether Dhjerga went or stayed. He was low, exhausted, hungry, and stuck on a planet that felt corrupted to the core by the Ghosts' vileness.

All the same he expected Dhjerga to stay, so it shocked him when Dhjerga said, "Right. I'll be back later."

He faded into thin air, and was gone.

CHAPTER 4

Megumi Smythe woke in her berth on the *Unsinkable* with her stomach tying itself in knots. She swung her feet to the floor and stumbled barefoot to the head. She vomited as quietly as possible, but when she unlocked the door, Axel Best was standing there.

"Are you OK?" Axel said.

She smiled and shrugged, although the truth was she hadn't been OK since Colm Mackenzie inexplicably disappeared from the *Unsinkable's* weather deck, 71 days ago.

That disused compartment still had sensor barriers around it and Marines standing guard 24/7. The Rat's people had scanned every inch of the uninteresting little room, trying to work out where the hell Colm had gone. They had found no clues. He'd pulled a Houdini so perfect, Houdini himself couldn't have managed it.

"It's the meds," Meg said, holding up her right arm. You really couldn't tell, but from the elbow down it was a vat-grown prosthetic. She'd lost her arm on a sentrienza ship, the day she killed the king and queen of Betelgeuse. "I know I have to take the stuff so my body doesn't reject the prosthetic, but man, it makes me sick as a dog."

Axel relaxed like he believed her. "Maybe you should go to the clinic. Request different meds."

"Yeah, maybe."

He put his arm around her. She said, "Don't kiss me unless you like the taste of puke."

He kissed her anyway. Someone applauded at the end of the corridor. Axel casually gave them the finger.

23

Peeling herself away, Meg saw Axel's crew. Axel flew a Vulture now. That was the new name of the fighters the Fleet had built by reconditioning luxury yachts, which had been built in the first place on the airframes of fighters that got cancelled because the sentrienza didn't like them. Humanity was done with dancing to the sentrienza's tune. But defiance had come late ... maybe too late. The *Unsinkable,* her sister ship the *Indomitable,* and their few auxiliary craft were stuck in the Betelgeuse system, in a standoff with the surviving half of the sentrienza's Betelgeuse fleet.

It would be a hopelessly unequal fight, except for one thing ... and that *wasn't* the Vultures, despite their crews' bravery.

"I had to get up for work, anyway," Meg said.

It was not easy for her to smile and casually say hello to the crew as she passed them on her way back to her cabin. The Marine Corps used to rely on the Navy for air support, but the Vultures were their babies. They wouldn't let mere sailors fly them. Meg had been reinstated into the Navy, in fact she was a second lieutenant now ... but she wasn't allowed to fly anymore. While Axel and his crew were about to go into action against a militarily superior foe, she had to stay on the *Unsinkable,* waiting it out, like some kind of damsel in distress.

She dressed in one of her damsel outfits—an ankle-length blue velvet dress with sparkly trim around the neck and cuffs—yanking the sash so hard that she couldn't breathe, and had to loosen it again. She detested these dresses, and the shoes which went with them—absurd pointy-toed things that made her slip around in the half-gravity on board.

Axel wolf-whistled.

"Are you *trying* to piss me off?" Meg said, her frustration escaping.

She turned away to fix her hair. In the mirror, she could see Axel shaving at the other hygiene unit. They shared this cabin, although that would normally not have been allowed. Axel got privileges because his father was Philip K. Best, one of the architects of the CHEMICAL MAGE project, now the governor of Juradis.

He buzzed the razor over his jaw with unusual care. His handsome, high-cheekboned face looked drawn, his eyes fixed on some distant place. She remembered that he was going into combat today, and regretted yelling at him.

"Walk me to work?" she said. "There's still a few hours before we get there, anyway."

After their successful assault on the sentrienza's Juradis fleet, the Rat had split his forces. The *Indomitable* had stayed at Juradis to guard the planet—and the half a million human refugees on its surface, as well as mara, shablags, and queazels. Meanwhile, the *Unsinkable* had burned directly away from Betelgeuse. Their destination was Noom, the second-largest of the Big Three terraformed planets which orbited between 60 and 70 AUs from the red supergiant.

But they hoped that to the sentrienza, it would look like the *Unsinkable* was running for home. If the sentrienza figured the *Indomitable* wasn't coming back, they'd hopefully commit all their forces to retaking Juradis ... leaving Noom and Barjoltan, the smallest of the Big Three, undefended.

So the *Unsinkable* had burned STL for almost two weeks, which was how long it took to get far enough out of Betelgeuse's gravity well to enter the zero-gravity field. They were now in the FTL portion of the journey, which was scheduled to take five hours. Noom lay 170 AUs away, on the other side of Betelgeuse.

Climbing through the grubby, weathered crew decks, Meg and Axel passed air support crew and Marines on their way to the flight deck, or to the sim suites for one last rehearsal of their date with death. The atmosphere was tense and gloomy. Although everyone talked a big game about kicking faerie ass, they could not really conceive of winning. This was the freaking sentrienza. The species that ruled most of the Orion Arm of the galaxy. Any victory in the Betelgeuse system would last only as long as it took the sentrienza to find out what had happened and send more ships from elsewhere.

That's why they *had* to capture Noom.

Meg suddenly noticed that they were going the wrong way. "Where are you going? I've got to be on the bridge in twenty minutes."

"This'll only take a second." They were on Deck 55. Sickbay. The *nice* sickbay, for company-grade officers, walls painted a soothing green, quiet music tinkling.

Meg had spent a week here after the battle on the *Ruddiganmaseve*. The place held painful memories in both the literal and the emotional sense.

"Those meds are making you sick," Axel said. "We're going to get you a new prescription."

He had so much anger inside. Anger at his father, at the Rat, at everyone who'd supported the desperate gamble of CHEMICAL MAGE. Now he'd finally found something it was OK to get mad at: Meg's meds.

But she had a lot of anger stored up, too, and she jerked away from him. "I'm *fine*, Axel."

"You're so fine, you've been puking twice a day." He strode into the self-serve pharmacy. "Megumi Smythe …" He gave her ID number. "It needs your eyeprint and voiceprint."

Meg stomped into the narrow reception area. Now that he had told the system she was here, she had to go through with the transaction, or it would be a red flag in her record. In the old days there would've been a pharmacist behind the desk, but now such non-essential positions went unstaffed, leaving the computerized prescription system wide open to abuse. Requiring biometric ID did not stop people from faking symptoms to get drugs.

"I do *not* need any new meds," she told the computer.

Behind the reception desk, a sensor-activated LED fixture illuminated walls lined with tiny lockers, stretching away into the darkness. A robot arm hung motionless between the lockers. The music had gone off, since there was no longer anyone in the corridor; the quiet filled up the space between Meg and Axel, like something solid with edges that could cut.

The computer said, "At present you have no active prescriptions, Lieutenant Smythe. Do you wish to report symptoms?"

Axel stared at her.

Meg flushed furiously. Caught out, caught out. She said, "It's a mistake." The truth was she'd finished taking the anti-rejection meds several days ago.

"But you said …"

Axel trailed off. The music had started up again in the corridor. They were about to be interrupted. Thank God.

But no one came in. Meg heard no footsteps. All the same, she started for the door of the pharmacy, eager to escape.

There was no one in the corridor.

Just the music, tinkle-tinkling, like a tune from a music box. *Für Elise.* It was really a horrible little tune. It used to drive Meg mad when she was stuck in here, hearing snatches of that tune every time someone opened the door of her room. It would get stuck in her head for hours.

The yellow-tinted lighting no longer looked soothing, but weak and unpleasant.

Tinkle, tinkle, tinkle.

A breath of cold stung Meg's face. She flinched against the jamb of the door.

Axel stumbled back. He'd felt it, too. Meg reached for her weapon—a reflex not hindered by the fact she wasn't allowed to carry a weapon anymore. Her prosthetic hand closed on empty air.

The lights in the far back of the pharmacy flickered on for an instant.

Meg gasped.

There was someone back there, pawing through the lockers like they weren't even locked.

Axel vaulted over the reception desk. "Hey! What are you doing?"

Half a pace behind him, Meg ducked under the motionless robot arm. Axel halted suddenly. She crashed into his back.

"Colm?" Axel said, sounding like a scared child.

"Collie Mack," Meg breathed. She squeezed past Axel on his non-gun side, hardly noticing that the protruding sensor pads of the lockers snagged and tore her dress.

Colm stood in the shadows at the end of the long aisle, pulling meds out of a locker. Blister packs and vials cascaded to the floor. "I can't find it," he said despairingly. His voice sounded faint and insubstantial, like the music-box tinkle of *Für Elise*. But the music had stopped now and Colm was here.

Or was he? As Meg instinctively moved towards him, she realized that she could see the wall through his body. The freckles on his cheeks were puncture wounds of shadow.

"Oh, Meg," he said. "I'm so sorry." Packets of pills dropped through hands made of darkness.

"You should be fucking sorry," she spat, forgetting to be afraid. She had forgiven him for so many things over the years, but she could not forgive him for disappearing. "You *vanished.* How is that OK? I'll tell you one thing, It's not OK with Admiral Hyland. If he ever sees you again he's going to space your ass."

"It's no good. They're not going to help us. I want to go home." Colm reached through the door of another locker and pulled out more meds, as if the door wasn't there.

"What are you looking for?" Axel said, with barely a quiver in his voice.

"Tropodolfin, of course."

Axel read the labels on the lockers and tapped his Void Eagle on one high up above Meg's head. "Here."

"Thank fuck."

Meg and Axel cringed back, crowding each other, as the shadow that was Colm surged closer to them. Listless sparks cracked from the robot arm overhead. Colm raked the contents of the tropo locker out. As before, everything fell straight through his hands. He cursed hopelessly.

"What's *wrong* with you, Collie Mack?" Meg burst out. "You came back from wherever just to get drugs?"

"It's a shithole," Colm said. "If you were there, Gunny, you'd want drugs, too. "

Axel reached for her hand. It was probably meant to be reassuring but static sizzled between their hands when they touched. She flinched away. His hair was standing on end. Hers would have been, too, if it wasn't done up medieval fashion.

"Where have you been all this time, anyway?" Axel blurted.

"All this time? It's not even been one day," Colm said.

"One day? It's been more than two months."

"Two bloody months. You're joking." Colm began to fade. "I'm losing it," he said, panic-stricken. She could read the labels on the lockers through him.

"What can we do?" she pleaded.

"Hold onto me. Oh God, Meg, hold onto me!"

If only she could hold onto him. That had been her heart's desire. She grabbed at his shadowy arms. But there was nothing there to hold onto. Her hands went through his flesh, with a prickling sensation as if she'd plunged them into a freezer, and closed on thin air.

The lights came back up.

Colm was gone.

She was standing in the pharmacy amidst a junkie's treasure trove of meds, with queasiness roiling her stomach and the normal hum of spaceship fans and plumbing in her ears.

The computer repeated, as if the power outage had never happened, "Do you have any symptoms to report?"

"Yeah," Meg whispered. "I'm pregnant."

CHAPTER 5

Colm came back to himself in the dark outside the blockhouse. It was snowing again. He was holding a pair of spoons. He threw them down in an agony of frustration.

He'd borrowed the spoons from the children after Dhjerga left. They were quite beautiful, with enameled handles, and the children's mother would want them back. He picked them up. But he did not move. He just stood staring at the ice slabs in the river.

It hadn't worked.

He couldn't fetch things without tropodolfin. And he couldn't get tropodolfin because he couldn't fetch things.

He was stuck on Kisperet.

Forever, the river seemed to say. *Forever.*

Day was coming at long bloody last. Gray brightened the clouds, in what wasn't necessarily the east because day on Kisperet meant that it had orbited to the dayside of its gas giant parent, not that Kisperet itself had rotated. Was it tidally locked, with the same side always facing the gas giant? Probably, as the gas giant had not budged from its position near the horizon. The little moon had moved across the sky, and was now a black pimple on the gas giant's bland face. Moons-of-moons were incredibly rare. Would be interesting to know the precise balance of gravitational forces that allowed Kisperet to hold onto its moon …

No. It would *not* be interesting. *Fuck* physics, Colm thought, clenching his fists. The mathematics of the cosmos were irrelevant to the Ghosts and they would be irrelevant to him from now on.

His feet had gone numb in his Fleet boots, and the wind cut through his inadequate dress uniform like it was made of paper. But still he did not move. The river was looking tempting.

The fear on Meg and Axel's faces haunted him. They had thought they were seeing a ghost. A *Ghost*. Ha, some Ghost I'd make; can't even flit …

I'd like to wring Gil's furry neck for getting me into this mess …

Two months had passed, Axel had said. Two whole months.

Insult added to injury, Ghost travel wasn't exactly instantaneous, after all.

*

Gilliam Tripsilion Nulth met Axel and his crew on the flight deck, wearing his EVA suit. It was a tubular, flexible garment with eight grippers on its underside, which he could manipulate with his eight dexterous paws. Queazels' clawed appendages served them as both hands and feet. Gil knew that the EVA suit made him look, to the humans, like a cross between a centipede and a silver sausage. Two of the Marines rubbed his helmet for luck as they boarded the Vulture. Gil half-wished he were not wearing the helmet, so that he could have bitten their fingers. On the other hand; vacuum.

In the unpressurized hangar, all six of the *Unsinkable's* Vultures perched on their launch platforms, attended by scurrying rampies who looked tiny from the height of the airlock. The Vulture's frivolous, needlenosed silhouette, with swept-back wings for in-atmosphere operations, ended in a drive powered by a 3 GW reactor. This was a serious spaceship. The humans had risen in Gil's estimation when he first saw one. It was *almost* as good as a queazel spaceship.

Of course, the humans, like the queazels, had got the key technologies from the sentrienza. Everything good came from the sentrienza … and they made you pay for it.

Gil's people had paid with the loss of their homeworld. They still had records of Uzzizriat. Gil drew pictures of Uzzizellan scenery sometimes, imagining that he was really there, not in this war-torn system.

He still believed that he, Admiral Hyland, and Philip K. Best had done the right thing.

As he settled into one of the couches lining the Vulture's stripped-down crew cabin, a pang of sadness shivered him from nose to rump. If only the CHEMICAL MAGE project had gone right, the war with the Ghosts would be over by now, and this war with the sentrienza need never have begun. But now that it was begun, they must finish it, even if that meant dying.

"Internal comms check," Axel said from the cockpit.

"Copy," said the Marines, and Gil.

"OK, guys and girls. Are you ready to kick faerie ass?! Lemme hear you!"

The Marines roared in the affirmative. Gil declined to join in the primitive morale-boosting ritual. He rested his chin on his hindquarters and mused that Axel seemed to be in a strangely good mood, considering the dangers they were about to face. Of course, Axel's moods were unpredictable at the best of times. But still.

The *Unsinkable* burst out of the zero-gravity field, barely 150 kilometers above the surface of Noom. Swirling gray clouds exploded onto Gil's personal screen. Sentrienza satellites pelted the carrier with queries, which the *Unsinkable* answered with computer-generated garbage that concealed pellets of malware. The humans had captured enough sentrienza gear on Juradis to be able to devise cyberweapons that would slow down the sentrienza's famed semi-sentient automated systems. The data war lasted 29.07 seconds. That was long enough for the Vultures to escape from the carrier.

Their drive plumes seared the closing doors of the launch bays. Streams of charged particles lashed the carrier's sides as the automated defense platforms recovered from their disorientation. Too late. The Vultures had already duck-dived towards the sullen clouds. Noom's radiation belt broke up the energy beams that chased them.

"Yee-haw," Axel yodeled, as the clouds blanked their screens out.

Gil opened a private channel to the cockpit. "Axel," he said. "Do you have a reason to sound as if you are having a good time?"

"We're on a search and destroy mission to take out the Duke of Noom's headquarters, which are said to be defended by the most advanced automated systems this side of Rigel. It's about time we had some fun on the job," Axel said.

"It's a suicide mission in all but name," Gil said. "I wish I had not come."

"Well, It looks like the Rat's head-fake worked," Axel offered. He was not really that gung-ho. He just acted it for the sake of the crew. "No sentrienza ships in orbit.."

"It will not take them long to return, once they realize they were tricked. Sentrienza drives are measurably superior to yours."

"Why *did* you come?"

Gil snarled quietly. The re-entry gees pinned him to his couch, but unlike the Marines in their steel battlesuits, he could move. Queazels were very hardy, despite their fragile appearance. He jerked a forepaw upwards in imitation of the human gesture commonly performed with the middle finger.

Instead of chiding him, Axel laughed. "I guess I might as well tell you. Meg's pregnant."

Gil's eyes widened. "Congratulations."

"I only found out this morning. I feel like a complete goof. She's had severe morning sickness, but it never crossed my mind ..." He was clearly bubbling over with happiness. "Keep it to yourself for now, OK?"

"Naturally." Gil sighed inwardly at the thought that he had missed his own chance to have a family. Even if any females would have had him, Gil had always believed it would be wrong to bring kits into a world ruled by the sentrienza. He resolved anew that Meg and Axel's baby should not live in such a world.

The Vulture tore through the underside of the clouds and screamed over Noom's largest continent. The other five Vultures had pierced the clouds at different locations. Defensive installations, bored into jagged mountain peaks, chattered fire. The Duke of Noom always had been a paranoid recluse. Missiles chased the Vultures, accelerating to follow their twists and turns. All six craft were still decelerating hard, heading for the same coordinates. A missile caught up with one of the other Vultures and atomized it. The Marines watched the fireball with no comment, but their fury charged the silence on the shared radio channel.

Axel jinked the Vulture from side to side, forcing Gil— whose harness did not fit—to dig his claws into the sides of his couch. The sooty, smoggy atmosphere of Noom made energy weapons next to useless, so the Vulture's charged particle cannon was deadweight. The ship also had a railgun, but they were saving their rounds for their targets. "Hold onto your guts," Axel said. "We're heading down to the deck."

The Vulture plunged into a dive that left Gil's stomach high in the troposphere. Levelling out, the ship scudded above a desert sprinkled with rock formationscarved into lacy arabesques by the wind, and oases where Noom's most numerous slave species, the quadripedal bisshengri, lived. Gil detested the bisshengri, and was pleased to see Axel spray a fragmenting round into a particularly large and ugly oasis. The frag rounds started off as solid metal slugs, but melted from the sheer acceleration the rails imparted to them. A million droplets of recooled metal shredded the flat-leaved trees and towering bisshengri mud nests. The wind instantly whirled the debris away, exposing a peculiarly regular hill … a sentrienza mound.

The Duke of Noom's dwelling-place was a closely guarded secret. However, Gil, as a former confidant of the late Queen of Betelgeuse, knew about it.

The Vulture decelerated at full throttle. As it dropped towards the desert, a number of cylinders, deceptively resembling chimneys, rose from the surface of the mound and opened fire.

Axel cursed and triggered the expanding foam inside the Vulture's Whipple shields.

Slugs thudded into the shields. The ship descended so fast that Gil thought for a melancholy moment the drive had been hit. Then Admiral Hyland said in his helmet, from the bridge of the *Unsinkable,* "Got you covered. We're jamming their targeting radar. Get in there before the orbitals counter-jam us."

"Yes, sir," Axel grunted. He dropped the Vulture onto the desert with a bump that threw Gil against his ill-fitting harness. The Marines hurtled out of their seats and deplaned in combat order. Gil got just a taste of the particulate-heavy air blowing in through the open airlock before he snapped his visor shut. He undulated to the top of the steps.

The semi-sentient guns popped out of the ground like so many corks out of bottles. They shot high in the air and came down, optically guided, heading for the Marines. One of the Marines did not dodge in time. The gun's tonnage crushed his battlesuit like a hammer cracking a nut. Standing on the bleeding mass of metal and electronics, the gun spat a revolving stream of lead at the other Marines. They returned fire with their combis, alternating grenades and rifle bursts. The GIMP team took cover behind a drift of fragmented tree trunks and poured ammo through the crew-served machine-gun. The Vulture aimed its turret-mounted Gauss cannon at the other guns that had landed here and there among the advancing Marines. The last gun landed on top of the Vulture itself, with such exuberance that it sank six inches into the fuselage.

Gil flattened himself to the floor of the airlock chamber and prepared to die.

A steel-booted foot came down beside his helmet. Axel picked him up by the midsection. Gil spat and clawed—uselessly, as his teeth and claws were encased in his spacesuit.

"Stop that," Axel said. "You're coming. You're the only one who knows the way."

The sentrienza guns' charge had left their holes empty.

The Marines skirmished towards them.

CHAPTER 6

On the bridge of the *Unsinkable,* Meg watched the Rat do his thing. Chewing up ships and crews like they were made of cardboard. Noom's mountaintop defences had taken out three of the Vultures. Axel's ship and two others had made it to the mound. After an intense firefight, 46 Marines, including Axel, and one queazel, had vanished underground.

Now they were out of radio contact.

Meg dug her fingernails into the heels of her hands. She fiddled with the end of her sash. She fought queasiness. She listened, and tried not to scream, as the Rat bantered with the Duke of Noom about the technological conundrums of empire in a finite but very large universe. The cool-as-a-cucumber admiral was on the radio with his enemy at the same time as their troops were fighting to the death.

So far, the Duke had explained that multiverse theory was a wish-fulfillment fantasy, that wormholes did not exist, and that you really could hear bluebells ringing if you were doing the right kind of psychotropic drugs. He had dropped more nuggets of technological wisdom in half an hour than humanity had got out of the sentrienza in three centuries. But he had not said where his fleet was.

The Rat rocked on his heels, thumbs hooked in his belt, the picture of confidence. Admiral Hyland was a lean, sinewy man who looked younger than his sixty-something years. He had a crisp English accent, very different from Colm's soft Scots burr. He stood in front of the command station, against a backdrop of desks arranged in concentric horseshoes. Wall screens displaying sensor data panned and scrolled. Staff officers, heads bent to their holo displays, appeared to be hard at work, but Meg knew they were all listening intently. She herself stood out of the camera's field of vision, leaning against a door with a hand-lettered sign on it.

The alien on the big screen facing the Rat looked enviably relaxed. Sentrienza were naturally thin but the Duke of Noom was emaciated, with his pale green hair braided into a crown so large it seemed his toothpick neck should not be able to support it. He reclined on a padded throne that appeared to be upholstered with zebra hide, in a room with a low bulgy ceiling; the hollows among the bulges shed a cold subterranean light. Sentrienza, human, and mara slaves attended him. Meg remembered—she could never forget— the Queen of Betelgeuse's audience room on her flagship. It had been spartan, dominated by a pyramidical throne of skulls. The Duke clearly had a different idea of luxury. But Meg had killed the queen on her throne, and she would kill the duke too, without a second thought, if she were there. She wished she had gone instead of Axel, or with him. She wished she hadn't lied to him about the baby.

A mara in a bronze bikini brought the Duke a drink. He launched into a   disquisition on the nature of dark energy.

The Rat waited politely until he paused for breath, and then said, "You'd really better surrender."

"Surrender to a slave race?" The Duke let out a high chittering cackle. Meg winced.

"Otherwise, I'll nuke you in your hole. Humans don't mess about, you know. No pansy airbursts for us."

"Your bombs could not penetrate my mound." The Duke's voice was the typical sentrienza kazoo-like buzz. "Try it and see."

Unfortunately, he was correct. According to Gil, the complex below the mound went down half a mile. The sentrienza's preference for living underground had a practical side.

"What strange, wilful creatures you are," the Duke said, "to imagine that you could defy the greatest empire in the galaxy!"

"Oh, give it a rest," the Rat said. "Your lot have been nosing around Earth for long enough; ever since we were building stone circles, and you came and danced in them by the light of the moon to give us a fright. Rings of toadstools, sour milk, sick cows, the evil eye—that was your first contact strategy. And you call *us* strange?"

Everyone on the bridge laughed, even Meg, in an explosive release of tension. It was not widely known on Earth that the sentrienza were the very same beings humanity used to dread under the name of faeries, *yokai,* or whatever. Scratch that, it wasn't known at all. Textbooks instructed children that the sentrienza were the good guys protecting us against the dangers of the galaxy, despite the obvious fact that the sentrienza hadn't protected us against the Ghosts—because it suited them for us to be weakened, so that we would make better slaves.

"Going to escape in a puff of smoke?" the Rat added, rubbing it in. Everyone laughed again, but not Meg, this time. She was remembering Colm in the pharmacy, her hands sinking through his flesh as if it were made of smoke. The sentrienza could not really work magic. But one ginger-haired Scotsman could.

The Duke of Noom smiled. It was a horrible sight, as the sentrienza had lots of pointed teeth. "Not necessary," he said, and snapped his fingers.

The sensors officer on the bridge of the *Unsinkable* shouted, "Craft detected. Altitude 400 klicks. 350. Two—five—seven of them!"

Immune to the panic sweeping through the bridge, the Rat raised an eyebrow. "Bit risky, coming out of the zero-gravity field that near a planet."

The Duke of Noom grinned. "Our ships are superior to yours, as we are superior to you."

The *Unsinkable's* tactical officer grunted, "They're targeting us, sir." Screens flashed urgent warnings.

The Duke said, "Your childish ruse did not fool *me*. I knew that you, Admiral Hyland, would never abandon your fellow humans, or the lesser sapients you risked so much to liberate. Therefore, I instructed my fleet to enter a flexible holding pattern in the zero-gravity field. Now, as you see, they are back."

Meg stared at the screen where composite imaging had acquired optics of the sentrienza ships. They looked like dead twigs, or pieces of coral, symmetrical from one perspective, asymmetrical from another, like those pictures that could be a face or a vase depending on how you looked at them. They made her head hurt. She remembered her time as a captive on the *Ruddiganmaseve,* and knew she'd rather die than repeat that experience.

Well, she wasn't likely to get the choice. Thorny protrusions turned into bristling guns. Targeting lasers pinned the *Unsinkable* from multiple directions. Noom lay too close to Betelgeuse for the old carrier to go FTL. There was no escape.

The Rat hesitated.

"Three. Two," the Duke taunted them.

Suddenly, a commotion erupted in the Duke's lair, deep below the surface of Noom. Smoke and dust clouded the screen. The slaves dived for cover. Muzzle flash sparkled. Part of the ceiling descended behind the throne like a gently shaken quilt, spraying debris across the carpet. The Duke turned on his zebra-hide throne.

A Walking Gun scuttled out from underneath the throne— and suddenly catapulted backwards, gripping a live grenade in its jaws. It reached the corner of the screen before it exploded. A shard of metal raked a bright track down the Duke of Noom's cheek. The Duke touched the cut and stared blankly at his fingers.

A human being in a battlesuit, dripping with filth, charged out of the dust cloud and jammed a combi against the Duke's braid-wrapped head.

"Surrender or die, you minion of the Gray Emperor, deceiver of peoples and destroyer of worlds!" squealed the silver sausage clinging to the Marine's shoulders.

The Rat smiled broadly. "The queazel has just taken the words out of my mouth."

Everyone on the bridge leapt up cheering, except for Meg. Horror paralyzed her. One Marine? *One* survivor out of 46 who had gone below ground? Who was it? Filth obscured his or her visor …

With supreme self-control, the Duke turned his slender neck until he was staring straight into the barrel of the combi. "So," he buzzed. "You may slay me. But if you do, my ships will atomize your primitive rustbucket. Then they will proceed to Juradis to liquidate your friends."

"At least we're at *if,*" the Rat said.

The Marine popped his faceplate. Relief flooded through

Meg. Thank God, thank God. It was Axel.

His clean, pale face contrasted with his damaged and dirty battlesuit … but his wild-eyed snarl made the Duke recoil. "You're in no position to negotiate," he yelled.

"But I am," the Duke said. "If you shoot me, my ships will open fire." He turned back to the camera. "Admiral Hyland, you know your history. So let us play a game that men and faeries often played in the old days. I shall pose three riddles. If you answer them all correctly, I will surrender. If you answer wrong, my ships will atomize you, as previously discussed."

"You're dead either fucking way," Axel shouted.

The Duke shrugged. "Well? Will you play?"

On the external imaging screens, the sentrienza ships drifted closer to the *Unsinkable,* turning broadside on. A targeting laser drowned one of the screens in a wash of icy blue.

The Rat glanced around at the mutely pleading faces that lined the bridge. Meg knew before he spoke that he was going to choose the hundreds of people on the *Unsinkable* over Axel. "OK, we'll play."

He paused the transmission and pointed at her.

"Smythe, you're up. Get me the answers. I needn't remind you that Major Best's life depends on it."

She sealed her lips tightly on her rage. She saluted and opened the door behind her. The sign on it said *FAERIELAND.* She walked inside.

CHAPTER 7

The servomotors and hydraulics of Axel's battlesuit held his combi rock-steady, six inches from the Duke of Noom's head. Just as well he still had juice in his suit, because he had none left in his muscles.

On his shoulders, Gil snapped and swore at the slaves cringing on the floor. The queazel held three pistols, taken from the bodies of dead Marines. Two full platoons had died so that Axel could stand here, in the heart of the Duke of Noom's mound, not shooting him. It was Majriti IV all over again. Despair and battle-sickness swirled in his mind, telling him he was the worst officer in human history.

The Duke, eyes fixed on the camera, said in a low voice, "Did you meet my Walking Guns?"

"Yes," Axel said.

"Did you see my Living Garden, where I keep the slaves who have displeased me?"

"Yes."

"And yet you did not turn back. Amazing. You smell as if you had fallen down the garbage chute, where they throw the bodies."

"I *crawled* down that garbage chute," Axel said. "I left half my men in your torture garden. But now I'm here. And only one of us will be leaving this room alive."

*

FAERIELAND. Abandon hope all ye who enter here.

The staff officers had put that sign on the door to make themselves feel better about what was on the other side of it … or rather, *who*.

Princess Emnl ki-Sharongat, the sole survivor of the royal family of Betelgeuse.

Meg closed the door behind her, hearing the *snick* as it automatically locked. She was unarmed, but she didn't need to be armed; the sentrienza were physically weak, and Meg was a karate black belt.

The sentrienza princess squatted on the floor with her upper body canted forward over her toes. Her knees bent backwards, like a dog's knees. Meg never had got used to that. "Hello, Emnl," she said. She settled crosslegged in front of the princess, deliberately adopting an unladylike pose. Petty, but Emnl made her behave in petty ways.

They had originally furnished this room with some potted plants, and a decorative carpet sourced from a sentrienza ruin on Juradis, to try to make it into a prison cell fit for a princess. Emnl had peed on the carpet, eaten one of the potted plants, and ripped the others to shreds. She was not upset about Meg's having killed her parents. She was upset that she hadn't gotten to take her mother's place as Queen of Betelgeuse. She was fine with the killing bit, she had explained, and actually held Meg in high esteem for having pulled it off ... which was why Meg was the only human being she would talk to.

That was the reason she had given the Rat, anyway.

"You're looking well, Meg-*sensei*," she piped. "You're practically glowing." Her gaze rested for an instant on Meg's stomach.

Why, why had Meg told her? For spite, she supposed. Emnl forced her to confront the least pleasant aspects of her own character. Meg had wanted Emnl to know that she did not give a good goddamn about any previous agreement they might have had.

FELIX R. SAVAGE

But now their lives depended on the odious little princess's cooperation.

"You've got to be bored," she said, shakily. "How about playing a game?"

"What sort of a game?" Emnl piped.

"Riddles."

"I have a better idea. I'll pee on the floor again, and make you clean it up."

To hell with being nice. Meg no longer cared that the Rat was listening. "Heads up, you freaky bitch. The Duke of Noom is threatening to slag this ship and murder everyone on board. That includes you. If you don't want to die, answer his goddamn riddles."

"Oh," Emnl said. "That horrid old pervert. He always did like the riddle game. All right. What's the first one?"

The Rat fed Meg the Duke's first riddle through her comms implant. She repeated, "What has no legs, and yet runs?"

"Blood, of course." Emnl yawned. "He must be losing his touch."

*

"Blood," the Rat said, from the tiny screen on the arm of the Duke's throne.

"Correct," the Duke said. "The next one is harder. We two weave a tangled web, with only one end."

We two weave a tangled web, Axel thought. Me and Meg. Meg and Colm. Colm and me. But it's ended now. Colm's gone. Only one end. And she's carrying my baby.

Sweat trickled down his forehead, tickling.

My baby.

The news of Meg's pregnancy, which had filled him with

46

such joy when she first told him, now seemed distant and unreal.

A child of mine and hers. What will he or she be like? Will I live to meet him, or her?

Only one end.

The armor held his arms steady. The helmet kept him staring into the crosshairs.

"What are we?" the Duke said, and smiled at the camera.

*

"What are we?" Emnl smoothed her *uwagi*. She was dressed in white karate *gi*, her uniform of preference, since proper sentrienza clothes were not available. "I used to think we were teacher and student."

"Not anymore," Meg said. She drew the line at continuing to teach Emnl karate, even though the alternative was dressing in damsel-in-distress outfits to satisfy Emnl's sense of propriety. "Anyway, that wasn't a question. It was the Duke's second riddle. A tangled web—"

"—we weave, when once we practice to deceive. Is there something you're not telling me, *sensei?*"

"The answer *can't* be Shakespeare."

"Why not? My three-times-great grandmother knew him. In fact she fed him a lot of his plots. He understood tragedy better than most humans."

"Yeah, maybe. But *only one end?*"

"There can be only one end to your rebellion. Your defeat. *That* would be a tragedy, Meg-sensei; and where is the modern Shakespeare to make a story of it? Not one human will remain to remember the past. But you could save your species, Meg. You could even save your homeworld. It would be so easy."

47

"I don't know what you're talking about," Meg said, terrified that Emnl would spill the beans about her pregnancy in the Rat's hearing.

"You have a boyfriend now, don't you? That man Axel? I like him. I think he would be a good father. What do you think?"

"Answer the goddamn question!"

"The answer is qubits, of course. Two quantum particles in an entangled state."

*

"Qubits," the Rat said.

The Duke's lips thinned. "That is correct. Let me see. I shall have to think of something harder ..."

*

"Where do the Ghosts come from?" Meg repeated the question the Rat had just fed to her, and felt panic squeezing at her heart. "That's not a *riddle!* That's not fair! I mean, the Duke doesn't know the answer, either!"

"Probably not," Emnl admitted. "But he *wants* to know. So do I, naturally. Where do they come from? Where do they get their arcane powers? Why do they look so much like you?"

"Is this really the time?" Meg could practically feel the targeting lasers of the sentrienza ships crawling over her skin.

"What better time could there be? If you do not answer the question under threat of death ..."

"We don't *know* the answer! If we did, don't you think we would have fried their asses by now?"

"They look like you, but not like *all* of you," Emnl pondered. "You come in many different colors. Your facial and musculoskeletal characteristics differ widely, as one would expect of a species that evolved in a variety of habitats.

However, the Ghosts all resemble the human phenotype known as Caucasian. They exhibit a remarkable uniformity. Their DNA, too, while very similar to human DNA, has not a thousandth of the population-level or individual variation seen among you. They appear to have evolved from a very small population ..."

"Actually," the Rat said over the speakers in the room, "my own theory, absolutely unscientific, has always been that the sentrienza kidnapped a bunch of people from prehistoric Europe and conducted a breeding experiment, selecting for unusual mutations like those carried by Colm Mackenzie."

"Sorry," Emnl said. "We didn't."

"Oh, well," the Rat said. "It was too neat a theory to be true, I suppose. He's starting to get impatient. Have you got any better ideas?"

"I do, actually," Emnl buzzed.

She stood up with an swaying backwards jerk. Meg scrambled to her feet.

"Patch me through to the sentrienza ships," Emnl said.

"And then what?" the Rat said suspiciously.

"Oh, *please* just stop asking questions, for once in your life, Admiral Hyland," Emnl said with a buzzing giggle.

The Rat let out a surprised bark of laughter. "All right. Not as if we've got any other options." *Click.* "You're through."

Emnl drew herself upright. She spoke in the sentrienza language, a slurry of hisses and buzzes.

The Flying Guns were hearing this. But what were they hearing? Meg felt as if her heart might stop. This much stress couldn't be good for the baby. Then again, it didn't much matter, if the sentrienza fleet was about to blow them all to pieces.

Emnl stopped speaking. There was a long pause.

Faintly, Meg heard cheering from the bridge. "What's happening?"

"They're no longer targeting us," the Rat said.

"Correct," Emnl said. "I told them who I am, and that they must obey *me* now. I told them to stand down and await further orders." As an afterthought, she added, "Shall I tell them to blow the Duke's mound to pieces, or will you do it?"

*

The Rat's voice crackled urgently from the tiny screen. "Stand down. Best, stand down."

The Duke of Noom slumped in Axel's crosshairs. His fleet had betrayed him. His louche defiance was gone.

Axel said, "What do you want me to do with him, sir?"

"Take him prisoner. He may have valuable intelligence, and he knows a great deal about cosmological science and tech—"

Axel shot the screen, cutting the Rat off in mid-sentence.

"What did you do that for?" said Gil, perched on the back of the throne, aiming his three guns in three different directions at the confused slaves.

"So that I can pretend I didn't hear him."

Axel would never forget the horrors he had endured this day. He would never forget the men and women who had followed him into the mound, and how they had died. Nothing could make up for their sacrifice. But he could even the score a bit.

"Guess you don't believe in God," he said to the Duke.

"God is a faerie tale," the Duke said, and actually laughed. He was not the ruler of a planet for nothing. "If you are going to shoot me, do it."

"You'd better hope the other guy doesn't exist, either.

Because if he does, you're about to meet him."

Axel pulled the trigger.

*

Later, back on board the *Unsinkable,* Axel and Meg lay squashed into one of the single bunks in their shared berth. Axel rested his hand on Meg's tummy, thinking about the miracle taking place inside. It helped to blot out his bitter ordeal in the sentrienza mound.

"Did you get in trouble for shooting the Duke?" Meg said.

"Oh yeah. The Rat tore me a new one."

"Ouch."

"Gil stuck up for me." He yawned. "Anyway, we've got the sentrienza ships. We'll be able to take them apart, reverse-engineer their drives."

"Yeah …"

Meg's ambivalent tone roused him. "What?"

"I'm not taking anything away from you or your guys. I'm just saying … Emnl didn't do that out of the goodness of her heart. She did it for her own reasons. God, I hate her." Meg sighed. "I'm not a very nice person, am I?"

"You're never complacent." Axel kissed her neck. "That's one of the reasons I love you."

"Oh, Axel." She didn't say she loved him back. She never did. He was used to that, but now that she was carrying his child, he'd hoped … Well, maybe she just needed time. Unwillingly, he thought of Colm in the pharmacy, Meg desperately reaching for him. He hoped Colm *stayed* gone.

"You know what else?" Her voice pulled him out of it. "When we boarded the ships? There were like three sentrienza on each one. And twenty Walking Guns."

Walking Guns were semi-sentient weapons, which walked.

And ran. And sometimes flew. And tore battlesuits apart like cheap chew toys. Axel had encountered several of them in the mound.

"Shit. I hope we spaced them with bombs strapped to their backs."

Meg shook her head, her hair brushing his cheek. "They're on board right now, with Emnl."

"No way."

"Yes, way. She's got them following her around like a bunch of lapdogs."

"That's crazy."

"The Rat said we'll need them."

They both fell silent, remembering that Betelgeuse was only one of the sentrienza's roughly 500 star systems. Their victory here would only sharpen the sentrienza's thirst for vengeance.

Trying to stay positive, Axel said, "Well, I guess he's right. Each Walking Gun is as good as another spaceship."

"*If* Emnl lets us use them."

"Won't she?"

"I sure hope so, but she'll want something in return." Meg rolled over, curling up with her back to him. "Remember, every gift that the sentrienza give has to be paid for."

He put his arm around her. "Try to think good thoughts for the baby," he whispered.

Meg let out a spluttery, miserable little laugh. "The baby. Yeah."

"*Our* baby."

"Yeah."

CHAPTER 8

Colm did not know how long he'd been standing on the river bank when a child's voice said, "Sir?"

He turned to see one of the little boys. Hralf's children.

"Lord Lizp is back."

"Who?"

The boy pointed to the blockhouse. The door stood open. White smoke rose from the chimney.

"Go on home," Colm said. "You'll catch your death." He fumbled in the pocket of his dress uniform. His fingers felt as numb as twigs unattached to his body. "Here, give these back to your mother." He returned the spoons he had borrowed.

He stumbled back to the blockhouse. The turbine thundered in its pit. The generator was still running. Blowing on his fingers, he followed the sound of voices to a room he hadn't noticed last night: a little break room off the passage between the turbine hall and the battery room. A cheerful blaze burned in a brick fireplace. In front of it sat Dhjerga Lizp and two strangers, a man and a woman.

"I didn't expect to see you again," Colm said.

"I told you I'd be back later," Dhjerga said. "Have a sandwich." He was eating a piece of flat bread rolled up around so much meat and cheese that it threatened to slide out onto his knees. He was no longer clad in grubby, worn khaki. He had on an extraordinary outfit of black leather drainpipe trousers, a bright blue shirt with bell sleeves, and a snow-white fur vest. He even had a fob watch on a chain. His shaggy hair was slicked back and secured by a gold band.

The other two people wore the same type of clothes—the woman had a split leather skirt instead of trousers. They looked to be in their late twenties, and shared the familiar Ghost look: pale skin, strong features, brown eyes and brown hair.

Colm had always reckoned there *must* be female Ghosts. Those little boys logically had to have a mother. You can't have people without women. But he'd never seen a female Ghost before. This one was frowning skeptically at him. Her fur-trimmed bodice outlined an hourglass figure. Gold pins held her caramel-brown hair in a knot, showing off an elegant neck.

Colm cleared his throat and said to Dhjerga, *"Lord* Lizp?"

"It's just a courtesy title. This is the Lord Prefect of Lizp Province." Dhjerga nodded at the young man, who was kneeling in front of the fire, singing bread on a bayonet. "My little brother. And this is my little sister. They're twins, if you couldn't tell." Colm did a double-take. "For fuck's sake, Dryjon," Dhjerga added, "at least say hello."

Dryon was gangly, long-limbed, awkward-looking. He met Colm's eyes for an instant. "You are the mage from Earth who will help us overthrow the Magistocracy?" His voice carried more confidence and authority than his wispy appearance suggested.

"Er," Colm said. "First I've heard about that."

"But you *are* from Earth?"

"Yes, but not recently. It's quite cold here, isn't it?" Colm shuffled nearer the wonderful warm fire. The smells of woodsmoke and toast were making him dizzy. His wet dress uniform steamed.

Dhjerga laughed, and reached under his stool. "I brought

you some proper clothes." He dragged out a bundle of leather and fur. "These are warmer, and you won't stick out as much."

"You can change in the washroom down the hall," the young woman said frostily.

In the freezing pissoir, Colm struggled with the Ghost clothes, teeth chattering. He felt a right berk wearing a blousy shirt and leather trousers, as if he were playing a part in some historical drama. The fur vest was nice and warm, but its toggle fastenings foxed him as he was accustomed to zips. He had even more trouble with the boots. During his military career, he'd worn EVA boots, combat boots, or dress shoes. As a civilian he had worn sneakers or shitkickers. *Normal* footwear, made of various smart polymers. Never had he touched, much less put on, a pair of boots all too evidently sewn from pieces of dead cow, creased into shiny ridges by someone else's feet, and smelling like someone else's feet, too, with side laces and tassels. He forced his feet in. They fit OK. He had a strange taste in his mouth. Rotten eggs. Bile. Panic. He laced the boots up and went back to the break room.

Dhjerga applauded. "Now you look like a human being." He kicked the young woman's stool. "Give him your seat, Diejen."

"No, really," Colm demurred.

"I don't mind standing," the young woman, Diejen, said. "We shan't be staying long, anyway." She stood up. Colm's exhausted body plopped onto the wooden stool of its own accord. A pile of rifles and shotguns lay underneath it. Diejen's voluminous split skirt had concealed them until she rose. Careful not to kick the weapons, Colm stretched out his hands to the fire. Returning sensation prickled his fingers, but he didn't feel the slightest twinge from his esthesia implant.

"Now then, sir, what's your name, and what can you do?" Dryjon said in a business-like tone, juggling his piece of toast. He stuck the bayonet into the other side and held it to the flames.

"My name's Colm Mackenzie." The Ghosts mouthed the unfamiliar syllables, and again Colm seemed to hear that strange echo of gibberish behind his own words. "As to what I can do? I can fly spaceships, and I'm a pretty good mechanic. But I can't do what I expect you're thinking of. I can't do magic."

"You said he was a mage," Dryjon said.

"That's what's so odd," Dhjerga said. "He *was.*"

"There are no mages on Earth," Diejen said, flatly. She was standing by the door with her arms folded. "And if there were, we wouldn't require their help."

"I think we do," Dhjerga said. "I'm on the run. If you try to hide me, you'll be in trouble, too."

"You could always go back to the front and do your duty," Diejen said, but she looked away as she said it.

"I suppose I could," Dhjerga said. "The Romans are human, you know. Every last one of them. We were told that we were only killing copies, but it isn't true." His hands shook, and bits of cheese fell on his lap as he bit into his sandwich.

Diejen said, "No one's saying that the war is right. I *hate* the war. I wish we had never begun it. The old ways were better! I wish we could turn back time to when we were little."

"Well, I gave up on trying to invent a spell to turn back time years ago," Dryjon said. He dropped his toast into the fire. "Oh, by Scota's grave." Colm leant forward and picked it out, half-blackened. "That was the last piece of bread."

"I'll eat it," Colm said.

"Really? Have some of this instead." Dryjon pushed a wicker trug towards him. It held meat, cheese, butter, and some rather wizened green apples. "Slim pickings, sorry."

Colm sank his teeth into an apple. He hadn't eaten a real apple in a decade. This one tasted heavenly. "Best piece of fruit I've had in years. Did you bring all this with you from …?"

Diejen said from the doorway, "You can't fetch *food.* It's neither living nor dead. We got these things from Hralf's family. What sort of a mage are you?"

"No kind of mage," Colm said, piling scraps of salt pork on the less charred half of the toast.

Dhjerga broke his brooding silence. "He *is.* A good meal, a bit of a rest, and he'll be right as rain."

Colm's voice was rough. He had to pocket his pride and disappoint Dhjerga at the same time. "I don't need food, I need tropodolfin. It's a … a medicine. I'm not a mage like you, it's … it's chemical." He tapped the left side of his skull, in reference to his esthesia implant, knowing it would mean nothing to them.

"And there I thought you were a druid, with that hair," Dryjon said. Again came the echoes of gibberish, but this time one of the echoes coincided with the word *druid,* like two instruments hitting the same note, and Colm understood it. *Draoi.*

"Are you speaking Gaelic?" he burst out in astonishment.

If only he'd actually studied Gaelic in school. If only he knew more than the few words his father had taught him.

Dryjon and Dhjerga both stared at him. Colm took their looks for incomprehension. But then Dhjerga said, chewing,

"Well, we're not speaking your English." *Béarla*. The Gaelic word for English. "And you're not, either. I know you think you are. I thought when I was on Juradis that I was still speaking the Teanga, and I was mystified that you all were speaking, it, too. But …" He waved the heel of his sandwich. "It's a part of the fix. When I got a fix on you, I also got a fix on your language. And now the same thing's happened in reverse, I'm guessing."

"We're meant to understand each other," Dryjon said with placid confidence. "And I believe you're meant to help us. Why else would you be here?"

Because I'm a Christing idiot, Colm thought.

Because I've never made the right decision in my life when I could make a wrong one.

Because I wanted to stick it to the Rat for fucking with me.

Because I didn't want to face Meg.

But among all the bad reasons he *did* have one good one. He wiped his mouth and straightened his spine in a vain attempt to look more like a representative of the Fleet. "The fact is we need *your* help."

"*Our* help?" Dhjerga said.

"Yeah. They sent me to ask you to come back and help us. Those bloody idiots have started a war on two fronts. Now we're fighting the sentrienza, too."

"The faeries," Dhjerga explained to his brother and sister.

Dhjerga had been there when Colm razed a sentrienza customs post on Juradis. In fact, Dhjerga and his reinforcements had done most of the razing. After that, things had got rather out of control. But Colm had started the rebellion against the sentrienza. So he bore at least some of the responsibilty for ending it.

"Right. So now we're fighting your buddies at home, and the sentrienza in the Betelgeuse system. And they've got an empire, whilst we haven't. So we're fucked, unless you come back and help."

Dhjerga covered his eyes with one hand. "Did you hear that?" he groaned.

"Yes," Diejen said. "You've been running wild, getting mixed up in other people's business. Pulling the ears of alien races we have no quarrel with. Isn't it bad enough to desert from the Mage Corps, without going berserk and making it worse?"

"In for a lamb, in for a sheep," Dryjon said, scraping his thumbnail over a piece of hard cheese. "The Magus has already sworn to execute Dhjerga if he gets hold of him."

This word, *Magus,* had no echo behind it. It fell like a stone, and the jolly little fire seemed to shrink and gutter, the tips of the flames breaking blue.

"Who's that?" Colm said. "The Magus?"

Diejen hugged herself. "Don't speak that name," she said harshly.

"You can't pretend him away," Dryjon said.

"No, but he can be killed," Dhjerga said. His eyes were red-rimmed. "Slay the Magus and the war ends."

"So," Dryjon said to Colm. "Will you help us?"

At the door, Diejen stiffened. "I hear horses. Damn it, damn it! They've found us."

CHAPTER 9

Diejen rushed towards the turbine hall. Dhjerga went the other way. After a moment's hesitation Colm followed him into the battery room.

The sun had risen while they were having breakfast. Morning light flooded over the tubs, the cisterns, the sacks of copper sulfate and the stacks of lead plates. The batteries had iced over, as had the puddles on the floor.

Two men in forest-colored livery stood on either side of the door, aiming their rifles at the tubs.

They were identical twins, jowly and red-cheeked.

Copies.

The Lizps had brought a pair of copies along, and not even bothered to mention it.

"My lord!" the copies barked at Dhjerga, without taking their eyes off the tubs in the middle of the room.

"Have to change the solution," Dhjerga said. "Drain out the clear water." He paused, one foot off the floor, head raised, as if sniffing the air. "No, no one's coming this way. *Yet.*"

He wheeled and dashed back the way they'd come. Again Colm followed, feeling totally at sea. In the corridor, Dryjon hopped on one foot, weapons sliding out of his arms onto a raised knee. Dhjerga snatched a shotgun. Colm saved the rest of the guns from falling to the floor.

"Can you shoot?" Dryjon said.

"Of course he can," Dhjerga answered for Colm. He grabbed a heavy satchel of ammo from Dryjon's shoulder. "Where he comes from, they have guns that can shoot hundreds of rounds a minute."

In the turbine hall, the air shook to the thunder of water rushing through the intake pipe below. A metal pole barred the front door. Diejen stood on the catwalk that ran around the room at head height, aiming a shotgun out of one of the slit windows. Hralf the caretaker, a short, wiry man in a forest-green cloak, covered the side of the building facing the river. His family huddled under the catwalk. A dumpy, sweet-faced woman. Eight or nine kids, including the two boys Colm had met last night.

Dryjon handed out guns to the caretaker's wife and the oldest children, and sent them all into the battery room. He, Dhjerga, and Colm climbed up onto the catwalk and joined Diejen at the window.

Outside, the sun perched on the hill beyond the river. The wind picked up flurries of dry snow from the patio. Footprints crisscrossed the white carpet. Colm saw the winding trail of his own footprints leading to the river and back. He scanned the forested hillsides on either side of the river. Nothing.

"I hear them," Dhjerga said.

The wind carried a faint jingling to their ears. It made Colm think of the spoons, and of Great-Grandpa Mackenzie, and for an instant he saw his mother squinting up into the sky, and then he was back on the catwalk, pressed to the crumbling brick of the wall, close enough behind Diejen that he could smell her hair and see a couple of pimples on her slender neck.

"Here they come," she breathed.

Colm peeked around her shoulder. An army was riding out of the trees.

Not the twenty-odd soldiers he and Dhjerga had left alive last night. *Hundreds* of men, it seemed to him in that stunned instant, and half of them were on horseback. And in the middle of them, pushing towards the front as the leaders reached the patio, rode two of the magistrates in their black cloaks. The whole straggling party formed up into a solid mass of flesh and glittering steel. The magistrates rode to the front. Another rider preceded them, holding aloft a tasseled banner like a scroll unrolled vertically, which bore the blood-red symbol of the two-headed eagle.

Dryjon sagged against the wall as if his legs would not hold him. "Where did this lot spring from?"

"They had a horse-powered generator," Dhjerga said. "They must have been running it all night. I wish I'd torched it, but there wasn't time."

"You spend your whole life wishing for things that can't be," Diejen said fiercely.

"Go!" Dhjerga said to her and Dryjon, as the magistrates trotted towards the blockhouse. "Go home! What are you waiting for? They don't know you're here. Let's keep it that way."

"Don't be ridiculous," Diejen snapped. "We're not leaving you."

Colm felt terrible. Dhjerga's brother and sister wouldn't leave him behind, and Dhjerga wouldn't leave Colm. His inability to flit was trapping them all, in the claws of this army. Perhaps after all there were only fifty men. That was still more than enough to slaughter everyone here.

The magistrates reined in, a stone's throw from the blockhouse. They were confident. "Hey, you in there!" one of them shouted. "Surrender to the authority of the Magus!"

"Will I fuck," Dhjerga yelled. He moved towards the window. He and Dryjon scuffled, as each tried to prevent the other from reaching the window.

Diejen darted behind them, ran along the catwalk, and pushed the caretaker away from the other window. She leaned out and shouted, "Go away! I am the sister of the Lord Prefect of Lizp, and neither I nor my brother has given you the right of passage through our lands!"

Dhjerga groaned. "That's torn it." Wild-eyed, he shoved Dryjon back against the guard rail of the catwalk. Shotgun shells rolled and tinkled to the floor.

One of the magistrates shaded his eyes. "Well, hello there. It's little Diejen Lizp. So you and your twin are sheltering the deserter? I might have known. Don't worry. He'll receive lenient treatment, if you surrender the human mage."

Colm cupped his hands to his mouth. "I'll give myself up!"

The whole mass of mounted soldiery seemed to sway in the wind as they saw him at the window.

"Don't bother." Wincing and holding his ribs, Dryjon bent for the shotgun he had dropped. "They have just declared war on us. It's been brewing for a while, to be honest." He picked up a handful of shells, broke the shotgun open, and fumbled to insert them.

Dhjerga shoved Diejen out of the way and emptied both barrels of his shotgun out of the window. The two magistrates fell from their horses.

Colm's jaw dropped. Dryjon groaned, "Oh, no." He seemed to be equally shocked by this casual slaughter. Dhjerga was acting like a Marine who'd been at the front too long. They would go berserk at the drop of a hat.

The horses cantered riderless back to the lines. The

flagbearer rode after them. Even before he reached the lines, bullets started crack-thumping.

Diejen let out a high, crazy laugh and returned fire. Dhjerga reloaded and smoothly took her place as she fell back.

"Those two," Dryjon said. "They egg each other on. They always have." He thrust his shotgun at Colm. "I'm going to fetch some more ammunition. We didn't bring enough for this kind of thing."

Left at the window, Colm squeezed off a shot or two. He had not much hope of hitting anything. Bullets sang past him, through the window, and crunched into the ceiling, or struck gong-like notes when they ricocheted off the generator housing, cracking the pretty enamel pictures. He hardly dared to look out of the window long enough to aim. He was no great marksman, anyway. Where he came from, the guns did the shooting for you.

When he ran out of shells, he edged one eye past the side of the window. The bleeding, torn bodies of men and horses littered the snow. But on the track from the caretaker's cottage, well out of shotgun range, stood a familiar covered cart. As Colm watched, another soldier slithered down the tailgate, and another. They sprinted forward to join the fray.

Colm tried to wrap his head around the logistics of a siege where both sides had unlimited access to men and ammo. It could theoretically continue until the enemy advanced to the power house behind breastworks of their dead. Until they climbed to the windows on a rampart of corpses.

Or until one side fell behind in the desperate race to replenish their assets, giving the enemy time to pounce.

One of the fallen horses shrieked, kicking in agony while its guts steamed on the snow.

Another scream pierced through the racket of gunfire. It came from inside the blockhouse.

Colm turned. Neither Diejen nor Dhjerga had noticed the scream. They were shooting, reloading, shooting.

Colm jumped down off the catwalk and ran to the passage at the back of the turbine hall.

One of the smallest children barrelled into him, wailing in terror.

Shots boomed in the battery room as Colm skidded in. Three soldiers lay bleeding into the blue-tinted puddles. They wore the khaki that Colm now understood to be the uniform of the Magistocracy. The Lizp liverymen and the caretaker's wife dragged them over to the wall, leaving slug-trails of blood. But how had they got in? This room had no door …

Dryjon was hauling a satchel of ammunition, too heavy to lift, clear of the icy puddles.

Colm shouted, "Where'd those guys come from?" But as he spoke, he got it. They were Ghosts. They didn't need a door. Just a power source. They had come from the *batteries*.

Dryjon yelled over the noise of gunfire from outside, "The idea isn't so much to inflict damage. It's a tactic to hog the foe's energy. If they're sending people through—even if we drop them immediately—we can't use the power source for our own needs. I managed to grab this much ammo before they keyed in on the batteries. Mind taking it to the others?" The air began to shimmer. "Oh, shit. Here they come again …"

CHAPTER 10

The ends of the hanging wires spat sparks. The Lizp liverymen levelled their rifles. Clots of unearthly brilliance in the air became mirages of men, and then—

BOOM. BOOM.

Two more soldiers dropped to the floor between the battery tubs, stone dead.

Colm felt like he was losing his mind. He reminded himself that this was only what Axel and the other Marines used to face when they were fighting Ghosts on the surface. But it didn't help.

The hanging wires sparked again. There were twenty tubs but Dhjerga and Colm had only hooked up ten of them. The other wires hung free.

"If there's anything at all you can do to help, now's the time," Dryjon said with a pale attempt at levity.

Colm stared at the hanging wires.

That might work.

He couldn't do magic, but he knew a few things about electricity.

"Have you got any spare cable around here?"

Dryjon stared at him. "You're hard to understand sometimes."

"Cable. *Cable*. Like that stuff up there, for God's sake. Wire with insulation on it."

"Oh. Lifelines. There are some spares in the storage closet, I think."

"Fantastic."

Rolling a heavy cable spool back to the battery room, Colm

heard more shots from up ahead. He ignored them this time. He kicked the end of the cable behind him. It was insulated, although the insulation just looked like a cloth binding dipped in tar.

"Throw that out the window of the turbine hall," he yelled over his shoulder. "And then tell them to stop firing."

*

The roar of shotguns from the blockhouse sputtered into nothing.

Outside, the last magistrate, observing the battle from the treeline—but visible, in his black cloak, to Colm, who was standing on the stepladder in the battery room, looking out the window—hand-signalled to his troops.

The khaki soldiers, now numbering more than when they had arrived, despite the dozens of corpses on the snow, ceased fire. For a moment no one moved. Silence returned to the valley.

Then harness and buckles jingled. The Magistocracy troops formed up into a wedge, with the surviving cavalry in the lead.

Colm turned from the window. A length of cable trailed over the sill beside him. His hand hovered above a switch improvised from two planks and Dryjon's bayonet. He hissed, "Is everyone standing on the table?"

"Yes," Dhjerga said, standing on one of the wooden stools in the doorway, eyes wide with curiosity. "Or on something else made of wood, like you said."

But the two liverymen were not standing on anything except the icy floor. They remained at their posts, ready to take out the next intruders. "Get them out of here," Colm begged.

The magistrate lowered his arm sharply.

The cavalrymen began to trot.

The footsoldiers jogged behind them.

Onto the patio, where the snow had been churned up into wet pink slush.

In that slush lay the end of Colm's cable, and another one dangling from the window of the turbine hall, which stretched through the power house to the battery room.

The riders picked up speed.

A volley of bullets slammed into the blockhouse.

They were all on the patio now.

They're just copies, Colm reminded himself. Just copies, just copies, just copies! But oh, the poor horses—

He threw the switch. Vicious sparks popped as the circuit closed.

The horses foundered as if their legs had been cut out from under them.

The riders dropped their weapons, slid from their saddles.

The infantry collapsed, and Colm hid his face in his hands. He had connected the batteries in series, maximizing the voltage of the generator's output … and hence the differential between the wet snow on the patio, a conductor, and the foe's feet. All that power was now coursing through the people out there, stopping their hearts and charring their flesh.

"Oh fuck," Dhjerga yelled. Colm turned to see the two liverymen staggering, jerking. As he had feared, the circuit ran through the battery room, too. Wet outside, wet inside. Their shoes offered no protection.

Just copies, just copies—

He threw the switch to break the circuit, half a second

before Dhjerga leapt off the stool, forgetting Colm's warnings.

Dhjerga shoved Colm aside and clambered to the top of the ladder. "Amazing," he breathed, staring out of the window.

Dryjon and Diejen crashed into the room. Diejen brushed past Colm and climbed the ladder, squeezing around Dhjerga to see out. "They're all dead," she said in wonder.

"Including ours," Dryjon said, glancing at the liverymen. "So you can do magic, after all." His gaze rested coolly on Colm.

"That wasn't magic," Colm said. He wrapped rags around his hands for extra protection, as he didn't really trust the insulation on the cables. He hurried from tub to tub, disconnecting the batteries before anyone else managed to electrocute themselves. "It was electrical engineering 101."

"I don't care what it was," Dryjon said. "You saved our lives and ended the Magistocracy's illegal incursion into Lizp Province. But if they broke the law once, they'll break it again. So I would like you to teach us that spell, and any others you know."

Colm had to step over one of the dead liverymen to reach the last battery tub. "Wouldn't you rather have streetlights? Trains? Telephones?"

The faces of the three siblings were blank. Diejen whispered to Dhjerga, "What's he talking about *now?*"

"Faerie machines," Dhjerga muttered.

"Oh, yes," Diejen said. "I know about those. Machines that do the work of people. Sorry, but we don't believe in that kind of thing."

"Well ..." Dhjerga said.

"No, never mind that stuff," Dryjon said. "It's this power

spell I'm interested in. Naturally, we'll compensate you for your help."

Colm climbed on the stepladder to hook the wires out of the way. "Wouldn't you rather have spaceships?"

"Ships for flying between worlds," Dhjerga murmured to the others.

"You've never flown," Colm said. "You've never seen your homeworld from space. It changes your life. You see how small and precious everything is." They stared at him blankly. "Flying! Flying!" he said impatiently, stretching out his arms like a kid playing airplane, to show them what he meant. His body ached for the esthesia prickle of the vacuum, the kiss of re-entry heat, all the sensations of speed and freedom. He had spent his whole adult life flying, first light planes and then jets and then spaceships. It had been about getting away. From home, from Earth, from his father. Now he'd got further away than he ever imagined … and he would never fly again. He jumped off the stepladder. "Anyway, I'm fucking scunnered wi' this," he said, picking up the ladder. "I'll not be helping you anymore."

Dhjerga caught his arm. "Wait. Could you build us a spaceship?"

Colm felt like throwing the stepladder at him. He set it down by the wall. "It's not that easy."

"If I fetched you all the materials and tools, could you do it?"

"Probably not."

"Come outside. No, come on." Colm was too despondent to resist. Dhjerga dragged him back to the turbine hall. The door stood open. The snow outside was littered with bodies. Hralf the caretaker and his family were on the far side of the patio, struggling with the abandoned power cart. Dhjerga hauled Colm outside and pointed up. "See that?"

The cold wind sliced Colm's face. He shaded his eyes. The sun was still just peeking over the horizon; it did not seem to have moved. The gas giant sat on the hilltop behind the dam, a pale ghost in the daylight. "What?"

"The moon." It looked like a tiny green-tinged soap bubble on the gas giant's pale face. "That's Atletis."

"So?"

"That's the Magistocracy's headquarters. There's only one power source up there, and it belongs to the Magus. When we visit HQ, we're not even allowed to go outside. We're gloved from the minute we arrive until the minute we leave. We can't surprise him ... *But if we had a spaceship, we could.*"

"Maybe," Colm said indifferently.

"So build a spaceship for us! Help us kick the Magus's face down his throat.

"Who is this Magus, anyway?" The word felt like a rock in his mouth.

"He's the one that started the war, back when I was a kid." The first Ghosts had appeared on Earth's colony worlds twenty-five years ago, when Colm was a kid. He and Dhjerga were about the same age. It fit. "Kill him, and the war ends."

"Really?"

"Yes." Dhjerga walked to the nearest corpse and rolled it onto its back. He straightened out the limbs, folded the fast-cooling hands on the chest, closed the eyes. "We're born to die. But there's too much dying among us these days. Everyone's tired of it."

"They're only slaves," Diejen said. Colm had not seen her behind him. Dryjon was there too.

"It has to end," Dhjerga said.

"You're just making more work for the caretakers," Diejen said.

Dhjerga straightened up. "Back on this world called Juradis, Colm freed all the faeries' slaves. He risked his life to liberate *aliens!* It was fantastic." He spun to face Colm. "Can you refuse to do the same for us? For them?" He gestured at the dead. The men Colm had killed. Just copies, just ... "People like you?"

"Oh, damn," Colm said quietly. He rubbed his knuckles over his mouth. "If I build you a spaceship ..."

"Then we'll help you get home, of course," Dhjerga said with a quick glance at his brother and sister.

Colm stiffened. He searched Dhjerga's face to see if he was serious. "There's a way? You can help me get back to Earth?"

Dhjerga grinned. "Where there's a will ..."

Colm sagged, realizing Dhjerga had no idea how he could get back to Earth, either. He was just hoping something would turn up.

"No, no," Dryjon said. He strode forward, sticking out his right hand. "We can do better than that." His open, earnest brown eyes met Colm's. "Help us save our homeworld ... and we'll help you save yours."

Colm thought glancingly about the difficulty, not to say impossibility, of building a spaceship on a planet where technological progress had not even got as far as steam engines. But he had to give it a shot, didn't he? Even if they could not help him return to Earth, maybe they could help Earth. The Ghosts had started the war; Ghosts could end it.

"All right, you're on." He stuck out his hand. Dryjon clasped his forearm in the odd gesture favored by the Ghosts.

Dhjerga and Diejen joined the clasp. They stood there for a moment among the corpses.

"So," Dhjerga said. "A spaceship. What do you need?"

CHAPTER 11

Barjoltan, the third and smallest of the Big Three terraformed planets orbiting Betelgeuse, was a shipyard.

It did not have a shipyard *on* it, or in orbit around it. It *was* a shipyard. Every inch of the surface had been strip-mined, or turned over to heavily polluting industrial processes. Pithead refineries and sprawling factories delivered materials to the fab clusters scattered over the planet's two landmasses, which produced components ranging from 5-nanometer semiconductors to 500-meter hull plates. The actual ships—as well as drones, satellites, and the semi-sentient weapons known as Walking Guns—were put together at the assembly plants ringing two large spaceports, one on each landmass.

It had been easy for Dhjerga to find the place.

He already had a fix on Juradis, and after that it was just a matter of looking for another blazing big power source nearby.

The hard part was finding what he needed.

He had discarded his own clothes and borrowed a uniform from a human. Not a copy. A human. There were a lot of them about, now that they'd occupied this world along with its two sister worlds. The uniform, a coverall with the blazon HRF GROUND SUPPORT on the back, fit all right, and the weirdly soft dark blue fabric did not show the bloodstains.

He had not wanted to kill its prior owner, but he had got so used to killing that he did it without thinking.

He blamed the Magus, who had trained and shaped him into a killer.

He also blamed the Magus for the feelings of confusion

and inferiority that assaulted him as he wandered through the shipyard. It had been bad enough on Juradis, which was a colony world like other colony worlds—farms, power sources, people to be killed. This was different altogether. His people had nothing like this. We are primitives, he thought. Peasants who know one thing and do it well. These people know *everything*.

He walked purposefully along corridors where the walls breathed and the floors shivered, and loitered as long as he dared in the vast workshops where the humans congregated in the glare of faerie lights. He was trying to overhear any word or phrase that might point him in the right direction. The humans gave him puzzled glances—not, he thought, because he looked wrong, for he did not look wrong. He was wearing the coverall, pretending to be one of them. No, what puzzled them was the fact that he carried a piece of paper, on which Colm had written down a long list of things he needed. No one carried *paper* here. They all had faerie books.

Colm had told him to get a faerie book. He could start there.

The things proliferated in here like rats in a granary— squatting upon desks, riding on people's belts, swinging from their lanyards, or clutched in the palms of soft plump hands, puffing melty fireworks into the air. He walked around a cavern where faerie machines thumped like thunder, hammering pieces of metallic stuff into impossibly delicate shapes. He saw a large faerie book sitting on an unattended desk. He took it.

There was a distinction between *taking* and *fetching*, which Dhjerga had tried to explain to Colm without success. When you *fetched* things—or people—their originals stayed at home.

But the resulting copies were, well, copies. Never quite as good. Liable to break. Which didn't matter in general, because they were *copies;* you could always make more.

But this time, it did matter. Betelgeuse was so *far* from Kisperet. It had taken him so long to get here. And it would take just as long again to fetch a replacement if this faerie book broke, because it was a copy and subtly flawed.

So he took the original. Who cared if they noticed it was missing? They'd just put it down to their own carelessness.

Ambling past the desk, he aimed a glance at the big, C-shaped faerie book upon it, tracing with his eyes the lifeline that ran to the power outlet in the floor. He snorted up some of the power under the floor. The faerie book vanished, lifeline and all. A small flurry of dust settled to the desk. Dhjerga wandered on, feelng a bit better.

They had no notion of security, these Earth humans. Power ran through the assembly plant like blood through a living body. It was not just that they didn't guard their power sources. This plant—this whole spaceport—*was* a power source, with lifelines woven through the walls and floors, every building studded with energy nodes that made the horse-powered and water-powered generators back home look like candles. All right, blame the faeries; but the humans were just as bad. When he was in the Kuiper Belt, he'd seen Earth from a distance, blazing like a bloody bonfire. They were asking for it.

That's what the Magus said.

Dhjerga shivered, and quickened his steps. He was done with letting the Magistocracy tell him what to think. He had believed the Magistocracy when they said that the humans from Earth were all copies ... they *acted* like copies, and poor-quality ones at that, neither following orders, nor doing anything interesting ... but that didn't matter! They were humans, just like him. He would *not* kill any more of them.

Half an hour later, he had to kill a woman who tried to prevent him from leaving the assembly plant. Then some more people came running, so he flitted a few hundred miles to Barjoltan's other landmass. He wound up in a sun-bleached scrapyard, coughing on hot, nearly unbreathable air. He flitted again to the inside of the faerie mound whose chimneys he could see in the distance. This seemed more promising: no humans, just loads of machines making bits and bobs and ferrying them to a shipping center. But he still didn't know where to find what he was looking for. He prowled around the shipping center, comparing the labels on boxes to the words on Colm's list, without success. All this flitting around had taken it out of him, and he had now killed two people without getting any closer to his goal. He sat down on an empty pallet and put his head in his hands.

A querulous growl snapped his gaze up.

The shipping center was built around a semicircular loading dock, where machines transferred things onto the motorized carts called, Dhjerga knew, *trucks.* A different kind of cart, the kind that they called *car,* had just pulled up at the loading dock. A five-foot furry alien, wearing clothes, stood on its hind legs behind the car's open door.

Dhjerga knew this alien, unless it was a different one of the same kind.

"Am I going to have to kill you, too?" he said to it.

"You left a fine mess over on Parsimine," the alien said, referring to the other landmass. "All the humans are running in circles, imagining sentrienza treachery. But when I saw the camera footage, I realized it was only you."

Dhjerga groaned. He had forgotten about the all-seeing eyes called 'cameras.' "And I thought I was being so fucking clever, disguising myself."

"Have you come alone this time?"

Dhjerga knew this was a reference to his visit to Juradis. He now also knew that this *was* the same alien. "Yes. Sorry about your castle, by the way." He and his lads had wrecked it.

The alien dipped his head. "It was old, and needed redecorating." He closed the car door, revealing a pistol in one of his middle claws. Even odds whether Dhjerga would have been able to reach him before he got off a shot around the car door.

The alien holstered his weapon and undulated towards Dhjerga on his two rearmost sets of feet, with the rest of him raised off the ground—an oddly elegant gait. It was hot in the shipping center, the air full of dust, not much better than outside. The alien let out a prim, cat-like sneeze. "Excuse me. What brings you back to the Betelgeuse system?"

Dhjerga decided to ask the alien for help. He hated asking for help, or admitting to ignorance about anything. But if the alien tried to nobble him, he'd simply flit. "This." He extended Colm's list.

"'All types of sensors,'" the alien read aloud. "'Gyroscopes. Inertial dead reckoning platform. Vernier controls. Don't bother trying to steal sheets of aluminum, or anything else we can make here. Tools to make tools: an electron beam furnace, a hot isostatic press ...'" Further down the page there was another heading, *Engine*. "'Combustion chamber. Niobium alloy engine bells, *not* the titanium alloy ones, they're rubbish.'"

The alien turned the paper over. "Drugs. Anything you can find. Cocaine. Morphine derivatives. But what I really need is tropodolfin …'" The alien's voice caught. "Who wrote this?"

"Someone you'll remember," Dhjerga said.

The alien dropped the list. The paper fluttered to the floor. "Colm is *alive?*"

"He is," Dhjerga said.

"Where?"

"On a colony world," Dhjerga said evasively. "I can't tell you exactly where." This rule of the Magistocracy's seemed wise to observe. An alien, after all, was an alien. "But he's very much alive, I promise you." He hoped it was still true.

"Oh, my friend," the alien said quietly. His black eyes shone. "He's somewhere safe, then?"

Dhjerga grimaced. "Is there anywhere safe?"

"Too true. Too true." The alien picked up the list with a hindclaw and transferred it to a front one. "This looks like a list of spaceship components."

"It is." Dhjerga did not mention where the spaceship would be flying to, if they got it built.

After a moment, the alien dipped his head. "What can I do to help? I have already taken the precaution of disabling the cameras in this facility."

"Thanks." Dhjerga pointed at the list. "Well, I'm not *exactly* sure what a hot isostatic press is…"

CHAPTER 12

That night, an automated inventory scan detected 193 separate items missing from the shipping center. The losses were not connected with the unexplained murders on Barjoltan's other continent.

By that time Dhjerga Lizp was far away.

And Gil was back in his car, on his way to see Axel Best, bursting with his news.

Axel had been seconded to the team managing the Barjoltan shipyards. The Fleet needed to build as many new ships as possible within the next three years. The nearest sentrienza system to Betelgeuse was Rigel, 18 months away by FTL—add in the time for drones to carry the news there, and you had a tight timeframe. The mood now was tense, but cautiously optimistic. They had beaten one sentrienza fleet. Perhaps they could beat a second one.

Civilian experts had been plucked out of the refugee masses and were working to master the sentrienza assembly processes. Gil found Axel in a towering vehicle assembly building, listening to a group of engineers explain the theory behind the antiquark drives used in sentrienza ships. Overhead, an almost-complete drive module hung in its cradle. The doors of the assembly building stood open; Betelgeuse shone in. Dry wind whipped the dangling lines and cables, and deposited dust on Gil's fur.

Axel said to the engineers, "OK, let me see if I've got this straight. It heterodynes the Q-field and the gauge field, flipping half of the down quarks in a given chunk of matter into down antiquarks. When that happens, the neutrons in the said chunk of matter decompose to an up quark and pure energy. Correct?"

Gil raised himself onto his hind legs. "In fact, you are considerably over-simplifying it. But yes, that is how it works. Antiquark power is superior to nuclear fusion on all key performance metrics, with the single exception that it is not easily weaponized. That is why the sentrienza continue to rely on nuclear bombs for anti-personnel applications."

"Hello, Gil," Axel said. "So you're an expert, too? "

Gil gazed up at the drive module. Like all sentrienza machines, it looked half-organic, like a cross between a giant geode and a termite nest. That lumpy shell contained some of the galaxy's most arcane applied physics. However, he had no doubt that the humans could reverse-engineer it. There was a reason the sentrienza had fast-tracked them as a future slave race: their minds were as sharp as claws. And if they ran into trouble, there were several queazel engineers in the group. "I suggest you let them get on with it," he said gently to Axel.

"What he *meant* to say," Axel told the engineers, "is that I'm due for a coffee break. Don't blow us all up while I'm gone."

"Fine, we'll wait until you come back," said the lead engineer.

"Screw you," Axel grinned. "I'll see if I can find any of those algae cookies." He and Gil walked across the assembly floor, between other modules waiting to be triple-checked before they were lifted into space. "I just can't help trying to understand everything," Axel said, ruefully pushing at his fringe.

Gil had observed the banter. The engineers had been laughing *with* Axel. Formerly, they would have been laughing *at* him. Axel had loosened up, got better around people, and

Gil thought he knew why. "How is Meg?"

"Grouchier than a rattlesnake," Axel sighed. But a smile spread from his eyes to his mouth. "At least she's over the morning sickness. But now she's starting to show, you know? Which means we're gonna have to tell the Rat. She didn't want to tell anyone. I'm like, honey, people are going to notice … But hey, taking maternity leave might be better than dancing attendance on the faerie princess. She hates that assignment."

Axel led the way into a break room with a claustrophobic low ceiling. Exhausted technicians sprawled on the overstuffed sentrienza furniture. A coffee machine stood on a side table. Coffee was one of Gil's healthier human vices. Axel pushed the button and filled two disposable cups. Gil remembered drinking coffee with Colm in the Uzzizellan embassy on Gna. The memory always brought a shiver of nostalgia. Now excitement tempered the sadness. He hugged his news, savoring the anticipation of telling Axel.

"I'm still trying to wrap my head around it." Axel said, cradling his coffee cup. "I never saw myself as a father, but …" He smiled dazedly.

"Have you told your own father yet?"

Axel's father, Philip K. Best, served as the governor of Juradis. Gil worked with him in his role as a liaison for the queazel community, and considered him a fundamentally decent man, whose yen for risk-taking was only what one might expect from the former CEO of an interstellar corporation. Philip was, anyway, a better man than his son gave him credit for.

"Nope," Axel said. "Guess I'll have to at some point." He shrugged.

"Then you are not thinking of naming the child after him?"

"It might be a girl! Anyway, no." Axel pushed a plate of algae cookies across the table. "These are awful, I'm warning you."

"What will you call the child, then?"

"Meg wants to name it after Colm."

The name made Gil jump. "You don't agree?"

"I'm just hoping it's a girl," Axel joked. His shoulders sank a fraction. "She misses him. I get that. I miss him too. But ..."

It was on the tip of Gil's tongue to blurt out his news. He had met Dhjerga Lizp. Colm was alive! But the sudden darkness in Axel's expression held him back. Gil had been a diplomat for years; he defaulted to discretion when in doubt. And now he doubted whether in fact Axel would welcome his news. He lapped a mouthful of coffee. It was not very good. "Do you think Meg misses him ... *too* much?"

Axel sighed. "That's one way of putting it."

"How else would you put it?"

"We all want things that aren't good for us sometimes." Axel raised his head and with a challenging stare turned it around on Gil. "You'd know all about that, wouldn't you?"

"This coffee is quite horrible," Gil said. "The blend has been adulterated. The best coffee in the Betelgeuse system comes from my own estate at the north pole of Juradis."

"I know. You introduced the crop yourself, didn't you?"

"I did. One of my small successes."

"You introduced tobacco, too, right?"

"Yes ..."

"And grapes."

"*Not* a success. The soil is too alkaline and dry. Anyway, our hawbrother berries make a superior beverage."

"So you're sticking to hawbrother wine these days? That's

good to know."

Gil wriggled his hindquarters in irritation. Axel had seen him at his worst, when he was a recluse, living alone at Castle Nulth with a bottomless supply of drink and drugs. "I have lost my taste for stimulants, if that is what you're asking." He had not touched tropodolfin, or any of the myriad other substances humans had invented to improve on nature's chemistry, since Colm disappeared. Now he felt a twinge of the old craving. It was Axel's fault.

"Colm was a junkie," Axel said brutally. "We caught him … well, never mind. It freaked Meg out." He gazed into his coffee cup, lips sealed.

Gil knew that quite well. *He,* after all, had encouraged Colm's tropodolfin addiction, for the sake of the CHEMICAL MAGE project. At Castle Nulth, he had shared his supply with him. Watched as the drug interacted with Colm's implant, unleashing his gift for magic. And he had gotten an illicit thrill—hadn't he?—out of sharing his most degrading vice with someone else. Having a companion on the road to hell.

A friend.

On Dhjerga Lizp's list, handwritten by Colm, had appeared the damning words: *Tropodolfin … or ANYTHING you can find …*

Colm must be suffering agonies, wherever he was. Gil had experienced the misery of withdrawal for himself, and queazel physiology was more resistant to addiction than human. He did not want to put Colm through that wretched cycle again.

So when Dhjerga had said, "And what about this stuff? Is it chemicals or what? Any of that around here?" Gil had said no. It was true, anyway—hard drugs were not found in spaceship component distribution centers. No, he doesn't *really* need that, he had said—and Dhjerga, believing him, had crossed those items off the list.

Gil had been there that night on the weather deck of the *Unsinkable* when Colm vanished. He shivered at the memory of the crazy glitter in Colm's eyes, and the rattling of the spoons … and that instant when he had found himself alone, with only a chill in the air.

CHEMICAL MAGE had been a mistake. It had accomplished nothing. It had inadvertently brought the Ghosts to Sol system, killed hundreds of innocent subjects, and wrecked Colm's life. Gil refused to be complicit in continuing the deadly experiment—and he believed that Colm's plea for drugs was simply withdrawal talking.

After all, Colm had also asked for spaceship parts.

A more than typically resourceful human, he was building his own ship.

He would be coming back the usual way, via FTL.

And that, Gil now decided, would be soon enough for Axel to know about his return. Axel and Meg had a chance to be happy. However unexpected and inconvenient, their child would bring them joy. It had already made a new man of Axel. His mental state would *not* be improved by the knowledge that his rival was on the way home.

"Was there any specific reason you came out here?" Axel said, with a determined smile. "It can't have been for the coffee …"

"No it was for the algae cookies," Gil said, swirling one up with his tongue. "Ugh. Quite disgusting."

"I warned you."

"How are the new builds coming along?"

"We're ahead of schedule. Five frigates and three cruisers completed. That's in addition to the ships we got from the Duke of Noom."

"The sentrienza's Rigel fleet is thirty ships strong. If they send the entire fleet …"

"We'll crush them." Axel spoke for the benefit of the civilians nearby. His eyes told a different story. He was worried. Even the Rat, Gil knew, was worried. And why should they not be? Even if they did crush the Rigel fleet, there'd be another fleet behind that one. And another. And another. How could the humans and queazels prevail against a 500-world empire?

Gil had had a thought in his mind for some time which he uttered now. "Sooner or later we shall have to take the fight to Elphame."

Elphame: the homeworld of the sentrienza, abode of the Gray Emperor. A fortress world in the Orion Cluster, more than 2,000 light years from here. Gil, of course, had never been there, but he'd been hearing about its impregnability since he was a kit.

"Damn straight. Show the faerie bastards no mercy," Axel said. He clearly took Gil's comment for bravado, and Gil left it there.

"The minefields around Noom and Juradis are almost complete," Gil said. The queazels had responsibility for those. "It would help if we had some Walking Guns to reinforce our defenses."

Axel grimaced. "Have to talk to Princess Emnl. Sorry, I mean *Queen* Emnl." The sentrienza princess had insisted on the title as a condition of helping the humans, even though it was meaningless, since she remained in the Fleet's power "The Guns are her big bargaining chip. She won't turn them over to our control without some major concessions. Meg is supposed to be negotiating that right now ..."

CHAPTER 13

Meg lay on her back beneath a beach parasol, watching seventy-two Walking Guns carve calligraphic tracks across the sky. They were *Flying* Guns as well. Beyond the parasol's shade, Betelgeuse pounded the white sand of Skaldaffi, an island in Juradis's northern hemisphere. Waves frilled on the beach. Children, wearing sun hats the size of truck tyres, romped in the foam, catching the pink pearl jellyfish that floated ashore at this time of year. Meg was watching the Walking Guns because she couldn't bear to watch the children. This time last year, the sight of human children playing would have brought an uncomplicated smile to her face. Now, it awoke the abiding horror that swamped her mind whenever she thought of the future. It had been downright cruel of Emnl to make her come here.

But of course, Emnl *was* downright cruel. She was dangling the Flying Guns like a carrot in front of the Rat's nose. They were skywriting now, spelling out the word *Victory* in sentrienza, human, queazel, and shablag script. The mara, the other slave race who lived on Juradis, were illiterate. But even they (there were a couple of mara on the beach, catching fish with their hands) gazed approvingly at the display. It looked like a promise: *Victory* … But *whose* victory? This aerobatic display ratcheted up the pressure on Meg to deliver the goods.

"Would it kill you to let us use them temporarily?" she snapped.

"You know my price," Emnl replied.

And the trouble was, Meg did.

Emnl's lavender hair trailed across the sand. She lay on a

stripy towel, swathed in a protective garment resembling a multicolored burkini. Sentrienza skin was even more vulnerable than human to the high levels of UV radiation from Betelgeuse. Large mirrored sunglasses hid her eyes, but Meg just knew the bitch was gloating.

"In fact, I'm doing you a favor," Emnl said. "Our contract, as initially formulated, was a fair exchange. In return for the life of Axel Best, you promised me your firstborn child."

Meg looked away, balling the material of her sarong in her fist. Back on Sakassarib, where she signed that contract, she had thought it was a sentrienza joke. If it got them off that damn iceball, she'd have signed anything. She never planned on having kids, anyway ...

Well, look at her now. The sarong tied high under her breasts hid the little four-month bump, but she felt the fetus moving every day now. The first time, it had scared the shit out of her. She'd gone to the clinic, thinking something was wrong. No, said the automated diagnosis system. Your baby is perfectly healthy. She'd been glad that day that there was no human staffer on duty. She'd related the whole episode to Axel as a joke, and he'd duly teased her about it. "I guess we're all dumb, when it comes to babies."

You got that right, Axel.

She felt so dumb, not just about babies but in general.

So dumb.

Sure, Smythe. A piece of paper, or bisshengri hide, or whatever it was, signed in a sentrienza mound on an iceball in the Betelgeuse system, can't possibly be enforceable ...

Except now it was. Because Emnl had the whole Fleet over a barrel. The Marine guards standing at the treeline, and the gunboat in the lagoon, were just window dressing. Emnl, though still a prisoner, held the whip hand. The Rat had authorized Meg to offer the sentrienza princess—OK, queen—pretty much anything she might ask for in exchange for the Walking Guns.

Emnl had asked for clothes, jewellery, and a tropical holiday, for starters, but Meg knew she was just toying with them. She only wanted one thing.

Meg's baby.

"You owe it to me *anyway!*" Emnl reminded her. "I'll throw in the Guns as a bonus." She made them loop the loop in the bright yellowish-blue sky. People applauded. "Out of the goodness of my heart."

Meg pushed herself up on her elbows. "The goodness of your heart? Don't make me laugh."

"You can have a caesarean section at seven months," Emnl said. "The Rigel fleet cannot get here any sooner than that."

"Why do you *really* want it? Why mine? I know you guys had a nasty habit of stealing human babies in the old days. But why be so picky? There are hundreds of kids around here." Meg gestured at the children wading in the surf with their dripping nets full of jellyfish. She felt bad for suggesting that Emnl pick on someone else, but she knew it wouldn't happen. Emnl was only interested in *her* baby, for reasons she refused to disclose.

"It is sure to be a nice baby," Emnl said placidly. "How could it be otherwise, with parents like you and Major Best?"

And she twitched her sunglasses down, and winked at Meg with her optical membrane, one eye transforming from a faceted golf ball into a luminous blue orb that reminded Meg of Emnl's mother, the late queen.

She knows.

Meg had never been sure on this point. After all, how could Emnl have gotten access to her medical records? But now she was certain.

She knows.

She got up, stumbling as the blood rushed to her head. She jammed her sun hat on.

"Where are you going?" Emnl said in alarm.

"To talk to Bella. She's right over there. I assume I'm still allowed to chat with my girlfriends?"

*

In fact, Bella Tan was Meg's only girlfriend. She was married to Suleiman Tan, the ex-Navy pilot who'd flown with Meg and Colm on Majriti IV, and then worked with them in the Kuiper Belt. When the shit hit the fan, you could count on Sully Tan to have your back. His rock-steady reliability was only matched by his wife's gift for making lemons into lemonade. Axel had helped Sully bring his family to Juradis. Now the Tans operated one of the krill fishing factory vessels that plied the planet's oceans, helping to feed the refugees who had formerly been prisoners on those very same ships.

The Tans' ship, the *Vienna,* lay offshore in the haze. They had arranged to call at Skaldaffi when they heard that Meg was coming. She hadn't asked them to do it, but now she was glad they were here.

She sank down in the shade of Bella's parasol, two minutes down the beach from where she'd been sitting with Emnl. "I can't fucking take it anymore."

Bella raised her eyebrows reproachfully. Her younger daughter, Zainab, age six, was building a sandcastle beside her lounger.

"Sorry. I swear like a sailor, I know. But I *am* a sailor. At least I used to be. I mean it, Bella: I cannot go on like this."

"She's a rhymes-with-witch all right," Bella said supportively. "The blood thing? That was just sick."

Emnl had requested a blood bath—literally a bathtub full of blood, to bathe in. Meg and Bella had brainstormed with the manager of the Drumlin Hotel, where they were staying, and ended up filling a tub with fish blood, while saying it was the blood of queazels as requested.

"Well, her mother used to hold court on a throne made of skulls, so like mother, like daughter, I guess," Meg said. "But that's not what I was talking about, actually." She hesitated. Then took the plunge. "I mean this."

She cupped her hands over her stomach. Her temples were pounding. Too much sun.

Bella swung her legs off her lounger and reached for Meg's hands. "Are you OK? You're not bleeding or anything, are you?"

"No." Meg drew on the anger that had been building up ever since Colm left. Since before that. Ever since she was a teenager. "I wish I *was* miscarrying. I—I can't have this baby, Bella. I need to get rid of it."

*

"Please *think* about this, Meg," Bella said desperately.

Meg had threatened to drown herself if Bella didn't help her. Now they were walking through downtown Skaldaffi, a sleepy strip of shops along the road leading to the village in the island's jungly interior. Meg still felt like she was on the way to drown herself. Like mother, like daughter? Meg's mom had committed suicide when she was a teenager. Meg had always resented her for leaving Meg and her father on their own. Now she felt like she honestly might follow in her mother's footsteps, if she couldn't get this straightened out.

White dust coated their sandals and feet. Local humans and mara lounged in the torpid shade of awnings. The only sound was the distant whine of Emnl's Walking Guns, still wasting fuel all over the sky. Crystal, Bella's elder daughter, scuffled behind them with Zainab, the two girls quietly squabbling, upset at being dragged away from the beach.

Meg had told Emnl she was going back to their hotel to get a snack. "Pregnant females eat a lot," Emnl had said understandingly.

In reality, they were going to the island's one and only medical clinic. Now that Meg had made up her mind, she was desperate to get it over with. She needed Bella's help, though, because abortion required the consent of both parents. Bella knew everyone here and would be able to persuade the clinician to make an exception.

Meg just wished she would stop trying to talk her out of it.

"I *have* thought about it, Bella. I've been thinking about it for months."

"I can't believe Axel is OK with this."

And there was the rub. Bella did not know that Meg had lied to Axel, lied to everyone. Yet Emnl had somehow found out …

Meg didn't want Bella to find out, too. That would really complete her fall from grace. She dodged the issue. "Axel knows how I feel. It's like I've got this little alien living inside me, making me fat and tired and sick and grumpy. I hate it." She wasn't even lying. Pregnancy was a major drag, and she felt zero emotional connection to the fetus. How could she, when someone else had a prior claim on it?

Bella rubbed her eyes with tanned knuckles. The sight of

her tears shocked Meg. Bella was as tough as nails. "You're not totally wrong. They *are* like little aliens at first. Cry, feed, poop, sleep, cry, repeat." She glanced back at her daughters. "But oh, Meg, it's the best experience you'll ever have in your life! The first time your child smiles at you, you'll forget all the pain and sickness and grumpiness. You will wonder how you ever could've thought of—of getting rid of it." They were standing in front of the clinic. "Please, please." Bella grasped Meg's wrist as she reached out to open the door. "Please give him or her a chance!"

Meg jerked away. Bella was making her think about the fetus, dammit. Think about it as if it were a child. This wasn't helping.

"I know you want your life back. But is that really a good enough reason to—to end the baby's life?"

"Mommy? Mommy, are you OK?"

Crystal and Zainab pulled at their mother's arms, their squabbles forgotten.

"Mommy, why are you crying?"

"It's OK, darlings," Bella said. "Auntie Meg felt a bit sick. But she's fine now. Aren't you, Meg?" She stared challengingly at Meg, daring her to enter the clinic in front of these two lovely, un-aborted children.

Meg went in.

Bella followed her and flopped down, stone-faced, on one of the benches. There were several people waiting ahead of them.

Crystal and Zainab made a beeline for the crate of toys in one corner. Meg stared at the screen on the far wall. A reminder that skin cancer was less costly to cure if caught early. The same went for pregnancy, obviously. Four months was pushing it. But it was still technically possible.

"Please don't give me any more shit, Bella," she said. "Please just *help*. I've gone round and round and round in circles and there's no other way."

CHAPTER 14

Axel threw the *Shihoka* in reckless S-curves through the sky of Juradis, showing off the power of the antiquark drive. The fighter was one of the latest ships to come out of the Barjoltan shipyards. The engineers had integrated a sentrienza propulsion system into an upgraded version of the Vulture airframe.

The sentrienza did not commonly manufacture fighters, as they had not had any enemies to fight for several thousand years. It turned out that there was another reason, too: at high velocities, the antiquark drive's specialized external heat rejectors produced a static buildup on the skin of the spacecraft, as they collected electrons from the ionized gas in space faster than they could be discharged. There wasn't *much* ionized gas in space, but when you were travelling at fighter speed, you bumped into enough of it that the electrons added up.

The human and queazel engineers on Barjoltan had hacked the static buildup problem by installing plasma contactor units, which grounded the new fighters to their space environments. It wasn't a real solution, but they didn't have time to pursue perfection.

Every pilot in the Fleet hoped for the chance to fly one of the new fighters in the defence of Betelgeuse system. Axel didn't know if he would be selected, after his ambiguous performance on Noom. Hopefully today's flight would count in his favor. He glanced aft, using the *Shihoka's* internal cameras, to see if his passengers were suitably impressed. They sat frozen in their couches, looking queasy.

Axel flipped the *Shihoka* over and dropped the ship into a dive. Nicholas Smythe grabbed for a barf bag.

Professor Smythe, actually.

Meg's father.

He had been a professor of English at the University of Tokyo, until the Ghosts conquered the city.

Now, newly arrived on Juradis, he sat next to Axel's father, Philip K. Best, rigidly watching his personal screen as the ocean hurtled at them. Nicholas was short and pudgy, with a receding hairline that testified to his scanty professor's salary; Philip, tall and personable, oozed money from every surgically minimized pore. They were not obvious soulmates.

Never mind. Axel was looking forward to springing Nicholas Smythe on Meg. Her father was the only family she had. His surprise arrival on the planet would hopefully give a much-needed boost to her spirits.

Axel levelled out close enough to the sea to make both passengers gasp, and decelerated to a vertical landing on the highest point of Skaldaffi, where a flexible asphalt platform had been put in. "Welcome to Juradis, Nick," he said. The professor had asked him to call him Nick.

Even Philip K. Best wobbled a bit as he descended from the airlock. "Very impressive flying," he commented dryly. Axel hid a smile. He knew he had acted like a rebellious teenager, but he just couldn't help it. Besides, his father had done terrible things. He deserved worse than a somewhat hair-raising deorbit flight.

"My implant's performing well," he said, guiding them across the asphalt to the thatched shack that served as a terminal.

Like almost everything Axel said to his father, this was a

thinly disguised jab. His implant had been a present from his parents when he was 17. It not only delivered high-end esthesia functionality, on a par with the implants issued to Navy pilots, but tweaked his brain chemistry to control the peaks and troughs of his moods. Sometimes he disabled it. He kept thinking he could make it on his own, without the tech. But he never had been able to cope without it, not long-term. Right now it was enabled. He couldn't afford to go into a downwards spiral when Meg needed him to stay positive.

"They don't know we're coming," he told Philip and Nicholas, in a half-apology that there was no vehicle waiting to meet them. They started down the steep hill from the two-bit spaceport, walking in the shade of the trees.

"Oh?" Philip said. "You mean this *isn't* for our benefit?" He nodded up at the Walking Guns arrowing in formation across the sky.

Nicholas said hoarsely, "They say it only takes one of those things to destroy a planet."

Axel had only heard that about a million times. But he was trying to get along with 'Nick' for Meg's sake, so he said, "Imagine all that power under *our* control! If Meg can successfully negotiate their transfer to the Fleet, she may have saved humanity."

"That's what she always wanted to do," Nicholas said. "That's why she joined the Fleet. I wanted her to stay in college."

He pursed his lips, and sidestepped an overripe spikefruit lying on the track.

Axel triggered his comms implant with a sideways flick of his eyes. He called the *Vienna,* using the *Shihoka* to rebroadcast his signal. "Sully?"

"You upstaged the Walking Guns," Sully Tan said, from the *Vienna,* a dark gray lozenge on the sea. "I'm sure that wasn't on purpose."

"The Eagle has an antimatter cannon," Axel said. "I'm tempted to try it out. Like shooting clays."

"Don't."

"Looks like the display is finished, anyway." The Walking Guns were dropping altitude, converging on the lagoon side of the island. "Are Meg and Bella on the beach?"

"I think so. Let me call Bella." There was a pause. Longer than Axel would have expected.

He walked faster, inhaling the smell of the alien jungle. He remembered his first visit here last year. He and Meg had been confined in a sun-soaked pit after asking too many questions about CHEMICAL MAGE. He glanced back at his father and Nicholas Smythe. The bald top of Nicholas's head had already turned an angry pink.

"Axel?" Sully's voice was urgent.

"Yeah, what is it?"

"Where are you?"

"On the way down from the spaceport."

"Get downtown as quick as you can. Meg's in the clinic."

"Jesus God! Why? What's happened?"

"Nothing … *yet.* Listen, it's none of my business. But I seriously think you should get there as soon as possible."

Axel broke into a run. His father shouted after him. Axel paid no attention. The thudding of his boots on the track echoed the beat of fear in his heart.

*

Nine and a half minutes later, Axel slammed into the dusty little wood-slat clinic. Bella Tan sat dejectedly on a bench while her daughters played on the floor. "Meg?" he gasped.

Bella straightened up and began to speak, but Axel was already rounding the desk, ignoring the PATIENTS ONLY sign. He charged down the hall, into the single operating room.

Meg lay on the cot with her feet up in stirrups. A medical robot arched its arm sinisterly above her pelvis. The female clinician studying the robot's screen said, "Hey! What the heck?"

"Meg!" Axel bent over the cot and awkwardly hugged Meg's shoulders, further alarmed by her stricken, angry expression. He couldn't see any blood. "What happened, sweetheart? Are you OK?" She clamped her lips shut and turned her head away.

The clinician said, "Are you the father?"

"Yes. Is she OK? Is the baby OK?"

The clinician looked relieved. It crossed Axel's mind that he'd met her before, but he was too distressed to place the memory. She beckoned him out of the room, telling Meg to remain calm, she'd be back in a minute. In the hall, she said, "She's in good health, and the baby is also in good health."

"Thank God."

"Are you aware she's requested an abortion?"

"What? No ... no. I was not aware of that."

"I agreed to make an exception to the paternal consent rule, since her friend testified that she'd threatened suicide."

"WHAT?"

"They said you were on Barjoltan. I decided it was too risky to wait until you could be contacted. But now that you're here—"

"I don't understand." Axel lurched back towards the

operating room. Before he could open the door, Meg herself came out, barefoot, holding her flimsy gown closed.

"If I can't have the baby, she can't have it, either."

"She? Who, Meg?" He tried to take her in his arms, but she shoved him away.

Then she told him about a contract, signed on Sakassarib, that stipulated the surrender of Meg's firstborn child to the sentrienza, in exchange for …

… the life of Axel Best.

It was his fault. Axel's mind reeled. The sentrienza had claimed his life in exchange for the water they took from Sakassarib. They'd been going to experiment on him, quite possibly while he was alive and conscious. He had known that Meg had somehow obtained his freedom. But he had not known about this.

"It's not a real contract," he said, thinking of his father's armies of lawyers. All abandoned back on Earth, of course. "She can't enforce it."

"You think not?" Meg snapped. "Did you see those things in the sky?"

Axel tried again to hug her. She pushed him away. Bella and the children joined them in the corridor. "Sorry," Bella said to Axel. "I didn't know what to do."

The clinician frowned. "This is something to do with CHEMICAL MAGE, isn't it?"

Axel suddenly remembered where he'd seen this woman before. She was one of the refugees from Majriti IV who had settled here after their colony world fell to the Ghosts. She had helped Axel and Meg when they came here to interview the metaphysicist Emile Zaragoza, whose research had underpinned the CHEMICAL MAGE project. And in return for her help, Axel had … hit her on the head, actually.

He tried a smile. It was meant to be charming but came out weak. "We've met before. I owe you an apology."

"You people from Earth always hit first and apologize later," she said. "The future of humanity isn't on Earth. It's right here. Which is why it would really suck if CHEMICAL MAGE is going to screw up our lives all over again."

"This is nothing to do with CHEMICAL MAGE," Meg said. "Can we please just do the procedure before Emnl comes looking for me?"

"No," Axel said. This was the one thing he was sure of. "I do *not* consent. We're out of here, Meg." He knew for certain that she would regret this if she went through with it. Hadn't they talked about the baby with nervous anticipation? Made jokes about how screwed-up it was likely to be? But it would be loved. *He* would love it. She just had to not do this. She'd thank him later for stopping her. "Come on, sweetheart. Where are your clothes?"

"Fuck you," she said, blindsiding him. "Go back to Barjoltan."

Axel looked at the other women for support. "I'm legally entitled to refuse consent."

"Please," Meg said to the clinician. "Please!"

The woman didn't move. Arms folded, she said, "And what happens when the faerie princess finds out?"

Seizing the moment, Axel steered Meg into the operating room. Her clothes were piled in a wicker basket. Just a bathing suit and a sarong. "I swear to you," he said, holding them out. "I will die before I let the sentrienza get their hands on our child."

"You will?" Meg grabbed one of the attachments for the

medical robot. It was just lying in a tray. This shitty little clinic didn't have good security, and probably did not even observe basic rules of hygiene. But the scalpel attachment in Meg's hand looked sharp. "Back the fuck up, Axel," she said in the cold, detached voice he knew too well. "I will do it."

He stepped back, raising his hands with her swimsuit and sarong still in them, his gaze glued to the blade. "Meg. Don't do it. We'll run away. We'll go where she can't find us."

"The sentrienza are *everywhere.*"

"We'll go ..." It came to him suddenly in a flash of rightness. "We'll go back to Earth."

CHAPTER 15

Before Meg could respond to his impetuous suggestion, Philip K. Best and Nicholas Smythe burst into the room.

Meg dropped the scalpel. Axel picked it up and tossed it into the corner.

"Dad?"

"Baby," Nicholas Smythe said, holding out his arms uncertainly.

"Oh, Dad. What the heck are you doing here?" Meg embraced her father with a long-suffering sigh. It was amazing the way she packed away the ferocity Axel had just seen. But her eyes, above her father's shoulder, were still dull, focused a thousand yards away.

"I guess this wasn't the best-planned surprise," Nicholas said gruffly. "Did we catch you in the middle of something?"

"There's never a good time," Meg said. She selfconsciously smoothed her hospital gown. "I can't believe you're here, Dad! I thought you were still in Tokyo."

"I threw in the towel after the Ghosts bombed the campus during my seminar on Byron," Nicholas said. "They'd bombed the trains, too, so I had to walk home. When I got there, I looked at the old place and just kept walking."

"Whoa, My father, the action hero!" Meg said. But her eyes still looked dead.

"Phil's people were kind enough to help me get a berth on a Hail Mary ship. That was twenty months ago."

"Tokyo is a Ghost city by now," Axel's father said. "London, New York, Shanghai, Mumbai? All lost. Modern Atlantises."

And it's all *your* fault, Axel thought, despising his father's pretence that he and his collaborators had nothing to do with the fall of Earth. But now was not the time to play the blame game. "Dad, ah, Nick? Maybe we could give Meg privacy to get dressed."

He made sure that Bella and the children stayed behind with her. With those sweet little girls in the room, she wouldn't do anything stupid.

Out in the reception area, Philip said, "Axel, exactly what the hell is going on?"

"Guess what, Dad? It's none of your goddamn business."

"It's happening on Juradis? Makes it my goddamn business. She's meant to be negotiating the transfer of the Walking Guns—"

"Screw the Walking Guns. This is about my child. Your grandchild."

Father and son stared murderously at each other. Nicholas intervened with surprising tact, changing the subject. "Axel, when I was boarding the shuttle to transfer to my ship, I overheard something funny. The prices of these fares, you know, are astronomical. They declined for a while, but now the supply of ships is running out, so ... The point is that everyone at the spaceport was extremely rich, except me. And the woman in line ahead of me was on the phone with someone. She kept saying, 'Yes, but should I stay or go? It was *supposed* to be safe in Betelgeuse system, until that cowboy Hyland effed it up for everyone ...' And I stood there wondering what she'd think if she knew I was part of the team that effed it up for everyone."

Yes, Axel had found out something unpleasant about Professor Smythe since he disembarked from the latest

105

overcrowded refugee ship to arrive from Earth. 'Nick' had been a consultant to the CHEMICAL MAGE team. That's how he had got a ticket to Betelgeuse.

Axel managed a humorless chuckle. "You'd probably have been torn limb from limb." Seething, he went to the window and looked out. The sun's rays were lengthening. On the other side of the street, a mara sprawled on the ground, soaking up the afternoon heat. It looked like a homeless person back on Earth. In fact, the mara had a natural habit of lying around like that. But the thought triggered complex emotions of longing and guilt. Axel had lived his life on Earth inside a bubble of wealth. New York, Washington, Geneva, Hawaii … he had no one specific place to call home. Yet now, suddenly, he yearned for all of it: the pulse of traffic on 5th Avenue, the crunch of snow on Alpine ski slopes, the smell of pot-stickers on a Shanghai street corner.

He wanted to go home. He'd give up his job on Barjoltan, his chance of flying a Vulture in combat. He'd give up everything, to get Meg and the baby safely back to Earth.

But how the hell could they get away?

*

Meg tied her sarong. She stooped to put on her sandals, avoiding Bella's eyes. She didn't want sympathy. She had tried her best, and been beaten.

The clinician touched her arm. "I just can't take the risk."

"I know," Meg said. "You've got children, too." She walked past the woman and went out to the reception area. Axel reached for her—couldn't he keep his hands off her for five seconds? She brushed him off. "I'd better go see what Emnl's doing. A lady-in-waiting's job is never done!"

Her father fell into step with her as they walked down the

road towards the beach. "So I'm going to be a grandfather," he said, almost shyly.

Meg dug her fingernails into her palms. "Looks that way, Dad." She was happy to see him, of course she was. But he looked so old it scared her.

They arrived at the beach just in time to see the Walking Guns land in the lagoon. They plunged into the water amidst clouds of steam. They were hot— they'd been burning around the sky for ages. "Each of them's got a tiny black hole in its belly, according to Emnl," Meg told the others. Surfacing, they bobbed around like seals, cooling down and replenishing their water reserves.

Emnl waded in the shallows, her multicolored wrap gathered over one arm, the tip of her braid trailing in the waves. She carried her sunshade folded now that the sun had set. Standing there alone, she looked oddly forlorn, despite all the people watching from the beach. Then she turned and grinned at them and the illusion vanished.

"Hello, Governor," she buzzed. "What an honor."

"Your Majesty," Philip K. Best said stiffly, slipping on the sand in his dress shoes.

"And who's this?"

"My father," Meg said. She mashed her lips together. She felt some kind of an outburst coming on. What had Axel said in the clinic? *Let's get away.* If only they could.

Emnl swayed out of the water and padded up to Nicholas on her wet, sandy, four-toed feet. "Do you teach karate, as well?"

"Ah, no. I teach English literature."

"'True Thomas lay oer yond grassy bank, and he beheld a ladie gay'?"

"Walter Scott."

"That lady was my six-times-great-grandmother. Her horse was a Walking Gun Her jewels were sensors."

"Fascinating!" Nicholas flickered an academic's automatic smile: on, off.

*

While Emnl was talking to Nicholas Smythe, Philip drew Axel aside. "Can you fly that ship of yours remotely?"

"It's not my ship, but yeah."

"It is now. Bring it down to the beach."

"What?"

"Sand makes a fine launch pad. Might fuse some. Who cares? The sentrienza are going to fuse it all when they get here, anyway."

"We're going to kick their asses," Axel said automatically. He was watching Meg.

His father sighed. "Son, we're not going to win. Long term, it won't make a lick of difference if we have those Walking Guns or not. Maybe we'll win a couple more victories, but at the end of the day, they have five hundred star systems, and we have one."

"Dad ..." Axel was shocked. His father wasn't meant to say this kind of thing. Being negative and defeatist was *Axel's* role.

"Just telling it like it is," his father said with a faint smile. Then he changed gears. "I heard what you said to Meg in the clinic. I want you to do it. *Go.*"

Axel stared at him.

"Take her back to Earth. You're right. There's one place in the galaxy where the sentrienza fear to tread, because the Ghosts are all over it like flies on shit. And that is Earth."

"I was talking out of my ass."

"No, you weren't. Quit underselling yourself, Axel." The crows'-feet around Philip's eyes deepened. He clapped Axel on the shoulder. "Now get that ship down here ... and save my grandchild."

CHAPTER 16

Meg hardly noticed the roar in the sky, as she'd been hearing a similar noise all day. Then she remembered that the Walking Guns had all landed. She looked up as Axel's spiffy new fighter lowered itself towards the beach. People scattered. The ship settled, blowing clouds of sand into the water.

Emnl broke off her conversation with Nicholas Smythe. When the noise died down, she buzzed at Axel, "You are going? Good. Please do not return. Meg does not require your presence."

Meg herself felt that way quite often, but God, hearing it from Emnl made her blood boil.

Axel moved slowly in the direction of the ship, looking back at her entreatingly.

She had to at least say goodbye. She started to walk towards him.

"No," Emnl said sharply. "Stay here."

"Excuse me," Nicholas Smythe said. He was already pink from the sun but now he turned pinker. "You've got no right to order my daughter around. Go on, Meggie."

Emnl chittered. "You have always loved your books better than you loved Meg. She told me so."

"Shut up!" Meg screamed at Emnl.

"Hush, Meg," her father said. "I love you."

Then he threw himself at Emnl.

He couldn't fight, Nicholas Smythe. He had never understood Meg's karate practise, let alone her career in the Fleet. Her mother used to whale on him when she got really upset; Nicholas would just stand there and stoically fend her off. He swung his fists at Emnl as if they were rocks that happened to be attached to his arms, and the only reason one of them connected with her face was because the attack completely flatfooted Emnl, as well as everyone else.

Then she whirled her sunshade, sending the parasol part spinning away onto the sand. What remained was a three-foot spear with a glittering point. She ran Nicholas through.

Philip K. Best caught Meg by the shoulders as she started towards her father. "Run," he said.

"Dad. *DAD!*"

"He's distracting her so you can get away. Go. Save my grandchild—and his."

Meg ran. As she neared the stairs of the ship, a Walking Gun loped out of the sea to intercept her. Then it fell on its side. Axel stood on the cockpit steps, aiming a combi. The Walking Gun—unhurt, of course—rolled over and picked itself up, but by then Meg was on the steps.

She managed one glance back. Emnl squatted over Nicholas's body. The ends of her lavender hair trailed in his blood, while the Walking Guns bristled around them, keeping the horrified bystanders at a distance.

Axel shoved her into the main cabin. She tottered to the nearest couch and sat down. Her mind was a vortex of white noise. The emotions stirred up by her father's sacrificial attack were so unbearable she couldn't feel them.

"Launching in three," Axel barked. "Two. One."

The ship lifted off in a boiling cloud of plasma.

The Walking Guns pursued it into the air.

*

"Keep going," Sully Tan said over the radio. "I've got your

back."

The *Vienna's* guns reared skywards. They spat flame. Heat-seeking projecticles cruised at trans-sonic speed through the evening sky and locked onto the Walking Guns. Fireworks dotted the sea as Axel climbed higher. Of course, the Walking Guns would be down but not out. That was good enough for Axel. He just needed to outdistance them.

"You're the man, Sully."

"You've still got a bunch of them on your tail."

"I see them."

Axel was dividing his attention. Esthesia made it possible for him to multitask. He felt the atmosphere thinning around his hull, the warmth of air morphing into the tingle of vacuum. He saw Meg lying with her eyes closed in a couch— the same one, in fact, her father had used. He also saw the evil hot spots of the Walking Guns climbing into the stratosphere behind him. He counted forty-two of them, their wings folded into stabilizer fins, their legs folded back along their bodies.

"Shit," Sully said. "Those fuckers are fast."

"They've got black holes in their guts."

"Yeah, that's what I heard."

That was why people said a Walking Gun could destroy a planet. If you fired a black hole—even a small one, as long as it was large enough to not spontaneously evaporate—into the center of a large mass, such as a planet, it was sayonara. The internal pressure of the planet would keep pushing matter into the hole, until it was all gone.

Axel wondered if Emnl would destroy Juradis in revenge for their defiance. His courage wavered.

Sully came back on the radio. "I'm patching Gil through.

If I don't talk to you again, Godspeed and semper fi, you crazy bastard."

"Hello, Axel," said the distinctive growly voice of the queazel. He had returned from Barjoltan with Axel to visit his estate at the north pole. "What sort of firepower do you have on your new ship?"

"Charged particle cannon," Axel said. "Medium railgun. Kinetic rounds, a few nukes."

"Use the nukes," Gil said.

"Gil. You cannot nuke a black hole. Whatever you throw at it just turns it into a bigger black hole." That was why few people tried to destroy Walking Guns, and no one ever succeeded. They literally soaked up kinetic impactors by allowing them to pass through the black hole containment fields inside their compact little bodies.

"I know that," Gil said. "You are not going to nuke them. Here is what you must do …"

*

The *Shihoka* soared into orbit. The Fleet carrier *Indomitable* was also orbiting Juradis at 150 kilometers, surrounded by a gaggle of Hail Mary hulks. Axel took the *Shihoka* higher, keeping the planet between himself and the fragile human fleet.

The Walking Guns accelerated to catch up. Axel allowed them to rise past him into a higher orbit. They crossed like a flock of starlings across the orb of Betelgeuse. They thought they were cutting off his escape.

He took a deep breath. "Meg?"

"What?" She was supine in the couch, floating in her straps, clutching something in her hands.

"Watch this."

Praying that Gil's information was correct, he launched all five of his nuclear rounds.

They streaked off the rails faster than the eye could see. Seconds later, they exploded amidst the flock of Guns—a shortlived fireworks display, washed out by the light of the red giant.

"You didn't hit any of them," Meg said.

"I wasn't trying to."

Nuclear explosions produced powerful electromagnetic pulses. At close range, the pulses would overwhelm the Walking Guns' hardened electronics. That would set off a cascade of failures …

With his infrared eyes, Axel watched the Walking Guns' heat signatures slowly fade. "It worked," he exulted. "It worked!"

The Walking Guns' black hole containment fields had failed, decoupling the inertia of the black holes from the inertia of the Guns themselves. Their own acceleration had pushed them into the black holes. They were being eaten from the inside out by their own ammunition.

Axel cued the comms. "Gil? It worked. We now have forty-two micro black holes spiraling out on a course that will eventually carry them out of the system. Warn the Rat."

"You might do that yourself."

Axel didn't think the Rat would be very happy to hear from him right now. Another concern thrust its way into his mind. "Could you get in touch with my father, as well? Tell him …"

"I already have," Gil said. "He said to tell you to expect a care package."

"A care package?"

"A resupply capsule, to be precise. You have not enough

food and water for the journey, do you? The capsule will contain everything you need. It will rendezvous with you before you reach the zero-gravity point."

Axel swallowed. "Thanks, Gil. Tell him … thanks."

He went back into the main cabin. Meg held up the object in her hands. It was a small computer. "Dad forgot his books," she said, and burst into tears.

Deciding that the *Shihoka* could fly itself for a while, Axel went over and held her.

CHAPTER 17

Ilfenjium was burning.

Smoke smudged the sky above the city. Paler explosions flowered where mortar shells fell short in the slums below the dam. Colm had seen this kind of thing on colony worlds when the Ghosts overran human settlements. Now it was happening to the Ghosts themselves. He felt shamefully glad that he was too far away to see the faces of the people running out of the burning buildings, only to be cut down in the streets.

He sat astride the sorrel mare the Lizps had given him, on the road that wound down from the pass into the Great River valley. Two miles away, Ilfenjium huddled below a dam built on a pharaonic scale from dressed granite. The suburbs metastasized into monoculture fields like nappy velvet, brown and green. The reservoir behind the dam was a bowlful of reflected clouds. Fancy villas looked down upon it. There was no one left alive up there. Ghost war was total war. Ilfenjium had been the most populous city on Kisperet this morning. By nightfall, it wouldn't be.

A deafening boom interrupted the thunder of the Lizp artillery from higher up in the pass. The mare put her ears back. Colm patted her neck, to steady himself as much as the horse. When he looked up, he saw soil and broken trees cascading across the road. Well, crap. Twenty feet to the left and he'd have been dead.

He rode downhill, guiding the mare around the landslide. He had got a lot better at riding. The Navy pilot who had landed here in a shivering heap five months ago would hardly have recognized the tough-faced horseman, his forest-green cloak flapping over a sword-belt, his knee boots shiny and his shirt snowy white, his ginger hair covered by a forage cap, who rode into the boggy hollow concealed behind a crag from the city. Only the quivering heart in his chest remained the same.

His power cart stood beside a stream that trickled through the hollow. It looked like a holiday caravan, with some branches tied on the roof—Diejen's idea of camouflage, after a few drinks. Every ten seconds or so, a soldier in Lizp livery scrambled out of the cart, clutching a rifle, and clomped through the mud. By twos and fives, they scrambled over the lip of the hollow and sneaked downhill to join the battle. All of them were gaunt, dark-haired men with thick eyebrows and a noticeable scar on their chins. They were older versions of the Ghosts that had invaded Kuiper Belt Object 11890 when Colm was working there. They were also identical to the man who sat on a camp stool under the trees, next to Diejen Lizp. He had a sad, beaten-down expression, and stroked the rifle across his knees as if it were a child. Diejen had her arm around his shoulders. She seemed to be comforting him. In reality she was copying him. One every ten seconds. A rate never previously achieved by mobile forces on Kisperet. And it was Colm who'd made it possible.

He shouted, "They've ranged in on this location. We've got to move the cart."

Diejen was concentrating, he knew, and hadn't really heard him, so he slid off the mare's back and floundered over to her.

"We've got to move the cart! These lads weren't careful enough staying under cover. The enemy spotters must've seen where they're all coming from."

This time the man sitting next to Diejen looked up. "Sorry," he said, abashed. "I'll be more careful."

"Too late now." Colm waded through the mud to the cart. He wished he had ear protectors. At close range, the violent thudding from inside the cart drowned out the artillery. The cart had double wheels on reinforced axles. A steel pipe stuck out of the top, belching white woodsmoke. Actually, it was quite possible that the Magistocracy's spotters had seen the smoke, although Colm had had a look through a telescope from the eastern approach this morning, and decided that it was impossible to distinguish it from the gunsmoke rolling out of the Lizp mortar positions a hundred yards higher up … especially if you didn't know what you were looking for.

Steam power had been unknown on Kisperet. The Magistocracy's war on humanity had come at a time when humanity's only reciprocating steam engines were in museums. The Magistocracy might have built steam turbines, copying those used in human power plants to this day, and in fact Colm had seen an entire coal-fired power plant, stolen piece by piece from the New Seattle Power Authority on Gliese 581g, languishing unused in a pig barn. Colm had tinkered with it while the slaves butchered the pigs, but had given up hope of getting it working. He had had a hard enough time building half a dozen wood-burning steam engines on the Lizp estate while he waited, with less and less optimism, for Dhjerga to come back.

He ducked inside the cart. Heat blasted into his face. The engine stretched the length of the cart. Pistons thudded and the flywheel whirred, driving a DC generator that fed a voltaic pile in the front of the cart. Two freemen, stripped to the waist, shovelled wood chunks into the voracious little furnace. Their teeth and eyes glistened in faces black with soot. Colm made them understand with sign language that he was going to shut the engine down. He topped off the boiler to draw down the engine's steam production—carefully, carefully. Two boilers had exploded during his prototyping phase, and in fact he shouldn't be doing this himself if he ever wanted to get home. Leave it to the slaves. But how could he ask a slave to do what he wouldn't do himself? He probably wasn't ever going to get home anyway. Dhjerga had been gone for months. The Betelgeuse system was a dangerous place for a Ghost. So, when they'd raked out the fire, Colm handed the mare's reins to a small Lizp cousin and swung up onto the bench of the power cart. He stroked the lash over the backs of the dray horses and drove the cart down towards the crucible of Ilfenjium.

Diejen caught up with him. She had Janz, the freeman she'd been copying, trailing after her on a broken-down gelding. "Where are you going?"

"Taking the cart closer to the Electrical Quarter."

The Electrical Quarter was the name for the bit of Ilfenjium directly below the dam, where the hydroelectric generators were. Every city on Kisperet had an Electrical Quarter. These, of course, were the source of the enemy's power. Colm knew the drill by now. Go in under cover of darkness, set fires, and send small squads to knock out the generators. It had worked great for a couple of months. Then the Magistocracy had started reinforcing their standing garrisons, and to hell with the harvest. Dryjon's forces had been bogged down in the city center all morning—two and a half standard Earth days, by Colm's increasingly unreliable body clock. So they'd brought up more artillery, but damned if that was doing the job, either. The mortars nibbled daintily at the colossal blockhouse below the dam. Even when the gunners landed a bullseye, the shells barely left scuff marks. Dryjon needed reinforcements in the city proper, and he needed them now.

The tree cover ended a mile from the city limits. Colm had planned to park the power cart at the treeline, but the lack of corpses in the fields gave him courage. And the houses he could see in the distance were no longer on fire. So he drove the cart across the fields. Sweet-smelling flowers foamed on the verges of the road. The millet was rotting on the stalk. It had rained a lot recently.

The horses clip-clopped through the blackened brick warrens of Ghost suburbia. The very mud in the streets steamed from the lingering heat of the fires. It was eerily quiet after the constant noise up at the artillery lines. Corpses, both burnt and fresh, littered the streets. Some of them were not dead yet. The Lizp troops paused to bayonet them as they passed by.

A stadium loomed over the rooftops like a rising granite moon. Colm had observed this from the hillside and wondered what it was. The freeman Janz glanced at it and smiled nostalgically.

Diejen said, "That is the arena where they held the Games. I wonder if there'll ever be Games again."

"Games?" *Iomacht,* his voice echoed, telling him nothing new.

"The War Games. Every fifty days—" that was about one standard Earth year, since a Kisperet 'day' was eight days long— "the Magistocracy used to hold competitions here.

Shooting, running, obstacle courses, that kind of thing."

Janz spoke up. "I beat everyone in my year in the shooting. Yes, I did."

"Yes, you did, Janz," Diejen affirmed, and muttered under her breath, "but that was years ago."

Colm felt as if he were back in the early days of his exile on Kisperet, when the things people said frequently did not make sense, although his brain faithfully converted their strange *Teanga* into English. "Friendly competitions? Like the Olympics?"

"Not exactly friendly. The winners, of course, would have the so-called honor of becoming soldiers in the Magistocracy's war."

"Like me," Janz said, cuddling his rifle.

"The Games *used* to be friendly." Diejen's green eyes grew wistful. "There were plays and poetry contests."

"Tell me about it," Colm said.

So she told him about the festivals where the best mages on Kisperet would compete to produce stunning effects, filling the skies with fish and the streets with stars, and little Diejen and Dryjon had ridden on their parents' shoulders and laughed and laughed at the comic poets who performed skits in between the contests, and ice cream dripped over their hands onto their best clothes. Dhjerga had been a wild teenager. They'd lose him and the parents would panic until he invariably turned up somewhere he wasn't supposed to be.

Colm shifted over on the bench and reached out to clasp one of the slender hands white-knuckling her horse's reins. "This'd be as good a place as any to set up the cart."

He meant they'd be safe from stray shells. The arena looked as ancient and impregnable as the blockhouse that the artillery had been pounding at without result. He wondered how long the Ghosts had been on Kisperet. Everyone he had asked said "Forever," but if that was true, why did they speak a corrupted form of Gaelic?

A plaza surrounded the arena, offering good sightlines. He drove around the colossal structure until he found the gate. Diejen directed him to the stable beneath the arena seating, a cavern which opened onto the stadium via a row of high arches. Even in here it smelled of butchery and smoke. Janz wandered around smiling at the garish fresco portraits of Games champions on the walls. Each one was wreathed in the colors of a Family. Colm knew most of the Families by now; there were only about a hundred on Kisperet. He added the capital letter in his mind to distinguish them from ordinary families. Of course the freemen had families, too, but as far the mages were concerned, *they* were the only actual human beings in the universe.

Half of them had joined the Lizps' uprising against the Magistocracy, and the other half had stuck with the devil they knew. But the momentum was on the rebels' side, thanks to Colm's steam engines. He had also written and distributed a handy manual explaining how to make voltaic piles, which were much more practical than either Leyden jars or bathtub batteries.

He sent a couple of the freemen to look for the water mains, and told the others to fire up the furnace again. Soon Diejen was back on her camp stool, cranking out copies of Janz. The artillery rumbled in the distance and the steam engine's smoke drifted out over the grass-furred running tracks. Before nightfall the city fell into the Lizps' hands.

CHAPTER 18

For the first time Dryjon had captured a Magistrate. He presented this man to the rest of the Lizps with an apologetic grimace. Colm soon understood why. Burly, with a square jaw, blue eyes beneath cropped blond hair, and a horrendous sword-cut across his forehead, this Geathla Moro had formerly been Diejen's fiancé.

This was a worse blow for Colm than he wanted to admit, even to himself. Lonely in his exile, he'd become entranced by Diejen's elegant profile, melancholy green eyes, and wry sense of humor. He'd even convinced himself that he loved her occasional fits of homicidal lunacy. They had travelled together, worked together, shared laughs and danger, and Colm had believed their moments of closeness meant something. *Now* he found out she'd been engaged to someone else all along.

She still cared for Geathla, too, judging by her reaction to his appearance. She went pale and sneered, "Were you too slow to get away?"

In previous cities conquered by the rebels, the Magistrates had always fled when they judged that the battle was lost. Being mages, they could simply vanish at the last minute, leaving their slaves and freemen to their fate.

"We caught him sneaking around the power cart on the eastern approach." Dryjon said. Three steam power carts had contributed to the conquest of Ilfenjium, including the one Colm was personally in charge of. "I assume the Magus told him to gather intelligence about these new power sources. Well, *that* didn't work out very well for you, did it, Geathla?"

Dryjon swung away, upending a bottle of wine to his lips, and stumbled over an ammunition crate on the floor. He was already drunk, Colm thought.

Diejen laughed wildly. "Now you'll be spending the rest of the war in gloves! We will all have to feed you and help you go to the toilet."

Geathla already wore huge unwieldy mittens, like leather oven gloves, that went over his elbows and were joined by a chain behind his neck. They were similar to the ones Dhjerga had been wearing when Colm freed him from the Magistocracy. They had a high-potential rubber lining. The Tegression knew about non-conducting materials, and used them as handcuffs for mages: with these on, Geathla could neither flit nor do anything else magical. The Lizps had taken the extra precaution of chaining the gloves to Geathla's belt, with only about six inches of play.

Geathla scowled and nodded at Colm. "Actually, I was looking for *him.*"

"No doubt, no doubt," Dryjon said. "He's the reason we're winning." He sat down by the fire. They were camping in the Lizps' own house on the lake. The Magistocracy had defaced the gracious villa with obscene graffiti and dogshit murals. They'd even taken the trouble to carve the two-headed eagle into every door and window in the house. When he saw that, Dryjon had set the slaves to ripping all the doors and windows out. The noise of demolition resounded through the house. With the windows gone, a chilly wind blew into this large, austere parlor, which faced the lake. Even in this temperate region of Kisperet, it got cold after dark. Slaves were tacking curtains, fetched from the Lizps' estate of Dam Lizp Hol, over the glassless holes. Dryjon uncapped another bottle of wine and offered Colm some.

"Thanks." Getting drunk seemed like a sound option.

"Where's your brother?" Geathla said to the twins.

"None of your damned business," Diejen said, and Dryjon just grunted. But the question resonated among the other Lizps and their associates who had begun to gather at the villa. Colm saw on their faces an echo of his own fear that Dhjerga was gone for good.

Geathla joined them for supper. The villa got quite crowded with cousins, aunts, uncles, and friends breezing in from other combat theaters, which might lie hundreds or thousands of miles away. The steam engine racketed away in the front garden, allowing the mages to come and go and fetch supplies from their distant headquarters. An atmosphere of febrile jollity took hold, partly as a result of the mead they had found in a cellar overlooked by the Magistocracy, and partly, Colm thought, for Geathla's benefit. The mages were terrifically proud and would never admit in front of an enemy what they all knew to be true: they might have conquered Ilfenjium, but that meant little as long as the Magus sat on Atletis, unhurt, untouchable, ready to spring a counter-offensive the moment they let their guard drop …

… if Dhjerga did not come back.

Colm watched pink roses bloom on Diejen's cheeks, and kicked himself for ever having thought she might be interested in him.

An entire pig roasted on a spit in the hearth, dripping into the fire. The meat was tough and tasteless. Colm's first meal on Kisperet of bread and cheese and apples was still the best one he'd ever had. The Tegression seemed to eat nastier things, the more money they had—eels, pigeons, offal, salads of flowers and bitter herbs, puddings of sour berries and honey. In the field, however, food was an existential problem. It could not be fetched. Why? "It's neither alive nor dead," the mages would explain, but that made no sense to Colm. He had once unpacked a crate of ammo with a disgusting oozing lump tucked in among the shells. Diejen had laughed and said, "Whoops! That used to be an apple!" Colm suspected the problem was related to the Ghosts' mysterious energy-mass conversion technique. All those proteins in food would have to be reassembled perfectly, and food had no sentience, so it couldn't 'remember' what it was supposed to be like. Nor did the Ghosts know what it was supposed to be like. They didn't have degrees in molecular biology.

This sentience problem obviously did not apply to animals. Therefore, armies in the field survived on a meat-only diet of chickens and pigs, which *could* be fetched, as long as they were alive. Any Tegression army camp witnessed the regular spectacle of thousands of slaves catching their supper as it staggered squealing and clucking out of the Shadow. And that's if the mages even bothered to feed them. Dryjon had explained to Colm that he and Diejen were actually breaking the law by feeding their slaves; the Magistocracy just let them starve when they were no longer needed. It was a form of social hygiene, to prevent the planet from being overrun by half-daft copies. .

It seemed only fair that the rulers of this hideous civilization did not eat much better than their slaves did. Tonight's tough roast was supplemented with porridge made from millet gathered in the fields, and one of those mouth-puckering salads.

Colm picked at it, and took away the taste with wine. On his third trip to the toilet, he found that Geathla was following him.

"If you think I'm going to help you get your dick out—"

"No need. I'm not the one who's been drinking like a fish," Geathla said. "They really knock it back on Earth, huh?"

"I'm the planetary drinking champion." Colm had taken to making up tall tales to put off people who asked him about Earth. "Where I come from, in the Highlands, we have cows that give whiskey instead of milk. We're a nation of inventors. You've got to do something when the weather's dreich, which is more often than not …"

"You're telling the truth about the weather, anyway," Geathla said. His blue eyes caught the light from the parlor. "When I was in Edinburgh—"

"You've been to Edinburgh?!?" That was only a couple of hundred miles from Colm's hometown in Western Scotland.

"I'm a senior Magistrate. I've been commanding our forces in Britain. I was ordered home a few weeks ago to deal with the Lizp situation."

Colm's mind filled with questions. As sometimes happened when his emotions were running high, his tongue got tangled up, and he couldn't form words because he kept noticing that his lips and tongue were shaping different syllables from the ones in his head. He finally managed, "So what's the news?" *Cad é scéal?* his own voice mocked him.

"We've won," Geathla said.

"That—that was quick."

"That's what Diejen used to say." Geathla winked at his own crude joke.

Colm went to the toilet. He hoped Geathla was just trying

to psych him out. But the stylized faces tiled on the wall of the pissoir turned into the faces of his family. Mam, Bridget, Dad … Were they all dead? Fear curdled his buzz. He clumsily did up the stupid button fly of his trousers and tucked in his newly fetched white shirt.

The villa was laid out like a five-pointed star, with covered archways stretching out from a central atrium. Colm crossed the dark atrium and stopped at the entrance to the hall that led to the parlor. Geathla was still there, leaning on the wall, shunned by the other people wandering by. The mages had total confidence in the gloves: with them on, Geathla was in a mobile jail. He couldn't get away.

But he was no longer alone.

Diejen stood in front of him, the light from the parlor outlining her slender waist and the fall of her specially fetched dress.

Colm couldn't hear what she was saying. They were having a sing-along in the parlor, and the power cart outside was still clattering away.

Suddenly Diejen and Geathla started down the hall towards Colm. He stepped back into the atrium. He hid behind a pedestal where a bust of the twins' father had been replaced with a crucified dog, which the slaves had removed, leaving only a stain. Diejen and Geathla crossed the atrium and went out. Colm followed them. He told himself that he needed to grill Geathla about the situation on Earth. He just wanted to be sure he wasn't interrupting anything.

Shadows lapped over the garden. It was twilight—the long twilight of Kisperet, when the tidally locked moon's orbit had begun to carry it to the dayside of its gas giant parent. Cerriwan bulged over the pass like a round mountain. The sun seemed pinned to the opposite horizon, shooting long shadows across the reservoir. Fruit trees, whose branches the Magistocracy had vengefully hacked off, cast their own mutilated shadows. The far side of the lake blazed with campfires.

Diejen and Geathla slipped away beneath a pergola hung with dead vines. Colm mooched down the drive, past the power cart. Two giggling Lizp cousins were fetching musical instruments for the ceilidh indoors. Slaves struggled with a harp; the strings twanged. The furnace roared and the pistons thudded. There were still plenty of people about. Colm's heart thudded like the steam engine as he saw Diejen and Geathla going out onto the road.

The garden had no wall. No house or estate on Kisperet was fortified in the sense Colm understood. He momentarily thought of the Free Church Manse, his great-grandfather's house on the Isle of Skye, which he'd wanted to buy and renovate. It would have been a safe refuge for his family when the Ghosts reached Earth. He clenched his right fist on the hilt of his sword—useless goddamn toy. He only carried it because no mage would be seen dead without one.

But what kind of a mage was he? No magic. Just a basic grasp of the principles of engineering. He hadn't even practised his conjuring tricks for months.

Diejen and Geathla walked along the road, back towards the dam. They were close together, but not touching. Between the road and the reservoir there was a strip of woodland. At least that's what Colm thought it was, until Diejen and Geathla turned in through an ornamental gate, beneath a sign in the Tegression's rune script. He half-closed his eyes and let them go out of focus. *Ilfenjium Zoo.*

Beyond the gates, tall trees flanked a downhill sweep of cobbles. Iron-barred enclosures cast jail shadows. At the bottom of the hill, a circular ornamental pond reflected the sunset. There was a nose-prickling smell of manure. Colm thought he had lost Diejen and Geathla, and then he saw them standing in the shadow of a brick building, maybe a concession or public toilet. The Magistocracy had not vandalized this place. He sneaked down the hill, staying in the shadows, feeling like a right Peeping Tom.

Diejen was talking. Geathla was gesturing with his grotesque gloves, his range of motion constrained by the chain securing the gloves to his waist. Colm couldn't hear what they were saying, and if he went any closer they'd see him. He stayed put beneath a tree rather like an oak, which grew everywhere on Kisperet. He had brought a flask of mead with him. He drank that, while Diejen got angry with Geathla. She looked her best, unfortunately, when angry. Her throat flushed and wisps of caramel hair came loose around her face, and several times during the past months he'd only barely restrained himself from kissing her.

She reached into the folds of her skirt. Colm hoped she was going to draw a gun and shoot Geathla dead. Her anger was always only a hair away from Ghost-style murderousness. But instead she drew out something small and bright. She reached for Gaethla's gloves.

It was a key.

The chains fell loose. Loudly, Diejen said, "Go, damn you! Now, before I change my mind!"

She walked back up the hill, looking neither to left or right.

Colm stood frozen in the shadows of the not-oak.

Geathla pulled off the gloves. He hurled them into the

enclosure behind Colm's tree. He massaged his fingers, staring up the hill after Diejen. He touched the cut on his forehead and muttered, "Fuck."

Then he called to Colm, "You can come out now."

CHAPTER 19

Colm was so surprised that he did walk out of his hiding-place. Geathla looked at his sword hand, and then at his other hand, which was still holding his flask.

"Can I have some of that?"

"It's all gone."

"This cut stings like a motherfucker."

"Why are you still here?"

Diejen had freed her fiancé. Colm supposed she had expected him to make off to safety.

"I wanted to talk to you," Geathla said.

"So talk."

"Let's sit down."

Gaethla turned his back on Colm's sword, displaying bravado. Shoulders rolling, he walked around the front of the brick building and pushed its door open. The squeak of the hinges underlined how quiet it was here, away from the hubbub at the Lizp villa, away from the war.

Colm weighed his options for a moment, then followed Gaethla into the building.

Gaethla was sitting on a bench, facing a glass window that ran the length of the building. Glass on Kisperet was Victorian style: hundreds of little streaky panes. Gaethla moved over to make room. Colm didn't sit. His heart was crushed. He felt stupid and full of hate. "She shouldn't have freed you."

"She's a good girl. We've been engaged since we were both knee-high."

"What would they have done to you?"

"Oh, killed me, probably after dark when they had more drink in them. Crucifixion, or maybe they'd have stripped me naked and thrown me in with this fellow."

Geathla gestured at the glass. The sun, shining through the high windows, reflected off it. Colm heard a dragging sound. He stepped closer and involuntarily recoiled.

A tangle of scaly limbs, like snakes with elbows, lay in a bare brick cell. Claws the size of dinosaur teeth. Dull, globular eyes staring out of the coils. He'd never seen anything like *that* on Kisperet, and he'd seen a lot of Kisperet at this point. All the animals here were Earth animals, with the exception of a few insects. And nowhere on Kisperet was hot enough for reptiles …

The nightmarish creature suddenly heaved itself into a different configuration. Its elbows flexed, raising its long scaly body a foot off the floor. It was a *dragon*. It pressed its blunt, scaly face to a grille set into the glass. "I'm hungry," it mewed.

Geathla laughed. "I bet you are. Well, you won't be getting *me.*"

"What the hell is it?" Colm said.

"I am a limethion," the creature lisped. Its mouth was overstuffed with teeth. "I come from Mitheikua. They're holding me captive. Please …"

Geathla raised his hand threateningly. "Shut the fuck up." He said to Colm, "It's an alien."

"Is this whole zoo full of …?"

"Aliens? Yeah. Hundreds of different kinds. We went to a lot of planets before we found our way home."

Colm shook his head. It was all too easy to imagine the Ghosts berserking their way across 8,000 light years, carrying off anything that caught their eye. The plight of the captive aliens horrified him. But worse was Geathla's admission that they had been searching for Earth all along.

Home …

"It took centuries," Geathla said. "There are so many stars out there! So many planets! And no one knew the way."

"Not even the Magus?"

"He's not *that* old."

"Who is the Magus, anyway?"

"I've already given you something for nothing. Now how about you tell me how to build those fire and water engines?"

"Steam engines," Colm said. "They use water as a working fluid to convert heat energy into kinetic energy. The kinetic energy drives a motor with an electromagnetic winding … The concept was invented by a Scotsman, James Watt." Colm didn't mention that he had actually got the idea from Tim Jenkins, a neighbor of his parents, who'd built a steam tractor. Colm had seen it on his failed visit home, when he met the Magus for the second time.

"You're talking gibberish," Geathla complained. "Tell me something, do the Lizps understand that chatter?"

Colm was fairly annoyed with the Lizps right now. Especially with Diejen. "They can fix rivets where I tell them to, and that's about all."

"Well, the old ways are the best ways." Geathla pushed himself up off the bench, wincing. "I'll be going now. Want to come?"

"To Atletis?" Colm was unhappy here, but it could be worse. It could definitely be worse.

"To Earth, of course," Gaetha said, going out. The limethion mewed hungrily behind them.

Outside, the shadows did not seem to have moved an inch.

The unchanging sunset gave a surreal hyper-solidity to the trees and the scattered cages, but it was getting colder. The wind wrinkled the ornamental pond. The sun *had* moved after all, because it had been shining on the water and now the pond lay in darkness, with the reflection of Cerriwan wobbling in it. Atletis was a dark spot on the gas giant.

Colm said, "Maybe Diejen didn't mention it, but I can't flit. I'm not that kind of mage. I got here from Lizp Province the old-fashioned way. On horseback. Thousands of miles, stopping at all the towns along the way to burn them."

In fact, he didn't know if it had been thousands of miles, but it had felt like it. Diejen had ridden most of the way with him, because she had Janz in tow, and the freeman couldn't flit either. They had travelled from the snowbound sub-Arctic where the Lizps ruled, through endless forests that made Colm think vaguely of Canada, camping out at night and exchanging stories about their childhoods. At last they had reached this somewhat more inviting climate where plantations covered the valley floors. He had not seen the sea yet. The Tegression had no need to transport things by boat; even their roads hardly existed. What mattered to them was power, so all their towns were built on rivers. All their energy went into the construction of dams. Their maps looked like database tables, with cities defined by the amount of 'work' their hydro plants produced—'work' being the sketchy unit of measurement they used instead of watts. Colm had no idea if Kisperet had more than one continent, or how big it was, or even if he was *on* a continent or just a large island. He had completely lost the perspective you got from flying.

"So come with me," Gaethla said. "This planet is a shithole, though I was born here. The rebels can have it. I've got loads of booze and food at my headquarters in Edinburgh. Girls, too." He winked. "You can show me how to fix those big power plants they have—"

"Are you deaf? I *can't FLIT!*"

"That's what they told you, is it?"

Colm hesitated. Geathla, standing in the shadow of the not-yew tree, smiled. He suddenly looked cunning, his big square face half-Scot and half-troll.

"I noticed you didn't eat your salad," he said.

"What the fuck's that got to do with it?"

"You should have eaten it." Geathla pulled down a branch of the not-oak and ripped off a handful of the small dark leaves. He stuffed them in his mouth and chewed. "Good for you," he said through his mouthful. "Try some."

Colm belatedly recognized that the leaves of the not-oak did, indeed, look like the side salads at Tegression meals, which he always left. He also remembered Dhjerga pulling leaves off bushes on Juradis, tasting them, and spitting them out.

"Is there something special about that tree?"

"You bet your arse there is. Oh, there's other special plants, too, but this is the tree we brought from the groves in the Great Flit." Geathla grinned. Bits of leaf stained his teeth. "Did they really not tell you?"

Colm shook his head.

"I'm not surprised. They didn't want you to flit off home and leave them. You're far too useful."

In a trance, Colm moved towards the tree. He ripped off a handful of leaves. Could it possibly be that these had the same effect on the brain as tropodolfin? He bit a fragment off one. It was as bitter as he remembered. His education cautioned him that bitterness meant poison. He ate a whole leaf, chewing thoroughly, and then another.

"Not too much all at once," Geathla warned. "We start on this stuff in childhood. By the time you get to be my age, you hardly need it anymore."

But Colm had been dosing himself with poison for years, off and on—in the form of pills, in his arm. He ate the rest of the handful.

The world sharpened. He felt a twinge of dizziness, and a heaviness in his head. He touched his stomach.

"It's working, is it?" Geathla seemed newly edgy. "Right, let's leg it." He reached for Colm's left hand.

"No," rasped another voice, faint and yet strangely resonant. The whole zoo seemed to fill with that whisper: *No.*

Both men flinched. They stumbled around to face the shadows under the tree.

Those shadows had thickened. At the foot of the tree sat a hump of tarry blackness. As Colm stared in horror, the tree shook slightly. A muddy boot slid out of the shadow. It came down with a perceptible thump between the tree roots.

Geathla muttered, "Oh fuck. The hypocaust heating system in the limethion house. It's battery-powered. Forgot to turn it off." Louder, he gibbered, "Sorry, sir. Sorry, sorry."

"He is mine," whispered the trees and the wind.

"Yes, sir. Sorry."

Geathla turned and fled uphill. Colm could not move. He was rooted to the ground with sheer terror, as he had been when he was six years old, when he saw the Magus for the first time.

"You are mine," the Magus whispered.

Hiding behind the settee in the living-room, Colm had

watched with his heart freezing in his chest as the shadow in the corner stretched out a bony finger to touch his baby sister. At least Bridget wasn't here now. She was far away in Scotland—dead, or alive?

"Come here," the zoo whispered, and blue glints flashed in the heap of shadows.

He'd screamed and his father had woken up. His father wasn't here now. The last words Colm had spoken to him had been hard ones.

"If you won't come to me, then I must come to you," whispered the shadow. Colm's mind shrieked *no, no, no*. But his tongue was stuck to the roof of his mouth. He swayed backwards as the shadow rushed at him.

It didn't hit him. It humped away in the blink of an eye to the far side of the pond, and rested there, quivering, a mound of blackness deep enough to drown stars. Those *were* stars drowned in it, or were they its eyes? It plonked a muddy boot on the low wall around the pond. The shadow leaned over the water, burgeoning like a mountain, with those two blue glints at the top. A finger stretched out of it. Colm swallowed a scream. The finger had at least six knuckles. But all it did was stir the water. The reflection of Cerriwan broke up.

"I will show you something you want to see," the Magus whispered.

Despite himself, Colm edged forward to the pond, keeping the water between them.

It was mirror-still now, despite the wind. As he watched it changed from dark to blue, and then to green. He seemed to be looking down from a height, as if the pond were a hundred meters deep, and he felt a spasm of vertigo—it had been so long since he flew, he had forgotten the feeling. Far below, it seemed, a rough green hillside fell into mist. A burn tumbled down the hill, and a woman trudged out of the mist towards it, carrying two jerrycans on a metal rod over her shoulders.

"She is stronger than you," the Magus whispered.

The woman reached the burn. She knelt on the stones to fill the first of her jerrycans. She wore a camouflage-print fleece over cargo pants and wellingtons. Her hair was pulled back into a bun. Dew-silvered, it was the same ginger hue as Colm's own.

"Bridget!" Colm yelled, recognizing his sister.

She looked up. Their viewpoint swooped lower, cranking up Colm's vertigo. Bridget dropped her jerrycan and rolled into cover between the stones. The rod on which she had been carrying the jerrycans was a rifle. She aimed it up at him and fired.

He flinched violently. The scrying broke up. He found that he was on his knees on the ground, sprawled over the wall, elbow-deep in the pond. Another few instants and his face would have been in the water.

He reared back, reaching for his sword.

The Magus's boot came down on the wall, inches from his hand. "She is a mage, too. But you are stronger."

His bones were freezing, his breath burning his lungs. So cold.

"I'll have her, and then there will be one. Then I will have you, and there will be no mages left on Earth at all."

He looked up. Straight into the shadow, and rolled onto his back, slashing out wildly with his sword.

The sky shook. The trees tossed. The water rose into little waves. Far away at the top of the hill, someone was screaming.

*

Colm half-ran, half-staggered up the hill. He reeled out of the zoo onto the road. He could still hear the screams. He thought at first that they were in his head but when slaves passed him, running, he realized that the screams were coming from ahead of him.

From the Lizps' villa.

He stumbled through the garden. The shadows doubled back at him. Firelight leapt between the trees. Slaves clustered with their backs to him. Colm pushed between them.

The power cart stood on the drive where he had left it. But the roof was gone. The boiler was gone. The flywheel was missing from the engine assembly. The furnace door hung open, bathing the drive in flickering light. Gaethla stood with one hand stretched towards the electromagnetic motor. He had returned to steal the steam engine.

Diejen's teenage cousins, who had been using the cart to fetch cushions and books and musical instruments, sat on the grass beside the drive. It was the youngest one who was screaming. Another moaned and thrashed in the third cousin's lap. Her face was severely burned.

The electromagnetic motor vanished. Gaethla dusted his hands together and studied the mutilated power cart as if deciding which piece to take next.

"You! Dog!"

Dryjon reeled out of the villa. The slaves on the front steps parted to make way for him. He waved his sword. Diejen, her hair falling all over her face, swung on his sword arm, trying to pull it down.

"How dare you fuck with my sister?" Dryjon bellowed.

"She can't resist my manly charms," Gaethla said.

"I'll fucking spit you like a pig! I'll drink toasts out of your skull, and the Magus can come take it back, if he dares!"

Dryjon's eyes were glazed, his gait unsteady. He shook Diejen off and made a rush at Gaethla, who sidestepped. The big man caught Diejen by the hair. "You should've come with me when I asked you to, sweetheart."

"I told you to *go!*" Diejen screamed, struggling. "I spared your life! And this is how you repay me? Traitor!"

"Traitor? No, that's the pair of you."

Dryjon whirled his sword in an overhead cut. Gaethla pushed Diejen in front of him. Dryjon pulled his swing just in time to avoid hitting her. Gaethla stepped outside his guard and grabbed his arm.

"I'll give your regards to the Magus," he called, catching sight of Colm.

The air shimmered.

Then all three of them were gone.

The furnace puffed smoke over the empty drive.

Too stunned to think clearly, Colm moved towards the cart. He needed to quench the fire, although it didn't really matter, with the boiler missing.

The voltaic pile was still there. It was a stack of silver and zinc discs, interleaved with paper, in a wooden barrel six feet tall. It had an output potential in the kilovolt range. Colm had been quite proud of getting the design to work. Diejen had copied all her jewellery to get enough silver for the piles, over and over and over until the original bracelets and necklaces faded to tarnished wisps.

The cousins stared in shock at the place where Diejen and Dryjon had stood.

Colm wanted to say he'd give all the silver on Kisperet to get them back.

But they weren't staring at him.

Behind him, someone cleared his throat.

Colm spun.

Dhjerga sat on top of the voltaic pile, where nothing and no one had been a second ago. He wore the uniform of a Fleet ground technician. The hi-viz stripes shone garishly in the sunset. "Well, I'm back," he said. "Did I miss anything?"

CHAPTER 20

Bridget Wilson, née Mackenzie, saw where the drone fell. She fossicked around in the wet heather until she found it, and put it in the pocket of her fleece. Then she picked up the jerrycans and headed back down to the caravan site.

She already regretted shooting the drone down. They used to see them swooping silently around all the time, and they would hold up handwritten signs: *13 Adults 8 Children. Need Meds, Toothbrushes, Propane, Nappies.*

That was last year. Now, if she had had a sign to hold up, it would have read: *6 Adults 3 Children.*

The Singhs had moved on, and old Mrs. Robertson had died. You didn't need Ghosts to kill you when a Highlands winter was knocking at the door, and arterial sclerosis had already taken up residence.

Need Meds. It wasn't just poor Mrs. Robertson, RIP. Bridget's own mother, Daisy, had arthritis, and Scarlett, her youngest, had a cough that wouldn't go away. It worried Bridget half to death. What if they'd eluded the Ghosts, only for her daughter to die of some unknown malady because they'd run out of antibiotics?

And they *hadn't* eluded the Ghosts, either. They still saw them on their rare foraging trips into Ullapool. The Ghosts had killed every soul in the picturesque fishing village. Now they lived in the Mariners B&B and patrolled up and down the A835. But they never came out to the coast, for whatever reason. That's why Bridget's group had survived.

And now, the first chance they had in months of being found and rescued, what did she do? Shoot the thing!

Which had been really daft for another reason, as well: they were down to their last crate of ammunition for the .22, and they depended for food on the rabbits that Bridget and Ted could bring in off the hills, when the sea was too rough to get any fish.

Need Ammo, Fishing Line, Sailcloth.

Tromping through the bracken, with the pines dripping down her neck and the jerrycans banging the small of her back, Bridget added more and more things to her imaginary list of wants from a government that no longer existed. *Razors, Brillo Pads, Toilet Paper.* She was mentally debating the merits of sanitary napkins vs. tampons as she squeezed through the hedge and came out onto the road at the end of Ardmair Point, where a row of caravans faced the sea loch. Her elder daughter and son raced up to her. They had heard her firing the .22. Had she got a rabbit? No rabbit? Oh, *Mam.* You're a crap shot ... *I* would have got it, said nine-year-old Ivor, puffing himself up. Morag, twelve, scoffed: you didn't even hit that sheep the other day ... Bridget smiled and rolled her eyes at her children's competitiveness. *Need Large Latte With Extra Shot,* she thought. *And a Chocolate Chip Muffin.*

It was the little deprivations that got to you. They'd adjusted to life without any electrically powered conveniences. At the end of the day it was not a big deal to lose the power, compared to losing one's life. They cooked on a wood stove, bathed in a tin tub, stayed warm with extra jumpers and sparing use of the propane heater. Bridget forced herself to appreciate the benefits of their medieval lifestyle. After all, she and Ted had seen this coming. They had prepared by buying the caravan, equipping it with the wood stove and a gravity-fed water filter, stuffing the trailer with essential supplies. They'd always dreamed of packing in their careers, living the simple life, getting back to their roots. Three generations under one roof ...

And there was Bridget's biggest problem, the *three generations* bit.

Oh, *Ted's* parents were fantastic. His father, Oliver, came to help her with the jerrycans as she plodded towards the caravan they used as a kitchen and dining-room. "Sunita's on lookout duty," he said. "Daisy's having a lie-down." Bridget forced a smile. Her mother, Daisy, spent all too many days 'having a lie-down.' It was partly because of the arthritis, but in her mind Bridget assigned causation for the arthritis, too, to her father.

It was no picnic living with Lloyd Mackenzie in the first place. And now that he was contending with his own 'little deprivations'—no booze, no fags ... look out.

She showed Ted the drone after the children were in bed. The elder Wilsons had gone to their own caravan. Lloyd remained in the young family's caravan, citing the need not to disturb Daisy's sleep, but in reality so that he could pester Bridget and Ted about going to Skye. This was his pet idea, which he would not let go of no matter how often she pointed out the impossibility of packing the nine of them and their goods into one small sailing boat, not to mention the dangers of the Minch. Ted put him off this time by saying they'd think about it when summer came. Peeved, he'd taken himself off to play one of his endless games of solitaire by the open door of the wood stove. But at the word 'drone' he was back, a towering scarecrow-like figure, blocking the kerosene lamp.

"Let me see it."

Bridget pointed to the little machine on the fold-down table. It was a microcopter with a stealth-black fuselage that had an odd form factor, sort of bristly, like a dead twig. It was no bigger than a starling. Her bullet had torn off one of its rotors.

"It's from the Fleet," Ted said. He was all lit up with this possibility, and heroically not blaming Bridget for shooting the drone down. "It'll have been looking for survivors."

Lloyd picked the drone up in his long deft fingers. No matter how much he drank in the old days, his hands had never shaken. Bridget was dismayed to see them shaking now. The wobbling shadows exaggerated the tremors. "It's not from the Fleet, you numpties."

"It is," Ted protested. "Who else could it be from?"

The Fleet was their last hope, given their implicit understanding that the government of Scotland, and probably every government on Earth, had gone the way of the hoteliers and shopkeepers of Ullapool. The Fleet had evacuated millions of people from the colonies, and then re-evacuated thousands of people from Earth. They could not possibly, said Ted, have left everyone who was *not* rich to die.

Yes, thought Bridget, they could have. Her father seemed to confirm her cynicism. "It's not got any weapons, just a camera, but that doesn't mean it's friendly. Why'd you shoot it?" he asked her.

"I had a bad feeling about it," Bridget said defiantly.

Lloyd turned the drone over. Then he walked away with it, back to the woodstove at the other end of the caravan where the children were sleeping. An unfinished game of solitaire covered the table. It was a funny kind of solitaire he played, with the kings opposing each other across the table, black to red, and all the other cards swirling around in the middle. He cleared a space for the drone.

Bridget scanned the sleeping faces of the children zonked out on the couches. "Jesus, Dad, not in here."

He paid her no attention. He sat down and held both hands out flat, about a foot above the drone. He did not move for several minutes, except to grimace and roll his shoulders to relieve the strain. Ted gave Bridget's waist a gentle pinch, which meant: *Your father's a complete nutter, isn't he?* Bridget nodded. It was easier for Ted, she knew, to believe that old Mr. Mackenzie was a crank than to accept the truth, which was that he was a magician. Not just a conjuror, which was how he used to earn a living. A real, honest-to-God magician.

The cards moved.

The king of spades sliced into the air. As if blown by a wind from nowhere, a wind they couldn't feel, it landed on top of the drone.

Lloyd grunted. The king of hearts rose off the table. It slid under the black king and flipped it upwards.

Ted's mouth hung open.

The king of spades fought back, slapping against the red king and pushing it away from the drone.

Several of the other cards joined the fray. They whirled in the air above the table, slicing at each other, black versus red. Lloyd's hands began to shake violently.

"Fuck's sake!" he said. "Help me hold my hands up!"

Bridget squeezed around one side of the table, Ted the other. Meeting one another's gaze with wide, frightened eyes, they planted their elbows on the table and supported Lloyd's arms while the cards darted around the caravan like birds gone mad. A two of spades hit Ted in the face.

"Ugh," Lloyd grunted. The king of spades flopped to the table, face-down. The other cards followed.

The king of hearts lay face-up on top of the drone.

"You can let go now," he added.

Ted straightened up, looking dazed.

Bridget caught movement on one of the couches. She panicked for an instant, thinking one of the children had woken up, and there she'd been thinking they had learned to sleep through anything—then she saw it was just Mickle, the cat, sticking her head out from under the edge of Scarlett's duvet. She bent and checked on her daughter. The rattle in her chest didn't sound good, but at least Scarlett wasn't coughing tonight.

Lloyd said, "Well, I've taken it off him. He'll not be spying on us *that* way anymore. That's the good news."

Ted cleared his throat. "Um, am I the only one who thinks that was rather odd?"

Bridget laughed. She tucked her arm around her husband's waist. How she loved him—naïve, English, ordinary. So blessedly ordinary.

Lloyd turned a bleak gaze on his son-in-law. "We've been invaded by teleporting aliens who look like humans, and you think *my* wee tricks are odd?"

Ted smiled, conceding the point, but he said, "You're a magician, aren't you, Lloyd? A real one."

Well, well. Not as naïve as she'd thought.

Lloyd grudgingly nodded. "A few hundred years ago, they'd have burned me at the stake. A few thousand years ago, I'd have been prancing around the oak groves in a white nightgown, cutting the living hearts out of prisoners of war."

"And Bridget's one, too," Ted said. He was thinking, she

knew, of the 'bad feeling' she'd had about the drone. Of her other 'feelings' in the past, including the one that had pushed him and her to move up north and go full prepper, at a time when other people were still telling each other the government would save them.

"No, I'm not," she said, low.

"It's in her blood," Lloyd said. "But she's not trained."

Too true, damn you, Dad, Bridget thought. And why? Because you never even tried to train me. You spent hours and hours teaching your tricks to Colm, and how did that work out? He ran away to space and never came back. *I'm* the one who stayed here to look after you and Mam, and what do I get for it? Nothing but grief.

Ted said, "All I want to know is if *they* … " He trailed off, glancing at the three sleeping children.

"No," Lloyd and Bridget said together. Then, for the first time in ages, they laughed together. Of all the people on Earth, Ted Wilson—born in Birmingham, former media manager at an outdoor goods company—was the least likely to share the taint of the fucked-up Mackenzies. Morag, Ivor, and Scarlett were safe. "You have to get it from both sides," Bridget explained. Ted relaxed a smidge.

Lloyd stared gloomily at the cards. Bridget tried to divine what he saw in the pattern in which they had fallen. The black and the red were all mixed up together. She wondered if it meant anything that the *other* red king, the king of diamonds, hadn't moved. The other black king, the king of clubs, lay all by himself on the far side of the table. "So what's the bad news?" she said.

"I need a drink," Lloyd said.

"You stopped the Magus from spying on us with the drone."

The Magus was a familiar bogeyman. It was Lloyd's way of referring to whatever intelligence motivated the Ghosts. "You said that was the good news. What's the bad news?"

"Ah. Is it not obvious? He already saw you. So we'll have to book it."

Ted jumped as if he'd been stabbed. "You think they're coming for us?"

"Definitely," Lloyd said. "But all is not lost. They don't like the sea, as you'll have noticed. Can't stand the bloody sight of it. Got no clue about boats. So we'll be safe if we cross the water."

"Dad—"

"I know what you're going to say, and I'm not saying we should go to Skye in that crapped-out dinghy. If you'd stolen a better boat, as I keep telling you … Ah well. The dinghy'll get us across the loch."

"To where?"

"There's an island closer than Skye. You can see it if you step outside. Isle Martin. Aye, sure, there's no nice cozy caravan site over there. But it's better than being dead, isn't it?"

Bridget was about to object. But then Scarlett coughed in her sleep. She rushed to her side, consumed by worry about her daughter.

She hardly heard Ted say, "So I take it you don't think the Fleet is coming to save us."

Lloyd replied curtly: "That drone isn't one of theirs. It's from the sentrienza."

CHAPTER 21

Dhjerga had taken all the stuff home to Dam Lizp Hol. Well, he hadn't known Colm was going to conquer the world while he was gone.

The stuff took up an entire warehouse at the Lizp steelworks. The artisans sidled unhappily around the spools of fiberoptic cable and precision-machined engine bells. It offended them to have all these barbaric objects invading their domain, he knew. The steelworks were a boutique operation, dedicated to one-of-a-kind excellence. A dozen metalworkers with lifetimes of experience between them might labor for days over a single gun barrel, not content to make anything less than the best and most beautiful gun barrel in the universe. Only a few dozen finished items came out of the works every year; but each of those could be copied thousands of times without significant quality loss, because they were so good to begin with. The artisans discriminated in their choice of materials, going themselves to the mines and forests to obtain the very best metal ores and timber. Fate forfend they work with materials from a source they had not personally vetted. They took immense pride in their work. Wherever attempts to introduce Earth technologies to Kisperet had been made, they had failed, nine out of ten times, in the face of passive opposition from these freemen.

"Suck it up," Dhjerga told them. "Starting today, we're going to be building a spaceship."

Then he had to explain what a spaceship was. Predictably, they didn't like it. Flying between worlds in a *metal tube?*

"The old ways are the best ways," sniffed a veteran machinist.

"That's what Lady Diejen always used to say," Dhjerga reminded them. "Now she's gone. That filthy louse she was going to marry kidnapped her and Lord Dryjon. He's taken them to Atletis." The artisans' faces crumpled in shock. They, too, knew that the Lizp-led rebellion had strewn corpses across Kisperet and—a worse crime—left thousands of illegal copies wandering around. The twins were under an automatic death sentence. They were not likely to ever come back from Atletis alive.

But Dhjerga didn't believe the Magus would execute them immediately. He'd keep them alive for a while, hoping to bait the rebels into trying to rescue them.

Dhjerga was eager to accept that invitation, and he wasn't going to let a bunch of bolshy freemen stand in his way.

Having leveraged the steelworkers' affection for Diejen to win their cooperation, he copied two dozen of them to Ilfenjium. He had also had to promise to copy their families with them, so he went into the town and explained the situation to the women and children and a few husbands. In the ordinary way of things, freemen would never let themselves be copied. It was at once a privilege reserved for the chosen few, like Janz, and a taboo rooted in a sound grasp of the health issues. Dhjerga ordered them to gather on the snow-blanketed cobbles of Electrical Square, and did it. Other townspeople stopped and stared and asked questions. Dhjerga answered them. It was just as well they should all know that the old ways were changing.

The whole operation was pointless, to be honest. When the copied artisans met their copied families at Ilfenjium, they would barely know each other. Copies retained their skills but little of their humanity; the adults would have to be told the names of their own children, and would not care much about them. The children, lacking skills, would be virtually helpless. They'd have to be fed and dressed and led around like imbeciles until they came to themselves. And when the mothers and fathers came to themselves, there was no guarantee they'd still want to be married to the same people … Yes, there were many good reasons why what Dhjerga had just done was a capital crime. But it was far from the first one he'd committed, and the way things were going it would not be the last.

He pulled some power from the steelworks and went home.

Dam Lizp Hol was named after, and overlooked, the same dam that powered the steelworks. You could see the snowy roofs of the town from the upstairs windows. The turbines of the hydroelectric plant were actually in the cellar of the vast, ancient castle. Because of this, they had something virtually unknown elsewhere on Kisperet—electric light. Dhjerga's mother had discovered incandescent lightbulbs on the first colony world they conquered, and to this day, one artisan spent all his time making incrementally more perfect glass bulbs that enclosed carbonized wood splints in a vacuum, in memory of her. It had been the family's first small defiance of the Magistocracy. Dhjerga changed out of his wet clothes beneath the lightbulb in his chamber. First the Magus had taken his mother and father. Now the twins. He was the only one left.

"Janz!" he shouted. He needed help polishing the lord prefect's torc and cleaning his mantle. Dryjon never used to wear them, so the originals had got tarnished and shelf-wrinkled, respectively. He hated to make copies of them in this condition.

One of his second cousins poked her head into the chamber, and pulled back with a scandalized yelp when she saw Dhjerga standing in his shirttails, his cock hanging out.

"I need Janz! Where is he?" Dhjerga yelled at the door, hurriedly pulling a pair of breeches on.

"Um, your freeman?"

Dhjerga rolled his eyes. He didn't really know any of his cousins and nor did they know him, since he'd been away at the front since he was seventeen. Still, it was inexcusable that this girl wasn't even sure of the name of the Lizp family's reigning champion. "Yes, my freeman! My *best* freeman. Where is he?"

He was suddenly afraid for Janz. They had been fighting together for fifteen years.

He put on his boots and went out to the corridor; no one there. He tracked his cousins down in Diejen's chamber, at the end of the wing. Their female slaves knelt on the floor, with kirtles and leggings and blouses draped over their outstretched arms and heads. He had a horrible feeling that his cousins had been trying on Diejen's clothes. But these girls were lionesses. They had helped to conquer the *world*. He was not going to fall out with them over a few frocks. Keeping his temper, he said, "Janz?"

"Oh, yes, I know who you mean," said an older girl. "Diejen took him south with her."

"Took *him?*"

"Yes. She said she wanted to look after him herself."

Oh, Diejen. It figured that her idea of *looking after* Janz was dragging him on a thousand-mile trek through the forest.

Dhjerga didn't know whether to laugh or cry. He settled on leaving. But before he left, he said to his cousins' slaves, "Stand up."

They did as ordered.

"Put those things on the bed, or on the chairs. Wherever you like."

They did so. A couple of them were too new to make sense of such a confusing order; they stared at him blankly, with kirtles hanging over half their faces.

"Now you can sit down—or go get something to eat—or go to your quarters and rest. Whatever you like."

"Hey!" his cousins said indignantly. "We're using them."

"Have you forgotten why we rebelled against the Magistocracy in the first place? They're not slaves anymore! They're free! Treat them like human beings."

He was aware of his own hypocrisy. After all, he had just made copies of a hundred people who'd served the Lizps faithfully all their lives. He didn't give the girls time to point this out. He pulled power from the generator in the basement, and flitted.

The nippy air of Diejen's chamber turned into warmth. Electric light turned into the flickering light of Magistocracy-approved kerosene lanterns. The steelworks at Ilfenjum dwarfed the Lizp operation. Giant forges and rollers loomed at one end of the factory floor. This was where they made tanks for the front—a recent and still controversial innovation, which had meant adopting the internal combustion engine. Dhjerga had already moved the spaceship parts here from Dam Lizp Hol. They lay scattered on the factory floor like a giant jigsaw puzzle, mixed in with tank armor and caterpillar treads. He saw his copied artisans poking at them, and then he stood among them.

There was always an instant's dizziness; a feeling of pins and needles in his bones. Then he was himself again.

He smelled hot metal and lubricant oil, and saw Colm sitting on the edge of one of the giant anvils near the unlit forges. Swathed in a Lizp-green mantle, Colm was drinking from a flask as he pored over the big C-shaped faerie book. He had not seen Dhjerga appear. Dhjerga regarded him across the factory floor for a moment. He saw Colm as their savior, a mage with an innate grasp of the principles of freedom, who could teach them all a better way to be. Yes, there was the slight hitch that he was not a mage at the moment. But that was a good thing. It made him easier to control.

"Hola," Colm called out, raising a hand.

Dhjerga went over to him, tucking in his shirt. In the end he'd forgotten to bring the lord prefect's gear. It was probably just as well. He was not the lord prefect, and it might get his allies' backs up if he started dressing like it.

Colm touched a button and the screen of the faerie book went black. "First priority is setting up a power supply for that. Once the battery goes, it's dead unless I can get AC current out of the generator. We'll have to build phase transformers, too. Have some bee juice." He offered Dhjerga his flask. Bee juice? Dhjerga took it and gulped. Mead. Dhjerga had had to get used to the concept of a savior who drank like a fish, but Colm looked really fried just now. "I keep thinking I could've done something to save them," he said. "I just stood there with my thumb up my arse. Real Fleet preparedness."

The words warmed Dhjerga. Colm missed the twins as

much as he did. "We'll rescue them," he said, wondering how on earth this chaotic collection of parts was ever going to turn into a spaceship. He pushed the doubts away. Colm could do it.

"Yeah, well, you're going to need to go back to Barjoltan," Colm said.

"What?"

"Fuel. I asked for LH2 and LOX. You didn't bring any."

"Oh. The queazel said there wasn't any at that place. It shouldn't be a problem, though. That kind of thing is always lying around …"

"Is that what he said? Sure, it's always lying around where *he* comes from."

Dhjerga did not even know what LH2 was. His ignorance frustrated him. He attempted to change the subject. "Have you seen Janz?"

"Yeah, he was just here." Colm pulled the list Dhjerga had brought back with him out of his pocket. He tapped it without unfolding it. "The O isn't a problem. There's oxygen all around us. We've got to liquefy it anyway, so I'll build the equipment, run it on air, and use a fractionating column to separate out the gasses. There's our oxidizer. But hydrogen? Oxygen boils at 90 degrees Kelvin. Hydrogen boils at 20 Kelvin."

"That doesn't sound like much of a difference."

"I know, but hydrogen is incredibly difficult to liquefy, and fucking dangerous. It leaks out of everything, embrittles metals. The cracks allow more of it to escape into open air, and then things go bang. I really don't want to mess with it. Did you at least bring the cryo-compression system?"

"I think so."

"Well, maybe I can make ethanol and react it with high-temperature steam." Colm unfolded the list. A few dark, dry leaf fragments fell to the floor. He said casually, "No meds, either?"

"The queazel said you didn't really need them." Dhjerga was looking at those leaf fragments. By Scota's grave, he hoped those weren't what they looked like.

"That goddamn furball." Colm helped himself to more mead.

A procession of slaves entered the factory floor, lugging ingots of aluminum. Colm jumped up and went to meet them.

Dhjerg picked up the leaf fragments. He rubbed them between his fingers and sniffed them. It was as he had feared. They were *doire* leaves. And Colm hadn't said anything to him about it. This was not good.

Janz came up to him. "My lord."

"There you are," Dhjerga said with a grin, attempting to conceal his shock. Janz looked thin—almost transparent, in fact. He was no longer the strapping champion who had accompanied Dhjerga, in a hundred thousand bodies, from one battle theater to the next. Bloody Diejen! She must have been using him profligately. Dhjerga had been going to make a new copy of him on the spot, but now he realized he could not take the risk. "You look as if you need some time off."

"Indeed, my lord, I'd rather not." Janz looked panic-stricken. "I'd be bored."

"Well, then, I've got the perfect assignment for you. Become Lord Mackenzie's bodyguard." He accorded Colm the honorary title out of habit, although if his suspicions were correct, Colm did not deserve it. "Whenever he leaves the steelworks, if I'm not there, I want you to accompany him.

Follow him wherever he goes … and when he takes his meals, you are to tell me what he eats, to the last mouthful."

A gleam of approval appeared in Janz's eyes. "That I can do, sir." He glanced across the factory floor at Colm. "Do I have your leave to start now?"

"Certainly."

"It's only I heard him talking about liquid hydrogen, my lord, and I thought I'd suggest kerosene for the first stage."

CHAPTER 22

Colm worked his ass off every watch. He had adapted to using the imprecise Ghost unit of 'watch' for a human waking period, what he used to call a 'day.' During the 'sleeps,' when his artisans and slaves got their heads down in the houses he had commandeered for them—when he could get away from reviewing the blueprints with woefully ignorant mages, or inspecting materials fetched from the ends of Kisperet—he went to the zoo.

He would've preferred to go alone, but Janz was always with him. Dhjerga said it was necessary for his safety. After all, he was now the most indispensable man on Kisperet. Colm appreciated the thought, but he felt like Janz was *watching* him, and taking note of any changes in his habits.

He still wasn't eating the salads. Instead, whenever he could manage it without Janz seeing him, he pulled handfuls of leaves off the not-oak tree. He never had caught its name. He called it, to himself, the *noak* tree. He stuffed them into his pocket to consume later, alone. But usually Janz stuck to him so closely that he didn't dare to approach the tree. On these occasions, he contented himself with visiting the limethion, the dragon-like alien he had met on his first visit to the zoo. It was only too eager for company, now that it was being fed pigs instead of criminals. Colm would sit in front of its cage and listen to its reminiscences of life on Mitheikua. "We'll get you home someday," he promised, while he was privately beset by a feeling that he and the limethion were in the same plight. He did not live in a cage, but he too was a prisoner.

Guards surrounded every power source in the steelworks,

vigilant for any attempt at invasion. A defensive perimeter enclosed the entire complex. Occasional probes from Atletis were met with volleys of fire that killed the invaders before they could see anything. The mages were sanguine, but it felt to Colm like they were under siege.

He had a place of his own now: an office at the steelworks, which he had equipped with a bed, chair, and desk. The bed was a typically fancy piece of Kisperet furniture, the headboard and footboard carved in the form of trees that met overhead and dangled diaphanous canopies around him. He would lie in there chewing noak leaves and thinking about Diejen until he felt sick.

Then his esthesia implant would come to life, and when he shut his eyes, he could feel the power flowing into the computer on his desk. Further away, he could feel the electron beam furnace, the hot isostatic press, his newly built milling machine for the hull plates, his die presses, and his new arc welding kits.

So there was definitely *something* happening. But when he pictured Bridget, all he could see was the glimpse that the Magus had shown him. Drop jerrycans, roll into cover, fire. Drop, roll, fire. That was not the Bridget he knew. She worked at a camping goods company. She'd married one of the sales guys, an Englishman. What had happened to her? What was happening to her *right now?* And what about his parents? And what about everyone he'd left in the Betelgeuse system? Axel, Sully, Meg … Gil …

Alone in the dark, after Janz finally went to bed, he would juggle or play the spoons until his fingers ached. No dice.

If the noak leaves contained a natural version of the key active ingredient in tropodolfin, it wasn't as strong. Maybe he had to build up a certain amount of the chemical in his bloodstream, and he couldn't get to the noak tree often enough to get enough leaves.

They'd stopped serving him salads.

"But you don't like them," Dhjerga had said, the one time he asked why.

So all he could do was throw himself into his work.

The computer Dhjerga had stolen from the Fleet came with the standard public knowledge base, containing petaflops of information about everything. Colm had been counting on this. Knowing a fair bit about early human spaceflight, he was basing his spaceship on the Saturn V, the rocket that had taken humanity to the moon for the first time ever.

Slowly, a copy of that historical marvel took shape in the yard in the middle of the steelworks. It looked more or less like the photos on the computer. In reality it was an unholy mash-up. Sentrienza electronics nestled in mechanical cradles fashioned by armorers and swordsmiths. Modern spaceships were precision-cast or printed by the module; Colm's ship was *sewn* together with thousands and thousands of arc welds. *Son Of Saturn*, he was calling it. A private, black joke. *SOS.*

*

He sometimes had to throw parties at the steelworks to keep the Families on board. The mages were very keen on parties. The wilder the better. They made a polite show of interest in the rocket, and then fell upon the food and drink laid on by Dhjerga, who spent most of his time struggling to feed their horde of workers and armed guards. He sent forage carts overland to plunder fields and orchards scouted out by the Lizp cousins. One of the cousins had recently hit the jackpot: an apiary. Bees made honey. Honey made mead. Mead, served up by the pint, in silver flagons cooled with ice straight from the snowy north, made Dhjerga and Colm the most popular men in Ilfenjium.

A few days ago Colm had held a static fire test of the *SOS's* main engine. He had adopted Janz's suggestion of using kerosene, in preference to ramping up several additional industries in order to get liquid hydrogen. The engine had not exploded. That was something. But the residues left in the combustion chamber and engine bell horrified him. His kerosene just wasn't pure enough to meet the rocket fuel standard. He'd run the whole lot over a bed of carbonized millet husks to get the sulfur out of it, but that might actually have made it worse. If he fired the engine for longer than a few seconds, it would clog the lines. Goodbye, Atletis. Goodbye, Earth. Goodbye, Diejen. The computer could not tell him how to get rocket fuel out of lamp oil.

He spooned up pork and turnip stew, brooding over the problem. Around him, the mages caroused. He had had tables and benches set out in the courtyard of the steelworks, where the test had been held. The rocket stage, in its wooden scaffold—minus the engine assembly, which he'd had removed for cleaning—towered above the throng. Summer had come to Kisperet: it was warm enough to sit out in shirtsleeves, and less windy than usual. Rho Cassiopeiae shone brilliantly overhead. Atletis was a crescent at the zenith. Cerriwan, in its usual place, glowered through the top of the *SOS's* scaffold. You didn't even need lanterns on a 'three-moon' night like this.

The scraping squeals of a fiddle penetrated the chatter. Colm smiled in relief—the ceilidh was starting. Now he wouldn't have to think about kerosene residues for a while. He hurriedly gobbled the rest of his meal. Janz hadn't been able to stop him grabbing some salad amidst the free-for-all of a Ghost dinner party. The bitterness of the noak leaves turned his mouth inside-out, and warmed his stomach. Now he could feel the electricity in the buildings around him. The fiddler launched into a fast-paced tune. A second later a percussionist joined in, climbing up on a table to whack on a skin drum rather like a bodhran.

The Ghosts loved music. All the mages could play some instrument, and they formed bands at the drop of a hat. Soon a harpist and another drummer joined in. The tables were pushed back and the mages began to dance. They stood in two lines, the men facing the women; they high-stepped in and out and changed partners with formal solemnity. The women wore ankle-length split skirts that belled as they moved, with wrap-around blouses that exposed quite a lot of skin to the air. The men wore tight trousers and colorful shirts with sleeves as wide as the women's skirts. Around the edges of the courtyard, freemen and even slaves danced too, men partnering men as there were not enough women to go around. All the mages wore a great deal of jewelry. When you could just copy it, there was no reason not to have three gold necklaces and diamond earrings the size of quail eggs. Even Colm wore several bracelets on each wrist, to fit in. The fiddle screamed, the drums hammered, high heels rattled on the cobbles, and Colm nodded his head in time with the music.

For an instant he thought he saw Diejen coming towards him. His heart turned over. But it was only one of the Lizp cousins, Sethys, who looked rather like her. "Come and dance, my lord!"

"Not yet, my lady," Colm said, smiling at her. "On Earth, we don't dance unless we're drunk."

"Then you must have another drink."

The mead worked its magic and before long he was shaking it with the others. The formal dances had ended by now and people were just stumbling around, yelling at the musicians to play faster, louder, more. Teenagers danced on the tables, stepping in the uneaten food. A swordfight broke out. More than one couple were having sex in the open air, up against a wall.

"Are parties on Earth this much fun?" Sethys said, swaying against him. Her hair had tumbled down. She was utterly captivating.

"There usually aren't any swordfights."

"Let's go somewhere quieter. Show me the factory floor."

So he did. The tour ended in his room. They could still hear the music and shouting from the courtyard. Sethys walked him backwards until he bumped into the bed and sat down. She plopped onto his lap. His head was spinning. He grasped her waist and pressed his face into her warm, sweaty cleavage. Her voice vibrated joyfully. *"Now* we will have fun."

"What would your husband say?" He knew that her husband was in the Mage Corps, away on one of the colony worlds.

"What do husbands say on Earth?"

"On Earth, we don't sleep with other people's wives."

He was making Earth out to be a place of morally upstanding perfection. But the truth was that Sethys was right. In some ways, Kisperet was more fun.

CHAPTER 23

Colm had been celibate for over a year. The woman in his arms could have been anyone, but in the dark, he caught himself imagining a face he hadn't seen in a long time. He cried out, "Ah, Diejen!"

Sethys Lizp laughed breathlessly under him. "I do look like her, don't I? Everyone says so."

"Sorry."

"If you are really sorry, you must make it up to me. Do that … yes, that … oh, yes!"

Some minutes later, as they lay drained, cuddling, the diaphanous canopies were ripped away from the bed. A man stood silhouetted in the faint starlight that fell from the skylight.

Colm had not heard the door opening, because it hadn't opened. The whole building was now so cluttered with cables, or lifelines as the Ghosts called them, that doors were obsolete: mages could pop up anywhere. He frantically reached for his gun. Then he recognized Dhjerga.

"That you, Sethys?" Dhjerga said. "Get out."

Sethys fled, leaving the air laced with her scent. Colm pawed around on the bed for his breeches.

"Did you know she's married?" Dhjerga said, his voice heavy with disgust.

Humiliation and outrage urged Colm to take a swing at him. But finding his trousers was a higher priority. By the time he got them on, his unthinking anger had worn off. He said coldly, "Yes, actually, I'm aware of that. Does it matter?"

He brushed past Dhjerga and hurried after Sethys, hoping

to catch her and apologize. He reached the courtyard but she was gone. Cerriwan shone coldly on the debris of the party. The harpist was throwing up in the shadow of the launch tower. A pool of blood glimmered black on the cobbles; the swordfight must've ended badly. Colm wandered along the tables, lifting flagons and putting them down, drinking from any that still had mead in them.

"You shouldn't have done that," Dhjerga said, behind him.

"What business is it of yours what I do?" Colm knew, in fact, that he shouldn't have done it. But Dhjerga's anger seemed disproportionate. It was as if Colm had personally betrayed him.

"You're supposed to be working on the spaceship."

"I can't work on it around the clock. Anyway, it's hopeless. We may as well scrap the thing."

"Scrap it?"

"I explained about the kerosene residues, didn't I? It was a good idea but it isn't going to work."

That, in fact, was why he'd got drunk and had drunken sex with a married woman. He was trying to adjust to the idea that he might never get off Kisperet. He was trying to decide if he could stand it here forever.

"Maybe you should have chosen a different design," Dhjerga said.

"Good God," Colm said sarcastically, slapping his forehead, "why didn't I think of that before?"

Of course, he had considered different designs at first. It would have been nice to go with the propulsion system he knew best, the standard Fleet nuclear plasma drive. But he wasn't mad enough to think he could build a water-xenon plasma engine with 19th-century technology. As for a thorium reactor, he didn't like the idea of Dhjerga and fissile material on the same planet. Colm had never forgotten the homemade nukes that wiped out millions of people on Majriti IV. Dhjerga had been on that planet at the time. He acted ignorant, but …

"It was either solid propellant or liquid propellant," Colm said. "And solid rocket boosters aren't reusable. Call me crazy, but I want to have at least a chance of getting back."

"Then we need a different rocket fuel," Dhjerga said.

"Give the man a gold star."

"You're the rocket scientist. You're supposed to be able to solve these problems!"

Colm laughed. "I'm not a rocket scientist. I'm just a guy with a computer. But as it happens, I do know exactly where we can get fuel." He pointed up. "What do you think that's made of, eh?"

"Cerriwan?"

"Bingo. If it's like other gas giants, and I've no reason to believe it's not, it's made of hydrogen, that's what. There's normally a sea of liquid hydrogen under the clouds of any gas giant. So you just fill a tank and fetch it back … before the gravity makes you drop like a rock to the center of the planet … and you die from the radiation … and by the way, you can't breathe, so you're dead anyway. Easy as falling off a log."

"All right," Dhjerga said. "I'll do it."

Colm stared at him. "I was joking."

"Well, I'm not." Anger radiated off Dhjerga like esthesia heat off a generator. He raised his hands to unpin his cape at the neck, as if getting ready to flit to Cerriwan this very minute.

Colm rushed at him and grabbed his arms. "What the hell is your problem? Have you got a death wish?" As he spoke Colm realized that Dhjerga had had a pretty thankless time of it recently. Perhaps his pent-up frustration was boiling out under the influence of alcohol and Colm's unwise taunting. Colm knew quite well that Dhjerga was very touchy about his own ignorance regarding technology. All the other mages were equally clueless but they just laughed it off or rambled on in a snooty fashion about the superiority of the old ways. Dhjerga *cared*. "Don't do it," Colm begged.

"I won't have to go all the way," Dhjerga said. I'll do this." He started to fade. Colm clutched his arms tighter in panic. His fingers sank through cold, prickly cloth and flesh. He could see the launch tower through Dhjerga's head. Then, all at once, Dhjerga became solid again. Colm flinched back, his fingers stinging. "Partly here and partly there. Not many mages can do that. The Magus, of course. And me. It's very difficult. The apple trees are still blooming at Dam Lizp Hol, by the way." A pale petal or two drifted out of his hair.

"Partly dead is still dead," Colm said, rubbing his static-bitten fingers. "We don't know at what altitude the liquid hydrogen starts. You'd have to make more than one trip to find the right depth. A *lot* of trips ..."

"I'll ride the lightning. That's what we used to do in the old days."

A new voice spoke. "No. I'll do it."

Janz limped out of the shadow of the launch tower.

Dhjerga rounded on him, finding a new target for his anger. "You were meant to be watching Lord Mackenzie!"

"Sorry, sir. I thought he deserved a little privacy." Janz winked at Colm. "Anyway, it will work better if I do it. You can send me as many times as it takes to find the right depth. Yes. We will probe Cerriwan, as if it were an enemy world. When I find the right place, I will tell you. You will go just once, for just a moment, to get your fix on the place. Then you can fetch the fuel straight into the tanks."

Colm took a deep breath. "We could make you an EVA suit," he said. "It would have to be extremely tough to withstand those pressures. Like a suit of armor. I dunno if we could make it completely radproof."

"I don't understand you," Dhjerga said angrily. Colm couldn't tell if he was talking to him or Janz.

"Do you have the tank ready?" Janz said, ignoring Dhjerga. "You will need at least 5,000 psi of cryo-compression."

"You know quite a bit about this, don't you?"

Janz smiled. "Many worlds. Many copies. Everything they know, I know."

"Ah. Right." That explained rather a lot … such as the Ghosts' lines of communication between Kisperet and the far-off front. "Well, the tank is ready." The cryo-compression system was a plug-and-play module from Barjoltan. But Colm wasn't 100% confident about the antiporosity of his improvised tank liner: he'd substituted carbonized chicken feather fibers for carbon nanotubes. "I'd like to fill it as close as possible to launch, so we don't risk boil-off. If you're really sure about this, we could start making the EVA suit now."

"I'm ready anytime," Janz said, sitting down on a bench.

Dhjerga grated, "No. I forbid it."

"Well, sir," Janz said, "you did say that we are not slaves anymore. We are free."

"You were already free."

"But now I am even more free. And that means I do not

have to obey you."

He smiled.

Dhjerga stormed out of the courtyard.

Colm watched him go. "What's wrong with him?"

"He misses Lord Dryjon and Lady Diejen," Janz said.

Colm sighed. "That makes two of us."

CHAPTER 24

T minus 1 watch. In the dark, acrid-smelling intertank space of the *SOS,* Colm checked the safety valve and heat exchanger of the LH2 tank one more time. He clambered out onto the scaffold, and waved down at the artisans watching from the rooftops. They seemed to be very far below. Fully assembled, the *SOS* stood 150 feet fall. It awed Colm what they had achieved—and make no mistake, this was *their* achievement, more than it was his. But it would all be for nothing if today's risky operation did not work.

Down in the courtyard, a scrum of mages buzzed around Dhjerga and Janz.

Janz was wearing an EVA suit made of leather and glass. He looked like an arctic explorer with a fishbowl on his head. He needed to be able to see but he did not need to be able to move. The suit had no air supply: he would just be breathing the air trapped inside it, until the gravity of Cerriwan crushed him to death.

Steeling himself not to think about the ghastly fate awaiting the copies, Colm gave his hand signal to the mages, and yelled, "Let's do it!"

Dhjerga stood behind Janz and rested his hands on his shoulders. It looked like nothing was happening. Then Janz removed his helmet to breathe, and shook his head. They resealed the helmet. The performance was repeated. Again. And again. And again. The watching artisans and mages suddenly let out a mass sigh as Janz's knees buckled. Sethys Lizp and Linc Terrious rushed over to help Dhjerga hold him up.

Everything they know, I know.

Did Janz also know his copies' pain? Was he experiencing, over and over, the agony of a living human body being ripped apart in a storm of hydrogen gas, or plummetting, still alive (for a few ghastly seconds), into Cerriwan's toxic internal ocean?

Colm dropped to his knees on the scaffold in unconscious imitation of the freeman. His knuckles whitened on the uprights. For an eerie moment it seemed as if everyone in the courtyard was experiencing the same pain as Janz, so intense was their empathy.

Then Janz collapsed.

The mages peeled him out of the EVA suit. Dhjerga put it on. He sealed the helmet, then did a slow flicker, the way he had on the night of the party. Fade, sparkle, back.

A mechanical bell trilled inside the intertank area. Colm hustled back through the hatch and down the ladder. He peered at the tank capacity dial. The LH2 tank was filling up, unbelievably fast. He didn't even need to look at the dial. He could feel the temperature dropping. In front of his eyes, ice formed on the outside of the cryo-cooled tank. The light had gone soft. He raised his gaze to the bright square of the hatch, seeking something, maybe God.

Snow was falling inside the tank. It landed on his hands and face. He licked it off his lips, and tasted metal.

When the dial stopped rising, the tank contained 200,000 liters of liquid hydrogen. Colm hadn't believed this could actually work. But it had. They had fueled a spaceship directly from a gas giant, without blowing anything up. His mind reeled at the possibilities. This could make the square-cube law and Tsiolkovsky's rocket equation obsolete. Chemical rockets would be competitive again. They'd be *faster* than plasma drives. And more to the point … the ability to refuel the *SOS* meant it had a good chance of coming *back* from Atletis. And he did, too.

He climbed back out onto the scaffold. "It worked!" he yelled to the artisans and workers standing on the roof of the steelworks, and the soldiers keeping watch. "It flipping *worked!*"

A cheer went up. Down in the courtyard, Dhjerga, still wearing the EVA suit, sat on the ground with Janz's head and shoulders on his lap. He tipped a cup of water to Janz's lips as tenderly as a mother feeding a child.

*

"Let's take the limethion," Colm said.

He was flushed with joy at the success of the fuelling operation. But he had not entirely stopped thinking objectively about his own situation. Janz was in bed, recovering, and Dhjerga was unlikely to leave his side for the time being. The *SOS* had to fly as soon as possible; the longer they left the LH2 sitting in the tank, the greater the risk that the cryo-compression would fail. For the next few hours everyone involved with the spaceship would be insanely busy.

"I'll go and fetch it from the zoo."

"Why?" said Quintana Terrious, an intimidating gray-haired mage who was also planning to fly on the *SOS*.

Colm thought for an instant that she was onto him. Then he realized what she was really asking. "Well, it's extremely vicious, isn't it? It might be useful if there's going to be fighting."

"If," Lady Terrious echoed, sarcastically. "Well, I do not see why not, if the creature will consent to be bound and muzzled while it is on the spaceship."

The limethion did consent. It even put the required muzzle on itself—it had capable claws. Its deft movements reminded Colm of Gil, although he was under no illusion that the limethion would turn out to be anything like so personable. It had already told him frankly that he looked tasty. "You're only to eat the enemy," he told it. "Not us."

"Understood."

With the limethion's leash looped around one wrist, Colm veered over to the noak tree and stuffed his pockets with its leaves. No one else was around.

"What are you doing?" the limethion said.

"Mind your own business, and if you tell anyone I won't let you on the spaceship."

"Consider me muzzled," the limethion said. "Literally."

The *SOS,* Colm calculated, could carry six. The limethion weighed as much as a man. The other four crew-members would all be mages: Dhjerga, Lady Terrious, her youngest son Linc, and another Lizp whom Colm did not know very well. He got back to the steelworks to find that this man had been kicked off the crew and Janz given his place.

"He wants to go," Dhjerga said glumly. "And I can hardly say no after he got us the fuel."

"Yes," Janz said. "I always stay at home while my copies travel the universe. This time, I want to go myself. Yes, I do."

Colm threw up his hands. "Up to you." He just wanted to do this before his tank liners failed and the whole bloody rocket exploded under them.

But the Ghosts had their own way of doing things, and a sense of ceremony that was not undermined by the ease of going and comings in their society. This would be a going like none Kisperet had ever seen, and mages from all the Families had come to Ilfenjium to watch. Colm begged them to stay in their villas and use spyglasses. They would be able to see perfectly well from there.

The crew boarded the rocket to the strains of a band. Snow fell in the sunlight, as the cryo-cooled fuels froze the humidity out of the air around the rocket. Their jewellery and boots picked up a dusting. Inside the cramped capsule, Lady Terrious took her boots off and settled into her goosedown-padded couch. "I hope you remembered the mead, Dhjerga. One does get thirsty on long journeys." The limethion lay down at her feet. "It is very cramped," it muttered disapprovingly. Colm stifled a howl. It was all so ludicrously unprofessional. None of them were wearing spacesuits. The EVA suit they had made for the fuelling journey had severe mobility issues, and it would've been impossible to make a suit for the limethion. But what did it matter? If the *SOS* did not reach Atletis, they were dead. End of story.

He buckled himself into his own couch, in front of 24th-century electronic displays set into a walnut dashboard crafted by a master cabinet-maker. "Ready to launch on my mark."

Despite everything, he felt childishly excited. He had sneaked a handful of noak leaves before they boarded. His esthesia implant fed the heat of the ship's systems into his body. He was like a kid on a sugar high. He could not flit, but he could fly.

The gas generator ignited. The main engine caught. The anchors fell away. Flame engulfed the courtyard, and *Son Of Saturn* howled into the sky with a boom that shattered every window in Ilfenjium.

CHAPTER 25

The original Saturn V had had three stages. Stages one and two fell into the Pacific. Stage three pushed the Apollo spacecraft towards the moon.

Son Of Saturn was a single stage rocket. Kisperet was slightly smaller than Earth, with a smidge lower gravity. Atletis was also smaller than our moon, and it orbited just 198,000 kilometers away, as best Colm could reckon it with a telescope and trigonometry. He calculated that he could get the *SOS* there with a single mighty push. Oh, it was back-of-the-envelope stuff. But he couldn't stand the thought of his lovely handcrafted rocket falling into the sea.

As it turned out this would not have happened anyway.

Kisperet had no sea.

Colm switched his gaze between the single, fuzzy camera feed and the porthole he had built into the crew capsule. He could not believe what he was seeing. Kisperet had shrunk to a globe. White and gray clouds hid a part of the northern hemisphere. Green land glimmered in the gaps between the clouds. This 'continent' was where they'd come from. It looked to be about the size of South America. But it was not a continent as such. Instead of ocean, it was bounded by desert. The rest of the planet was a dead, dull, uniform brown.

"By Scota's grave," Dhjerga said quietly, floating beside him. "It *does* look different from up here."

Colm remembered his claim, long ago, that flying gave you a new perspective on your homeworld. It had certainly given him a new perspective on Kisperet. "Where's the sea?"

Dhjerga stuck a finger in his ear. "I can't hear you properly."

"You know. *Sea*. Lots of water in one place. Like on Juradis." Juradis was a water world with two small polar continents and a scattering of islands.

Lady Terrious drifted up to them. She was coping well with the novel experience of freefall. It had taken years off her lined face, and the Kisperet-light from the porthole turned her gray hair silver. "There used to be a *sea,"* she said. "There is still a small body of water—can you see it?—near the equator. Ah, it is hidden by the clouds. It has grown smaller and smaller over the centuries. Our world is losing its water. That is why the Magus decided we should go back home."

Home ... A bell rang in Colm's mind. He ignored it, fascinated and horrified by the dying world below. Kisperet's slightly lower gravity, and maybe a weaker magnetic field, were allowing its water to escape into space. That kind of process was exponential on a scale of aeons. It happened slowly at first, then faster and faster. "What about the rivers?"

Lady Terrious understood what he meant. "You have not visited the mouth of the Great River. It is a wonder of the world. The water pours over a cliff—and vanishes! There are mages constantly on duty, fetching it back to the frozen north." A shadow crossed her face. "I am afraid some of them left their posts during the war. This rebellion has cost us many, many works of water."

Colm shook his head in amazement. The mages of Kisperet were keeping their homeworld's water cycle going, literally by sheer willpower. It really testified to the power of the human spirit.

Kisperet shrank into space, a brown pimple on the face of Cerriwan.

*

The *Son of Saturn* covered the distance to Atletis in a day and a half. All the mages eagerly gazed at the little moon as it got bigger.

Its green and white coloration had not been an illusion. Atletis was covered with trees. Clouds massed over lakes and sparkling polar ice caps.

"But it's tiny," Colm said. Smaller than our moon, how did Atletis hold onto its air? Could this, too, be magic?

Lady Terrious shook her head, her silver halo of hair swaying. "It is a heimdall."

"A what?"

The elderly mage folded her lips shut. She could not or would not say.

Colm saw no sign of human habitation. The forests looked as deep and dank as the Cairngorms. It would be a challenge finding an LZ that wasn't covered with trees. As they orbited the little moon, he pieced together camera images into a map of the surface. "Where do you want to land?"

Dhjerga, Lady Terrious, and the young Lord Terrious had all been to Atletis, of course, in the days when they worked for the Magistocracy. But they didn't know *where* on Atletis they'd been. The horrible thought came to Colm that they may not have been to Atletis at all. The Magus might have lied to them to conceal the location of his headquarters.

Dhjerga stared at the map. "I don't even know what this picture *is!* It's pretty …"

"It's a map," Janz said. "There was a lad who saw one like it once at headquarters. Innismon is here." His forefinger came down on the map.

"Good thing you came along, Janz," Colm said in relief.

Innismon, the Magus's headquarters, was not visible from

orbit. It must be hidden beneath the trees.

"But there must be *something* we can see from here," Linc Terrious said. "The Magus's power source: a river, a dam …"

"There's no river on this map, Janz," Dhjerga said. "Are you sure you've got the location right?"

"Yes," Janz said with stolid confidence.

Colm chewed his lip. "How about landing somewhere else?" He didn't want to sacrifice the hope of getting away from Atletis alive. That meant looking after the *SOS*. Keeping it intact. It would be hard to do that if he landed on top of the enemy's headquarters.

"I am hungry," the limethion said darkly.

Lady Terrious settled the debate. "Wherever we put down," she said, "they will find us instantly. This ship, after all, is a power source. Therefore I suggest that we land at the location Janz has identified. We have a single chance at victory. We must assault Innismon with overwhelming force, and capture the Magus's power source, just as we did at Ilfenjium."

*

Colm made the best of it. On Majriti IV, on Ross 458 c, and on Mu Arae d, he had often employed the Navy pilot's favorite tactic against the Ghosts: vaporize 'em. A ship's drive, after all, was its most powerful weapon. The pilots of the Unsinkable used to brag about the number of Ghosts they barbecued on their drops. Colm decided to take out as much of the Magus's infrastructure as he could with the SOS's drive.

Guiding the ship down into the atmosphere of Atletis, he had a sense of déjà vu. He was landing on a moon occupied by hostile Ghosts. Just like the old days. To put the cherry on the cake, Atletis was a moon orbiting a gas giant … well, a moon orbiting a moon of a gas giant … and as on Majriti IV, static-electric discharges sparkled through its upper atmosphere. This would make for a hairy landing. He remembered Meg singing, *I see lightning, I see lightning!* There was no point sharing his misgivings with the Ghosts around him. They barely understood physics.

He mentally crossed his fingers, and initiated the *Son of Saturn's* final de-orbit burn.

Once again, his luck held. They were descending onto the dayside of Atletis. Lower, lower. Down through the clouds. The forests took on texture, and now Colm glimpsed fields in clearings. The moon really was inhabited. "Where's the *river?*" Dhjerga said, confused. A stream crossed the fields, a mere silver thread. Cottages huddled around a green square. Chimneys puffed. Hell, Innismon was just a village! Above it, a line of unusually massive trees marched along a high ridge.

Colm made the split second decision to land in the village square. The computer said it was the only place flat enough. He could see people running around, staring up.

Imagine that you're back at war. Those people down there? They're Ghosts. *Aliens.* Not human.

Just like the old days.

Down we go.

The *Son Of Saturn* speared down out of the sky. It did not produce jets of plasma. It produced a single jet of white-hot flame. In terms of lethality, there wasn't much difference.

CHAPTER 26

Colm opened the airlock. A blast of cold wind carried smoke into the crew capsule. The sounds of clanging bells, screams, and neighing horses pierced the murk. He had expected micro-gravity. In fact, he felt about as heavy as he used to on the *Unsinkable,* which meant this tiny moon had half as much gravity as Earth. How was that even possible? Never mind. "Go, go, go!" Dhjerga was screaming, pushing at his back.

Colm checked the strap of his assault rifle—another handy toy he had had built at the Ilfenjium steelworks—and started down the ladder. He wished he had not followed the Ghosts' example of changing into his best clothes, including shiny leather boots with slippery soles. Good thing he had his riding gloves on, though. He could feel the hot metal charring their palms. The *SOS* swayed on its fins. The wind blew the smoke away. Glancing over his shoulder, he saw a ring of flattened, charred, and burning buildings. It looked like a bomb had gone off in the middle of Innismon.

As he neared the ground, bullets pinged off the *SOS*'s hull. He glanced over his shoulder again. The trees up on the ridge were clanging in the wind. They were *spinning*. They were not trees. They were mighty wind turbines, painted green. So this was the Magus's power source: wind power, rather than water power. If only he'd known! He could have destroyed at least some of the turbines with the *SOS*. Now it was too late.

The turbines had wide trunks like trees, spreading out at the bottom. And now Magistocracy soldiers emerged from among the trunks. One, two, twenty, two hundred ... They formed up and charged down the ridge towards the invaders.

Dhjerga jumped off the ladder above Colm's head, vanished in mid-air, and reappeared on the ground. Around him, copies of Janz multiplied. They spread out through the wreckage, seeking cover. The squat frog-faced champion of the Terrious family joined them, times a hundred. Each of the rebel soldiers had an assault rifle like Colm's. The weapon was based on the famous AK design that he remembered Meg carrying in the Kuiper belt. Now, as then, the Ghosts' bolt-action rifles could not answer the AK's superior rate of fire. A horizontal metal hail of bullets ploughed into the Magistocracy's soldiers.

The charge wavered and petered out.

Dhjerga and Linc Terrious breathlessly shouted orders.

The rebel soldiers advanced across fields of cabbages and turnips blanketed with ash, and waded across the stream.

Colm, who had watched the exchange of fire spell-bound, suddenly remembered that he was exposed up here. He crabbed the rest of the way down the ladder, panting. His ears rang. His throat hurt and his eyes watered from the smoke. A boot came down on the same rung as his hand. He wrenched his head back and saw Janz.

"Oi," he gasped. "You're meant to stay on board."

"Lady Terrious thinks the rocket might tip over. She's coming out, too."

"It won't tip over."

Janz smiled. "Lord Lizp leaves me behind every time. He's not leaving me behind *this* time, no." He jumped off the ladder and ran in search of Dhjerga.

Colm followed them across the fields. He was a pilot, not an infantryman. He had never felt comfortable in ground combat situations. Ahead of him, the rebel army multiplied into a sea of Lizp forest-green and Terrious sky-blue. It lapped up the slope and almost attained the ridge before clashing with a new wave of khaki. The gunfire sputtered out as the soldiers met in a hand-to-hand melee. Now Colm knew why Dhjerga had insisted on putting bayonets on the AKs. The soldiers jabbed and hacked without a sound, the way the Ghosts always had. Now, however, Colm understood the eeriely perfect coordination of their wedge attacks and flanking maneuvers. All those soldiers were really just a few men.

Deafened, he leaned against a tree. He smelt the sun-warmed bark, and watched some ants crawl out of a crack. The evergreen foliage reminded him of the noak leaves in his pocket. He pulled out a handful. As he chewed them, the limethion lolloped across the field and crouched at his side. "It is rather loud here," it said uneasily.

"How did you get down the ladder?"

"Very carefully."

Colm laughed. "Here, I'll take that off for you." He unfastened the limethion's muzzle, freeing its fearsome jaws. He ate some more noak leaves. Then he saw Dhjerga and Janz kneeling behind a hedge on the far side of the fields.

Janz slumped with his head on Dhjerga's shoulder. One hand, hanging down, jerked spastically.

"Come on," Colm said to the limethion. They floundered over the crushed cabbages to Dhjerga and Janz.

Dhjerga's eyes were wet. "I've used him up." Janz's eyes showed white under half-closed lids. "He's dying, the useless piece of shit."

Colm grabbed Janz and lowered him onto his back on the

grass. Horrifyingly, he could see the grass through him.

"I *told* him not to come!" Dhjerga said. "I should've brought someone else."

Bullets whined over their heads. The rebel advance had bogged down. Now that Dhjerga was no longer throwing new copies of Janz into the fight, the tide would turn at any minute.

"Hmm," the limethion said, sniffing the air. "Smells good. But I do not want to get bulleted."

"Copy this guy," Colm said to Dhjerga. His ears were ringing awfully. He could feel the heat of the *SOS's* fuel cells in his belly. They were still close enough to the spaceship to use it as a power source.

Dhjerga glanced indifferently at the limethion. "Want to try?"

"Yes," the limethion said, licking its lips.

Dhjerga laid one hand on the limethion's head. With his other hand, he gestured in the direction of the battle.

Nothing happened.

"I can't copy it." Dhjerga said angrily. "I suppose it doesn't work on aliens." His face crumpled. "We're finished. The Magus will keep creating soldiers as long as the wind keeps blowing."

"It's all about the numbers, aye?" Colm said cynically.

Linc Terrious sprinted across the cabbage field and threw himself down beside them. "Fetch someone else!" he yelled at Dhjerga.

"We've no one else as good as Janz," Dhjerga said.

"You must have! Go and look!"

"I can't leave him!"

"Then I will!" The terrified young man vanished.

"He won't be back," Dhjerga said.

Colm wiped his bloody hands on his trousers. He pulled the mag release lever on his AK and shook five rounds out of the magazine. He began to juggle them. Up and down and round and round they went, glinting. The ringing in his ears thickened into silence.

He saw Meg cleaning the disassembled pieces of her AK clone. She was alone in the main cabin of the *Shady Lady*. Hadn't the *Shady Lady* been destroyed years ago? Perhaps this was only a memory. But Meg's *face* …She looked tormented. Her hair slid aside, exposing the pale nape of her neck, as she bent over the neatly laid out gun parts.

He reached out to tap her on the shoulder.

CHAPTER 27

Meg felt someone tap her on the shoulder. It startled her so much she dropped the grip bolt she was holding. She twisted around, ready to yell at Axel for sneaking up on her like that.

No one there.

She was alone in the cabin of the *Shihoka,* a space fighter named after Axel's mother, which had been her home for the last seven months, and would be for eight months more, if not forever.

The fans hummed. The lights flickered.

Meg shivered, feeling cold.

She glanced at the electronic bracelet she wore. It indicated a relaxed, slow pulse, in contrast to her own. She sucked her lips, holding in tears. Then she went back to her pointless, time-killing task.

*

Although the *Shihoka's* main cabin resembled the old *Shady Lady's,* the aft crewspace was laid out differently. In addition to the cabin where Axel and Meg slept, and the small galley, there was a gun room. This was meant as a place for crew on longer missions to store and maintain their battlesuits and weapons.

Axel and Meg were midway through a longer journey than the designers had ever anticipated. When they left the Betelgeuse system, the gun room had been entirely filled with extra food and supplies. Slowly, they'd used up the stacks of stuff nearest the door. Now the empty half of the room served as a nursery. A single battlesuit stood by the door, like a metal sentinel.

Axel sat in the nursing chair, sewing. He had cut up his spare flight suit and was using the material to make tiny t-shirts and shorts. He enjoyed this activity more than he would have expected to. At least he was doing something useful, as opposed to endlessly breaking down and reassembling a gun, or running unneeded checks on the *Shihoka's* weapons systems.

On the table next to Axel, Nicky slept peacefully in his cot. The cot was actually a gun locker, cut loose from the wall, turned on its back, and strapped to the table. Axel paused in his sewing and tucked a blanket over the chubby three-month-old. It felt kind of cold in here.

A shadow fell across the baby.

Axel looked up.

Darkness engulfed the far end of the gun room, resisting the weak overhead lights. Crates and fabric bags of supplies, stacked to the ceiling, bulged out of this shifting, living pool of dark. Two blue glints shone in it, high up. The darkness itself cast a shadow, and the shadow was the shape of a man.

Axel dropped his sewing and moved between the shadow and the cot. It did not occur to him to call Meg, or to grab Nicky and flee the room. They were on a spaceship, in the zero-gravity field, halfway between Betelgeuse and Sol. There was nowhere to flee to. Without taking his eyes off the shadow, he slapped his palm on the biometric reader of the locker behind the cot. This was still a gun room, after all. He reached into the locker and grabbed a combi. He pointed it at the bulging, shivering darkness.

"It's me," came a whisper.

Colm? Axel said angrily: "Stop scaring the baby." *Stop scaring*

ME.

"Can you see me?" At the bottom of the shadow, the light reflected on something brown. It looked like a leather boot.

"Kind of," Axel said.

"Meg couldn't see me."

"Maybe it's too bright in there."

"Maybe." Colm chuckled, an eerie hoarse sound, and the shadow shivered like something solid. "Why are you sewing in the dark?"

"Don't want to wake the baby."

"The baby ..." Colm breathed. The shadow swayed and toppled forward. It moved past Axel and leaned over the cot.

Nicky's forehead wrinkled. His tiny rosebud lips parted. He was thinking about crying.

Axel put down his combi and snatched Nicky up, blanket and all. He did this partly because his new mission in life was to keep Nicky safe, and also because he was now sure that he did not want Meg bursting in here, and if Nicky started crying, she might.

Held in Axel's strong arms, Nicky relaxed and slipped back into peaceful sleep.

The shadow started laughing. It really was Colm. "Axel, what the mortal fuck are you doing with a baby?"

"He's mine." Axel paused. "And Meg's."

"Are you serious?"

Axel smiled. "Yup."

"Well, congratulations." The shadow settled against the wall, rising and falling. Its oscillations hurt Axel's eyes. "He's a cute wee fellow. What's his name?"

"Nicholas. Nicky. We named him after Meg's father," Axel said, thinking: Thank God I didn't let her name him after *you.*

A glimpse of riding boots, a shadow, a pair of gleaming blue eyes ... Was this what had become of Colm? When they saw him in the pharmacy on the *Unsinkable,* he'd at least looked like himself. "Are you a Ghost?" Axel blurted.

"No!"

"What are you doing here?"

"I'm *not* here."

"Then where are you?"

"A long way away."

"What do you want?"

"You."

∗

"You want me," Axel repeated, keeping his voice low so as not to wake Nicky. "Is this some kind of sick joke?"

"I was going to ask Meg. But it doesn't seem right, if she's a new mother, with the baby to look after ..."

In fact, Axel handled most of the baby care. He knew that Meg loved Nicky—she obsessed endlessly about his health, whether he was hitting his growth metrics, if they should be giving him vitamin D supplements—but she never wanted to spend any time with him, apart from breastfeeding. She would have put him on formula, if they had any. Meanwhile, Axel would've been happy to breastfeed the baby, if he had breasts. He patted Nicky's back. "Again, Colm, what do you want?"

Then the shadow told him about a distant moon, the Ghosts' homeworld, and an even smaller moon that orbited it— "I think it's artificial; it's got half a G of gravity and it's covered with *trees.* It shouldn't exist—" and the shadow that brooded under its surface, plotting the destruction of humanity. "They call him the Magus. Don't laugh, Axel, but they say he's thousands of years old. He's very strong."

"OK," Axel said. "Okayyy …."

"But we're stronger than he is. I know we are. Us. The Fleet. The Marines."

Axel was not a Marine anymore. He backed towards the door.

"Will you hear me out? You're a better warrior than any fucking Ghost."

"Even when I was a Marine, all I ever did was get good people killed."

"On this operation, the only people getting killed would be yourself."

Axel's hip bumped into the table. He stumbled and recovered his balance, too late. Nicky's face reddened and he started to bawl. The electronic monitor bracelet on the tiny, kicking ankle went wild. "Shush. Shush, shush," Axel said, making a silly face at Nicky—which was pointless, as his eyes were tightly closed.

"You won't have to leave the wean for even a minute," Colm pleaded. "You'll still be here. You might just feel a bit under the weather for a while …"

Meg's voice came faintly through the door. "Is Nicky OK?"

"Fine," Axel yelled. Lowering his voice, he gritted, "Go away, Colm!" He reached behind him and locked the door. He could not have Meg seeing this.

A second later, she tried to open the door, and couldn't. "What the fuck, Axel?"

"If you won't help, I'll have to ask her," Colm said.

Axel's blood ran cold. He believed everything Colm was saying. That was the trouble. "You're an asshole, Mackenzie."

"Thank you," Colm said faintly. "I try."

Axel kissed Nicky on the forehead and laid him in his cot, still yelling his head off. "What do I have to do?"

*

Three minutes later, Axel opened the door of the gun room. Meg, who had been banging frantically on it, reeled back from the warlike monster that walked out: a Marine in a battlesuit, holding a loaded combi in one gauntlet.

"Pick him up," Axel said through his suit's external speaker, gesturing at the screaming baby. "I'm gonna have to stay like this for a while."

With a hydraulic sigh, he lowered himself onto his haunches, cradling the combi as if it were a child.

CHAPTER 28

The air around the *Son of Saturn* shimmered. Battlesuited Marines pounded through the ruins of the village, spreading out with Fleet-trained tactical savvy. Their visors were down, hiding their faces, but Colm knew that every one of them was Axel—one of the best Marines in the whole damn Human Republic.

He grinned for joy to see them, but he felt the esthesia warmth in his belly fading. He was rapidly draining the fuel cells in the rocket, which ran on hydrogen and oxygen. He could replenish the LH2 with Dhjerga's help, but he couldn't think of any workaround for the LOX that did not involve running the condenser and evaporator for hours. He couldn't do that in the middle of a battle. He needed to capture a new power source.

Staying in the cover of the hedge he yelled, "The wind turbines!" He pointed up the hill.

There were two thousand Magistocracy soldiers in the way.

The Marines crashed into them like bullets going through paper targets.

Dhjerga shouted, "Never thought I'd be glad to see those guys."

"It's one of my friends," Colm said. "Well, about a hundred of him. A company of Marines is a match for ten thousand Ghosts." An old Corps saying. *Until they run out of ammo …* But these Marines came with their own, endless supply.

As they ran uphill, some of the Marines stopped to give Colm the extra item he'd asked Axel for: a blister pack of tropodolfin. He lined the packs up on the grass, gloating over them. *Finally.* No more horrible bitter noak leaves. He popped a single pill out with his thumbnail and crunched it. Artificial sweetness filled his mouth, and energy filled his veins. At long last, he'd be able to go home! But he couldn't leave the Marines on their own just yet, after he'd fetched them here. He stood up to cheer them on.

Lady Terrious ran across the cabbage field and pulled him down behind the hedge before he could get shot. "You *are* a mage, after all," she said. Then she kicked Dhjerga, who was sitting on the ground next to Janz's body. *"Go.* This was your rebellion. You started it. Go and finish it."

Dhjerga's face reddened. "What can I do that those big armored bastards can't?"

Colm observed that the surviving copies of Janz were leaving the fight as the Marines relieved them. They limped down the hill and flung themselves face-first into the stream that flowed between the village and the fields, drinking greedily. Dhjerga was conserving them, now that there would never be any more.

It was up to Colm now. He didn't want to get killed on the very point of going home, but he had to make sure they won. He left the Ghosts and ran up the hill, zigzagging between the dead and dying. On top of the ridge, the battle raged around the wind turbines. Colm took cover behind some bushes.

The Marines' combis were simply mowing the khaki soldiers down. Well-placed grenades vaporized a dozen at a time, spraying flesh shrapnel over the hillside. Meanwhile the Ghosts' bullets bounced harmlessly off the Marines' battlesuits. It would have been a grotesquely unequal fight, except for the same factor that had often defeated the

Marines on human colony worlds: the fuel cells in their own battlesuits. New khaki soldiers spawned on their backs and shoulders, driving them to the ground with the sheer weight of their bodies.

Colm saw that he was going to have to do something more. He was now close enough to the wind turbines to feel the esthesia heat from the generators in the tops of their trunks.

Desperately, he turned out his pockets. He had nothing useful except one of the thongs the Ghosts used as bootlaces. That might do. Fumbling in his haste, he knotted it into a loop, slipped it over his pinky fingers and thumbs, and began to weave a cat's cradle.

Over. Under. Through and let go.

His father used to be able to make all sorts of designs with cat's cradles. Everything from the Eiffel tower to an owl to the golden arches of McDonald's. That was when they were driving back from Edinburgh, Colm and Bridget hungry enough to eat a wolf, and miracle of miracles, there was a McDonald's at the next rest area.

But Colm wasn't trying to conjure burgers.

Over. Under.

In a trance of concentration, he wove the thong into a jagged bolt of lightning.

Pulled it taut—

—and lightning answered his call.

Static electric discharges from Atletis's upper atmosphere arced down like whips out of the clear sky. They struck the wind turbines one after the other, with bangs so loud that Colm was left opening and shutting his mouth, convinced he had lost his hearing.

One of the wind turbines toppled sideways and crash onto

the corpse-littered hillside.

Where it had stood, a dimly lit hole gaped in the top of the ridge.

"Shit," Colm breathed. "That's why we couldn't see the Magus's headquarters from the air!" It was *underground.*

The Marines rallied. As one man, they charged into the pit.

Axel, it appeared, also wanted revenge on the nemesis of Earth.

*

Colm brought up the rear of the Marines' charge. Lady Terrious joined him. They picked their way down a wooden staircase, cracked by the weight of the battlesuits, to a long, not-quite-straight tunnel which sloped gently down.

Colm felt an unpleasant shock of recognition. Red and yellow stripes wound horizontally along the lumpy walls. Stalactites hung from the ceiling, dripping. The gray, indeterminate lighting seemed to come from everywhere and nowhere.

"It can't be," he muttered. "A sentrienza mound?"

Midway down the corridor, the Marines were exchanging fire with a fresh horde of khaki soldiers.

"So this is the Magus's headquarters," Lady Terrious breathed. "It is not as I remember it!"

"It's a faerie mound," Colm said. He ventured into the middle of the corridor to see if he could see around the curve to its end. His boots squelched on squashed land urchins.

Lady Terrious gave him a curious stare. "Faeries? There are no faeries on Atletis. That I can personally attest to—beware!" Stray bullets were zinging past them.

Colm lunged back into cover. Too late. Pain seared his right hand. He sat in a heap at the foot of the wall, staring in disbelief at the bloody mess on the end of his arm. A bullet had gone through his right palm and out the other side. Bone poked out of the pulpy red exit wound. He started screaming.

Lady Terrious knelt at his side. Bandages magically appeared in her lap. She bit a length off. "You may be a powerful mage, but you are also an idiot."

Colm sealed his lips to stop any more screams from getting out. Below them, the battle raged on.

CHAPTER 29

The *Vienna* had dropped anchor in the harbor at Haravalding, one of the islands on the equator of Juradis, to sell fish meal and krill oil and take on fresh water. The factory ship did not require refuelling—it was nuclear-powered, and only needed an overhaul every century or so. Gilliam Tripsilion Nulth tore himself away from his work in the planetary administration center and went out to the ship to see his friends Sully and Bella Tan.

Bouncing across the harbor in a water taxi, he noted a lean human male waving to him from another taxi. They reached the *Vienna* at the same time. It was Admiral Hyland. "What a pleasure," Gil said warily. He had worked closely with the Rat during the active phase of the CHEMICAL MAGE project, but they had not seen much of each other since, as each had his own duties and they were rarely on the same planet.

"Skiving off?" the Rat said with a hollow laugh.

"I have a capable staff," Gil said defensively.

"Just joking," the Rat said. "I know you're the hardest-working queazel on Juradis." They climbed the companionway to the foredeck. The ship boomed gently under their feet as unseen supply vessels tied up and cast off. Admiral Hyland strode into the sunlight. "Sully! Long time no see. Where are those girls of yours?"

Sully Tan, wearing a salt-stained wifebeater and shorts, visibly braced himself, determined not to show deference to his former commanding officer. "Down below, helping. Crystal says she wants to be a ship's captain when she grows up." His smile was strained. "It's crazy when you think about it. We were born on Mars. Now we're fishermen in the Betelgeuse system. I feel like this should be our happily ever after. The girls think it is. Are we going to have to run again?"

The admiral mopped his forehead with a handkerchief. "I'm doing everything in my power to ensure that you don't have to run again, Sully."

Gil felt his carefree day off slipping away. Were they no longer even to have the luxury of pretending for a little while that everything was all right? "Hello, Sully," he said. "I have brought some presents for Bella and the children." He rose onto his hind legs and held out a bag. It contained cimes from the north pole, some little toys, and a drawing that he had done himself.

"Oh! Gil! Didn't see you down there ..." Sully took the bag, looked inside, and grinned. "Cimes mean margaritas. Hang out while I make them."

As he vanished, the Rat called after him, "The queen?"

"I'll try and get her to come down," Sully called back, with an edge of anger.

"It cannot be easy for them," Gil said delicately, "playing host to Emnl ki-Sharongat."

Since Meg and Axel fled the system, the sentrienza princess had been living on the *Vienna*. Bereft of her Walking Guns, she was no longer a threat but only an inconvenience.

"She may still be useful," the Rat said. "That's why I'm here, in fact." He and Gil sat on deck chairs in the shade of the ship's superstructure. The Rat took out a computer and switched on its holo display. The Betelgeuse system sprang into life above the table, not to scale, surrounded by a selection of the nearest stars. The Rat drew a red aurora with his forefinger around Rigel, where they expected the next wave of sentrienza reprisals would come from.

There were six deck chairs around the table. Only two of them were occupied, by the Rat and Gil. Then, suddenly, a third person was sitting at the table.

Gil and the Rat jumped.

"I remember this ship," Dhjerga Lizp said. "Hello, queazel. You get around, don't you?"

Gil gripped the edge of his deck chair tightly in his claws, ready to spring. But the Ghost just sagged, smiling dazedly. He wore a baggy forest-green uniform. His boots were very muddy. He had a scruffy beard.

The Rat found his voice. "Who—*what* are you?"

"You ordered Colm Mackenzie to go and ask us for help. He did; so here I am. I forgot how hot it is here." Dhjerga undid the top buttons of his shirt and fanned air inside it. At that moment Sully came back from the bridge, followed by Bella and the girls, with a tray of margaritas.

"Dhjerga!" Crystal squealed. She ran at Dhjerga and hugged him. Chuckling, the Ghost rose, picked her up, and swung her around.

"You've got about one more year of that before you get too heavy," he said.

"Me, me!" Zainab begged.

Gil relaxed. Dhjerga Lizp was a violent and dangerously ignorant man. But at this point he was starting to feel like a friend.

Not, evidently, to the Rat, who snapped, "Where's Lieutenant Mackenzie?"

"He took a bullet," Dhjerga said, sitting down with Zainab on his knees. Gil's heart skipped a beat. "Only through the hand." He helped himself to one of the margaritas.

"And what, exactly, do you think you can do for us?" the Rat said. Hostility tinged his voice. Gil cringed. These two men were on opposite sides of a titanic clash that had left millions of humans dead. Bygones could not be bygones, while the Ghost army still threatened Earth.

"That's what I'm hoping you'll tell me," Dhjerga said, wiping his lips.

A high voice buzzed, "There is nothing you can do to stem the vengeance of the Gray Emperor. Nothing!"

They all looked up. Emnl ki-Sharongat was leaning out of a porthole in the superstructure.

"The Rigel fleet will arrive here in less than one Earth year. That is how long you have to live. Enjoy it!"

Sully grimaced. "She's been like this," he said in a low voice.

The porthole slammed, not before Gil heard a flurry of shrill yelps from Emnl. The sentrienza girl was crying.

"A hostage?" Dhjerga said.

"To meet the definition of hostage, she'd have to be useful," the Rat said. "I was going to ask her about the fleet—ship numbers, weights, armaments, and so forth. I thought she might have changed her mind about talking to us It's her own life on the line, too, after all." He shut his computer with a snap, extinguishing the holo stars. "I could strangle Meg Smythe for leaving us in the lurch like this."

Bella Tan said, "Don't tell me you wouldn't have done the same for your child, sir."

"I haven't got any."

"Nor have I," Gil said. "But I see no value in rehashing what has been done, and cannot be undone." His gaze rested for a moment on his drawing of Uzzizriat, which lay unheeded on the table. The Rat had put his drink down on it.

He was guilty of what he denounced: he regularly spent hours dwelling, with pen in claw, on the past—on a planet which had been destroyed centuries ago. Sometimes when he was drawing he *almost* felt as if he were really there, perching on a frowsty crag above a silver waterfall. But Uzzizriat was no more. All that remained was to save Juradis.

Though he wanted to ask Dhjerga about Colm, he refrained from doing it in the presence of the admiral. "Rather," he said, "we should discuss Mr. Lizp's offer to help us defend this system."

"That's it," Dhjerga said. "The queazel's the most practical of you all. What're we talking about, then? Spaceships? Lots of them?"

"Yes," the Rat said.

"Hmm." Dhjerga's gaze turned inward. Gil sighed to himself. The Rat's skepticism was well-founded, he thought. The Ghosts might be unstoppable on a planetary surface, but they were helpless against spaceships. Dhjerga just didn't want to admit it. "I'd have to think about that," he said evasively. "These things need planning. But there's still time, you said?"

"A few months to a year."

"Right. In that case, maybe I could trouble you for some supplies in the meantime?"

The Rat let out a loud bark of laughter. "You slaughter millions of our people and then come asking for supplies. Good God!"

"We're fighting a war of our own, you know," Dhjerga said.

"Really? I had no idea." The Rat slotted his computer back into his bag and rose. "I'm afraid I can't stay any longer. I came to talk to the queen, but it looks like that's a non-starter."

Gil accompanied him to the head of the gangway. He obscurely felt that he should apologize. "Do come and visit me at Kevesingod."

"Make sure that bastard leaves. And don't give him anything. Especially not weapons, for God's sake."

When Gil returned to the foredeck, Sully was showing Dhjerga a GIMP crew-served machine-gun.

"We've had this on board since the uprising," he said. "You're welcome to it. Not as if we'll be able to use it to shoot down the sentrienza fleet."

The girls were playing with a piglet. It was skidding all over the deck and squealing. Bella held out the toys Gil had brought and shouted to them, "Why don't you play with these?"

"We're calling him Pinky," Zainab screeched back.

Bella said to Gil, "Sorry. Nothing can compete with animals, apparently. Last time he brought them a rat."

Gil dipped his head in a deprecating gesture, pretending not to feel hurt that his gifts had been rejected. The margaritas were all gone, too. "Is Sully giving him that machine-gun?"

"Looks like it."

"And explosives," Dhjerga said to Sully. "Colm specifically asked for explosives. What do you call them, shaped charges?"

"We might have some of those in the hold," Sully said, rubbing his hands.

Gil followed them down the cool, echoey companionway. Belowdecks, the pungent smell of fish pervaded the ship. They climbed down to the cargo deck, where Sully unearthed some crates of explosive, detonators, and fuses. "All yours. Hope it helps." He screwed up his stolid, goodnatured face.

"I hate to think of Colm marooned out there—wherever *there* is."

"He's not alone," Dhjerga said with a mysterious smile. "He's with us."

Gil could restrain himself no longer. "Is Colm all right?" He swayed on his hind legs. "You said he was wounded ..."

They were crossing the reactor deck on their way back upstairs, walking in single file along a catwalk, Sully in the lead. Below, the reactor's cooling system rumbled. Dhjerga stopped and looked down at the tangle of machinery. "Is that a thorium reactor?" he said.

"Yeah," Sully said, raising his eyebrows. "You know about reactors?"

"I know someone who does."

He had to be talking about Colm. Gil stretched himself to his fullest height, so that Dhjerga could no longer ignore him. "Colm?" he persisted. "When is he coming back? Last time you were here, you said he was building a spaceship—"

Dhjerga looked down at Gil. "Yeah, he did. It's a beauty."

The queazel's heart filled with anticipation. "Then, he will be returning soon?"

Dhjerga reached out and rubbed Gil's head roughly behind the ears. Gil recoiled indignantly. "You might have to get used to the idea that he won't be coming back."

"What?"

"The place for a mage is with other mages. The place for a warrior is a battle."

"Colm, a warrior?" Sully snorted. "He's just a spaceship mechanic! I might call him a pilot if I was feeling generous ..."

Gil was frightened. He no longer trusted Dhjerga. "He must come back! I miss him," he said, startling himself. At the same time he wondered whether he *should* wish for Colm's return. Everyone in Betelgeuse system was living under a death sentence.

"I'll pass it on," Dhjerga said.

He suddenly vaulted over the rail of the catwalk, and disappeared. He reappeared a second later, standing beside the reactor.

"Tell your wife thanks," he yelled up to Sully. "I'll be back for another of those margaritas."

The air shimmered.

Seconds later, he was gone.

And so was the reactor.

A shiny square on the deck indicated where it had stood. Water dribbled from the end of a neatly severed coolant feed pipe.

"Fuck," Sully swore. "My fucking reactor! Goddammit!"

Gil sank back onto all his legs. "I think he was telling the truth," he said limply. "We will never see Colm again."

CHAPTER 30

Meg stood in the cockpit of the Eagle, absently bouncing Nicky on her hip.

Axel sat in the pilot's couch. One of the screens in front of him counted down the seconds to their exit from the zero-gravity field.

The numbers stopped whirling. Sensors poured information onto the screens that had been blank for so many months. "Hello, Sol," Meg murmured, waving at the composite optical feed.

Nicky did not notice that anything had changed. He was an interstellar baby, born in the zero-gravity field.

"There's your home, sweetheart," Meg said to him. "Look. Third planet from the sun."

They had emerged at the inner edge of the asteroid belt, 50 degrees out of the plane of the ecliptic. This was the closest available zero-gravity point, but it would take them another couple of weeks to reach Earth.

Axel stretched and sighed. "Well, I guess my fighting days are over."

"Fingers crossed," Meg said. It worried her how tired and sort of *faded* he looked, although the *Shihoka's* diagnostic robot said there was nothing wrong with him.

This was the first time in six months she'd seen him out of his battlesuit, except when he took it off to grab a quick bite of food or a few hours' sleep. The rest of the time he had to be 'on call' in case Colm needed him. Meg often wished Colm would pay them another visit so she could tell him what she thought of his goddamn using ways. But he never had, and now he could not. At least, not until they reached Earth.

Nicky was wriggling and fussing in her arms. "What's up, little guy?" Axel reached for him.

"He's probably wondering why you shrank," Meg said dryly. "At this point he thinks his father is that damn battlesuit."

But Nicky quieted down when Axel took him. Following them into the main cabin, Meg felt a pang of emotion too complicated to process. She admired the unthinking competence with which Axel handled the baby, carrying him one-handed, echoing back his babble: "Goo? Ga. You got that right, buddy. Ga ba ba. Oh, you need a change, huh? OK. Do we have clean diapers, Meg?"

"Yup," Meg said. "Washed them this A.M." And wasn't *that* a fun way to spend the morning. "They should be dry by now." While Axel was on call, she had had to get good at the whole changing, feeding, cleaning-up routine. But she still got the feeling that Nicky loved Axel best. And why shouldn't he? He must be able to sense the passionate protective love that Axel showered on him ... on the child he believed to be his son.

Oh God.

Please let him never, ever find out.

They'd hardly finished changing Nicky's diaper when the comms alarm went off.

"I'll get it," Meg said. She went forward and played the transmission over the PA system.

"*HRF Infinite Jest* to unidentified small spacecraft in Belt Sector Two high." A flat female voice read off the *Shihoka's* coordinates. "Identify yourself and advise your intended course and destination."

"*Infinite Jest,* I copy you," Meg said. "This is the *Shihoka,* from Juradis, intending Earth orbit insertion and de-orbit in thirteen days and eight hours." The *Jest's* signal originated from LEO. "So I guess we'll see you soon. You can share the jest at that point."

Her lighthearted teasing sprang from relief. The Fleet was still here, still fighting! Her worst nightmare had been that they would reach Sol system only to find the radio waves dead, the system overrun by Ghosts.

She knew Axel had been worried about the same thing. She said to him, while they waited for the *Infinite Jest's* reply, "So what do you think? You actually stopped them?"

Axel's face darkened. Meg kicked herself for bringing up the topic of the distant war on Kisperet. At the same time, she resented Axel for being unwilling to talk about it. Only the future of humanity was at stake, after all.

"I don't know," he said eventually. "We've killed a lot of them." He seemed to run out of words after that. He lifted Nicky out of the acceleration couch they used as a playpen— Axel had crafted the soft side walls out of empty rice and flour sacks, while still in his battlesuit—and set him on his thighs, facing him. He played wih the baby's arms as if Nicky were piloting an imaginary spaceship. Nicky smiled beatifically.

"But have you *won?*" Meg said, tired of Axel's evasions. Thinking for the hundredth time: Why didn't Collie Mack take *me?*

"I wouldn't know," Axel said. "We're just the slaves."

"Ugh."

"Yeah."

The *Infinite Jest* did not get back to them until they had almost reached Earth. Axel was in the cockpit, monitoring their deceleration burn. Meg was in the main cabin, showing

Nicky the globe of Earth on the big screen. For her it was a tearjerking sight.

The voice of the *Infinite Jest's* comms officer crackled over the PA system. *"Shihoka,* do you read me? Orders follow."

"Orders?" Meg muttered.

"Proceed to Aldrin Station." The comms officer named the largest of the orbiting fuel depots and personnel transfer points that the Fleet operated in LEO. Axel split the big screen and threw up a long-distance composite image. Half a dozen carrier-size ships and many more small ones orbited in sync with the station, or docked with it. "Do you copy?"

"I copy you," Axel said. "And thanks for the invitation. However, we respectfully decline. Our destination is Earth, not LEO."

"Too bad," the comms officer said. "We are requisitioning your spacecraft."

"Requisitioning?!" Meg yelled, startling Nicky.

"What you see on your screens is the final stage of the evacuation of Earth."

At that moment, Earth set beneath the *Shihoka.*

They were orbiting over Asia.

That whole huge landmass, which used to blaze with city lights, was dark.

"Oh, baby," Meg said, bowing her forehead to Nicky's. "Oh sweetheart." She shouted through to Axel, "Guess you haven't won. The Ghosts have."

"Don't give up," Axel said to the *Infinite Jest's* comms officer. "Keep fighting! Listen, the Ghosts *aren't* unstoppable…"

"Didn't you say you came from Betelgeuse? Yeah, so I'm guessing you haven't been here in a while. Take a look at Beijing, or New York, or Tokyo, and tell me if they could've been stopped."

Tokyo. Meg flinched at the mention of her hometown. But Tokyo meant nothing to her now that her father was not there. She glommed onto the fact that the officer had only mentioned large cities. Out in the countryside, people were surviving, regardless of what the Fleet said.

"So this is the final evacuation," Axel said. "Where're you heading to?"

"Juradis, of course."

Meg gritted her teeth at the bitter irony of it. The sentrienza were going to get exactly what they had wanted all along. A compliant, manageably small remnant of humanity living as slaves in the Betelgeuse system. She wondered if the Rat would stand up to them, and how long it would take them to casually obliterate his fleet. Or maybe they already had.

"Hey, Meg," Axel said. "Are you sitting down?"

"Huh?"

"Hence," the officer quacked, "we have placed a requisitioning order on your ship. It belongs to the Fleet, anyway."

"Sit down," Axel said, and to the officer, "Belongs to the Fleet? Ma'am, I *am* the fucking Fleet. My father is Philip K. Best. Admiral Hyland appointed me captain of this spacecraft, and I have nothing more to say to you than this: If you want it that bad, come and get it."

Meg whooped approvingly. She lurched into the nearest acceleration couch with Nicky on her lap as the drive spun up to a thunderous throb. Axel opened the throttle and dived towards Earth.

"Axel, I love you," she said, and at that moment she meant it.

She could hear the grin in his voice. "They're shooting at us."

"For real? Mother*fucker.*"

"Just low-strength energy beams. They know that stuff can't get through the Van Allen belts. It's just warning shots. Thanks for the warning, guys ... and I will now proceed to ignore it."

Meg remembered how naively enamored she had once been of the Fleet's purported ideals. Honor, justice, mercy. Now, it had all degenerated into an ugly scramble for survival of the fastest and richest. She was probably better off without her naïve faith in humanity, but she still grieved its loss.

She worked frantically to strap herself and Nicky in as Axel pulled a defensive trajectory change. Loose items flew around the cabin. "Whoa, cowboy."

"Sorry. Habit."

Meg fastened the last buckle and glanced at the screen. Earth spun. The dayside came back around. The Atlantic. North and South America. As the *Shihoka* de-orbited into the troposphere, Axel said, "I'm gonna scan the civilian radio bands, see if we can pick up anything from the ground."

Meg hugged Nicky. "Axel, I'm starting to wonder if this was such a great idea. What if there's *no one* left down there? Only Ghosts?"

They had endlessly discussed what they would do if this was the case. Their answer was: Put down anyway. But now Earth looked less welcoming. The Atlantic stretched out cold and gray.

"I'm picking up Ka-band chatter," Axel said. "There are survivors, all right. Barbados, Antigua, Malta, Gibraltar ...

They're all on islands."

"And this woman? Have you picked up anything from her group?"

"Not yet."

The Shihoka screamed down out of the clouds over the Atlantic. It broke the sound barrier a hundred miles west of Scotland and decelerated at full throttle. Axel's carefully calculated burn brought the ship to a stall above an island less than a square mile in area, a lopsided triangle covered with birch and pine trees. The *Shihoka* dropped vertically, on a column of flame that sizzled in the rain, onto a stony beach. The seaweed was too wet to catch fire.

A dingy sailboat bobbed off-shore.

A whitewashed cottage stood behind the beach.

Smoke was coming out of the cottage's chimney.

Meg gave Nicky to Axel, took her AK, and scanned the beach from the open airlock. The fresh, wild, salty air almost knocked her over, it tasted so good. She aimed her weapon at the cottage. On the *Shihoka's* IR screen, it had looked like a bonfire.

A woman walked out of the cottage. She had bright red hair. She carried a hunting rifle.

Meg descended the airlock steps. They approached each other warily. Meg's heart knocked against her ribs. She said, "Are you Bridget?"

CHAPTER 31

The Magus's headquarters on Atletis extended for miles under the ground.

The rebels had fought for every square inch.

It turned out that the wind turbines had only been a backup for the Magus's power grid. A deeply buried, and quite modern, hydrothermal generator ran the lights and air circulation in the underground maze. There were caverns full of machinery so rusty that it fell apart at a touch, and even Colm couldn't tell what it had been designed to do.

The Mage Corps Headquarters occupied a small area within the complex. In this maze-within-a-maze, the spongy walls had been paneled over with wood, pictures hung, and candle sconces installed, to fool the mages into thinking the place was human-built. The Magus had been too proud to let it be known that he was squatting in a disused sentrienza base.

The Magus's inner sanctum was a covered hall, like an ark plopped down in one of those great caverns, wired for power. Here the Magus made his last stand, flinging soldiers at the attackers faster than bullets fired from a machine-gun. The piles of corpses blocked the tunnels. Old ones at the bottom, fresh ones at the top. Colm ended it by having his Marines tunnel down 200 meters and drop charges down the shafts of the hydrothermal generator, blowing the pumps and shutting off power to the whole complex.

They found Dryjon and Diejen, along with several other prisoners from the Families of Kisperet, chained to the Magus's throne like dogs.

After that no one wanted to spend another minute in the

complex. With the power down, the air circulation had failed. The smell of rotting bodies was overpowering. They trekked back to the surface. Colm instructed his Marines to lay more charges in the egress tunnels, burying the dead where they had fallen. He half hoped the Marines themselves would be buried, too—he had come to hate them, unfairly, for their ruthless skill at butchery. To his disappointment, several of them clawed their way to the surface, emerging like beetles from the shallow end of the tunnel on top of the ridge.

During the battle the rebel forces had camped in Innismon, around the *Son of Saturn*. The rocket towered over their victory banquet, as it had once towered over parties back on Kisperet. Colm, the man of the hour, accepted toast after toast. The mead they had liberated from the outlying villages, where a small population of freemen had grown food for the Magus's headquarters, packed a punch. Colm's euphoria gradually dulled into misery, a reaction to the months of slaughter he had personally ordered and witnessed. He stumbled off into the fields and puked behind a hedge. He wiped his mouth, groaned, and straightened up. Then he looked around.

The limethion was watching him.

The creature was a puzzle to everyone, since it could not be copied, but *could* be taken from one place to another, as if it were a mage—but it was not. It was just an alien. It had become a sort of camp mascot for the Ghosts, who found its scavenging ways hilarious. Colm, personally, had gone right off it the first time he saw it dining on a bloated corpse. "What do *you* want?"

"I like this place," the limethion said. "I do not want to go back to Mitheikua. I shall stay here."

"Good for you," Colm said grumpily, although he actually did know what the limethion meant. It was the beginning of Atletis's long day. Birds sang in the hedges. Bees droned. Music drifted from the pavilion. There was a tender, damp warmth in the air. The pale ghosts of Cerriwan and Kisperet overlapped in the sky, a sight you'd never see on Earth, yet ironically, out of all the alien planets and moons Colm had visited, Atletis felt the most like home. "Is that all you had to say?"

The limethion swished its scaly tail through the tall grass. "Dhjerga wants to talk to you."

"Oh, he does?" Dhjerga had only been at the banquet for a few minutes, and had then returned to his own camp in the forest. He had not taken much part in the war at all. Fair enough, he'd been gone for a while, fetching explosives from Juradis. But ever since his return, he'd been hiding out in the forest most of the time. He had shown up for the final battle but not helped with the mop-up. Once a deserter, always a deserter, Colm thought uncharitably. "Well, I'm not hiking all the way out there. Tell him if he wants to talk to me he can come here."

He walked away from the limethion and sat down on a wheelbarrow, which had been used to transport lettuces. At any given point during the war, half of the rebel forces had been fighting and the other half farming. Colm was wearing brand new clothes fetched from Kisperet: fawn leather trousers, the same snowy shirt that every other man had on, and a sheepskin gilet with embroidery on it. Now he had a mucky arse. So what? Mages did not do laundry. They just threw shit away, or gave it to the slaves and fetched new stuff.

He lay back in the wheelbarrow, with his boots on the

ground, and closed his eyes. The sun reddened his eyelids. Maybe the mead would help him get some sleep. He'd spent most of the battle hopped up on tropodolfin, sleeping very little. He was worn out, but instead of drifting off, he thought about the blisterpack of tropo in his pocket. It was his last one. When it was gone, he'd be back to noak leaves.

Something tickled his nose.

His eyes popped open. He hit out reflexively. Diejen leaned over him. She had been tickling him with a daisy. She danced back out of the way of his clumsy swipe, laughing.

"Do I not even get to take a nap in peace?" Colm said, although his spirits rose at the sight of her. She was wearing a new outfit fetched from home, one of those elegant split skirts with a tasseled blouse. She was thin and pale from her long captivity, but her eyes shone. The long sleeves covered the marks left on her wrists by the Magus's high-potential gloves.

"You weren't sleeping." She sat down beside him. "Everyone's having a lovely time."

"Even you?"

"Even me. I can still hardly believe I'm walking free under the sun." She lay back and basked in the rays of Kisperet's no-name star.

"Now you know how the faeries live," Colm said.

"Yes, the stories say they don't like sunlight."

Colm had shared his surmise that the Magus's complex was an old sentrienza mound. Perhaps the sentrienza had once discovered Kisperet and then forgotten about it again, although that didn't seem like their style. In fact, Colm suspected Atletis itself was an artificial body. Lady Terrious called it a *heimdall*. If it had been formed with plenty of iron and other heavy metals in the core, that would explain the gravity, as well as the magnetic field that helped it hold onto an atmosphere. An artificial origin would also explain the one-in-a-million orbit that prevented it from either crashing into Kisperet or spiraling away. But the machinery he found in the caves had clearly been thousands of years old. There was no sign that the Magus had been in contact with the sentrienza.

Diejen interrupted his thoughts. Her eyes were closed, her face bathed in sunlight. "Are you going to leave us now?" she said in a careful tone.

For the first time, Colm opened his heart to her. "I don't know. I don't know what to do. I don't know what I *want* to do. I feel like shit, Diejen."

"You won a historic victory."

"That was mostly Axel."

"You slew the Magus—"

"But did I? *Did I?* We never found his body—"

"Yes, Dryjon said the same thing," Diejen admitted.

"What if he flitted?"

"Or maybe we did find his body, but we didn't recognize it. After all, no one knows what he looks like." The Magus had never revealed himself to the Mage Corps, always issuing orders, praise, and censure from the darkness of his throne. Colm had seen this repulsive piece of furniture when they finally took the Magus's hall. It was the size of a fourposter bed, with clawed golden feet and double layers of fur curtains around it. Even when Diejen and Dryjon were chained to it, they had only ever seen the Magus's boots.

"He's probably buried with his slaves," Diejen said. "You could go and dig them out if you really want to be sure." Her lips twitched in amusement at the idea.

Colm remembered those last awful moments in the Magus's hall. They had broken though after the power went out. Smoky pine torches and the Marines' headlamps had lit a carpet of corpses and ruined battlesuits, heaving like stranded jellyfish, seeping blood. Colm had stepped on men who were still alive. He writhed at the memory of how they'd twitched under his boots. Dhjerga had leapt forward and cut his brother and sister free, while Colm hacked down the curtains around the throne, expecting to face the shadow that had haunted his childhood … and all he'd found was a wooden chair, with armrests the size of tables, and a depression in the seat shaped like a very large rear end. A faint whiff of sulfur lingered, layered onto the reek of death.

Diejen patted his hand, bringing him back to the present. "It's all right," she said. "Today is a day for celebrating, not worrying."

Not worry? She might as well have told Colm not to breathe. "Diejen, if he's flitted, he may have gone to Earth. My family may be in danger." He had never forgotten the evil promise the Magus had made him that night in the zoo, when he showed him a scrying of Bridget. *I'll have her, and then there will be one. Then I will have you, and there will be no mages left on Earth at all.* Colm had told Axel roughly where to find Bridget, but he did not know if Axel and Meg *had* found her, because he'd lost contact with them after they exited the zero-gravity field. Five tropo pills left. He glumly feared he would waste them like he'd wasted the rest of his supply, just staying awake and cheerful. Juggling? Conjuring? Coin vanishes? He couldn't do a goddamn thing left-handed.

"And how are you to help them," Diejen said gently,

reading his thoughts, "with this?"

She moved aside the lacy cuff of his shirt and touched his right hand. A lump of scar tissue marred the middle of his palm. The bullet he took on the first day of their invasion had shattered two of his metacarpal bones. They had healed, but not properly. He was lucky he hadn't lost the hand, given that the mages scarcely had any medical knowledge, and relied on their dubious healing magic. He didn't have a full range of movement in his middle and ring fingers anymore. And he was heavily right-handed.

He playfully tugged a lock of her hair. "If I was the suspicious type, Diejen, I'd think you deliberately let my hand heal wrong …"

Her eyes popped open. "Me? I wasn't even there!"

"Lady Terrious. Dhjerga. *Didn't* they heal it wrong, so that I wouldn't be able to flit? They know I'm not like you. Magic doesn't come naturally to me. I've got to conjure it."

"That is a serious accusation!"

"I'm Scottish," Colm said, thinking to himself: and you are, too, aren't you? All of you are. "I'm naturally suspicious. And I've not forgotten that none of you ever told me about the noak leaves." The Teanga echo behind the word said: *doire*. They called it a *doire* tree. *Doire:* oak grove, sacred grove.

Diejen's pale cheeks pinkened. "I never lied to you."

"No, you and your brother just didn't give me the information I'd have needed to get home."

"You can go home now." She was gazing up at the sky, keeping her cool. "If you can manage it."

Yeah, Colm thought. Now that I've taught you how to build rockets, and steam engines, and machine-guns, and chainsaws. While his hand was healing, he'd kept busy the same way as before, designing and building equipment for the troops. His most recent innovation had been chainsaw bayonets. He could hardly close his eyes without seeing those abominable things spinning up. The Marines had wielded them with little show-offy flourishes, the way Axel did everything. It was worth it, Colm had told himself. They needed to win. Now they *had* won, but the Magus—he felt surer than ever—had escaped.

"All right," Diejen said. "It's true. We did not need another mage. We needed *your* magic."

"It's just engineering!"

"Call it what you will, it won the war for us." She opened her eyes and turned her face towards him. *"You* won the war for us. Won't you stay and enjoy the peace?"

Their faces were very close. Gazing into her green eyes, Colm felt himself losing it. Her scent filled his nostrils, tantalizing him. Her beauty, he felt, could wipe out the horrors in his memory, if they just held each other for long enough. He slid his left hand into the caramel waves of her hair, and gently kissed her lips.

The lips tensed. Her eyes narrowed.

Then she kicked off from the ground, throwing her whole weight backwards, so that the wheelbarrow tipped up the other way. They both slid out in an ungainly backwards somersault.

Colm, his reflexes slowed by alcohol, landed in a heap in the grass. Diejen nimbly jumped clear. She pulled him to his feet. "That will teach you to molest a lady," she said, laughing. The laughter sounded a bit forced.

"I've never been turned down quite like *that* before," Colm said glumly, yet hopefully. He was not yet sure she actually had turned him down.

She removed any lingering doubt. "My dear, I owe you my life. So does Dryjon. All the Families owe you a great debt. But I am still engaged to Gaethla Moro. He may not ever turn up again. Maybe he lies dead … down there." She pointed at the ground. "But maybe he went back to Earth. If so, I mean to find him. Maybe I will kill him. Maybe I'll kiss him. Maybe I'll dump him out of a wheelbarrow… I don't know yet. Anyway, it's a thing I have to finish."

Colm had completely misunderstood. He had thought she was inviting him to stay with *her*. He now realized that if she was not here, Atletis wouldn't be so charming. In fact, it was only for her he had come here, and stayed so long.

"Well," he said, trying to make the best of it, "shall we travel together? Your magic, my pills. No molesting, promise."

"Well …" Diejen glanced around with a panicky expression.

"No," said Dryjon's voice. He rose up from behind the hedge, rather red in the face, but wearing the look of nervous determination that Colm knew so well, because it was just like Diejen's. The twins had played him. Dryjon must have been there all along—and must have witnessed Colm's clumsy pass at Diejen. Colm flushed, recalling how Dryjon had reacted the last time someone messed with his sister.

But Dryjon wasn't wearing a sword today. He wasn't even drunk. He struggled through the hedge, catching his shirt on the twigs. "Sorry, Colm. You are not to go to Earth. You must stay here and help us rebuild."

"Must?" Colm echoed, staring from one to the other of them. *"Must?"*

"The power sources need to be mended," Dryjon said

bravely. "You're good at that sort of thing."

Colm held onto his temper by his fingernails. Icily, he said, "I seem to recall that you made me a promise. If I helped you liberate your homeworld, you would help me liberate mine."

"We're not breaking our word!" Diejen exclaimed. "We *will* liberate Earth. Now that the Magus is gone, it only requires talking our friends in the Mage Corps around … or kissing them … or tipping them out of wheelbarrows," she finished, with a pale attempt at humor.

"And actually, er, we never promised to take you home," Dryjon said.

"I don't need taking," Colm snapped. "I'll just go." Pain shot through his right hand as he clenched his fists. He was talking out of his ass. He couldn't go anywhere on his own unless he learned to play the spoons left-handed. The twins remained tactfully silent. "Oh, fuck it," he breathed, and turned on his heel. He stomped away through the meadow, the twins following him at a distance.

The limethion slunk up to him. "Are you going to go talk to Dhjerga now?" it lisped.

"Yes, I am." Would Dhjerga take his side against the twins? It seemed like a pretty long shot, but he had no other hope.

CHAPTER 32

Colm had only visited Dhjerga's camp in the forest once, several months back, and had forgotten where it was. The limethion led the way. Dryjon and Diejen trailed behind them. Little grew on the forest floor between the crowded, unhusbanded birches and noaks. The leafy canopy overhead was full of life. Red squirrels crashed through the branches overhead, and crows called. It was eerily like the forest on the south shore of Loch Ness, and Colm wondered if the Magus had planted it from memory. Then he noticed a familiar smell.

Decomposition.

Moments later he saw the first corpse, lying on the leaf mould, slightly chewed.

It was a Janz.

Behind him, Diejen pointed it out to Dryjon. Colm heard their surprised voices, and turned. "Janz died on the first day of the invasion. But Dhjerga made as many copies of him as possible before he croaked." He tried to keep his disapproval out of his voice. "Since then he's been making copies of those copies. Putting off the evil moment, so to speak."

"No wonder they're dying like flies," Diejen said tartly. "Copies of copies are always poor-quality."

"We're going to ban this sort of thing," Dryjon said. "I want to ban copying altogether, although I'm not sure if everyone will go along with it."

"We managed on Earth for thousands of years without any copies at all," Colm said.

"Yes; I don't know how."

They followed a trail of corpses, assisted by the limethion, whose nose led it unerringly from one ripe body to the next. Suddenly it stopped dead. "I am not going any further. There's a bad smell beyond here."

"I can't smell anything except *you,* alien," Diejen said, but her laughter was brittle.

Colm gestured for quiet. He could hear the faint hum of machinery, and now his esthesia implant prickled. He strode forward, guided by the warm pull of the power source hidden in the trees ahead.

Sunlight pierced the trees. A makeshift workshop occupied a clearing. Beneath the slat roof, Janzes bustled around a nest of pipes and heavily shielded containment housings. And there were the surviving Marines, monitoring a large piece of equipment with a hatch like a spaceship airlock …

"Where is he?" Dhjerga's voice came through the trees behind him. "Colm! *Colm!* Come back! Don't go too close!"

Colm needed no telling. He now knew what he was looking at. He turned and ran.

"You could have warned us!" he said to Dhjerga, when he caught up with the Lizps. They were a quarter of a mile away, walking back towards the village.

"I tried," Dhjerga said.

"I don't get it," Dryjon complained. "What are you doing out there?"

"He's making nukes," Colm said.

He studied Dhjerga, looking for signs of radiation poisoning. Dhjerga didn't look sick, only unkempt and depressed.

"I've limited my exposure," Dhjerga said. "The Marines have taken over on-site management. Their suits protect them."

"Nukes?" Diejen said.

"Improvised nuclear bombs," Colm said. "The most effective weapons of mass destruction my people have ever come up with." He stared narrowly at Dhjerga. "You fetched a thorium reactor."

"Your friends gave it to me."

"You've been running it to extract uranium from the fuel. I suppose you've got it set up somewhere out of the way."

"At home in Lizp Province."

"And you're fetching the uranium to that little workshop back there. Sintering it into hemispheres ... Making bombs."

"It's really Janz doing it. He's the one who knows about that stuff."

Colm nodded, remembering Majriti IV.

Diejen burst out, "Dhjerga, Janz is *dead!* Those slaves are not Janz! They're just copies!"

"I know that," Dhjerga grated.

They came out of the trees within sight of the village. The *Son of Saturn* impaled Cerriwan. Tension simmered among the three Lizp siblings.

"I've had it with this place," Colm said. "I've had it with you lot." Dhjega's workshop seemed to presage the next phase of Ghost atrocities. Now they were going to start nuking each other. "I'm finished," he said. "Done. I'm going home, one way or another. Dhjerga, will you help?"

Dhjerga, caught flatfooted, stammered, "Well ..."

"No!" Diejen said. "You mustn't help him! We need him *here.*"

"What," Colm shouted, "so I can help you build ballistic missiles?"

"The nukes aren't for us," Dhjerga said. "They're for your

friends!"

"I just bet they are," Colm said. In a passion of loathing and frustration, he strode away from the others. A stunted apple tree grew on the edge of the forest. Colm jumped, caught a branch, ripped unripe apples off it. Three. Four. Five.

The Lizps watched him with identical worried expressions.

Breathing hard, Colm put down the apples and fished out his tropo blisterpack. He popped out all five pills and tossed them back. Two and a half times the recommended maximum dose. If this didn't do it, nothing would. The rush practically ripped the top of his head off. Dizzy, he picked up the apples and began to juggle.

The apples cascaded out of his hands ... and fell to the ground. His right hand was just too stiff. It was useless. All the same, he tried again and again.

"I can't watch this," Dryjon muttered. "By Scota's grave, man, give it up."

"Don't you like it here?" Diejen said. "Don't you like us?"

Dhjerga turned on his brother and sister. "No, he doesn't. And I know how he feels. I don't like you two right now, either." He stepped forward. Colm was just picking up the apples again, shaking with determination and despair. "Here," Dhjerga said, holding out his hands.

Colm stared at him for a second.

Dhjerga grinned the old crazy grin that Colm remembered from Majriti IV. "Use my hands."

All right.

With his left hand, Colm threw an apple to Dhjerga.

Dhjerga threw it back.

Another.

Another.

Another.

Like any good team, they quickly got into a rhythm. Throw and catch and throw. Colm's right hand might be unusable, but between them they had three hands. The apples arced through the sunlight, green and glowing. Colm focused his thoughts on Bridget, the sister he hadn't seen in almost ten years. He saw a hooded figure in a black mac, trudging along a rainy beach. She looked very small from here.

Faster, faster!

The obelisk of the *SOS* blurred.

He could feel the rain.

Everything went silent.

He smelled the salty scent of the sea.

CHAPTER 33

Bridget Mackenzie walked along the beach of Isle Martin, rain driving in under her hood, muttering four-letter words. Much as she tried to stay good-humored, she'd had just about enough.

Her father was driving her round the bend.

He'd been easier to live with—for a while—after they picked up and moved to the island. And she too felt safer with the sea between them and the Ghosts. Their food situation had not deteriorated as much as she'd feared. Birches and pines covered Isle Martin, left over from the re-wilding craze of the late 21st century, which had seen forests planted all over Scotland. Wildlife flourished on the island, so their diet now included squirrel as well as fish and potatoes. Better yet, the tourist center where they were camping had had a little convenience store. It still made Bridget smile to remember the joy on her children's faces when they saw all those chocolate bars and packets of crisps.

But then the *Shihoka* had arrived. Friends of Colm's! How could she say no, go away, we can hardly feed ourselves? She couldn't, not after she saw their baby. So she had just said, gruffly: that ship is a power source, you can't keep that here. Axel had ended up parking the ship in the channel between the island and the mainland. There it stood now, thirty yards out from the beach, up to its belly in the tide, painted in the green and blue colors of the Fleet.

It'll be fine there, Axel had said. The Ghosts don't like the sea. (With total confidence, like he *knew* what the Ghosts liked and did not.) They won't go near it.

And so far, he'd been right. But Bridget couldn't look at the ship without seeing a reminder of how the Fleet had abandoned Earth. And unfairly or not, Axel was a living reminder of the same betrayal.

Meg was easier to get along with. She was teaching the kids karate. She bagged more squirrels and rabbits than anyone, and the one time they saw Ghosts moving around on the mainland, she had dropped them with that fearsome Fleet rifle of hers. A full kilometer away, in the mist. Meg was a lovely lass, but a bit scary.

Which brought Bridget to the problem which had sent her out of doors in this dreich weather, to stomp along the beach with a fishing rod over her shoulder for an excuse, but lacking the calm and focus it would take to go fishing, much as they needed the food.

Meg was not the maternal type. In theory, Bridget had no problem with that. These two awful years had opened her eyes to just how much pampering children *didn't* need. So Meg preferred hunting and patrolling to childcare? Fine. Others would look after little Nicky.

The trouble was that *others* included Lloyd Mackenzie.

He would not leave that baby alone.

Although Axel was a wonderful father, Lloyd was forever criticizing the way he handled the baby. (Lloyd considered Meg a lost cause.) When Bridget's daughter Morag, now 13, babysat, Lloyd would hang around barking at her—be gentler with him! Put another pair of socks on him, he's cold! Can't you see he's hungry? It was downright funny, Bridget had observed to Ted. When she and Colm were little, Lloyd had never so much as changed a nappy. Now he was the world's expert on babies? But it didn't *feel* funny. Bridget had lost count of the number of times she had waked in the night and seen Lloyd sitting up by the fire with Nicky on his lap, shuffling that dogeared old pack of cards to amuse the seemingly hypnotized child.

Today, she had caught him and Nicky playing with a pair of spoons.

Her boots crunched on the pebbles. She was nearing the headland, where the beach ended and the cliffs began.

At the very end of the beach, something white lay half in and half out of the lapping waves.

Maybe it was a sentrienza drone. The bloody things did not even pretend to be stealthy now that there were so few humans left on Earth. Bridget supposed the sentrienza were nervous about the Ghost takeover, and wanted to see what the Ghosts were up to. Good luck to them. The drones were powered equipment, and so they couldn't last long in Ghost-infested areas. Several of them had previously washed up on Isle Martin, intact, but powerless. Ted's mother, Sunita, was good with electronics. She'd built their hand-cranked Ka-band radio from drone parts.

Bridget walked towards the drone, planning to salvage it.

The driving rain lifted for a moment.

Dammit.

Not a drone.

A human body.

It would hardly be the first time one of those had washed up here, either. Now she'd have to lug it up the cliff and throw it off, so that the currents would carry it away and the children wouldn't see it. Pathetically, she was still trying to protect them from the collapse of their world.

Always preferring to play it safe rather than sorry, Bridget approached the body cautiously. An adult man. Face down. A white shirt stuck to broad shoulders. Tight trousers. Bare feet. Seaweed in his longish, water-darkened hair.

A wave came in, and the body moved.

Dragged itself higher up the beach, floating on the tide and at the same time clawing with its hands at the pebbles.

Not dead!

The water slurped back out and the man's head fell to the side.

"Colm!" Bridget screamed.

Not a scintilla of doubt obtained. This was her brother.

She dropped the fishing rod, grabbed him under the armpits, rolled him on his back. He was unconscious. His skin felt like ice.

He coughed. Opened his eyes. His pupils were pinpoints.

"What the hell are you doing here, Colm?"

"Came to save you from the Ghosts, of course."

Bridget laughed so hard that tears came to her eyes. "Did you swim from the mainland?"

"Only from the ship," Colm mumbled, and seemed to pass out again. His chest rose and fell shallowly. Bridget slapped his face in fright.

His eyes opened again. She recoiled from the naked fear in those shrunken pupils. "Help me, Bridget. I'm so sorry. I've taken an overdose."

*

"But where've you *been,* Colm?"

He thought the voice was Diejen's. He tried to answer but his lips seemed to be glued shut. One minute he'd been juggling apples in a field on Atletis and the next minute he'd been drowning in the sea beneath the tail of a spaceship. The current was strong. He'd barely made it to shore.

"Where've you been?"

The agony of the transit gripped him again—a vivid memory, replaying as a dream, but it felt so real. He knew now how the Ghosts flitted. They deconstructed themselves into zero-gravity, zero-mass entities—*souls,* you might say—and travelled at the speed of thought … not *quite* instantaneously … not fast enough to escape the tearing, wrenching sensation of being naked in the zero-gravity field, stripped of skin and bones and everything, your soul exposed to the primeval violence of this fallen universe.

"Colm! Colm …"

He suddenly recognized the voice. It was his mother's. He opened his eyes and tried to smile. He was lying on a red vinyl couch in front of a fire, with a blanket over him. "I've been with the Ghosts, Mam. Listen, they're not so bad ..."

Daisy Mackenzie's face fell. Colm pushed himself upright. The shivering and shaking of withdrawal had passed off. He felt human again. People surrounded the couch. His family. Axel and Meg. An older couple he didn't know. He started to explain about Kisperet, about Dhjerga Lizp and the Families and their rebellion against the Magus, but he could see it wasn't taking. They thought he was raving, or if he wasn't, that would be worse. They said it was great to see him awake, and hopefully he'd feel better soon, and then they drifted away.

Only Axel stayed behind. "So it all really happened," he said.

Colm struggled off the couch. He didn't know how to express his gratitude for Axel's free gift of his body and expertise. "What's the last thing you remember?"

Axel screwed up his face in thought. "The chainsaw

bayonets," he said eventually.

Colm grinned. "Those were awesome, weren't they?"

"You're not a real Marine until you've used a chainsaw bayonet," Axel answered, and then he said, "But the memories are fading." He drove his hands into his trouser pockets, hunching his shoulders to his ears. "They can't fade too soon for me."

Meg came back into the room, carrying the baby. "Ah, he's adorable. Hello, Nicky," Colm started. The baby was a lot bigger than when Colm had last seen him on board the *Shihoka;* a toddler, actually. How long had Colm's transit from Kisperet taken? Nicky looked about two. He had dark blond curls and a grubby face. His brown eyes regarded the stranger with distrust. Meg handed him off to Axel, without acknowledging Colm.

"I'm going out hunting."

Colm leapt at the chance to reconnect with her. "I'll go too, if that's all right with you."

"You're a junkie," Meg said, with withering contempt.

"I'm feeling fine."

"You can't shoot."

"I'm a lot better than I used to be."

"There's only one rifle."

Colm realized that she didn't want him along. He was about to back down when she shrugged off her raincoat.

"Fine, you can go instead of me. Don't waste ammo." She tossed him the raincoat and went back upstairs.

Axel said, "The ammo's almost gone. But Meg's got a backup plan. She's made a bow out of PVC pipe and rawhide. Now she's making arrows out of rabbit bones!" His eyes pleaded with Colm not to take offense at Meg's tetchiness.

"Why don't you use the ship to fetch more ammo? And anything else you need?" Colm said.

"Colm … the Magus won."

"No, he didn't."

"We may have won on Atletis, but it took too long. An army of Ghosts can do a whole lot of damage in a few months."

"You're saying everything's gone?"

"Dunno," Axel said. "Maybe not everything. But I'm not gonna risk the ship, and my life, to find out. I've got this little guy to think about." He turned his face away, blowing a raspberry at Nicky to make him smile.

CHAPTER 34

If this was the end of the world, Colm's first choice would have been to get drunk. That clearly wasn't an option, so he decided he really would go hunting. He headed for the boot room.

This building was not actually a house but a visitor center formerly run by Scotland's tourism agency. Bridget had explained that a couple of Visit Scotland employees used to live here during the tourist season. The Mackenzie group had taken over the upstairs flat, the shop, the waiting room—that was where the fire was—and the kitchen behind the shop, where everyone was presently hanging out around the gas stove. Colm smiled awkwardly at them.

Wellies and coats crammed the entryway. Colm's waterlogged boots stuck out like a sore thumb for their fine workmanship and the colorful tassels around their tops. He borrowed someone else's wellies, and took the .22 hunting rifle down from its shelf.

"Want some company?"

His head jerked around. There stood his father, togged up in waterproofs. Oh, *no*.

"All right."

"You don't know your way around yet. I'll give you the grand tour."

They climbed up from the beach into the forested interior of the island. Although Lloyd Mackenzie looked thinner and grayer than Colm remembered, he sustained a spanking pace. Colm struggled to keep up with him. As for shooting squirrels, the rifle felt too heavy to carry, let alone fire. He caught his father grinning, at his unfitness, he thought. They came out on top of the cliffs, facing west across the sea. The rain hid the outer islands.

Lloyd pointed. "There's where I want to go," he said. "Skye."

Colm gave him a surprised glance. His great-grandfather had owned a house on the Isle of Skye: the Free Church Manse. In his Fleet days, Colm had dreamed about saving enough money to buy it and fix it up. He had never mentioned this ambition to his father. "Do you think there're Ghosts on the island?" he said.

"Doubt it," Lloyd said. "They don't do boats. There used to be a bridge but the government took it down years ago, when there was that mania for putting everything back the way nature intended it ... bloody nonsense." Lloyd shaded his eyes against the rain. "The wolves'll be taking over the place soon enough. It was a mistake re-introducing those bastards. Maybe they'll eat the Ghosts."

Lloyd paused. Colm felt that he was expected to defend the Ghosts. He did not. Instead, he said, "I wonder if Great-Grandfather's house is still there."

'That's where I want to go. That house is warded against evil." Lloyd's eyes gleamed with a hint of vulnerability. In the old days, Colm would have scoffed or walked out if Lloyd ever said anything like that.

"The Ghosts aren't evil," he said neutrally. "They're just people who lost their way. People like me." He paused. "People like you."

Lloyd spat off the cliff. "Then off you go to the mainland and convince them of that."

Colm hefted the rifle. "Give them time," he said, seething

inside. "They'll come to themselves, and then they'll be all right." He hoped this was true. Didn't know if it *would* be true, as long as the Magus remained on the loose. He pretended to shoot at the birds swooping above the sea. "I wonder can you eat seagulls?"

"Fucking nasty," his father said. "We've tried."

Everyone was thin and cross. It wasn't just Meg, although she was the angriest of all, refusing to so much as meet Colm's eyes, much less talk to him. The rest of them, though, weren't specifically angry with Colm. He realized quickly that they had no spare mental energy to worry or be curious about his bizarre return. Every moment was dedicated to finding food or thinking about ways to find food. His mother and Sunita Wilson doled out half a potato and a chunk of mackerel to each adult and child for supper.

Burning with anger at the situation, Colm bunked down on the floor in the waiting room. The couch had only been his while he was recovering from his overdose. Now he slept on the floor with Axel, Meg, Bridget, Ted, Morag, and Ivor, in a miasma of unwashed human bodies and potato farts. Scarlett and Nicky had the couch. The older generation had the single bedroom upstairs. The fire burned low and Colm drifted off to sleep while wondering if there might be some tropo left on the *Shihoka*. He might swim out and have a look ...

He awoke suddenly.

The fire was dying.

His parents' new cat, Mickle, lay on the hearth. Her eyes gleamed in the dark.

Beside the fire, on the vinyl chair that matched the sofa, sat Lloyd and little Nicky.

The toddler sat astride Lloyd's lap, his face pressed into

Lloyd's cardigan, the material bunched in his tiny hands as if he were holding on for dear life.

Lloyd had one arm wrapped around Nicky and with his other hand he was doing magic. Two sticks, tied together with twine in an X shape, floated up and down and back and forth in front of him, following Lloyd's hand movements. He was levitating the sticks.

The shadows on the other side of the fireplace bunched deep and dark.

Colm silently untangled himself from his sleeping bag, eyes peeled in the gloom.

Something scraped in the shadows.

Mickle danced to her feet, hissing.

Lloyd moved the sticks faster, teeth bared, body hunched around the child.

Scrape. Scrape.

The toecap of an enormous boot slid into the firelight, and at the same time the fire sank low, guttering, as if a cold blast of wind had crept down the chimney.

Colm rose to his feet. He stepped over the sleeping Bridget and vaulted over the sofa. He grabbed the little rake that lay in front of the fire and drove it into the grate, scooping up embers.

Turning, lunging, he dashed the embers into the shadow's unseen face.

His momentum carried him stumbling into the wall. The bricks were so cold that they burned his hands, and then there was nothing.

Nicky started to cry.

Lloyd hissed, "Pick up those fucking coals before you burn the place down!"

Colm hastily raked up the embers that had scattered in the corner. "That's him sorted," he said, while inside he was crying out: No, oh no ... not *here!* Not my family, you fucker!

"I had it in hand," Lloyd said. "Now you've scared the wean!" He stroked Nicky's hair, comforting the terrified child with a tenderness Colm had never seen from him.

Bridget rose from her sleeping-bag. Taking in the situation in one glance, she plucked Nicky off Lloyd's lap and deposited him on the floor between Axel and Meg. "He had a nightmare," she explained in a whisper. Axel sleepily slung an arm around the boy and pulled him under the covers. Bridget came back to the fire. "All right," she whispered. "I've had just about enough of this. Enough! What the hell is going on?"

Colm threw a glance into the corner. "It was the Magus." He stretched his cold hands out to the fire.

"Is that what you call him, too?" Lloyd said.

"He's a Ghost," Colm said. "He's the one I've been fighting all this time."

"Aye well then, you need to raise your game," Lloyd said. "He's been hanging around us for months. Years! Recently it's been every bloody night. He's after the child."

"Why?" Bridget said.

Lloyd shrugged. "I can handle him. He's only an auld magician."

"What were you doing with those sticks?" Colm said.

"Praying," Lloyd said, with a croaky laugh. He picked up the X of sticks and tossed it into the fire. "Praying like our lives depend on it. Which they do."

"Fire works, too," Colm said.

"It works only because of you." Lloyd hit Colm lightly on

the shoulder. "You've come on …"

"I need tropo," Colm muttered. He felt hobbled without it, his magic locked up in his brain. "*You* don't need chemicals, Dad. You don't have an implant …"

"Is that what they did to you? The fucking bastards."

Lloyd was the first person ever to react the same way Colm had. *The fucking bastards.* "Yeah. But I can't do anything without drugs …"

"You still have a lot to learn," Lloyd said, in a tone that was almost kindly.

Bridget slapped her thighs. "This is ridiculous. You can't keep on doing this every night, forever!"

"No," Colm said. "You're right, Bridgie. We can't stay here. We need to move to Skye."

Lloyd rose from his chair to coax Mickle the cat back to the fire. Colm remembered what had happened to the last cat they had. The memory fanned his hatred of his father all over again.

Lloyd picked up the small tabby and stroked her. "Aye, I'm all for it. But how are we to get there?"

"That's easy," Colm said. Here was something he *could* do. "We'll go in the *Shihoka.*"

CHAPTER 35

Dhjerga looked up at the *Son Of Saturn*. Timber chocks caged its base, to ensure it wouldn't fall over. They looked flimsy beside its stupendous bulk.

"Just put them anywhere," he shouted up to the Janzes, who were shepherding his nukes up the ladder in rope cradles.

He and the spaceship were alone in the field outside the village. Over the last few days everyone had scattered. Some had gone back to Kisperet, others to seek their friends and relations on the conquered worlds. The twins had gone, too. Lady Terrious and one of her daughters were staying on Atletis; they had gone upstream to look for somewhere to build a dam. Looking for a way back to the past.

Dhjerga knew the old ways were dead. The pavilion flapped in the wind.

"Sir?"

Alone? He wasn't alone, of course. Several hundred copies stood in the field, the newer ones blank-faced, the older ones visibly confused by the lack of orders to follow. They couldn't understand why their masters had gone away and left them. Among them, the surviving Marines had removed their battlesuits and were scrounging amidst the rubble of the banquet. At five months old, they were the eldest copies on Atletis, and had more or less come to themselves. They could manage the others.

"Sir? What are our orders?"

He turned to the not-Janz that had addressed him. His face was so familiar, and yet soon he would be someone else. "No more orders," he said roughly, and started to climb the ladder.

He passed the other not-Janzes on their way down without a word.

He reached the top, panting with exertion, and looked down. Vertigo tickled the backs of his eyeballs. Innismon appeared so tiny. The ridge, like a giant barrow. The grave of the Magistocracy. The slaves, staring up at him. He permitted himself a flight of fancy: perhaps they were marvelling, in their half-formed minds, that he, Dhjerga Lizp, had mastered these alien technologies, the magic of nuclear reactions and computers.

Colm didn't have what it took. Disappointment still rankled in Dhjerga's heart when he thought about him. He had seemed like a man of principle but really he'd just been looking for a way out, and had flitted first chance he got. The twins had been furious with Dhjerga for helping him. He had tried to explain to them: he isn't our savior, he's got no sense of honor, you're better off letting him go.

I'll keep my promise, unlike some.

And maybe, just maybe, along the way, I'll become the greatest mage that ever lived.

He flapped his arms at the watching copies in go-away gestures. Then he swung into the crew capsule and shut the door. He had no idea how the controls worked, but so what?

Seconds later, the watching multitude saw the *Son Of Saturn* vanish. The timber chocks toppled into the empty place where it had been, and crashed onto the flattened yellow grass.

*

Gilliam Tripsilion Nulth scuttled along the hot earth between ragfruit bushes. He raised his front half off the ground and squeezed an unripe fruit between two claws.

"Hmm," he said to his estate manager. "What do you think? Will these ripen before the sentrienza destroy the planet in a storm of nuclear fire?"

The estimated arrival of the Rigel fleet was just ten days away. Gil was certain that the sentrienza would arrive more or less on schedule. They never lied.

The estate manager, a human, gazed over the rows of bushes. "Perhaps our fleet will prevail," he said, hopefully.

Gil said, "Perhaps," but he had inspected the newly built fleet for himself. Fine ships ... but not enough of them. To make matters worse, the logic of space combat inherently disadvantaged the defenders. They would have to disable every single sentrienza ship, counter every single attack. The attackers only had to get through once.

His heart heavy with forebodings, he had come home to his family estate at the north pole of Juradis, to tread one last time upon the land where he had been born. There had been good things, after all, about the Uzzizellan exile on Juradis. Rich soil, sweet water, warm sunshine. He inhaled the scent of the bushes, and wondered if their ashes would fertilize new crops, someday, for the next hapless species to be lured into the sentrienza's embrace.

The estate manager let out a cry of shock.

"What is it?"

He pointed back towards the coast. Gil scrabbled up the trunk of the nearest bush. Clawing the leaves aside, he peered in the direction of the Kevesingod fjord.

The parapets of Castle Nulth broke the flat horizon.

Beside the castle—twice its height—stood a rocket.

*

"It's got a sort of antique charm," said the Rat. "Does it

actually fly?"

Gil had summoned the admiral immediately. The Rat had come down from the *Unsinkable* in his personal shuttle, which was now parked near Dhjerga Lizp's rocket. The sleek, modern spacecraft contrasted shockingly with this prehistoric-looking obelisk. Gil circled the rocket, sniffing the faint odor of steel forged on an alien planet. Its stabilizer fins and angled legs were discolored, less than smooth—and cool to the touch.

"It flies all right," Dhjerga Lizp said. "But I didn't fly it here. I just brought it. Much faster."

Gil asked the question whose answer he was dreading. "Where is Colm?"

"I told you he wouldn't be coming," Dhjerga said. He wore an outlandish, foppish outfit that he said was the garb of his own people: baggy sleeves, tight trousers, billowing cloak. He held a blocky little device with an antenna. He calmly watched the Rat's technicians climb the rocket's access ladder.

"If I hadn't dishonorably discharged him already," the Rat said bitterly, "I'd do it now, in absentia." He was clearly unimpressed, with the rocket; with Dhjerga; with Colm's non-appearance. "What's his excuse?"

"Drink and drugs," Dhjerga said succinctly. Gil winced.

"Sir!" one of the human technicians shouted down from the airlock at the top of the rocket. She was waving a handheld scanner. The display could not be read from the ground, but the fear on her face could. "He's got a nuke in here!"

"Three nukes, actually," Dhjerga said.

The words galvanized everyone on the ground. The humans ran for their shuttle. The queazels ran for the castle.

Neither refuge would protect them if the nukes went off, so Gil stayed where he was. So did the Rat. He strode up to Dhjerga Lizp, and would probably have punched him if not for the radio-control detonator in Dhjerga's hands. "What the hell are you playing at?"

"You wanted help. I've brought it."

*

Gil cajoled the humans into the castle and served them drinks in the library, hoping this would foster a more amicable atmosphere. Admiral Hyland ignored the Ghost, tapping on his computer. Dhjerga Lizp poured Gil's hawbrother liquor down his neck with gusto, while keeping his radio control device on his knee. He would have slouched extravagantly, Gil thought, as he did on the *Vienna,* were that possible, but when sitting on a bench less than a foot off the floor, a human's only option was to sit bolt upright with the legs inelegantly splayed. The whole room, of course, was queazel-sized. Shelves held books written by Gil's ancestors, and ornate frames displayed Gil's own pictures of Uzzizriat. The humans were incongruous. So too were the three steel cylinders lying on the flagstones behind Dhjerga.

The Fleet technicians had scanned the nukes and reported that they were implosion assemblies with uranium cores. They'd grudgingly confirmed Dhjerga's assertion that the devices were well shielded. Yet the nukes were so crude—and powerful—that this was scant comfort. One stray chirp on the wrong frequency and Castle Nulth would slide into the fjord. Gil's back fur clumped into tufts with nervous sweat.

"These faerie spaceships," Dhjerga said. "Where are they now?"

"In the zero-gravity field, fast approaching Betelgeuse,"

Gil said.

"What do they look like?"

Gil sighed, and searched the castle computer. "Here. This is one," he said, flashing an image of the late, unlamented *Ruddiganmaseve* up on the screen. It looked like a dead branch, with more spikes.

"Ugly as sin, aren't they?" Dhjerga said.

"Yes."

"What about the inside of the ship? Where do they keep the engines?"

Wondering what the point of this was, Gil searched for interior images. He had a library of schematics from the Barjoltan shipyards. While he was selecting the best images, Admiral Hyland said to Dhjerga, "Why are you interested in the interior layout of sentrienza ships?"

"I'm going to help you," Dhjerga said.

"You're very confident, aren't you? You defeated us; that doesn't mean you'll be able to defeat the sentrienza."

"We didn't win that war," Dhjerga said. "You lost it."

The Rat sighed. Confirming Gil's high opinion of him, he acknowledged, "You may be right. We kept expecting the sentrienza to come and save us."

Dhjerga nodded. "We should have been fighting them all along. But I didn't know that until I came here."

"*I* knew it," Hyland said bitterly. "But how can we fight them? I've got us into a war that can only have one outcome. Our obliteration." The crisis had cracked his professional shell, leaving only raw, self-aware honesty.

"Chin up, sir," Dhjerga said. "I've got a trick or two up my sleeve." He thrust his head forward, focusing on Gil's images.

Puzzled, Gil resumed his lecturer's role. "This is a capital ship," he said. "But they are all much the same, with a greater or lesser number of modules." He had stitched the schematics together into a virtual tour. On the screen, their viewpoint slithered through uneven tunnels, and into a cavern filled with the machinery of an antiquark drive. "This is the drive module."

"The bit that makes it go?"

"Yes."

"And what about the bit that ..." Dhjerga's forehead creased. "That makes it travel between stars?"

"The zero-gravity field generator." Gil moved their viewpoint to the other side of the cavern, and tapped the screen with a claw. "This unit. It runs off the power generated by the antiquark field, as does the drive, so they are in the same module."

"Good." Suddenly, Dhjerga smiled fiercely. "I'll be back."

Before Gil or Admiral Hyland could say a word, he had vanished.

The nukes remained, their hand-burnished surfaces catching the light from the screen.

Dhjerga had taken the detonator.

Man and queazel stared at the devices for a long moment. Gil wondered if they were going to go off. The Rat spoke into his computer. "Phil? Yeah, this is Bastian. Guess there's no hurry, after all."

CHAPTER 36

Betelgeuse, dipping close to the horizon, stretched the shadows of *three* spaceships across the hillside: the *Son Of Saturn,* Admiral Hyland's shuttle, and the sub-orbital spaceplane in which Philip K. Best had arrived with an escort of Marines. The soldiers were not there to protect Governor Best. They were there to guard Best's companion, Emnl ki-Sharongat. Best had scooped her off the *Vienna* to see what she made of the Ghost's claims. "But where is the Ghost?" she said scornfully. They had no answer except to point to Dhjerga Lizp's ship.

The nukes remained inside the castle. Gil had thought it prudent to evacuate his household as well as his guests. They all regrouped four kilometers away, behind a hill which would protect them in the event of a blast. After a while, Gil sent two servants back to the castle to fetch refreshments.

Hyland and Best spoke about evacuating Juradis. It was a recurrent topic but a futile one. Even had they the ships to transport everyone, where would they go?

Gil climbed to the hilltop to await the return of his servants. He curled himself on a sun-warmed rock. Looking seawards, he could see the little town of Kevesingod at the mouth of the fjord. The bay sparkled in the midnight sun. Inland, his ragfruit orchard and the edge of his barley fields furred the land. His castle's towers flew the brave flags of Uzzizriat and the Human Republic.

He grabbed his binoculars and screwed them, trembling, to his eyes.

Two queazels had just come out of the gate, walking on

their hind legs, carrying picnic baskets. And between them limped a man.

*

"I told you I'd come back," Dhjerga said, when he reached the others. "A mage keeps his word."

Although everyone else was standing, the Ghost had sat down on the ground. He looked worn out. Gil prodded a servant to offer him something to drink. Dhjerga drained half a bottle of orange fizz in a single gulp.

"I'm done in. That was a lot of flitting."

So they all sat down on the rocky hillside, and the servants, not knowing what else to do, spread out the picnic.

"Where've you been?" Admiral Hyland demanded.

"Achar feadha's feadh achair," Dhjerga replied, helping himself to mutton stew.

"What?"

"Colm showed me the magic of space travel, the *tekne*. So I looked for these faerie ships you described. I found thirty-seven of them. Was that all?"

Emnl ki-Sharongat said in her high voice, "That is the shipcount of the Rigel fleet."

"And then, Ghost?" the Rat growled.

"Then I fetched my nukes into their engine parts and I set them off." Dhjerga gave a tired, triumphant grin. "It was very tricky, the timing of it! I had to be in and out—" he snapped his fingers— "like *this!* There were faeries all over the place, of course." He gave Emnl a hard cold look. "I was the last thing they ever saw."

This claim stunned the humans into silence. It was left to Gil to say, "Are you serious? You blew them all up?"

"I felt the heat from the explosions," Dhjerga said,

touching his slightly reddened cheeks.

The humans shouted aloud and high-fived each other. The Rat whooped, "Get this man some rad pills! He's singlehandedly destroyed the Rigel fleet."

Emnl buzzed, "Our ships are modular! An explosion in one module, even if it truly occurred, could not destroy the whole ship."

"Maybe not," Hyland said. "But if the ships lost their zero-gravity field generators in the middle of interstellar space, the result'd be the same, wouldn't it?"

Everyone crowded around Dhjerga to hug and thank him. Gil's servants ran in circles like kits, chasing each other for joy. Had Gil not had his position to think of he would have done the same thing. And yet the experienced diplomat in him wondered if it was too good to be true.

Dhjerga took a computer out of an inside pocket of his embroidered vest. It was not a human or a queazel computer. It looked like a rusty geode. "I got this from the first ship," he said. "I had to flit away to a different part of the ship before I set off the nukes. So I picked this up from the place with all the faerie books."

"The bridge," Hyland said, grabbing it.

It took them the rest of the night to get into the sentrienza computer, with Emnl's grudging assistance. What they found on it, decoded and translated, cast a pall on the celebratory mood.

"'Extinction protocol authorized,'" the Rat read in a hoarse whisper. "This is a letter from the Gray Emperor himself. 'Target: *Homo sapiens.*"

"Do you think that includes us?" Dhjerga said.

"Of course it does, Ghost," said Philip K. Best. "Of

course it does."

They had returned to the castle and were sitting in the refectory, with a crackling fire going. The translation on the screen of the computer made it feel icy cold. Gil scanned the words. The Emperor's letter said nothing about queazels. His species had been relegated to the status of collateral damage, too unimportant even to mention.

"The protocol is to be applied to the following planets," he read. "Juradis, Barjoltan, Noom, Gliese 581g, Kepler 442b, Ross 128b, Mu Arae d, Monoceros f, Majriti IV ..." The list included every single one of Earth's former colony worlds, now Ghost colony worlds. Gil reached the final entry: "... and Earth."

Emnl ki-Sharongat broke the stunned silence. "But what about *me?*" she said plaintively.

Gil took a certain pleasure in saying to her, "The Gray Emperor has clearly decided that you are to be relegated to the role of collateral damage, too unimportant even to mention."

"The Rigel fleet was armed with planet-killing weapons," Hyland read on. He sat down on one of the too-low benches and rubbed his face with his hands.

"Walking Guns," Emnl buzzed. "Just one of them can destroy a planet, you know."

"And now they are to be loosed on Earth." Hyland looked at Dhjerga. "What you did to the Rigel fleet. Could you could do that again? Could you ... *keep* doing it?" Gil saw how much it cost him to ask this of his former foe.

"I don't know," Dhjerga said. "There's only one of me and there's lots of them, aren't there? And I can't be everywhere at once." He brightened. "But I know people all over the colony worlds. I could teach them the *tekne* of space travel. I *think* they'd help."

The Rat did not seem encouraged by this vague promise. He said to Best, "We must return to Earth."

"It's an 18-month voyage," Best said despairingly. "By the time we get there, Earth will be a black hole."

Emnl buzzed, "The process is not that rapid. It would take an estimated twenty-one standard Earth months from the introduction of a miniature black hole into the crust of an Earth-sized planet until the planet was consumed."

"Thanks for that information," Best growled. "Is that supposed to make me feel better? My son and grandson are there!"

Dhjerga said, "Don't fret! I'll sort it."

He did not inspire confidence, sagging by the fire, hiccuping.

Admiral Hyland said, "Regardless, we have to go back. We have to do what we can, even if all we can do in the end is say a prayer over Earth's shrunken corpse." He jumped up, seemingly ready to embark for Earth on the spot.

Gil rose to his full height. "No, Admiral," he said. "Governor Best." He met the eyes of the two anguished men. "I understand your feelings. You face the loss of your homeworld. Nothing is more frightening. But your place is here. Millions of humans, mara, and shablags depend on your leadership and protection." He held up his foremost legs to forestall their protests. *"I* will go to Earth. And if all that can be done is to say a prayer over a dead planet ... then I shall say it."

*

It took him the rest of the night to talk them into agreeing.

Weary, but triumphant, Gil left the castle at dawn to break the news to his estate manager. He climbed into his car and bumped along the dirt road that skirted the cliffs above the fjord.

Betelgeuse was so low in the sky that other stars could—just—be perceived at the opposite horizon. As Gil drove, a sparkling in the purple empyrean caught his eye. He stopped the rover and looked up. Gone; no—there it went again! And again, and again!

The computer in his vest pocket quacked. He took it out and said, "Hello, Admiral. Have you been watching this peculiar meteor shower?"

"Now we know what an antiquark drive looks like when it explodes," the Rat said. "The Ghost was right. They were *big* ships."

"Yes; and only a few light hours away."

"Yes."

They rang off. Gil drove on soberly.

When he reached the ragfruit orchard and parked in the employee parking area, the first thing he heard was Dhjerga Lizp's voice.

"You're married, then?"

Gil eased out of the car. Quietly, as only a queazel could, he crept around the trees at the end of the parking lot, and climbed one of them, digging his claws into the crumbly bark. Peering between the leaves, he could see over the fence into the orchard. Dhjerga Lizp stood outside the estate manager's cottage, talking to the estate manager himself.

"I'm sorry." Dhjerga Lizp spoke in an altogether different tone from usual—no bravado, nor exaggerated confidence. "I didn't mean to wake her."

"Oh, she's always awake at this hour," said the estate manager. He was holding his baby daughter, a chubby five-month-old, named—much to Gil's embarrassment—Gilliam, after Gil himself. "It's her mum sleeps like the dead. I get up with Gillie in the night; it's easier!"

"Her mum …"

"Yes, my wife," the estate manager said.

From his perch in the tree, Gil could see into the bedroom window of the cottage. The woman in question lay in bed inside. She was very pretty, for a human, even if she *was* sleeping with her mouth open. A refugee from Earth, she had found new love and a new purpose in life here on the Nulth estate. Gil felt proud that he had made that possible. He also felt proud of Janz, the estate manager. The human had turned up in Kevesingod after the uprising, ragged and penniless and unwilling to discuss his past. Gil had taken a chance on him and been amply rewarded.

"Sorry, sir, do I know you?" Janz said with a hint of perplexity. "It's just I keep thinking you look familiar."

"N-no. I just … saw you from a distance … and wanted to say hello."

Janz scratched his head. Baby Gilliam was beginning to grizzle. "Well, it's time for breakfast. Care to come in and have a bite with me and the Mrs.? Any friend of Lord Nulth's …"

"Thank you, but no." Dhjerga turned aside. He took a couple of paces towards Gil's tree. The queazel saw him covertly wipe tears from his eyes. "I have to be on my way. It was … good to meet you."

He vanished.

*

The next day Gilliam Tripsilion Nulth embarked for Earth

aboard the *Unsinkable*, with a skeleton crew of humans and queazels.

CHAPTER 37

Colm had begun taking the *Shihoka* on long-range flights in search of food and supplies. Unlike Axel, he did not have a child to think about, and he needed to do something to help the family. His destinations were usually spaceports, which tended to be deserted by humans and Ghosts alike. In the post-apocalyptic quiet, he worked by himself, overhauling and refueling the *Shihoka*. Then he would scrounge around the warehouses and spaceport concessions, and go home with the ship's hold full of food and useful bits and bobs.

Today, however, he had flown to a different destination: Tokyo.

He had a specific goal in mind, and an address scribbled on the screen of his computer. He walked for hours through the empty streets, using his computer's sat-nav function to find the way. Earth's satellites were still in operation, although the Fleet had gone.

Prior to the final panicked evacuation, the Human Republic authorities had carried out a planetary-scale campaign of power source denial. All over the world, solar panels and wind turbines lay in wreckage, broken turbines spun futilely in rivers, nuclear power plants were in cold shutdown, and generators leaked fuel into the ground. The lesson of the lost colonies had finally been learned. This orgy of destruction had come too late to stop the Ghost invasion. Fuel cells were the big culprits—there were billions of those scattered over Earth, and no way to run them all down in a hurry. But fuel cells couldn't be recharged without a working grid, so the Ghosts had been drawing down a resource they could not replenish. They were the masters of a world swiftly hurtling back into the Bronze Age. Colm suspected this, too, had been part of the Magus's plan. The Magus had wanted to restore Earth to an era when electricity was solely accessible to mages who knew how to fetch the lightning.

These grim thoughts brought him to an alley in the North Shinjuku district of Tokyo. The address he was looking for belonged to a small box of a house in a row of boxes, with fake brick walls. Grass grew in the middle of the street and kudzu climbed to the second-storey windows. This was what the Ghost victory looked like. Silence, weeds, and the sinister smell of rot.

Colm tried the door. It was not locked. "Hello?" he called out, for form's sake, and started to climb the stairs, pistol in hand.

"Get out!" yelled a panicky male voice. A silhouette appeared at the head of the stairs, pointing a rifle at Colm.

Colm threw himself backwards. "Calm down," he yelled from around the corner of the hall. "I haven't come to arrest you."

Silence.

"Can I come up?"

"Are you from Lord Moro?" the voice demanded.

Lord *Moro?* Colm blinked. "No."

Another voice—a woman's—called out, "All right! *Te o agete agatte kudasai!*"

Colm did not speak Japanese, but he took a chance on ascending the stairs. In the cozy family room at the top, he found a pale, big-nosed, brown-haired Ghost, clad in un-Ghost-like jeans and a Tokyo Giants sweatshirt, and a young Japanese woman. When the Ghost soldiers came to themselves, they often turned out not to be warlike at all. It was the woman who held the rifle.

Colm realized that Tokyo was probably not as empty as it looked. He might have been watched all the way here. It had been the same in London and Glasgow. As the Magistocracy collapsed, the Ghost soldiers had deserted by the thousand. When they came to themselves they usually went into hiding, fearful that they might be enslaved.

The chaotic cessation of hostilities had come too late for many of Earth's people, but not for all of them—witness this Ghost's girlfriend.

"What you want?" she snapped.

Colm wanted to ask her where her family was and what she'd suffered before winding up here, but he just said, "Calm down." He looked around the room. Nicholas Smythe's books were spread out on the table. On the verandah outside the window, the familiar leaves of potato and rice plants sprouted from pots. Colm pointed at random at a framed photograph hanging on the wall. "I only want that."

"Take," the woman said, giving him the photograph. "This not our house," she added, scrupulously.

"I reckon it is now," Colm said. "I'll leave you in peace." Before he left, he turned to the Ghost. "You asked if I was from Lord Moro."

"You said you weren't."

"No. I was just wondering—*Gaethla* Moro?"

"Yes."

"Is he here?"

The Ghost fidgeted nervously. "Yes. His HQ is in Shibuya."

"Shibuya?! The Shibuya Star Port?"

"That big dome. Don't tell him you saw me. Please."

"I won't." Colm left the house with the photograph in the pocket of his anorak, feeling a bit panicky. Gaethla Moro was at the Shibuya Star Port! That's where Colm had left the *Shihoka*. Fuck, fuck, fuck. He started to run.

The Shibuya Star Port was not actually a spaceport. It was a huge shopping mall roofed by a geodesic dome, with parks radiating out in all directions where streets had run in an earlier, traffic-clogged era. These parks were just right for launch pads, so Colm had put the *Shihoka* down on one of them. He had been planning to raid the mall later for supplies. He felt a surge of relief when he saw the ship still standing on the charred weeds in the park. He decided to take off straight away. Fuck the supplies. He could stop somewhere else on the way home.

Then he hesitated.

It's a thing I need to finish.

He stood by a slime-choked ornamental pond and scowled at the dome. The tiles were solar cells. The power would still be on somewhere inside.

He rationalized it to himself. Power might mean food in freezers. Drugs that needed refrigeration. Fully charged fuel cells.

Fuck it.

He nipped into the ship and exchanged his handgun for the combi he had borrowed from Axel. He also grabbed a duffel bag—Meg's, the one she'd had ever since she was in the Fleet. Then he started toward the dome.

It was eerie walking through the mall, among the deserted shops. Thanks to the solar roof, the lights were still on.

"Gaethla?" he shouted, gripping the combi tightly. "Gaethla!"

No one answered him. Nothing moved except holo advertisements, shimmying along empty corridors. All he heard was muzak dripping from sensor-activated speakers as he walked.

Inside the shops, mannequins and display tables lay toppled, consumer gizmos scattered. The Ghosts had conducted their usual smash-and-grab looting operations. But they always missed the really useful stuff. Alert for any noise, Colm stuffed his duffel with snacks and sweets for the kids, toiletries, gloves, razors, disposable computers that hopefully came pre-loaded with books and music, and several sizes of hiking boots.

He hit the jackpot at a boutique pharmacy. The drugs safe was biometrically locked, keyed to the biodata of some long-dead employee. Colm aimed his combi at the lock and shot it.

The solar-powered electronics died. The safe swung open. Colm scooped the contents pell-mell into his duffel. Drugs for arthritis and asthma, antibiotics, painkillers—he'd be a hero back home. His gaze snagged on an industrial-size bottle of tropodolphin tablets.

He had not taken tropo since he got back to Earth. Shamed by the overdose that had brought him here, he'd resolved for the hundredth time to get clean and stay clean.

But now his resolve wavered.

If he kept on nosing around the not-so-deserted cities of the world like this, he would run into trouble. If not today, sometime. It would be really handy if he could simply flit to safety.

Of course, he'd need to work on his conjuring before that would be a real option. His right hand was still stiff. He could pull a trigger now, but he'd never get back the full range of movement in those fingers, short of reconstructive surgery. Maybe Lloyd would be able to show him a one-handed trick he could do with his left hand …

As he hesitated, he heard distant voices and running footsteps. The Ghosts must've heard his shot. Talk about tempting fate.

Right, well, he'd known this might happen. He'd been asking for it. Now he was going to find out what he'd asked for.

He tipped the bottle of tropodolfin into his duffel, slung it over his shoulder, and walked out of the pharmacy. His calm posture belied his thudding pulse. He held the combi low at his side.

The running steps got nearer. Khaki figures darted out of the electronics emporium across the corridor. Colm put the combi down on the floor as raised his hands.

A PA speaker nearby suddenly boomed, "So it's you. I thought you'd show up sooner or later."

The voice was Gaethla Moro's.

"Don't shoot him, lads. Bring him to the club."

Colm relaxed incrementally. There was still a connection between them, he thought.

CHAPTER 38

The soldiers hustled Colm through the corridors of the mall, hissing at him to make him move faster. One of them had taken his duffel, another one his combi.

The mall's central atrium rose three storeys high. Neon pulsed over the doorways of various theme restaurants and fast food outlets. The soldiers shoved Colm beneath a sign that said, in English, *Aquarium.* They passed through a sound-baffle door into hammering electronic music, the reek of cigarette smoke, and watery light coming from, yes, aquariums all around the walls of the room. Plush carpet sucked at Colm's boots. Sofas clad in extravagant blue and green faux fur ringed a dance floor and an island bar.

It figured that Gaethla Moro had set up his headquarters in a nightclub.

"Wasn't Edinburgh good enough for you?" Colm shouted over the music.

Gaethla sprawled at a table covered with empties, watching the strobe lights play on the empty dance floor. "The power ran out. But—" Colm couldn't catch the rest. The music was too loud.

"I can't hear you," Colm yelled. There were soldiers all around the room, pointing their guns at him. A few frightened-looking Japanese girls were working behind the bar, serving the soldiers not presently menacing Colm.

The music went off. Into the silence, Gaethla said, "I'm learning to control this stuff. I'll have the power back on soon."

A chill shot through Colm's gut. If Gaethla was not bluffing, that was bad news.

"Is this what you wanted?" he said.

"Sit down," Gaethla said. "Have a drink. Have a smoke."

Warily, Colm sat. Gaethla looked tired, and a bit bloated. There were bags under his eyes. He was wearing a business suit, open at the neck, that didn't quite fit him. One-handed, he took a cigarette from a pack and turned it between his fingers.

"The Magus promised us a planet flowing with milk and honey," he said. "A fat land, where food grows on shelves, every home has a lifeline, and power flows through the land itself."

"But you wrecked it all by conquering it."

"He said that mighty weapons would bend to our hands. We'd all be rich, and there'd be girls coming out of our ears." Gaethla cast a glance at the girls behind the bar. Colm winced. Were the girls sex slaves? He had been afraid the Ghost conquest might take this ugly turn. But Gaethla looked regretful, rather than horny. Could he, too, have grown a conscience?

Heels rang on the dancefloor.

Colm turned.

Diejen Lizp walked across the dancefloor. Unlike Gaethla, she still wore her Ghost finery, including dangly earrings and abundant gold bracelets. They clanked as she folded her arms.

Colm found himself tonguetied.

Diejen tossed her head and said to Gaethla, "Get those little whores out of here." The girls behind the bar cowered and fled for the exit. The soldiers stayed put. "Where did you find him?"

"He walked in," Gaethla said.

"I came looking for you," Colm said to her.

Diejen's face twitched. For a moment she looked very young.

"Ha! As I thought." Gaethla drew a pistol from under the table. He must have been pointing it at Colm the whole time. He reversed it and held it out to Diejen. "Would you care to dead him yourself, my lady?" His tone oozed irony, but held a edge of barely controlled rage.

Diejen didn't take the pistol. "I tell you plainly, Gaethla, as I have told you before: I have *not* been with him. I wouldn't lower myself."

Colm realized he'd really put his foot in it. Gaethla thought Diejen had cheated on him with Colm, and Colm's stupid comment about having come to look for her had made it worse. All he could do now was back Diejen up. "She's too young for me," he said, shrugging.

"And yet you came armed into my fortress," Gaethla said. "It's a good thing you are no mage. Over there." Colm hesitated. Gaethla jerked the pistol at the dance floor. "Go stand over there!"

Colm rose and backed across the dance floor.

"You wanted to revive the old ways, my lady," Gaethla said. He took a swig of cognac and shoved his chair back from the table without getting up.

"Our old ways were better," Diejen said. "Why did you let the Magus lead you into folly?"

Colm answered for Gaethla. "Girls, guns, and gold." If he was going to die, he might as well say what he thought. "Everyone falls for it." He laughed, really laughed at Gaethla's bloated, scowling face. "Having the fiancée along kind of harshes the vibe, doesn't it?"

Gaethla thumbed back the hammer of his pistol. "Our old

ways *were* better. For instance, in the old days, a man would kill another man on the spot for messing with his betrothed." He aimed at Colm's heart and fired.

Colm knew for a heartstopping instant that he was dead. Then he realized he had heard the report. He couldn't have heard anything if he was dead. Trembling, he followed the awed gazes of the soldiers around the room.

Gaethla's bullet was flying like a bird, skipping slowly over the tables. It circled the room, returned to Gaethla, and fell into his outstretched hand.

"You see," he said to Colm, "I am a *real* mage."

Colm glimpsed naked admiration in Diejen's eyes. In Ghost society, a real mage was a real man, and vice versa. And here Colm stood with the substance that would make him into a real mage lying in the duffel bag near Gaethla's table.

"Where's Dryjon?" He had to try twice before his voice worked.

"He's gone to look for Scota's grave," Diejen said, grimacing.

"What?" Colm remembered how Dhjerga and the other Ghosts would swear by Scota's grave. He had thought it was just an expression.

"Scota was the Magus's true love," Gaethla said. "Like Diejen is my true love." His irony seared. "She's buried somewhere near Edinburgh. I was supposed to look for her grave, but fuck that. What's the use of a lot of dusty bones?"

"You have *no* respect for the old ways," Diejen said, "none."

"Oh, I do, I do. Shall I prove it to you, my lady?" Gaethla made a performance out of aiming his pistol at Colm again, squinting through the sights, his cigarette smouldering in the corner of his mouth.

Colm saw how this was going to go. Gaethla would toy with him for a while, to mess with Diejen's head, but eventually he would fire the fatal shot. Every game of Russian roulette needs an ending.

He thought about the likely futility of making a break for the exit.

Then the strobing disco lights jerked into alignment, shining a rainbow spotlight on the dance floor. The light shimmered, and Dhjerga stood between Colm and Gaethla, coughing, gripping a combi.

"Dhjerga!" Diejen screamed—in joy, Colm thought for a second: then he realized she was afraid.

Dhjerga glanced around, orienting himself. He fixated on the stunned Gaethla. "Ha! Here's luck! Got you at last," he said, and in one swift motion he tucked his combi against his hip and pumped a burst into Gaethla's torso, point blank.

The high-power rounds erupted from the back of Gaethla's chair. Gaethla slid bonelessly to the floor.

"Now we're even, fucker," Dhjerga said, striding over to gloat down at Gaethla's spasming form.

Blood gushed from Gaethla's lips. He raised a trembling arm and pointed at Dhjerga. He spoke words that Colm could not catch, but even so, the grating gurgle of Gaethla's voice drove a chill through his veins. Everyone in the room stood petrified. An expression of absolute horror came over Dhjerga's face. He stumbled backwards, dropping his combi.

Gaethla fell back, dead.

Dhjerga crumpled. His head hit the floor with a sickening clunk.

Diejen rounded on Colm. "You have done this! It was your coming that broke everything! Now Gaethla has laid his death curse on my brother, and you, *you* are to blame!"

Tears spurted from her eyes. She wrapped the lights around herself and vanished.

With a pop, the overloaded strobes went out, leaving the club lit only by the aquariums.

There was a dead silence, broken after a moment by the shuffling of feet. In ones and twos, Gaethla's soldiers were backing away from the two dead men and leaving the room. Very soon Colm was alone.

He laughed, shortly, to himself. In the silence of the deserted club, it was a crazy sound. He shuddered, ambled over to Gaethla's table, and took a long drink straight from the bottle of cognac.

That gave him the strength to circle the pool of blood around Gaethla's body and go to Dhjerga. They had fought together, fought with each other, and accomplished scarcely imaginable things. This was one hell of a way for it to end. He dropped to his knees and rolled Dhjerga onto his back, the way Dhjerga had once rolled over a dead copy in the snow of Kisperet, saying: *There is too much dying among us.* You got that right, my friend. Colm folded Dhjerga's hands on his chest.

One of the hands twitched.

"Dhjerga?!"

Colm lowered his face to Dhjerga's mouth. Warmth tickled his cheek.

He took Dhjerga's pulse: faint, but steady. Dhjerga was alive!

But no matter how Colm shook him and spoke to him, he did not respond. He was in some kind of a coma. Colm dragged Dhjerga into a sitting position. It was like moving a corpse, but warm. He grabbed Dhjerga's wrists and hoisted him onto his back. Dhjerga's feet dragged on the floor. Colm seized his duffel, hung the strap around his neck, and struggled out of the club, bowed down. He left the weapons.

*

The flight back around the world took three hours on a sub-orbital ballistic trajectory, topping out at Mach 3. Colm had never been so glad to see the north Atlantic and the friendly green islands that dotted it, like little fish grouped around the big fish of Skye.

He usually landed offshore, respecting the prohibition established by the Skye islanders: no power sources on the island—and waited for someone to come out with a dinghy. Today he didn't have time for that crap. He put down in the field behind the Free Church Manse.

The *Shihoka*'s drive crisped the daisies and charred the grass. The sun was rising—they had overtaken the dawn. The steam from the engine bells blew away on the wind. Colm inhaled the salty sea breeze as he dragged Dhjerga down the steps.

"Help!" he yelled in the direction of the Free Church Manse. A stern gray two-storey house, it stood on a rise amidst a windbreak of neglected pines. The smaller building beside it, with a peaked roof, was a disused Lutheran church. Maybe no one was awake yet.

But as he hauled Dhjerga across the field, Meg came to meet them, combi in hand. "Who the fuck's that?"

"Friend of mine from Kisperet."

"What's wrong with him?"

"Death curse, apparently."

"Okayyy."

Colm rolled his eyes.

Meg slung her combi and took Dhjerga's legs.

They carried Dhjerga along the footpath through the pines, to the scraggly back garden where Bridget had started planting potatoes. The back door was open. Lloyd stood in the doorway with his arms folded.

"Out of the way," Colm panted.

He had one foot across the doorstep when Dhjerga began to spasm. He made gargling noises in his throat and kicked his legs, forcing Colm and Meg to drop him. Meg leapt back.

"Ah," Lloyd said. "That's Grandpa Mackenzie's wards." He pointed at Dhjerga in a dramatic biblical pose. "He's got the taint of evil on him."

"He's sick!" Colm shouted. "He needs to lie down."

Behind Lloyd in the kitchen, Daisy picked little Nicky up. "No, sweetheart, you cannae go out. Not yet." All the Mackenzies and Wilsons had caught Lloyd's paranoia. Nicky had to stay in the house at all times unless it was broad day and several adults were with him.

"And *he* can't come in the house," Lloyd said. "Take him in the church. That's not warded. I suppose my granddad thought the Lord would protect it, but it's been deconsecrated for years."

Dhjerga was moaning and thrashing. Not knowing what else to do, Colm dragged him away from the house. Immediately he quieted down.

Wards? The taint of evil? Really?

Axel came out of the house and helped Colm carry Dhjerga into the church. They made him a bed by pushing two pews together face to face and laying sleeping bags on them. The sleeping bags were a fruit of Colm's previous foraging missions with the *Shihoka,* as was the gas heater that

Axel turned on and placed near Dhjerga. *"What* did you say was wrong with him?"

"Search me," Colm said. "Hope that heater's safe."

"No electricity. It's safe unless he knocks it over."

Dhjerga was no longer moving at all. He had sunk back into a deep coma.

"I'll stay with him," said Sunita Wilson, entering the church. "You go on and have a sitdown. Colm. You look done in."

"Thanks, Sunita."

Axel said, "I'll go move the ship."

"I don't think it matters anymore. Gaethla was the last of the Magistrates, and he's dead."

"I have no clue what you're talking about, so I'll move it anyway."

Colm didn't have the strength to argue. He went inside, sank into a chair and gratefully accepted a mug of instant coffee from his mother. Meg stood by the door, watching Axel walk towards the *Shihoka*.

"Hey, Meg," Colm said, suddenly remembering. He reached into his pocket. "I found this for you."

He held out the framed photograph. It showed Meg, aged eight or nine, with her parents.

Meg's face crumpled as she stared at it. *"Fuck* you, Collie Mack," she breathed.

"I thought you'd like it ..." Colm had wanted to make it up to Meg, even though he still didn't know what he had done.

"That's my mom and dad."

"I know, I—"

"It doesn't help, OK? We need *food,* not family pictures! We need meds, tools—"

"I got meds—"

"I just bet you did."

"What did I do, Meg? Please just tell me. Why are you so pissed at me?"

"I can't believe you need to ask!"

"Well, I did bring food," Colm muttered. He kicked his duffel, which someone had brought in from the ship.

Meg fell on her knees and opened it. "Oh my God," she said, lifting out a box of Pocky. Her voice wobbled. "I used to love this stuff."

Suddenly they heard shouting in the garden. Everyone jumped up. Meg was first out of the door with Colm close behind her.

Dhjerga struggled up the garden path on his hands and knees. Sunita was trying to hold him back. "Must tell him," he gasped.

"Dhjerga, for fuck's sake go back to bed," Colm howled.

"I didn't come to dead that fucker. That was just—luck."

"Some luck."

"Came—to warn you." Dhjerga's eyes were glazed. Colm squatted down in front of him, afraid to miss a word. "Hope—not too late …"

CHAPTER 39

Extinction protocol.

Target: Earth.

It was too much to take in at first. They all sat around the kitchen table, exchanging futile expressions of incredulity. Colm thought about how stupid it was, how he'd assumed he had got away from the war. All his repressed guilt about deserting from the Fleet came back. He had left everyone in the Betelgeuse system to fend for themselves, and now Earth was in the sentrienza's crosshairs.

He had forgotten what it was like to fight a foe that had *spaceships*.

Dhjerga had collapsed again as soon as he delivered his news. They'd put him back to bed in the church. Colm looked around at his family and friends and saw that they were all hoping it was a mistake or a misunderstanding.

Best to clear that up. He got on his computer. He knew there were a bunch of military satellites still in orbit, as they would automatically ping the *Shihoka* when he went sub-orbital. "Axel, do you still have Fleet clearance?"

"As far as I know."

"Can you talk to these sats? I want to see their observation data. Everything in the outer system."

Axel took over. "I'm in," he said, and a few moments later: "Data dump on its way … This is gonna take a while to crunch."

Outside the kitchen windows, across the back field, some of the locals ringed the *Shihoka* with their guns pointed towards the ship. Little did they know that they no longer needed to worry about Ghosts. They needed to worry about dying in a hail of fire.

Nicky toddled around the table, offering Pocky to everyone, as if he hoped that might cheer them up.

Daisy boiled water on the gas stove and made more coffee. Colm thought: I can do this.

Dhjerga had told them what he did at Betelgeuse. He had a strange way of describing it—the *tekne* of space travel—but Colm knew what he'd meant. It was normally impossible to flit to moving objects, such as spaceships. But Colm had visited the *Unsinkable* and the *Shihoka* while they were moving ... *in the zero-gravity field.*

True, he hadn't really flitted to either ship.

He wasn't the mage Dhjerga was.

But now, he'd *have* to equal Dhjerga's feat.

He played with his coffee mug, hovering his left hand above it and levitating it a few millimeters into the air.

"Done," Axel said abruptly. "Here are the observations." Colm let his cup go, startled. It spilled. No one noticed. They were all crowding around the computer.

"Oh, this is bullshit," Meg said after a moment.

Axel's finger rested on a loose constellation of ship icons outside Jupiter's orbit, on the other side of the solar system from the gas giant. They'd come in at an angle to the ecliptic, minimizing their in-system travel time. "Those are sentrienza ships. They're *big,* like the ones that Dhjerga said attacked Betelgeuse."

"We need to wake him up," Meg said. "Get him to stop them." She moved towards the door.

"No," Colm said. "Won't work. They'd have to be in the zero-gravity field, and they aren't. They're already here."

A pall of despair settled over the kitchen. Axel remotely commanded the satellites to track the sentrienza ships as they burnt inward towards Earth. They must have exited the zero-gravity field just a day or two ago. "It looks as if they planned their attacks on Betelgeuse and Earth to come off at the same time," Colm muttered.

"They'd have wanted to be sure of getting us all," Axel said. "What about the colony planets?"

"They're probably going to hit them, too." Colm was trying to levitate his mug again, and failing. His concentration was shot. The little icons on the screen had a hypnotic effect. Faerie lights. Each one of them armed with microscopic black holes, which would eat Earth from the inside out, crumpling the planet's crust, loosing stupendous flows of magma, boiling off the seas ... Think, Mackenzie, *think*.

He looked around for Meg's duffel. There it was, by the cat's water dish. He pawed through it for the tropo bottle. He popped two tabs, washing them down with water from the jerrycan on the kitchen counter. After his weeks of sobriety, the rush hit fast and hard.

The fog of despair that had filled his mind cleared away, leaving the answer shining out like a star.

"The *Shihoka!*" he shouted.

"What about it?" Axel said.

Colm didn't have time to explain. "Ghost magic plus human technology. This'll work. I know it." Then he slumped. "No, it won't."

"What? Why?"

"Haven't got any nukes."

"Yes, we have," Axel said.

"Huh? No, we haven't."

Axel looked slightly embarrassed. "Before we left Betelgeuse, your friend Gil sent us a care package. An unmanned supply capsule. It was packed with life support essentials ... and some extra rounds for the railgun. Including a couple of nuclear rounds."

Colm gaped in astonishment. "And they're still on board? I've been flying around the world with nukes in the boot, without knowing it?"

Axel eked out a smile. "I didn't tell you in case you went and used them or something."

*

"No," Daisy said. "You are *not* going to fight the entire sentrienza navy singlehanded without having breakfast. They're two weeks away. It won't make any difference if you sit down and have a bowl of porridge. And you may as well have a nap, too."

Colm's heart filled with love for his mother. He bowed to the inevitable. Exhausted by his adventures in Tokyo, he slept longer than he planned; it was getting on for evening when he woke. He gobbled a quick meal, followed by a couple of tabs of tropo. Then he asked his father to give him a bit of coaching. Lloyd silently showed him how to do the levitation thing properly—Colm had been holding his fingers wrong.

When he had it down, he crossed the back field to the *Shihoka*, carrying an empty mug. It had a picture of the Loch Ness Monster on the side with the legend NESSIE LIVES.

Axel was standing by the steps. He'd been checking the ship over while Colm slept. "I'll go with you," he said.

"You can't." Colm had explained what he was going to do. "Do what you did before. Copy me."

Colm studied his friend, taking in the lines around his

275

mouth, the gray hairs at Axel's temples. Were those normal signs of age? Or was Colm using him up? "No, Axel. I'm through with that. It's black magic. I'm doing no more of it." He tried for a jokey tone. "My dad won't let me in the house again if I keep on acting like a Ghost."

"Our lives are at stake!"

Colm shook his head. He didn't know how to thank Axel for his offer, so he just said, "I'm going by myself. I don't think it'd work with anyone else on board." This was an excuse. If he failed, he wanted to die alone, rather than watch his family and friends die later.

He suited up and settled into the *Shihoka's* cockpit. Esthesia poured rich sensory feedback into his nervous system as he ran through the preflight checks. And wasn't it also true that he *had* company? Him and the ship. A perfect duo, joined at the mind. This was all he needed.

Up he went. Launch gees pinned him in his couch, while friction heat rasped at his hull, and the pressure of the atmosphere gradually lessened, until he leapt free. Relishing the liberty of freefall, Colm waggled his wings for sheer pleasure, and then cut the main drive. Vacuum prickled his skin. He stretched his sensors into the void, all his telescopic and radar and infrared eyes on stalks, searching for the enemy.

*

Back on the ground, Axel unclamped his hands from Nicky's ears. The *Shihoka's* contrail of water vapor faded into the sky. Everyone had retreated a safe distance down the track to watch the launch. Now they aimlessly drifted apart. The elder folks returned to the house to see if the vibrations from the launch had broken any windows.

Bridget said, "Shall we take the kids down to the beach?"

Axel and Meg looked at each other and shrugged. The weather was fine, for a change, and this seemed as good a way as any to spend what might be their last afternoon on Earth.

Although the water was far too cold, in Axel's opinion, to go swimming, the Wilson kids took off their shoes and waded. Nicky kept toddling towards the waves, eager to join them. Axel pulled him back over and over, thinking of Colm, somewhere out there, hunting sentrienza ships, and being hunted by them. *Why didn't he take me? He took my ship, but not me. That's* two *ships he's taken off me without even asking.*

Meg stalked up and down, stepping from stone to stone, with her combi slung on her back. This was her way of coping, being constantly on the watch for danger. She said to Axel, "Do you think this would be happening if we'd let Emnl have Nicky?"

"You aren't saying we should have—"

"God, your expression. *No,* I'm not saying we should hand him over, or that we should have handed him over. I just wonder if that has anything to do with it."

"It can't have," Axel said after a moment's thought. "These orders must've come from the Gray Emperor. Elphame's supposed to be 20,000 light years away, after all. Even the fastest sentrienza drone couldn't do that in less than four Earth years. So we've been under a death sentence all that time. They must have initiated the extinction protocol as soon as they found out about CHEMICAL MAGE."

"Your goddamn dad," Meg said. "And the Rat." Pause. "My dad, too."

"They were trying to save Earth."

Further down the beach, the Wilsons were skipping stones.

Bridget was winning by a mile. Fifteen skips, twenty, thirty, her stones flew like little spaceships.

Meg followed Axel's gaze. "She's one, too, isn't she? Bridget."

"It's genetic," Axel said. He picked Nicky up and lifted him into the air. "We're just normal human beings, huh, buddy? Nothing wrong with that."

But *was* he a normal human being, with his implant stabilizing his moods, smoothing out his emotional reactions?

On an impulse, he disabled it. If this was to be their last day on Earth, he wanted to experience it without a technological barrier in the way, just as himself.

CHAPTER 40

Scudding around Earth, Colm identified his targets and ranked them in order of priority. There were twenty-one ships on their way in from the zero-gravity point. Three heavy cruisers the size of the *Ruddiganmaseve,* and the rest were even bigger. They hadn't reached the asteroid belt yet.

But they were coming fast, making no attempt to be stealthy. Of course, the sentrienza thought the Fleet had abandoned the system.

They didn't know Earth had one ship left. Just one.

And even if they could see the *Shihoka* in its low orbit around Earth, they'd never think it could hurt them. That little thing?

To be honest, Colm wasn't sure this *was* going to work. But there was no point dithering. He loaded the railgun, using esthesia to place the first nuke in the launch cradle with the robot arm. He armed the launch circuits.

He magnified his composite view of Target #1 as much as possible, until the image of its plume broke down into pixels.

Then he stuck his Nessie souvenir coffee mug between his knees, extended his left hand, and levitated it.

In freefall, it was *easy.*

The mug flew in a circle around the cockpit, like Gaethla Moro's bullet had flown around that nightclub in Tokyo, Nessie winking from its side.

And Colm flitted.

Hot plasma washed over the *Shihoka's* hull. Colm screamed in pain as esthesia reported damage to his forward heat shields.

Jesus God, I've flitted right into the end of their fucking drive plume!

Not the middle of it, or I wouldn't be feeling anything.

Fuck fuck fuck that fucking hurts!

The pain short-circuited any temptation to hang about and line up his sights just right. He mashed his right forefinger on the firing button, sent the Nessie mug on another flight around the cockpit, and flitted again, this time to a 'safe' power source he'd identified in advance, a fab complex on the large asteroid Vesta. Like all of humanity's outer-system outposts, Vesta had been taken over by Ghosts who had then starved to death or died because they could not work the life support systems. So the fab complex was a coffin, but its solar arrays were still working, feeding power to its giant storage batteries. The *Shihoka* landed right outside the plant, so close that the ship's nose smashed through the end of a long wall of solar panels. This ship-flitting was a dicey business. Colm multi-tasked for dear life, muting the feedback from the scorched heat shields, assessing the damage, and—finally—reviewing the last few minutes of footage picked up by his external cameras.

There it was, 3 seconds in.

"Boom," Colm whispered, smirking triumphantly at the flash on the screen. "Got him right up the arse."

His nuke had not just disabled the sentrienza cruiser, it had *vaporized* it.

"And then there were twenty."

He had travelled to Vesta faster than the light from the explosion. Almost 3 seconds faster. The implications sank in. This was even bigger than refueling a chemical rocket from a gas giant. It would completely revolutionize spaceflight.

If he survived the day.

The other sentrienza crews must be freaking out. He had no time to waste.

"Let's try *not* to land in the drive plume this time," he murmured to the *Shihoka*. "I don't tan well ..."

Boom.

Boom.

Boom.

Now he had only one nuke left, against 17 sentrienza ships. Time to resupply. He jumped out of his couch, retrieved the last missile from the ammo bay with the mechanical loader arm, and deposited it in the cargo hold. He sealed his helmet and dived through the airlock into the brightly lit vacuum. Every second counted. Maybe he should've brought someone else along, after all. He wrapped his arms and legs around the fat cylinder and replicated it. He had seen Diejen and other mages doing this during the war. It was just fetching without going anywhere. *One. Two. Three. Four* ... The lights flickered, the fans choked, and the cargo hold filled up with nukes. Colm scrambled around, using his own arms in concert with the robotic cargo handler arms to secure the missiles so at least they didn't bump into each other. The Rat would have had his head on a stick for this. Colm had once been severely punished for nuking a train full of Ghosts. What would his old commanding officer think if he saw him nuking a whole fleet of sentrienza ships?

They hailed him after number 18. He picked up their signal at Vesta, where he was resting for a minute, gulping canned miso soup while he loaded his last nuke but three into the launch cradle.

"Unidentified human ship on Vesta." That's where they

thought he was. "Are you aware that you cannot destroy a black hole?"

"Whoa! No shit," Colm said, rolling his eyes.

"Eighteen of our ships have now been destroyed. Each of them was armed with a black hole cannon. In all cases, the containment of the black holes was breached. Thus, eighteen small but deadly black holes are now wandering freely through your solar system."

Colm held up a finger. "Wait," he said, and finished his soup. Tossing the can into freefall, he said, *"Wandering?* Nice try. In fact, all those black holes are on trajectories which will miss Earth by a comfortable margin, and travel out of the solar system without hitting anything." He was just guessing, but space was big and all the bodies in Sol System were small, relatively speaking. Anyway, it wasn't half as risky as *not* destroying the sentrienza ships would have been. "That's what you get for being clever and coming in at a 30-degree angle to the ecliptic. I've got to go now. Cheers."

Boom.

Boom.

Boom.

Colm radioed the last surviving sentrienza ship, just to see what they'd say. "Any last words?" he enquired.

"Spare us," buzzed a sentrienza voice. "Please. There must be something you want."

Colm laughed. He was floating in the cockpit, feeling a bit loopy. "I've got everything I want." For a fleeting second, he thought of Diejen. *No.* "Oh, there is one thing I want, actually."

"What?"

"To see you join your buddies in hell." He loaded the last

nuke. He would be happy to get rid of it. A copy of a copy of a kiloton-yield bomb was not a good travelling companion.

"Wait! Wait! We can offer you the gift of eternal life!"

"Ha, ha; not interested."

"Your planet is already doomed! We launched our missiles after you destroyed our flagship. They are speeding towards Earth as we speak."

"Oh yeah?"

"But *you* need not die! We'll take you to Elphame. The Emperor himself will give you the gift of eternal life—"

Boom.

Returning to Vesta one last time, storing video of the last explosion, Colm remembered that the sentrienza did not lie. The lethal missiles were already on their way to Earth.

Shit.

CHAPTER 41

Back on the beach in Scotland, five-year-old Scarlett Wilson slipped and fell over in the little waves. Drenched to the skin, she started to howl. Ted picked her up. "Oh God. We'd better head back," Bridget said. "Kids! Morag! Ivor!"

Far down the beach, the two older children were playing an elaborate game with stones and seaweed. Meg said to Bridget, "It's OK. You guys head back. We'll watch them."

"Are you sure, hen?" Bridget said, but she was already following Ted up the track. Little Scarlett was always catching colds, and in a world without hospitals, her parents fretted about her delicate health.

Meg shaded her eyes, watching Morag and Ivor. "When I was their age," she said wryly, "I was usually glued to a screen."

"Me too," Axel said.

"If Colm fails—if the black holes hit the planet—do you think we'd notice?"

"If the missiles entered the atmosphere near here, we'd probably see them. Like meteors."

"But if they hit on the other side of Earth, we wouldn't even know it." Meg shivered. The sentrienza doomsday weapons might be devouring Earth already. She did not have confidence that Colm's crazy plan would work.

Unnoticed, Nicky toddled towards the overturned dinghy that lay on the beach.

Axel grasped Meg's shoulders and rested his forehead against hers. "You'll survive," he said quietly. "Colm'll bring the *Shihoka* back, whether he pulls this off or not."

"So we should just take off and leave everyone?" She

recoiled, outraged at the idea of leaving the Mackenzies and Wilsons, who'd been so kind to them.

"Not everyone. Just me."

"Axel!"

"Colm won't leave his family behind. But I'll make damn sure he doesn't leave you and Nicky."

"It's *your* ship!"

"It's OK, Meg. I know you love him."

She shook Axel's hands off, shocked. "He doesn't give a damn about Nicky." Her shock was profound and internal. It came from the realization that she really, truly did not love Colm anymore. Perhaps she'd stopped loving him on the day Bridget dragged him in from the beach on Isle Martin, a drugged-up, half-drowned mess. She'd been furious with him, but only now did she understand why: her anger had been the death throes of her long, stupid crush on Collie Mack. Now she knew that he would never be what she wanted him to be, because what she wanted him to be was … *Axel.*

*

Nicky, still unsteady on his feet, toppled forwards and caught himself on the side of the overturned wooden dinghy. Sun-bleached barnacles pricked his fingers. He made a face, but did not cry. Instead, he staggered around the dinghy, exploring.

The gunwales of the dinghy were buried in the shale. He could not get inside it. But around the other side of the keel, there was a ragged hole in the boat. The lower edge of the hole came up to Nicky's waist.

The faint smell of rotted seaweed wafted out of the hole. It was impenetrably dark in there, in contrast to the sunlit beach. But down there in the darkness, something gleamed blue.

Entranced, Nicky reached into the hole.

Far away at the other end of the beach, Morag and Ivor continued their game of castles.

Much nearer, but on the other side of the dinghy, Meg and Axel stared at each other, emotions running high.

*

"If you leave me," Meg threatened, "I'll shoot you." She gripped her combi's stock, swinging it around between them like a metal barrier.

"I'm letting you go!" Axel said. "Isn't that what you want?"

"No! I want to be with you!"

"Why? I'm a failure. I've failed at everything, up to and including saving Earth."

Meg suddenly recognized the darkness in his eyes, the pinched inward set of his face, and the tone of merciless self-examination in his voice. She had not seen this Axel for years. Had thought he'd gone away forever. "Oh, dammit, Axel. You've disabled your implant again, haven't you?"

"Yeah. If this is it, if it's all ending, I want you to know the truth about me. You deserve to know who I really am."

"I already know who you really are! Jesus! I should shoot you for being so fucking *stupid!*"

Axel hesitated. "Am I being stupid?"

Meg lifted the strap of her combi off over her head. Her fingers automatically safed the gun as she laid it down in a hurry.

"Yes," she said.

"Oh."

"But so am I," she said. "I have been. Really, really stupid."

He looked at her bleakly. "When you met me, I was

286

working for Dad's corporation. I had fuck-you money. I guess I seemed pretty slick. You didn't know you were actually getting a screw-up with a defective brain. That's not stupid. That's just unlucky."

"Nope," Meg said. "When I *first* met you, you were flying a gunship into a hot zone to rescue people you'd never met. *That's* the guy I fell in love with." Dammit, she was choking up. "And that's who I see in front of me right now."

"I don't deserve you."

"You know what they say, Axel, when you're in a hole …?"

She wrapped her arms around him, rising on tiptoe to kiss his mouth. He froze for a second, then opened up to her. The world shrank to their embrace. Warts and all, this was the man who loved her, who she loved. She faced it. Accepted it. So this was what it felt like, not being detached from her own emotions. Pretty damn good.

Suddenly, Axel stiffened.

"Nicky," he said. He wrenched away from her.

*

Nicky reached into the hole in the dinghy, trying to grab that fascinating blue gleam.

It blinked at him. There; gone. Blink. There again.

Peek-a-boo.

Nicky giggled, and reached further into the hole.

The stones next to his tiny sneakers shifted with a quiet clatter.

The toe of an enormous, salt-scalloped boot squeezed out from underneath the boat.

*

"Nicky!" Meg screamed, sprinting after Axel. How could she have let him wander off? Where was he?

Axel rounded the old dinghy that lay on the beach. "Nicky!" he exclaimed in relief. "There—"

There was a crunching sound. Axel threw himself headlong at the far side of the dinghy.

Meg crashed into him, just as Nicky's legs and feet vanished into the hole in the side of the boat.

She thrust her arms into the hole, while Axel tried to lift the boat. They lost a few seconds like that, working against each other, screaming at each other, and then Meg added her strength to Axel's. They dug their fingers into the rotting gunwales and heaved the boat onto its side.

A hollow in the shale held a mat of kelp and bladderwrack, which swirled in blackness like water, shrinking, vanishing. Meg saw her son's face in the seaweed, his eyes huge, his mouth stretched into a soundless wail. She fell on her knees, reaching for him. Her hands touched icy cold … nothing.

She clawed at the stones, screaming.

Nicky was gone.

CHAPTER 42

Colm tracked down all the missiles heading for Earth. They each had a power source, of course. It took a lot of energy to contain a black hole. They seemed to show up great on his infrared scans, and only after the first dozen or so did he realize that actually they didn't. They were not radiating heat, after all. He was 'seeing' them on the screen the way the Ghosts 'saw' power sources without screens, because esthesia made the *Shihoka* into an extension of his body.

Oh, well; whatever works.

He took the *Shihoka* alongside each of them in turn. He was out of nukes, and the nukes had been so heavy he could not bring any conventional rounds, so he just EMPed each one with the charged particle cannon.

They were still in the asteroid belt, 3 AUs from Earth. At this distance, hitting a target the size of a planet required flawless trajectory control. With their electronics fried, the missiles would not be able to point themselves at Earth. They'd fly harmlessly out of the system.

After number 50, he fell asleep in the cockpit. Woke, panicked, looked at the time, calmed himself down, drank canned coffee from a Tokyo vending machine, and went back to work.

After number 113, he ran another infrared scan and found … nothing. That was it. He'd sorted all of them.

Time to go home.

He flitted the *Shihoka* to Aldrin Station in LEO. The Fleet had left the lights on, and water in the storage tanks. He used that to top up the *Shihoka's* reaction mass tanks. He also on-loaded 50 freezedried kgs of Pink Slime, the long-haul emergency foodstuff, just because it was there. Then he spent a few hours exploring the station. He had passed through here on multiple occasions during his Fleet deployments. Now the concessions were stripped bare, the holos gone, the halls empty of the cheerful clamor he remembered. The air smelled stale and the artificial gravity was off. Rubbish floated in mid-air. On the walls, posters still displayed Human Republic flags and slogans. Colm drifted around aimlessly, thinking about the dead.

So many dead.

Catching himself getting morose, he snapped himself out of it. Time to go home.

He returned to the *Shihoka,* undocked from the refueling stand, and pulsed the attitude thrusters to separate the ship from the dead space station. Then he flipped the ship like an Olympic diver coming off the board, and plunged down towards Earth.

*

"Well, that's that."

Colm took off his helmet, and coughed. The vapors from his landing mixed with misty rain. Only one person had come out to meet him: his mother. Daisy Mackenzie stood bareheaded in the rain, her face drawn.

"What's wrong, Mam? You look like a wet weekend." Colm laughed uneasily. "It *is* a wet weekend …"

"Did you win?"

"Yes! Earth's safe!" Colm grinned. "I tried to radio you, but the Ka-band wasn't on, I suppose. Is it broken again?"

"No, it's not broken."

Colm hadn't expected a tickertape parade, but a smile

wouldn't have been out of place. "Well, we'd better get in out of the rain."

He started towards the house. His mother walked alongside him. The compressed shape of her mouth struck fear into Colm's heart. She looked the way she used to when Lloyd was being a bastard, but worse than that. She looked the way she had when Lloyd murdered Sprite, the family cat.

"Mam, what *is* it?"

Daisy stopped under the pines. "Colm, is there something you haven't told us?"

"Is it something I did?"

"Apparently so," his mother said meaningfully.

"Apart from saving Earth?"

At last she smiled. "Aye, you did that, didn't you? I'm so proud of you."

"All in a day's work."

"No need to be modest." She stretched up and kissed him on the cheek. But her smile vanished as quickly as it had come. "I'd better tell you before we go in. Nicky's missing."

"*What?* Nicky? How did that happen?"

"They took him down the beach and I suppose they took their eyes off him for a moment."

"I thought he wasn't allowed to set foot outside."

Daisy shrugged. "He's their child, not mine. Or so I thought."

"I don't understand."

"I don't, either." Daisy searched his face. Then she sighed. "All right, you don't want to talk about it. I respect your privacy, Colm. I always have. But I'm warning you, your father's going to bring it up. And I don't want you walking out on us, like you always do."

"'Like I always do'?" Colm objected, weakly. He *had* walked out on them, hadn't he? He'd run away to space. But he was back now. "What's Dad going to bring up?"

His mother didn't answer. She crossed the back garden, treading heedlessly on the lumpy rows where they had planted potatoes.

Colm followed her into the house.

Meg sat at one end of the kitchen table, sagging over an untouched mug of instant coffee. Everyone else stood around awkwardly, except for Lloyd, who sat in his usual place by the hearth with Mickle on his lap, seemingly asleep. That was odd enough but Colm scarcely registered it. The atmosphere of dread and sadness overwhelmed him. Meg glanced up at him, and looked away again. She seemed … frightened. Meg? *Nothing* scared her …

… but the loss of a child. Yeah, that'd do it.

Colm crossed to her and hugged her shoulders. "I've heard what happened, Meg." It was like hugging a rock. "I'm so sorry." He mutely asked the others with his eyes: What *did* happen? How do you lose track of an almost-two-year-old on the beach? Jesus, he didn't *drown*, did he? That wasn't what Daisy had seemed to be saying. *He's missing …*

Axel spoke. Leaning against the wall with his arms folded, he looked ten years older. "The Magus took him."

"Ah, no," Colm said.

"He was under that old boat," Lloyd said, speaking with his eyes closed, his jowls resting on his chest. "These two idiots didn't notice. Weren't paying attention. To their own child."

Axel's jaw clenched. Meg started to cry silently into her coffee. Colm wanted to hit his father for gratuitously hurting her, on top of what she was already going through.

But then Lloyd went on: "Except he *wasn't* their own child, was he?"

Daisy gripped a chair-back and rolled her eyes to heaven. "Will you shut your trap?"

"I'll not," Lloyd blustered, opening his eyes. "It needs to be said, and if a certain woman—" he jerked his chin at Meg— "had seen fit to tell the truth much earlier, this would never have happened. Aye, greet your eyes out. This is your doing more than anyone's."

Colm exclaimed, "Fuck's sake, Dad, leave her alone!"

Lloyd stared at him with a crafty gleam in his eyes. "Maybe *you* should have left her alone."

Oh, *no,* Colm thought. Oh, no.

Axel said, "Meg? What's he talking about?"

Meg shook her head. Her elbows were on the table, her fingers driven through her hair, the heels of her hands over her ears, as if she could shut them all out.

"She still doesn't want to tell you," Lloyd said. "So I will. I'm very sorry to be the bearer of bad news, Axel, but Nicky is not your child. I'm guessing he's Colm's."

Colm stood frozen. His single night with Meg, on the *Unsinkable,* repeated on him in tones of the starkest horror. That had been two and a half years ago, a bit more. Oh God, the timing fit. "Did you *know,* Meg?" he asked.

She nodded.

"Why didn't you *say?*"

He was moving towards her when a brick wall collided with the side of his face. He staggered and fell, catching himself on the table, knocking cups and plates to the floor. Axel had punched him with all the force of a Marine's fist. He grabbed Colm's shoulder with his left hand and swung him upright, hauling off to punch him again.

Ted grappled Axel from behind, trying to pin his arms.

Colm let his hands fall to his sides, offering his aching face. "Go on, Axel. Hit me again. I deserve it."

Instead of taking the invitation, Axel let out a raw howl. He shook Ted off and stalked out of the house. The back door slammed behind him, rattling the windows. Meg started up as if to follow him but then sank back.

Bridget broke the silence. "I'm not apologizing for my louse of a brother, but Dad, are you sure you're right? Nicky doesn't look like us at all."

"Of course I'm sure," Lloyd said. "I guessed it the moment the Magus first came sniffing around the child. He'd not have been interested in him if Nicky didn't have magic in his blood. The last son born of the last druid family on Earth. As to his looks, he's got a Japanese grandmother, has he not?"

Meg said in a dead voice, "It's true. I had a DNA analysis done when I got pregnant. He's not Axel's. And I haven't been with anyone else except ..." She threw a glance at Colm. It held no love, nor hate. Just emptiness.

Colm crammed his hands into his eyes as the truth hit him over the head like Axel's fist. He had visited the *Unsinkable,* and the *Shihoka.* He *hadn't* replicated Dhjerga's amazing feat of finding ships in the zero-gravity field. He'd just ... had a fix on Nicky. A mage whom he had met, so to speak, even before he was born. Because he was *his child.*

"It's blindingly obvious," Lloyd said. The old bastard was enjoying this. "The Magus took him. He didn't fetch away a copy of him and leave the child here. He *took* him. And you can't do that with normal people, can you?"

"Nope. You can't," Colm said.

"He could not have done that unless the child was a mage." Lloyd leaned forward, grasping the cat around the middle, addressing Meg. "What I'm puzzled about is your side. Is there magic in your family? On the Japanese side, maybe?"

"I can break concrete with my bare hands," Meg said, in the same quiet, dead voice. "And I bet I could break your neck, too, Mr. Mackenzie. And I will, if you don't fucking *SHUT UP!!*"

Lloyd sat back, blowing out an exaggerated breath. "All righty then."

Colm pulled himself together. It felt like jamming together the pieces of a broken machine. He would never be the same again. "Never mind all this shite. We've got to get Nicky back, obviously. Where's the Magus taken him? Oh, it doesn't matter, I'll find out." He picked up his helmet.

"Hold on there," his father said, dumping the cat off his lap. "I'm coming."

CHAPTER 43

Colm stared at his father. Lloyd was seventy-two, skinny as a wraith, and he'd been an alcoholic most of his life. "Dad, I hate to break it to you, but you're going to be fuck-all use in a fight."

"It depends what kind of fight," Lloyd said. He put his coat on. It was an old thing left over from his days performing as The Marvellous Mr. Mackenzie, a black duster with loads of hidden pockets.

Daisy sneered, "What are you gonnae do, Lloyd, juggle at the Magus?"

"Maybe I'll turn him into a frog."

Colm threw up his hands and went out to prep the *Shihoka*. While he was doing that, Meg came and talked to him. She talked for quite a long time, and by the end of it, Colm knew exactly what an oblivious, overbearing, selfish, unreliable asshole he'd been. All he could say was, "What did you ever see in me then?"

Meg snorted. "Something better than what was really there."

"I'm sorry."

"'I'm sorry, I'm sorry.' Are you even listening to me?"

Colm had been running systems checks while she was talking. But he'd been listening, oh yes, he had. He looked around and saw her standing in the middle of the cockpit, fists clenched at her sides. Her old Fleet duffel lay at her feet. It was the one he'd been using on his foraging expeditions. He suddenly remembered the day they'd both been discharged from the Fleet, when she had turned up at that Hawaiian-themed bar on Gna with the same duffel over her shoulder. That was the night he'd met Zhanna. He'd have sold his soul to be able to go back in time and change his own behaviour—change himself—see what was in front of his eyes. If that night had gone differently, Zhanna would still be alive, and Colm and Meg might be living with Nicky and his theoretical siblings in a cozy little house on ... well ... a planet long since conquered by the Ghosts. So, no. Scratch that. All the same, he yearned for what might have been.

To say what he was thinking would only lead to more futile rehashing of the past, and Nicky was missing. So he said, "What's in the bag?"

"My stuff, of course. I'm coming with you."

"Ah, Meg ..."

"I've got magic in my blood, apparently. What the fuck ever. But I don't know how to do the flitting thing. So you have to take me."

"And get you killed, as well?" It popped out. Meg's face contorted with grief and rage.

"He is my fucking child!"

"Where's Axel?"

"No idea. Ted said he took the boat."

"That doesn't sound good."

"He'll be all right," Meg said bitterly. "I wish he hadn't disabled his implant, but—"

"He disabled it again?" Colm groaned. He had too many memories of Axel doing self-destructive shit. He got up from his couch, careful not to go too close to her. "Meg ... I've no right to ask you for anything. I'm an unreliable, selfish, oblivious asshole, as we've established ..."

"And a user. Did I mention that? Look at the way you used Axel to fight your war."

"That's why I'm asking. Please go after him. Make sure he's OK."

"He can look after himself."

"Maybe, but the others can't. My mum, Bridget and Ted, the kids. Can I ask you to look after them while I'm away? Please, please?"

A heavy tread sounded in the companionway. "I hope and trust we're not taking Missy Fibs-A-Lot," Lloyd said.

Meg reddened. "I see where you get your charisma," she spat at Colm. Quailing from Lloyd, she picked up her duffel and left without another word.

Colm shouted after her, "I won't come back without him. I swear it on my life!"

"Don't make promises you can't keep," Lloyd said. With his camera eyes, Colm watched Meg go down the airlock steps and trudge back towards the house. If cameras had tear ducts, the image of her small, hunched back would have been blurry.

"Goodbye, Gunny," he whispered, and closed the airlock.

Lloyd was in the cabin. "Where should I put the cat?"

"You brought the bloody *cat?!*"

On the internal camera feed, Mickle scrambled out of Lloyd's satchel, evaded his hands, and climbed the webbing on the aft wall.

"Kitty!" Lloyd wheezed. "Kitty, kitty!"

Colm lost patience. He grabbed his Nessie mug, stormed back into the cabin, hauled Mickle down from the webbing, and shoved her at his father. Then, spinning the mug on a boomerang-like trajectory around the cabin, he flitted.

*

He had had Nicky's face in his mind, the living image of the child, dark blond curls matted with water, almond eyes red-rimmed. Nicky was sitting on sparkling white sand. His mouth wobbled woefully. In the background, waves bubbled up some unknown beach. But when the wrenching agony of the flit ceased, and Colm's body put itself back together, with the *Shihoka* around him like a second skin, he was not in that grove, wherever it was. He was floating in space, with vacuum prickling his hull.

Off to one side there was a star. Colm instinctively turned his back on it. He knew now what the Ghosts meant about being dazzled by stars. It was so bright it made it hard to see anything else at all. But he had a solution for that. He staggered forward to the cockpit and initiated a scan with the *Shihoka's* instruments. *They* would not be blinded by the electrical charge that built up in a star's corona.

Lloyd lurched into the cockpit. "Jesus, that was fucking awful. I need a fag."

"I'm actually surprised you're here at all," Colm said. He had half-expected to leave his father sitting on the dirt in the back field.

"You must have some fags," Lloyd said, poking into the lockers. "I can't believe you came back from Japan with twenty boxes of chocolate and no cigarettes ..."

"That's what I don't get, Dad. You're sober ..."

"Not by choice."

"And *you've* not got a next-generation esthesia chip in your head."

Lloyd smiled craftily. "No, but I've got something just as good. Here, Mickle, Mickle!"

Mickle padded into the cockpit. Colm wondered if it *was* Mickle, or a copy. No way to tell.

Lloyd scooped her up. "My familiar," he said.

At the sight of his father petting the cat, old emotions surged up. Anger spilled out, like pus from a wound that had been festering for thirty-plus years. "Are you going to murder her, like you murdered Sprite?"

Lloyd suddenly sounded old. "Murder's for people. You don't *murder* a cat …"

"Are you denying you killed her? I found her flipping body in a box! You had her stuffed, like a trophy!"

"You were so upset, I thought having her stuffed would make you feel better. But then your mother explained what a fucking terrible idea it would be to give it to you. I've been more fortunate than I deserve, being married to Daisy."

"That's the truth anyway," Colm said. He was white-knuckling the arms of his couch, blind to the screens in front of him. "But *why,* Dad? You loved Sprite, too! At least I thought you did."

"I did," Lloyd said heavily. "That's what made the sacrifice work."

"Huh?"

"Colm, your sister was very sick. I don't know if you recall. It was when you were eight."

"When Sprite died."

"Aye. Bridget caught multiply resistant tuberculosis. It was one of those things, she picked it up on a routine doctor's visit. After that I said no child of mine is going near a hospital again. But it was too late. They had no drugs they could give her. She was dying in front of our eyes. Your mother and myself were losing our minds, and I said all right. There may be one thing I can do. I heard about it from my father." He shrugged. "It worked."

Colm was silent for a minute. He hadn't known Bridget had

been *that* ill. There was so much you didn't pick up on as a child. "She got better."

"Yes."

"It was after that your career started going downhill."

"Yes."

"You'd lost your familiar."

"Yes."

"Did Gramps do ... animal sacrifice?"

"Yes. He was a black magician. Fortunately he was nae fucking good at it. He only managed to hurt and alienate everyone he knew. Your great-grandfather, the first Colm Mackenzie, who built the Free Church Manse, disowned him on account of it, which is why I hardly knew my own grandfather as a child."

These revelations rocked Colm. Not knowing what to say, he turned his attention to the screens. The results of the scan were coming in.

"I swore I'd never be like my father," Lloyd said. "No black magic for me. I only broke my rule that one time. Never again." His voice turned harsh. "All the same, I blame myself. I wanted to pass on the good to you and not the bad, but I suppose it's two sides of the same coin. So I taught you my tricks ... and you went away to space and came back sacrificing *human beings.*"

Colm turned in his couch. Lloyd's eyes were twin beams of searing judgement. Colm opened his mouth to deny it but then gave up. Of course Lloyd was right. Making copies, only to sacrifice them in battle? What else was that but human sacrifice? Kisperet had been drenched in black magic like a bandage drenched in blood. If it was all right, Colm's conscience would not so insistently have told him it was wrong from the very start. The amazing thing was that Dhjerga, reared to black magic, steeped in it, had known it was wrong, too.

"I've given that shit up now," he said. The composite imaging screen tugged at his attention. "Dad—"

"You'd better have," Lloyd said. "We can't defeat the Magus with black magic. It's no good playing these bastards at their own game. They always win."

"Dad, look at this."

They seemed to be in orbit around Atletis. An extremely elliptical orbit. The *Shihoka* was now approaching apogee, 50,000 kilometers out.

"What's that?" Lloyd said, pointing at the small, green-dappled moon.

"It's …" Colm trailed off. "Not Atletis," he muttered.

It looked the same, but there was no gas giant anywhere to be seen. The spectrum of the nearby star revealed it to be a dim red dwarf, not a G-type star like Kisperet's. This little sun was much *closer* than Kisperet's star. And most damningly, the 'moon's' equatorial and polar orbits were chock-a-block with spacecraft and orbitals.

"It's not a moon." He remembered the alien machinery he'd found in the caverns of the Magus's headquarters on Atletis. His suspicion that Atletis was an artificial body. "I think it's a … *heimdall.*"

"What's that when it's at home?"

Colm zoomed in on the captured images of spacecraft in orbit. They did not resemble human or queazel spaceships. They looked like dead twigs. Lengths of dry brambles, with complicated axial symmetries.

Looking inward towards the star, dozens more power

sources shone bright in the blackness. Looking outward, there were hundreds more power sources. *Thousands.* Yet he could see only a single, small, rocky planet in the system. It whipped around the dwarf star in a tight orbit that would take only seventy Earth days to complete.

"I think …" he said slowly. "I think this might be Elphame."

CHAPTER 44

The light woke Dhjerga up.

Just one of the stained glass windows in the old building remained intact. The others were broken, boarded over. The surviving window depicted a man holding a fish in one hand and a loaf of bread in the other. The man wore a plain gold crown that seemed to float above his head. Dhjerga had puzzled over this figure in his half-conscious moments. Now the afternoon sun shone straight through the man, onto Dhjerga's face, and he realized: Oh, of course, he's wearing a crown of *light*.

He lay motionless in the bed they had made for him, which was stiff, slithery quilts on two benches pushed together. The crack between the benches ran down the center of his spine. When they gave him water he imagined it running through the crack and dripping onto the floor. A dead mage could not drink.

He sensed he was being watched. At first he thought it must be the man in the window who was watching him, but then he decided that was silly. He propped himself up on his elbows.

An old woman sat on another bench, staring at him, chin in cupped hands.

"What do you want?" Dhjerga said.

"I want you to get up."

Dhjerga laughed. It surprised him that he was able to laugh. After all, he was dead. He lay down again.

She came and stood over him. She was haggard, her eyes bloodshot pits, her gray hair dragged back in a ponytail. A white plastic raincoat swathed her frail form. She said, "Get up, you lazy bastard."

"I'm dead," Dhjerga told her. "Gaethla Moro laid his death curse on me."

She grabbed his arm. She was uncommonly strong for a woman her age. She hoisted him stumbling over the ends of the benches. His knees crumpled under him, and he was like to fall on top of her, but another woman came up and caught his other arm. This one was younger with red hair. She said, "He's in a bad way."

"I'm in a bad way," Dhjerga echoed. "In a bad way." The death curse sat in his chest like a rusty nail, bleeding evil into his bloodstream.

"Cry me a freaking river," said the younger woman, and the old one said, "I've lost my husband, my son, and the grandson I did not know I had, all in one day. Now tell me how you're hurting."

The two women dragged him up to the front of the church. There was a table there, which had a thing on it, an X made of sticks standing on one of its long ends. It balanced there without being propped up. This annoyed Dhjerga. He swiped clumsily at it, knocking it over. The red-haired woman muttered under her breath and swept out a hand, making the thing sway back to the vertical again.

"Hold him," the old woman said.

There was another thing on the table: a bottle in the shape of a woman with a blue cloak. While the red-haired woman held Dhjerga upright, the old one uncapped the bottle. Fear suddenly took hold of him. He struggled. He was weak from days without food and almost water, but he was still a man and a soldier, and he gave the young woman enough difficulty that she shouted, "Sunita! Give us a hand!"

Another old woman, dark as soil, came in and helped her to hold him. Dhjerga thought fleetingly of his cousins on Kisperet: mages, healers, killers. He had learned early in life that one woman might be reasoned with but there was no use opposing a group of them. He gave up struggling. The dark woman said to the other old one, "Where did you get that?"

"I think it's been here for the last hundred years. It's from Lourdes." The old woman came up to Dhjerga and tipped the woman-bottle over his forehead, while with her other hand she made a strange gesture, side to side and up and down. Water trickled into his eyes and mouth.

It was a good thing they were holding his arms. The death curse reacted as if the water had been boiling oil. He roared and thrashed. He hit out wildly, forgetting that they were women, forgetting everything he knew. He had swallowed some drops of the water. He was coming back to life and it hurt like flitting, only a thousand times worse. It felt like life itself was killing him. He flung the women off him and plunged towards the door, desperate to get away. He was almost there when his legs suddenly vanished from under him and he went down face-first. His forehead hit the stone floor. He saw stars, and when he was able to open his eyes, he saw a pair of the funny puffy silver boots that came from the Fleet.

His gaze travelled up jeaned legs, over a camouflage jacket, to the pale face of Megumi Smythe.

"I guess I haven't forgotten *everything,*" she said with the ghost of a smile, dusting her hands together.

"That was brilliant," the red-haired woman said. "Remind me to never get on the wrong side of you."

Hitting his head on the floor had hurt so much that it drove out the other pain. Dizzy, Dhjerga sat up and felt his forehead. They stood around him in a half-circle, two old women and two young ones.

"How are you feeling?" said the pale old woman. She looked, Dhjerga thought, rather like his mother would have, if she'd had a chance to grow old.

He could have said: my head hurts like fuck, but instead he said: "Better." He tested his arms and legs. They moved normally. He was not dead anymore. He said in amazement, "What did you do?"

"Magic," the old woman said crisply. She glanced up at the single stained window. The sunlight had gone. And so had Gaethla Moro's death curse gone from Dhjerga's heart.

They took him inside the house. The wards no longer stabbed him like a wall of brambles, but welcomed him in. He sat in a steamy kitchen and ate two helpings of everything they gave him, and drank a gallon of coffee, telling them it was the best he'd ever tasted, even though it was just hot water with a trace of flavoring. The pale old woman turned out to be Colm's mother, the red-headed one was his sister, and the dark one was her mother-in-law.

Dhjerga's appetite failed as Bridget, the sister, told him everything that had happened. "So they've gone to look for the Magus," she concluded, "but I'm afraid they may've gone to the wrong place."

"The wrong place?" Horror and regret consumed him. While he had lain under Gaethla's curse, the entire war had flipped like a coin. The Magus would raise a new race of Ghosts from Colm's son, he thought, and it would never be over. Never.

Colm's mother turned to Meg, who sat on a hard chair with

her arms around her knees like a child. "Show him the picture."

Meg uncurled one arm and pushed a slim plastic rectangle across the table. Dhjerga looked at it. It showed a man, a woman, and a little girl on one of the Earth contrivances called *boats*.

"That's where we think the Magus is hiding," Meg said.

"I don't understand."

"That holo was taken thirty years ago. That's me and my mother and father, on a sightseeing boat on Loch Ness. They do cruises—I mean, they used to do cruises—where you can go and pretend to spot the Loch Ness Monster."

"The what?"

"Oh, it's just a fairy tale. Then again, the faeries turned out to be real, so who knows? But anyway, my parents weren't interested in Nessie. My dad was a professor of English literature. He specialized in the study of myths, specifically the myths about faeries. My mother was … woo-woo." Meg twirled a finger at one temple. Her mouth crimped. "But they had this passion in common, and that's how I ended up celebrating my fifth birthday on a Nessie-hunting boat."

Dhjerga shook his head in frustration. "I don't understand."

"Oh, you see, Loch Ness is *really* deep. And there are rumors that there might be caves down there, which are only accessible from underwater. That's why the Nessie myth won't die. But my parents' thinking was, we know there used to be faeries in Scotland. There are all these stories about them. And if they're still around, where better for them to hide? … That was before we knew the faeries *are* real, and they're just sentrienza."

"I still don't understand."

"So we went out in this boat with sonar imaging equipment,

and lo and behold, there really are deep cracks and trenches, which look a lot like the entrances to underwater caves. Well, that's as far as we took it. Dad published a paper. Nothing came of that, except that people laughed at him. And two decades later, the CHEMICAL MAGE group contacted him to help with their research. But then, the day Nicky w-w-was …"

Abruptly, Meg stopped speaking and put her hands over her face. Her body trembled.

"Daisy," she cried out, "you did a miracle for Dhjerga. Why can't there be a miracle for me?"

"I did not do it," Colm's mother said. "God did."

"Oh, fuck it."

Bridget went over and hugged Meg as she sobbed.

Sighing, Colm's mother picked up the thread. "Dhjerga, you said that your brother and sister went looking for Scota's grave."

"Did I say that?"

"You did. You were talking in your sleep. Maybe it wasn't true. Is it?"

Dhjerga nodded jerkily. He remembered the last conversation they'd had on Atletis before the twins flitted. It had been an angry one. He'd mocked the twins' ambition to find their ancestral home. Where were they now? That momentary glimpse of Diejen he'd had in Gaethla Moro's lair taunted him. He could not sense her or Dryjon at all. That might be because they were not near a power source. Or it might be because … His mind shied from the other alternative.

Huskily, he said, "They thought Scota's grave was at a place called the Ridge of the Bridge. I don't know where that is.

Maybe Gaethla knew; he might have told Diejen …"

"The Ridge of the Bridge," Colm's mother nodded. "You said that in your sleep, too. And I know where it is. It's where I used to live myself. It's a town called Drumnadrochit."

"Which happens to be right next to Loch Ness!" Meg said. Her eyes were wet and her nose red, but her voice was once more steady. "So, putting it all together, we think there really are caves under Loch Ness … or *something*. And that's where the Magus has taken Nicky. He's taken him home."

*

"But I can't help you," Dhjerga said. He felt weak again. It was dark and a wet wind blew over the hill. He followed Meg back into the church. She gave him an electric torch to hold while she rooted around in the piles of useful things Colm had left behind. "I've lost my magic."

The death curse had gone, but it had left him damaged. He could not flit. One had heard of this. He was as weak as any slave.

"That's OK," Meg said, backing into the light. She lugged a jerrycan that looked heavy. "Here's some gasoline. Axel took the boat, damn him—but we've also got a dinghy with an outboard motor. It'll get us to the mainland."

"Axel?" Dhjerga realized he had not seen the brave Marine in the house. "Where's he gone?"

"Who knows? He walked off, as usual. He's probably gone to kill himself," she said with dreadful flippancy. "But you know what?" She unwrapped a tarpaulined object. "This, my Ghost friend, is a Gauss gun. 12,000 rounds per minute, and it's lighter than an AK clone." She flashed a grin. "Who needs a man, when I've got this?"

Lioness, she-wolf, warrior—Meg, Dhjerga decided, was

the most terrifying of all the women in this clan. And he was going to be journeying with her to face the Magus, on foot, unaided.

He could have had worse company.

*

They packed their rucksacks first thing in the morning. Dhjerga sighed gloomily as he hefted his pack crammed with food, ammunition, and camping equipment. There was another Gauss gun for him, which added more weight. He was used to travelling light, with nothing but the clothes he stood up in—you could always fetch more stuff later. But now he could not fetch anything, and he had to travel inch by inch, like a slave.

They hauled the dinghy to shore and got in. The outboard engine sputtered into life. The Mackenzies and Wilsons waved from the beach. The prow bounced over small waves. Meg, at the tiller, turned the boat towards the mainland. "I figure we'll put in at the ferry port at Kyle of Lochalsh," she said. "How are you feeling?"

Dhjerga shrugged. "The same."

"I meant does your head hurt?"

"Oh. A little."

Meg felt in the pocket of her jacket. "I brought these for you," she said, taking out a handful of blister packs.

"That looks like the stuff Colm used to take."

"It is. Tropodolfin."

"It was killing him," Dhjerga said bluntly. Would he ever see Colm again? He and Meg might be heading to the wrong place. The Magus might have flung the child halfway across the galaxy, to some secret hiding place he'd discovered, just as he had discovered Kisperet so long ago. Colm and his father might have—no, almost certainly *had*—flitted into a trap. And Dhjerga, crippled, could not save them.

But maybe he could still save the twins.

He put the sheets of white pills into his pocket, and gazed across the waves, towards the land his people had come from thousands of years ago.

CHAPTER 45

The *Shihoka* swung past apogee and began to fall back towards the heimdall. The little artificial world on the screen drew incrementally closer.

"No more time to waste. I'm going in," Colm said. Nicky was somewhere down there. Get in, grab him, get out.

But there was a problem. Once he flitted away from the *Shihoka,* he wouldn't be able to get back. Because once he left the ship, he'd lose touch with the instruments that allowed him to sense and flit to fast-moving power sources. Catch twenty-fucking-two.

"Dad, you'll have to take the ship into the zero-gravity field." His heart sank. Initiating the zero-gravity field generators was a complicated operation. To make matters worse, the ship would need to burn further away from the star to reach the zero-gravity point. So Lloyd would need to start the antiquark field generator, go through all the steps of ramping up the output, plot a course to the zero-gravity point, and enter the field—that's if he didn't get wasted as soon as he throttled up the drive and the sentrienza saw him ...

Lloyd regarded the acres of buttons, dials and screens in front of the couch with distaste. "Save your breath. It's a recipe for disaster."

"You said it," Colm sighed.

"*I'll* fetch the child. I know him better than you do, anyway."

Lloyd stooped and called for Mickle. He coaxed the small tabby into the pocket of his duster, which made it hang down lopsidedly.

"Dad, no. This is my job."

"Your job is to fly this ship. Put it where I can reach it again." Lloyd petted the cat, whose head stuck out of his pocket. In his other hand, a pair of spoons had appeared. They rattled out a cheery rhythm, bouncing off the back of the couch and off Colm's head.

"Ow!"

"Now you see me …" Lloyd vanished. "Now you don't." His voice stayed behind, a sibilant echo.

Colm was alone in the cockpit.

He groaned, and swept a hand over the switches, enabling the antiquark field generator. It killed him to be left behind like this. Now he knew how his parents must have felt when he ran away to space.

Throttle up.

The *Shihoka's* powerful drive roared to life, hurling the little ship out of orbit. Colm had calculated the shortest trajectory to the system's zero-gravity point. It would take him past several more of these heimdalls. They orbited at all inclinations, not just in the plane of the ecliptic, and they undoubtedly hosted powerful weapons systems. If that rocky little world *was* Elphame, it was the best-defended planet in the galaxy … and by lighting up his drive, Colm had just alerted the sentrienza to the presence of an intruder in their midst.

His nose prickled with an esthesia alert, a bad smell, like dogs fresh from rolling in the mud.

Hostile craft approaching.

Well, that didn't take long.

He opened the throttle. This was a fighter. Maybe he could outrun them to the zero-gravity point. Acceleration pressed him back into the couch, giving a sense of speed that the blackness outside did not provide. The heimdall shrank into space, but the hostiles gained on him, and with his radar and infrared eyes he watched them swoop out of space. Spiky wings spread, they scrambled through the vacuum in a formation that changed shape by the moment. A murmuration of Walking Guns.

In half a human heartbeat, they surrounded the ship and landed on the hull like a hundred little airplanes touching down on curved runways. Colm felt their sharp legs digging into his skin. It was like ants crawling all over his body, biting and pinching. They chewed his sensor arrays, spat junk data into his radio and radar antennas. His composite vision got patchy. He screamed, clawing at his eyes. With his left hand he reached for his Nessie mug—

—and flitted—

—and thumped back into space on the far side of the system, 2 AUs out, with the Walking Guns *still* clinging to him! Another heimdall filled his single functioning screen. Click-clacking black legs obscured its orb. The smell of wet dog choked his nostrils. More Walking Guns scuttled up from their various orbits around the heimdall, converging on him, as if they'd been lying in wait. Come to think of it, they probably had been. He'd blundered into a living, semi-sentient minefield several AUs wide, and he could not escape, because the only power sources were these fucking heimdalls, so he was never going to reach a usable zero-gravity point by flitting, not without being eaten alive. He sobbed curses, and flitted again.

And again.

And again.

And again.

315

*

Lloyd grunted in pain as his boots thumped down on lush, damp grass. Jesus, that hurt! Before today he had not flitted in donkey's years. It was good to know he could do it without the booze. But where the hell was he?

Looked—and smelled—like a tropical paradise. He had never been big on travel, but he and Daisy had spent their honeymoon in Bali, and the dripping greenery and gaudy flowers reminded him of that.

He grabbed for Mickle as she escaped from his pocket and chased a fluttering butterfly. "Here, kitty, kitty!" He blundered after her through the trees, getting eyefuls of water from cup-shaped flowers. "Mickle!" His familiar, his precious. With her at hand, he didn't need the booze. It had been a long time after Sprite before he could even think about getting another cat, and it had surprised him how quickly he came to love her. And depend on her. They had to stay together to have any chance of getting out of here alive.

She caught the butterfly.

It had eight wings.

"Christ, don't eat that," Lloyd said. He glanced around and muttered aloud. "Where the hell is this?"

At the foot of a nearby tree sat a furry pale green octopus, reading a book. "Shangri-la," it said.

"More like Alice in fucking Wonderland," Lloyd said.

Another tentacle held a cigarette. The octopus languidly exhaled smoke from its beak. "In Xanadu did Kubla Khan," the octopus declaimed, "a stately pleasure-dome decree … There is no dome here, but the principle's the same."

"Yeah, yeah. Would you have another fag on you?"

"In Shangri-la," the octopus said, "or Xanadu, which are

both synonyms for the Land of Eternal Life, cigarettes cost *the earth.*"

"Dammit," Lloyd said. He wandered on, carrying Mickle, until he came out of the trees onto a beach.

A broad expanse of pristine sand stretched for miles and miles. Sparkling swell sluiced over and through a breakwater of half-submerged black rocks a few yards offshore. Breaking on the beach, the waves looked too foamy, as if the water were mixed with washing-up liquid. Maybe this was the place people once called Faerieland—or *a* Faerieland. The Faerieland of the furry green octopi.

About half a mile away, a peculiar rock stood on the beach. Lloyd mooched towards it with his hands in his pockets, one thumb stroking Mickle's fur. When he got close to the rock he stopped. It was ten feet high, gleaming like wet basalt, shaped like a sagging pyramid. When Lloyd closed one eye and turned his head sideways, so that the rock barely flickered in his peripheral vision, it looked like an enormous man sitting on his haunches, clothed in shadow.

"We meet at last," Lloyd said. He was shaking with fear and trying to hide it. "Where's my grandson?"

"Go home, Mackenzie," whispered the Magus. "It's over."

"It's not over till it's over. Where's the child?"

The Magus heaved towards him, squat-walking, kicking out his legs like beams, leaving a six-foot-wide snail trail in the sand. Lloyd involuntarily staggered back, feeling that the Magus was about to fall on him, crushing him. The Magus halted, leaning over him. "There."

Now the rock was no longer blocking Lloyd's view, he saw Nicky sitting on his bottom, wearing nothing but a nappy, digging in the wet sand near the waterline. His heart skipped a beat. "Nicky!" he shouted. "I've come to take you home! Come here to me …"

The Magus surged to his feet. The edge of his shadow rose off those horrible huge leather boots. He was still swathed in darkness, so Lloyd could not get a proper look at him, but he stood at least nine feet high. Fear chilled Lloyd's soul. They say that in the old days, men were giants …

"Go home." The words battered at Lloyd like a cold gale, raising gooseflesh on his skin, although he still stood in sunlight. "Go home, go home! Or stay—and *pay* …"

Lloyd frantically searched his pockets. Cards, coins, a silk handkerchief … That might work. He whipped it out and turned it into a seagull. It was only a trick, really. There were electrical conduits running under the beach and through that breakwater out there—power to spare. He just grabbed some of it, the same way he used to leech off the wiring in homes and theaters when performing for a crowd, and fetched a seagull from Skye, where there were loads of them. Chuck the handkerchief away and Bob's your uncle. You just had to be careful where 'away' was. He and Daisy had messed up their Vanishing Lady act once, thirty years ago, before the kids were born. Daisy was supposed to reappear in the middle of the audience, but she wound up in the parking lot, shivering in her spangly bikini. That had happened because he'd been drinking, of course. He should have been more careful. Shouldn't have drawn attention to them … to Colm. But now it was too late. His hubris had brought agony to his son and destruction to Earth, so Lloyd no longer gave a shit, and his seagull landed on the Magus's head and had a good go at pecking his eyes out before the Magus tore its head off and flung both halves into the ocean. Blood droplets fell onto the sand.

"You're scaring the child," the Magus said.

'I'm scaring him?" Nicky was crying. Head down, tears dripping onto the sand. Lloyd lunged towards the helpless little figure, and the Magus blocked his way.

"You've not even changed his fucking nappy."

"It matters not," the Magus said, wearily.

A spike of cold horror pierced Lloyd like a nail driven down through the top of his head. "What are they going to do with him?"

"That is none of your concern, nor mine."

Atrocious visions thrust themselves into Lloyd's brain. With an immense effort he stopped himself from making another lunge for the child. The Magus was faster than him, thanks to years of beer and Dunhills.

Breathing hard, Lloyd said cunningly, "What've they offered you for him?"

"He is theirs already, gifted and paid for."

"Aye, but there's got to be a finder's fee."

The Magus had gone back to looking like a rock again. Remotely, he said, "They have promised to give me Earth."

"And you believe that? Jesus, how can you be so gullible?"

"They do not lie."

"No, but it's what they're *not* saying. They can promise to give you Earth, but that won't matter when they have their own chemical mages, wired to obey them—human Walking Guns, making cannon fodder by the millions, to conquer the galaxy in the Gray Emperor's name. And you'll have one wee planet in the ass-end of the Orion Arm."

"Earth is all I ever wanted," the Magus said.

Lloyd felt the same way. But he said, "You've not got very

grand ambitions for a two-thousand-year-old druid."

The rock shrugged.

"Look, can I change his nappy at least?"

A moment passed. The rock breathed. Lloyd sweated.

At last the Magus said, "I'll have hold of you all the time, and if you flit, I shall be with you, and then I will tear your body into a thousand pieces and scatter them into the void."

"I've got no doubt of it."

Lloyd swiftly crossed the sand to the weeping toddler. Nicky stumbled into his grandfather's arms, bawling. For a long, sweet minute they just hugged each other, Lloyd on his knees, the boy folded against his chest, and the Magus's long index finger digging into the side of his neck like a bone fishhook.

At last he said, "Let's get you clean, wee lad." He knew where the nappies and the wipes were at home. One of the few things Colm had done that was actually useful was to bring the world's supply of disposable nappies to the Free Church Manse. Before that Meg and Axel had been using tea towels and washing them. Lloyd fetched the stuff, pulled off Nicky's nappy, and wiped his bottom. He put a clean nappy on the boy and then spent a long time bundling up the dirty one. Nicky had done a number 2.

The world that Lloyd had named Faerieland was a thin crust atop an underground cluster of machines, all pulsating with power. The sentrienza lived down there in the dark. They would come up only at twilight—like rabbits, Lloyd thought. Down there in their warrens. *Smart* rabbits, masters of all the technology under the sun. Except magic. That was the only thing they couldn't do, because they simply weren't built for it, any more than a rabbit can play the guitar. But they had air machines down there and water machines, boring and tunneling machines and gravity machines and computers out the arse. They'd made this heimdall thing from raw materials and they'd put a drive on it. That crater on the far side was a spaceship engine the size of a continent, so the heimdall could boost itself into a different orbit if necessary. Lloyd, however, didn't care what all the machines were for. It only mattered to him that they were brimming with power.

Humming to himself, he fetched copies of Nicky's dirty nappy into every machine he could find. Computer? Have a sopping clout right in your works. Generator? Ditto. Baby poop and wet recycled hemp padding landed on live circuits and squashed themselves into compartments full of sensitive electronic components. Short-circuits multiplied. Fires started. Alarms sounded. Lloyd picked up the pace, one hand resting on Mickle's back, the other kneading the bundled-up nappy. Nicky, watching, grinned as if he sensed what his grandfather was up to.

"What are you doing?" the Magus said.

"Just giving them a few little presents from Earth." Kill all the computers. That'd disable whatever guns they'd got, and then Colm'd be able to land the spaceship. That was Lloyd's plan.

But as the words left his mouth, the breakwater moved. Those black rocks grew heads. Angular bodies reared out of the waves, howling. They were not rocks but Walking Guns. They splashed to shore and ringed the three humans, their eyeless snouts raised to the sky. Their moaning howls seemed to resonate with the very tissues of Lloyd's brain, scrambling his thoughts, forcing him to stop his magical mischief. He clutched his head and groaned in agony.

That went on for a few minutes and then a sentrienza ship fell out of the sky like a fiery thumbtack. It struck the beach a quarter mile away. Battlesuited sentrienza jogged down the beach to the humans, the Walking Guns slinking around their legs.

"Get up, humans," a blank faceplate buzzed. "The Gray Emperor has deigned to take an interest in you."

"That," Lloyd muttered, "sounds very bad."

CHAPTER 46

Axel reached Drumnadrochit in the afternoon. The small town was a bleak, abandoned knot of streets around a castle. A few Ghosts shot at him from the castle's parapets, but their bullets bounced harmlessly off his battlesuit. He jogged on. As long as he kept moving, he didn't have to think about all he'd left behind at the Free Church Manse.

But when he reached the shore of Loch Ness he had to stop and think about why he was here.

Dryjon Lizp had spoken of this place. The *Ridge on the Bridge,* with an echo that said *Drumnadrochit.*

Axel had to concentrate hard to remember her exact words. He sat on the edge of a wooden jetty with boats tied up at it—*Nessie Hunter, Braveheart II*—and sorted through his jumbled memories of Atletis ... no, not *his* memories. The men who'd had those experiences were either dead, or not him anymore. But wearing the battlesuit, he felt close to them again, and he remembered Innismon. A 150-foot rocket standing in the middle of a medieval village. Benches and tables set out on the green. The lords and ladies of Kisperet drinking to their victory, while the slaves—including him— waited patiently for the leftovers. So fucked-up.

And yet he was fucked up, too, because he missed it. He missed the place where he had experienced the bloody highs and despairing lows of battle, all without the responsibility of looking after other people, because he was just a slave. Just a thousand slaves. One for all and all for one ... and that one, the one who made the tactical decisions, was not him. It was Colm Mackenzie.

And there Colm was, seated in the best chair, wearing the ruffles and the cloak and the jewellery of a Ghost, and the sword to go with it. Like Colm would know how to use a sword if you gave him a manual with numbered steps. Everyone complimented and flattered him, and now he got up on the table, swaying back and forth, stepping in a pie dish, to deliver a toast, all about how much he loved them (but what he meant was that he loved Diejen Lizp) and how sad he'd be to leave them. Drugged up to his eyeballs, as usual. "I *love* you guys …" and not a word about the slaves watching from their places on the grass, who had actually won the war.

Except they hadn't won the war. Because now Colm stumbled away from the feast. He never noticed the Marines following him. You made surprisingly little noise in a battlesuit, if you knew what you were doing. Colm cursed weepily to himself and sat down behind a hedge, and Axel hid in the trees. And after a little while Diejen Lizp came and started to work on him, while her brother concealed himself on the other side of the hedge. Diejen knew exactly what Colm wanted, it was obvious. It was also obvious (to Axel, watching stonily from the treeline) that she had no intention of giving it to him.

And then Colm did his vanishing act. And people accused *Axel* of bailing on difficult situations.

After Colm was gone Dryjon talked for a long time about *our ancestral home,* while Diejen harped on about *the old ways,* and Dhjerga spluttered about *our obligations,* and the upshot was they went away. All of them went away, leaving Lady Terrious and one of her daughters in charge of the slaves. The war was over as far as the Terrious women were concerned. They set the slaves to work clearing the forest, planting crops, and exploring upstream to look for a river worthy of damming, and they fetched women from Kisperet so that the new freemen could have wives and one day children ... and Axel wished to fuck he was still there, with that cheerful little brunette he had not had time to get to know properly, instead of sitting on a Scottish jetty, bereft of everything that had meant anything to him.

But.

The Ridge of the Bridge.

Drumnadrochit.

Scota's grave lies beneath the Ridge of the Bridge.

And this Scota had been the Magus's true love.

Didn't it make sense that the Magus would have taken Nicky to her grave? As a tribute, or ... a sacrifice?

Colm may have contributed a casual spurt of jism, but Nicky was *Axel's* child. He was going to rescue him ... or die trying.

He pushed to his feet. The weight of his battlesuit made the jetty creak. It had been Marines who won the war on Atletis, not mages. and it would be a Marine, not a mage, who finished it here on Earth.

He clomped out to *Braveheart II*. He was in luck: the boat had a solar array on the roof of its cabin, which continually charged its fuel cell. The Ghosts had either not bothered with this particular power source or, more likely, they were wary of this place. Axel knew how they felt. Steep green hills fell to grey water. Evening shadows had already begun to slither across the loch. It was eerily quiet.

Universal connectors were a thing, so he charged his suit from the boat's fuel cell. While the juice meter ticked up, he ate a canned bacon sandwich he found in the boat's snack box.

Yes, a canned bacon sandwich. Freaking Scotland. It was actually better than it sounded, so he had another one. He might not get the chance to eat again for a while.

Suit power: 100%.

Air supply: 100%.

Time to go.

He'd left enough power in the fuel cell to start the boat's engine. To someone with experience piloting spaceships, this vessel was as easy to handle as a child's tricycle. He piloted it out into the middle of the loch and then headed south, following the shoreline, until the power gave out. By now the sky was lavender and bats darted through the air.

Axel climbed up on the prow.

If a Marine battlesuit could stand up to outer space, it could definitely stand up to a bit of water.

He sealed his helmet and jumped.

CHAPTER 47

Meg drove a 10-tonne truck cautiously down the winding road from Drumnadrochit to the shore. She and Dhjerga had found the truck on the pier at Kyle of Lochalsh, being recharged by beamed power from some still-functioning orbital solar array. As recently as last month, Meg wouldn't have dared go near an electric truck, much less drive it across Scotland. But Dhjerga said it was safe. There were no Magistocracy loyalists left alive to exploit power sources. "I killed them all," he stated flatly. "Gaethla was the last one." Anyway, no Ghosts popped out of the truck's engine compartment on their way to Loch Ness.

When they passed through towns and villages, Ghosts had taken potshots at the truck, sure. Ghosts gotta Ghost. Meg had laid the hurt on them with the Gauss, per SOP. In other places, Dhjerga had restrained her from shooting at Ghosts ploughing the fields, or herding sheep. "They're coming back to themselves," he had said. "Look. That one there, that's not a Ghost, that's a local."

"They're mixing with us?!" Meg had said in outrage. "How can people stand it? The Ghosts *invaded Earth!*"

Looking pained, Dhjerga had said, "They're often quite nice when they come to themselves."

Meg had said nothing to that, but she'd quit spraying bullets at random Ghosts. She would save her ammo for the Magus.

Now, here they were. She parked in front of a ticky-tacky visitor center whose sign said *Loch Ness Monster Hunter Cruises.* They got out. No sign of hostiles. No sign of life at all.

The windows of the visitor center were broken. A single boat bobbed at a wooden jetty sticking out into the loch.

"We didn't start our cruise from here," Meg said, recalling that long-ago holiday. "We started from Fort Augustus. I think. It shouldn't make any difference. All these boats have sonar imaging equipment."

"Ye gods, please no, not another boat," Dhjerga said.

"Fucking man up," Meg said. She went into the visitor center. She was hoping for scuba equipment. She turned the place upside down and was going through stacks of life vests, hope fading by the minute, when she heard Dhjerga coming into the visitor center.

She rose to her feet as he entered the room. He was a homely guy, with his sticky-out brown hair and big nose, and now a fading goose egg on his forehead, thanks to Meg herself. His physique would put a Marine to shame. He carried his Gauss like it was made of balsa wood. His weird illness had not left any physical traces. But ever since he recovered, or Daisy healed him, or a miracle happened, or whatever, he had had an oddly uncertain manner.

Now that air of uncertainty was gone. He was grinning the same grin that used to creep her the hell out when they worked together on Juradis. "Any luck?" he said.

"No," she said tiredly.

"You were right," he said.

"Huh?"

"I manned up. I took these pills." He opened his fist. The blisterpack of tropo she'd given him for his head. Two pills were missing. "It works! I fetched this from Skye as a test." He took a handheld computer out of the pocket of his jacket. It was a flimsy little thing, solar-powered, that Roger Wilson played solitaire and chess on.

But a cheap computer wasn't what they needed now. Meg returned his grin, a mere spasm of her facial muscles. "Great. Can you fetch us some scuba equipment?"

"I understand now why Colm was such a fiend for this stuff! It's better than eating *doire* leaves."

"Yeah, but watch out for the crash."

"I feel like a warrior again."

"I'm happy for you. Now, scuba equipment? Do you know what that is? Probably not. It's for diving underwater—"

"We won't need that. We can travel like human beings now. No more trucks, or boats, or your 'scuba.'"

"Are you talking about flitting?" Meg flinched. But this was for Nicky. There was nothing she wouldn't do for him.

Dhjerga nodded. "Give me your hand."

"Hold on … Where are we flitting to?"

Dhjerga's grin broadened. "You were right. There *are* caves … and there is something drawing power down there. I can feel it, deep below our feet. It must be the Magus's lair. We will surprise him."

Meg swallowed. She involuntarily looked down at the mouldy carpet tiles between her boots. "I'm gonna take my gun, 'kay? I can do that?"

"I wouldn't dream of asking you to leave it."

She had brought her Gauss in with her. She picked it up. She looked into Dhjerga's eyes and slowly placed her hand in his.

Me, a mage?

Ki ga tsuyoi. That's what Mom used to say about me. Your *ki* is strong. She meant, why can't you act more like a girl sometimes?

Sorry, Mom.

You left me, but I'm not like you. I'm not going to leave *my* child on his own. Wherever he is, I'll—

OW OW OW—

She crumpled, screaming. Her body felt like it had been pulled apart and put back together wrong. Her prosthetic arm felt different, prickly, like the neural feedback electronics had gone screwy. And her eyes weren't working. She couldn't see a damn thing.

"Dhjerga! *Dhjerga!*"

A lighter rasped. Dhjerga's face, spookily lit from below, emerged from the darkness. Her eyes were OK. There just wasn't any light. As in, none at all. Tar soup.

Well; *caves*. Duh.

"Shit," she muttered, flexing the fingers of her prosthetic around the stock of the Gauss. "And I thought childbirth hurt."

"You get used to it," Dhjerga said. He was waving the lighter around. Wet rock walls. Tumbled boulders. They seemed to be in a cavern about the size of a small car. "So where's this power source?" he muttered.

The lighter gleamed on curved steel armor. Meg whipped her gun up, and a second later lowered it again.

A Marine battlesuit lay on the floor.

It was empty.

CHAPTER 48

Axel had had to take his battlesuit off to fit through the last crevice. It was such a tight squeeze that he left some skin on the glacially smoothed granite. Now he was barefoot, in a ripped t-shirt and tighty whities, wet with sweat and the moisture that clung to the walls. It was *cold* down here. At least the physical exertion was keeping him warm.

The battlesuit's helmet lamp could be detached—the Fleet thinks of everything!—so he had that on his forehead now. The elastic strap dug into the soft skin behind his ears. He also had his combi. He poked it ahead of him every time he came to a blind corner.

Once or twice, he thought he heard Meg's voice, faint and distant. But he knew that was just his mind playing cruel games with him. And when he stopped to listen, all he heard was the blood sighing in his ears.

He had swum down to the deepest point of Loch Ness. The lake's floor was absolutely smooth, like a bathtub. The sides were continuations of the steep slopes above. He'd used his suit's environmental imaging function to find the cave entrance. Then he'd swum in and up until he popped into the air. It was good air, to his surprise, indicating that there must be vents to the surface. Loch Ness lay on the Great Glen Fault, an area of ancient seismic slippage. The granite around here must be riddled with cracks and chimneys.

As he struggled upwards on hands and knees, he found himself remembering that fjordside cave on Juradis, and the rock chimney he and Meg had climbed to escape the Walking Guns. She'd saved his life that day, not for the first time. She had said she loved him but she'd been lying. Thinking about that made him want to sit down and die. But—*Nicky.*

He climbed on, and after a while the tunnel kinked like a bendy straw, and he was climbing downwards again.

There could've been other caves. Other tunnels. He might not be anywhere near the right place.

But what could he do except keep going? Lowering himself from one angled shelf to the next, he pressed on until the tunnel narrowed once again, and this time it *stayed* narrow. He could either go feet first or head first. He opted for gun first. He soon regretted it as the blood rushed to his head. Gravity was pulling him downwards, while the rocks digging into his body held him back. The planet seemed to be closing around him like a fist.

He grunted, gave a metaphorical middle finger to the Great Glen Fault, and squirmed downwards, shoving the combi in front of him like a blind man's stick, until suddenly it met no resistance.

He tumbled out of the crevice headfirst onto smooth rock. The echoes of his combi clattering told him it was a *big* cavern. He picked the combi up, picked himself up. Heart racing, he shone his headlamp around.

"Nicky?" His voice echoed back to him, mocking him. "Nicky!"

Water splashed.

Something slithered on rock.

Axel swung around, flipping up the laser scope of his combi, auto-syncing it with his infocals.

The specter in his crosshairs challenged his sanity.

A serpent humped up out of a black pool at the end of the cave. It was as long as a bus and it hadn't even come all the way out of the water yet. Instead of a head it had a spiky club, and all the spikes wavered towards Axel like the feelers of a sea urchin when food appears.

"Holy crap," Axel whispered.

The Loch Ness Monster was real.

And it was slithering towards him.

*

"Where'd you go?" Dhjerga said.

Meg, in the lead, said, "Right here."

"I can't see you."

"Yeah, you should have fetched a flashlight while you were at it."

"I did not know it would be so dark."

"Feel down and to your left."

His fingers brushed her ankle. "I'll never fit in there."

"Where there's a will there's a way." She dug her fingers into the rock, hauling herself on and down. Fingernails, who needs 'em? She could mute the damage signals from her prosthetic hand, so it didn't hurt, but the whole arm still felt funny. Tingly. The roof of the tunnel pressed the Gauss into her spine.

Damn, this was a tight squeeze.

"Axel can't have come this way," she muttered.

"What?"

"Axel." She'd thought he might have come this way, after she saw the battlesuit. It had sure *looked* like his. Now she had changed her mind. "He couldn't handle this. He's no good with enclosed spaces. Especially underground."

"He fought like a demon on Atletis, and that was all underground."

"But that wasn't *him*—"

333

"But he knows what they knew."

"Oh, your damn magic." She hauled herself over a sharp shelf, so she was hanging almost upside-down, and the strap of the Gauss got caught on a protrusion in the tunnel roof. "Shit."

"Are you stuck?"

"No …" She tried to jack-knife her body back up again, but her weight was now hanging from the strap and she couldn't get either arm around behind her back to free it. "Yes. Strap's caught."

"Hang on."

Somehow or other, Dhjerga crawled forward until he was lying alongside her in the tunnel. He reached up and freed the strap. Meg flopped down into the lower part of the tunnel.

"Axel's a good man," Dhjerga said. "One of the best."

"That's when his implant is enabled. Thinking back, I actually fell in love with an implant, not a man." As she spoke, she heard something from below her. A clattering noise. "Ssh! Listen!"

Silence.

"Did you hear something?"

A sudden storm of echoes bounced up the tunnel.

"Fuck," Meg gasped.

She'd know that noise anywhere. It was a combi firing on auto.

She fought onwards faster, no more time to talk, no time even to think. Smaller and lither than Dhjerga, she left him behind. She practically slid down the last, steepest, narrowest bit of the tunnel. It suddenly opened up. Muzzle flashes split the darkness. Half sliding, half falling, she braked her descent with her prosthetic hand and let her feet fall over her head, so she landed right way up, amidst the racket of gunfire. She went prone with the Gauss.

She could hardly make sense of what she was seeing. Gleaming black coils whipped across the floor of the cave. Pale in night-vision green, Axel stood with his back to the wall, firing into a mass of smaller tentacles. Between one breath and the next he ran out of ammo. There was an instant's ringing silence, broken by the slither of the monster's wet sides on the stone floor, and then Axel reversed his combi and struck out at the small tentacles, but there were too many of them, they spasmed around Axel's arms, and he let out a scream of pain—

Meg fired into the nearest coil. The monster dropped Axel and whisked around, unbelievably fast. The tentacles reached for her. There were thousands of the wiggly arms, getting smaller towards the middle, like a jellyfish's tentacles, and in the middle gaped a toothed maw.

She dodged. Running and firing at the same time, because the thing was too fucking big to miss, she zigzagged across the cave towards Axel. Behind her, Dhjerga dropped out of the crevice. The deafening pop-pop of rounds going supersonic filled the cave.

Meg slipped in a puddle of sticky ichor and skidded up to Axel. He'd dropped his gun. Was leaning against the wall of the cave, his arms hanging oddly at his sides. She pushed him behind her and poured rounds into the monster's body. Slime flooded out of its shredded sides. By the time she and Dhjerga stopped shooting, the Gausses had practically torn it in half.

Her ears were ringing but she heard Axel say, "Let me know when you get tired of saving my life, Meg."

She shook her head, gaping at the dead monster. "What …
the *fuck* … is that?"

"I'm guessing the Loch Ness Monster."

"It was real."

"Are *you* real?"

"We found your battlesuit." She remembered the suit's
power meter hovering at empty. She and Dhjerga had drained
it when they flitted in.

Dhjerga skirted the monster's still-twitching head,
stumbling in the dark. "Hello, Axel," he called.

"Yo," Axel said, twitching one arm.

"What's wrong with your arms?" Meg said sharply.

"Nessie stung me. Numb. I'm hoping it'll wear off."

"Poisonous like a jellyfish. Fuck."

"I think Nessie's an alien," Axel said, screwing up his face
thoughtfully. Or maybe in pain.

"No shit, Sherlock."

"So how'd she get here?"

"This is me not caring." Chewing her lip, Meg watched
Dhjerga wander away, using his Gauss's night scope to see
with. The cavern looked to be completely barren and empty.
She had told herself she did not really hope to find Nicky at
the end of this nightmare caving expedition. But she *had* been
hoping, all the same, and the disappointment bit deep. She
detached from it. She had to think about how they were going
to get out of here, with Axel Nessie-stung, unable to use his
arms, and his battlesuit out of power.

"There's a tunnel back here," Dhjerga called.

"Any wider than the other one?"

"Yes." Pause. "It has a concrete floor."

CHAPTER 49

The sentrienza let Lloyd keep Nicky on his lap during the flight, but the Magus must have told them how to disable a magician, for they put gloves on him. For a while in his younger days he'd gone around in two pairs of Rubbermaids, trying to train himself out of it. Never really worked. But these were not rubber dishwashing gloves. They were made of slinky gold fabric, came up to his elbows, and numbed his gift entirely. It was like losing one of his senses. "Grandpa's quite the fashion plate," he said to Nicky. The toddler didn't smile, but at least he wasn't crying anymore.

Poor wee lad.

It was probably for the best that he didn't know what was coming.

Nor did Lloyd but he knew it was going to be bad, so he didn't relax when the sentrienza spaceship touched down on the system's single planet and them stil alive and unhurt. They disembarked on a stony gray desert and stumbled between hydrocarbon seeps like little craters full of black soup. Sand blew in the air, hazing out the horizon. Lloyd, carrying Nicky, covered the boy's face with his duster. The occasional feeble sprig of purple vegetation pushed between the stones. Otherwise there was no sign of life whatsoever, until a steel chimney rose out of the ground and opened into curved petals. Their sentrienza escorts pushed them inside.

It was a lift. Down they went, fans whirring the dust out of the air. Lloyd coughed and hacked phlegm onto the floor. "Jesus, the air was foul up there. What did you do to this poor planet?" His ears popped.

Nicky, riding on Lloyd's hip, rubbed his eyes red. "Go?" he said hopefully.

That was Nicky's way of saying he wanted to go home. You and me both, laddie. Lloyd should've flitted when he had the chance, even if it meant abandoning Colm. He should've taken his chances against the Magus.

Where *was* the Magus?

The lift dumped them into a dark and slimy corridor with fist-sized mushrooms growing out of the walls. The mushrooms glowed, providing a dim bluish light. As he struggled to balance Nicky on his hip, Lloyd glanced back and saw a shadow oozing around the corner behind them.

There he was.

Clearly the Magus wasn't going to let Nicky out of his sight until he saw how this shook out.

The sentrienza glanced back, buzzed to each other, and swayed along faster. Lloyd studied them and decided they didn't know what to do about the Magus exactly. They could not get close enough to put gloves on *him*. He had the knack of the glamor, wrapping spacetime around himself like a shield and cloak in one. You'd never even see his face if he didn't want you to. He could do the scrying, too, and probably other tricks besides, according to Lloyd's father, who had tried several times to have a proper conversation with him but always got lost in the Magus's enigmatic, old-timey way of talking. As for Lloyd, he would have jumped in the Minch before he'd have conversed with the Magus, before today.

But maybe the Magus was not the evilest being in the universe after all.

The corridor ended abruptly in a grove of gray trees and yellow grass. The boughs of the trees creaked, hung with red

...

Lloyd crushed Nicky's face into his shoulder as he realized what he was seeing. His gorge rose. Bodies hung from the trees, flayed, dismembered, connected to tubes and wires ... they were still living! It was a torture garden. All he saw for the first seconds was red, red, red, and then his brain reluctantly identified the bodies as sentrienza and alien. No humans.

Yet.

He could practically feel the agony of the prisoners. It puzzled him that they made no sound until he saw that their mouths were sewn shut.

"Put the child down," said a sweet, high, buzzing voice.

"No," Lloyd said. "Don't make him look at this. It'll traumatize him for life. Please."

Buzzing laughter. "'Life'? What is this state we call life? It is a question I have explored for centuries, yet am none the wiser. Here you see a few of my ongoing experiments. I used to think that experience was the enemy of ignorance; now I know it is its handmaiden. Each experience further sweetens the fine wine of unknowing. Put the child down."

The battlesuited sentrienza wrenched Nicky out of Lloyd's arms and set him on his feet. Nicky immediately wailed and buried his face in Lloyd's legs.

"So you are *Homo sapiens,*" the voice said. "I have heard so much about you. A promising species—but troublesome. In fact, I distinctly remember signing off on something ... yes, an extinction protocol. One does not forget *that* easily."

"And yet here we are," Lloyd said.

"Yes. How did you get here? Don't tell me; you are another of these *magicians.*"

"Got it in one. Not gonnae offer us a drink? I thought faerie hospitality would be better than this."

More laughter. Trilling voices multiplied. A gust of air touched Lloyd's face. Before his eyes, the tortured prisoners vanished off the trees, and sentrienza in fancy dress appeared beneath them, seated at long tables groaning with food and drink. Strings of faerie lights in the branches replaced the overhead glare. Lyrical music played. Lloyd rubbed his eyes like a rube. He knew it was just an illusion, probably managed with screens and holo projectors, but it was disorienting. Nicky peeped in awe.

A sentrienza girl sashayed up to them with her knees bending in the wrong direction, and offered Lloyd a tray. On it stood a sippy cup of orange juice and a pint of dark beer with a creamy head.

Lloyd had never been so tempted by a drink. Not only had he travelled thousands of light years and seen horrors beyond his imagining, he'd been unwillingly sober for years. He could practically taste the hops and feel the foam coating his lips. A little moment of relief to make this game of living easier.

But suspicion sounded a shrill alarm in his head, backed up the memory of his grandfather's voice:

"These days they call them sentrienza and people grab their gifts with both hands. But I'm telling you, my lad, never take *anything* a faerie offers you."

Truer words never said, and yet the beer was stronger than Lloyd. He reached out for it.

Mickle scrabbled out of his pocket, clawed her way up his duster to his shoulder, and leapt onto the tray, knocking the beer and the orange juice to the ground. She bounded clear, hissing.

The sentrienza girl shrieked and turned into a prisoner with a flayed face, one arm missing, propelled on her grotesque mission by a remote control box crudely implanted in her skull. Nicky burst into heartrending sobs.

Lloyd dropped to his knees, gathering the child in. "Good kitty," he said fervently to Mickle. She'd saved him. No doubt the drinks had been drugged. "No more of your fucking games!" he shouted at the sentrienza nobles carousing under the trees. "What do you want?"

The illusory banquet vanished. In the harsh clinical lighting, the tortured puppet wobbled back to her place, and another sentrienza body fell from the tree nearest Lloyd. This one was in better shape: it had all its skin. However, deep cuts scored its limbs, and bruises marred the pale gray skin of its throat. Its abundant gold hair was so matted with blood that it stuck together in a single big dreadlock. As it approached, its reek seared Lloyd's nose.

"That's simple," it said. "I want to know how to do magic. You will teach me. If not, the child will."

"You're never the Gray Emperor?"

The hideously wounded sentrienza laughed the same buzzing laugh as before. "I prefer the title Emperor of Experience."

Lloyd's neck prickled. The light seemed to dim, and he knew the Magus was behind him.

"You will keep your promise, Your Imperial Majesty," the Magus said in his slushy whisper. "Give me Earth."

"But of course," the emperor said carelessly. "The promise is already made. And as you know, we sentrienza never lie."

CHAPTER 50

Colm stopped flitting. He was wrung out, his heart racing, his eyes popping out of his head. Every time he jumped around the Elphame system, from one heimdall to the next, the *Shihoka* had seemed to get heavier. The Walking Guns had stayed with him all the way, and not for a second had they paused in their work of destruction. They were dismantlng the ship around him. His sensor eyes had gone blind, and he'd had to mute all the esthesia feedback from his implant, because it felt like they were flaying him alive. A few minutes ago they'd got through the hull in the cargo hold. His internal camera eyes saw a pack of them floating in there, training their laser eyes on the pressure door that led to the main cabin. Vaporizing metal glowed red-hot. It wouldn't be long until they broke through.

Anticipating depressurization, Colm already had his helmet on. He checked the seals of his leathers, grabbed his gun and his Nessie mug, and flitted out of the ship. He had to see how much damage they'd done.

Huh?

He could not see the *Shihoka* at all. He was floating in empty space, facing away from the sun, having instinctively put it at his back. All he saw was blackness, studded with the bright dots of heimdalls.

The blackness heaved and sparkled.

Colm grunted in disgust. He saw them now, with his eyes and esthesia. Walkiing Guns. Hundreds of them. They'd literally buried the *Shihoka,* like ants on the corpse of a bird. One wing-tip stuck forlornly out of the seething mass of metal.

The sight filled Colm with rage and guilt. That beautiful ship had deserved better than this.

The Walking Guns spotted him. A dozen of them broke away from the ship and powered towards him, spurting fiery tailfeathers.

Exhaustion delayed him for a moment—just a moment.

Strange to say, the Walking Guns did not shoot at him. They circled him, wisping out tiny jets of plasma. Blunt heads butted his legs, sending him into a tumble. He spun among them, the sun flashing in his faceplate as they butted him this way and that, as if playing some rough game.

Oh. I see. You fuckers are sentient enough to have a sense of humor, is that it?

He bounced the Nessie mug off the nearest one's snout, and flitted.

*

"Dad?"

Colm stared around wildly, trying to orient himself. A sentrienza grove, like the one on the *Ruddiganmaseve,* but with bonus corpses. Jesus, that's horrible. Battlefield smell, hospital lights.

Two sentrienza in battlesuits dragged Lloyd away by his arms. He was kicking and thrashing, his face purple, he'd give himself a heart attack … He was wearing golden gloves. They'd neutralized him.

Further away, a naked, wounded sentrienza squatted on its haunches, in that dog-like pose they favored, hands cupped around Nicky's face. The child stood stock still, obviously paralyzed with terror.

"Nicky!" Colm bellowed. Forgetting his exhaustion and

confusion, he started towards Nicky. In his peripheral vision, sentrienza guards tracked him with their guns. What were his chances of reaching the boy before he got shot?

The repulsively wounded sentrienza lifted Nicky's face, dragging the child onto his tiptoes.

"Come any closer," it buzzed, "and I break his neck. It would not make him any less useful to me."

Colm stood frozen on the yellow grass, mindlessly noticing how it was splashed with dried blood.

"So," the sentrienza said, "there are three of you. Stay still. The nanosamplers are assessing your DNA ... My, my. Three generations of one family. I could not have asked for a better-designed experiment."

A raspy voice slithered through the air. "Then, you will not only give me Earth, but also my son?"

Colm swivelled his eyes without moving any other part of his body. The lights did not reach into the far corner of the grove. The trunks were sunk in shadow, and two specks in that darkness gleamed blue.

The Magus!

The Gray Emperor moved his shoulders in a way suggestive of a shudder. He said briskly, "Of course. That is part of our bargain. Everything and everyone on Earth shall be yours, forever and ever, including your child. Would you mind awfully going away now?"

Lloyd stopped fighting his captors. He yelled at the darkness, *"You've* got a child, you old monster?"

"Yes," the Magus sighed.

"And why should he not?" the Gray Emperor said. "I am older than he—three thousand, two hundred and eighteen Earth years old, to be precise—and I still have children all the time. These are some of them, in fact." He waved at the living corpses hanging from the trees.

"Jesus Christ," Lloyd grunted.

The emperor laughed. "He commanded His followers to drive out demons in His name. But on your lips, the name lacks power."

"It's a question of faith," Lloyd muttered.

"No doubt. What *is* this state of consciousness you call faith? Perhaps this experiment will shed light on that, too."

Colm saw two more battlesuited sentrienza advancing through the trees. One of them carried a pair of gold ribbons. He had no doubt those were high-potential gloves. If they got those on him it'd be over.

"For myself, I have faith in nothing," the Magus whispered. "Least of all in you, Your Imperial Majesty."

"Understandable, understandable."

"So I want it in writing. The Earth, and my son."

"Oh, damn you," the Emperor said. "Very well! *Then* you will go away. Yes?"

One of the guards left the grove. The other one trained its gun on Colm but did not attempt to approach him. He had a moment's breathing space. He fought to think about anything other than Nicky, crushed against the Emperor's scabby ribcage, tears trickling down his poor little cheeks. He remembered the Walking Guns butting him with their heads, like they were playing a game with him. Each of them a planet-killer, powered by a tiny black hole.

"They've promised to give you Earth?" he yelled at the Magus. "Did you know they just tried to destroy the whole planet? I saw them off. They were going to turn Earth into a black hole! There'd have been nothing left."

"Not true," the emperor said swiftly. "There would be a black hole. Its event horizon would still contain everyone and everything on Earth. So, not a lie." He glanced into the shadowy corner, then back at Colm. Membranes slid down over his eyes to make them gentle and lustrous. "You defeated my extinction squad? Really?" Of course, they wouldn't have got the news at Elphame yet. "I *must* know how you did it."

Colm was tonguetied. The Magus whispered menacingly, "You tried to trick me?"

"Tit for tat, you horrid ghoul," the emperor said. "Anyway, the extinction protocol seems to have failed. So you shall have the planet in its natural state, humans and all. Is that acceptable?"

The darkness breathed. "Yes," the Magus grumbled softly. "But I want it in writing."

"Oh, for God's sake," the emperor said. He winked at Lloyd. "See, I can take that name in vain, too … Bring writing materials!"

A guard brought a piece of what looked like parchment, and a stylus whose end glowed red-hot. The emperor clicked his fingers. A Walking Gun loped through the trees and crouched in front of him, flattening its back to serve as a writing desk.

The emperor blew on the end of the stylus, and then tested it on Nicky's arm.

Nicky convulsed. He drew a huge breath, face reddening, and screamed piercingly.

That scream shredded any other ideas Colm might have had. He took a single stride forward, knelt on the grass, and choked, "Let him go! Take me instead! I'll be better for your experiment. I'll cooperate. I'll do whatever you want. Just let him go. Please."

The emperor tilted his face on one side. "Well, well. Is this the state of consciousness called *love?*"

"I'm begging you. Let the child and my father go. Keep me." Colm stretched out both hands, palms up, offering them for gloves. Finally, he understood why he was here. Why he'd been made this way. It was so he could make his death count for something.

CHAPTER 51

Meg, Axel, and Dhjerga cautiously ascended the tunnel that sloped up from the Loch Ness Monster's cave. Meg took point, carrying her Gauss, senses extended into the greeny dark. The tunnel was wide and high enough for the Loch Ness Monster itself. She wondered if it had ever come up this way.

An odor of dead fish tinged the air. It got progressively stronger and more repellent as they walked. The walls grew paler and paler green and then turned dark gray. Meg's night vision had automatically taken itself offline, because there was light coming from up ahead. Not the welcoming glow of human LEDs, but a bluish gleam. Its source came in view: a cluster of fungi on the ceiling. The fungi were phosphorescent.

Meg and Axel startled at the sight.

"I've seen these somewhere before," Meg said gloomily.

"Yup," Axel said.

"In the sentrienza mound on Sakassarib."

"Yup."

"And on board the *Ruddiganmaseve.*"

"And in the Duke of Noom's mound."

But what were sentrienza star fungi doing in a cave under the bank of Loch Ness? The question answered itself.

"I guess now we know how Nessie got here," Axel murmured.

"Yeah," Meg said. She reversed her Gauss and swung it at the fungi, smashing their fleshy petals off. Phosphorent fragments fell to the floor. "The sentrienza brought it."

They walked on. There were more clusters of fungi. Meg gave up—she couldn't smash them all.

"But this cave is *old,*" Axel said. "And the legend of Nessie? *Thousands* of years old. I think she was first spotted in the fifth century."

"An alien monster could be long-lived," Meg said. "The sentrienza are pretty long-lived themselves. I think Emnl's dad was five hundred or something. He was like ninety percent bionic."

Dhjerga broke in. "Our legend of Scota's grave mentions the faeries. It's said that faeries guard her grave."

Meg and Axel stared at him. "Thanks for mentioning that earlier," Meg said. "How about fetching us some more ammo, before these faerie guards come to see who's trespassing?"

Dhjerga spread his hands. "No power," he said quietly.

And who ever heard of a sentrienza mound without power? Unless it was … deserted.

Meg did not relax, but when they finally reached the end of the tunnel, she removed her finger from the Gauss's trigger guard. A mat of star fungi on the roof illuminated an installation of machinery, dominated by a large tank. It had clearly been here for a very, very long time: the fungi had grown down from the ceiling in stalactites that actually encased the top of the truss holding the tank in place. The displays were dark and dead.

"No one's home," Meg said, half-relieved, half-disappointed.

"What *is* that?" Axel said.

Meg shrugged. Unexpectedly, it was Dhjerga who provided the answer. He circled the installation, brushing his fingers along a torpedo-shaped unit installed near the tank. "I've seen

349

one of these before. It's a thermal depolymerization plant."

"A what?" Meg said.

"This is a generator. It runs on biodiesel, which is produced from waste." Dhjerga knocked his knuckles on the upright tank.

Something knocked back.

Meg crossed swifly to the tank. She banged the stock of the Gauss on it, and listened.

"Help!"

A faint human voice.

"Help …"

Two human voices.

The tank stood on stilts. Its top was three meters off the floor, too high for them to reach. Meg, the lightest, stood on Axel's shoulders, while Dhjerga steadied them both. She heaved at the tank's lid, realized it was spring-loaded, slammed the release. The lid flew back.

The smell of rotten fish hit her like a punch.

The tank was half full. In a soup of lakewater, weeds, dead fish, and mud stood two people, a man and a woman. The water was up to their necks. "Help," the man said.

Meg hung over the edge of the tank, the metal cutting into her stomach, reaching for them. When the man grabbed her hands, he almost pulled her in, too. She managed to help him get a grip on the edge. He reached back for the woman. Meg knotted her prosthetic hand into the woman's soaked clothes, and somehow both of the prisoners heaved themselves over and out of the tank.

Meg sprang to the ground amidst glad cries. Dhjerga had his arms wrapped around the prisoners. The three of them danced in circles, weeping and shouting and hugging like they'd never let go.

"Does Dhjerga know them?" she muttered to Axel.

"Yes," Axel muttered back. "They're his brother and sister. That's Dryjon and that's Diejen."

The Lizps' joy was contagious, and Meg caught herself smiling, while her eyes grew damp. Against all expectations, Dhjerga had found his missing loved ones. But where was Nicky?

She cleared her throat. "Um, guys, hate to intrude, but ..."

Diejen broke away from Dhjerga, rushed at Meg, and hugged her, too. She kissed her on both cheeks. "Thank you," she exclaimed. "I am getting you all dirty and wet. Do you mind?"

Diejen's elation suddenly infected Meg. She seized the Ghost woman's hands and they spun around like children, laughing, until Meg saw that Diejen was falling-down tired, and probably dehydrated and maybe sick from standing in that tank for *how* long? She put her arm around her. "What the hell were you doing in there?"

"I thought our doom was upon us," Diejen said, shivering. "Dryjon came here looking for Scota's grave. I came after him. We got in here but then we could not get out. There is a ... ward? Something ... We could flit out of the tank, but not out of the cave. And every time we left the tank, the monster would find us, and sting us again, and put us back in."

"We ended up staying in the tank because it was the only place the monster would not attack us," Dryjon said. He looked around nervously. "Where is it?"

"Back that way, dead," Meg said, noting that the twins had been stung multiple times, and were still alive. Good news for Axel.

Dhjerga was fiddling with the computer controls. Suddenly the tank's lid snapped shut and a grinding noise came from inside.

Diejen went pale. "If we were still in there ..." Meg finished the sentence in her mind. Diejen and Dryjon would have been ground up with the fish and lakeweed to make biodiesel.

Dhjerga rubbed his hands on his jeans. "Once, I put corpses into a machine like this. In those days I didn't care. I just didn't care."

Meg cleared her throat. She noticed that the generator's display had lit up. "So the monster's job was to fill the tank. With fish. Um. People. Whatever. The grinder would probably come on automatically when it sensed that the tank was full."

Dryjon nodded. "The monster kept throwing more fish and things in on top of us."

"Then it would power the generator," Meg went on. "But what does the generator do?"

"I think I've found it," Axel called. He was over by the wall of the cave, inspecting the rock. "There are metal filaments embedded in the rock. This whole cave is a Faraday cage." He turned to the twins. "That's why you couldn't get out."

"It's a trap," Dryjon said. "I should have known. Honestly, I feel so stupid. Scota's grave." He shook his head.

"I'm not sure it was designed as a trap," Axel said, returning to them. "I mean, why would they expect anyone to come here? No one knows about this cave. We used to have powerful scanning equipment. We'd have noticed a TDP plant running under the bank of Loch Ness, even if it was only turned on occasionally. The Faraday cage is there to *hide* the plant ... How did you get in, anyway?"

Dryjon sighed. "We found a cave and went in. And further in, and further in. I know. Stupid."

Meg yelped, "So there's a way out?" but no one heard her, because Dhjerga, still fiddling with the machinery, let out a cry of shock.

They all rushed to him. A knobbly black unit, next to the tank, connected to it by pipes, had begun to spit brown cylinders into a metal container. Meg smelled a yeasty odor that reminded her of that all-time favorite shipboard food, Pink Slime.

Axel picked up one of the cylinders. His arms were working again, kind of. He had to use both hands to lift the small cylinder. He sniffed it.

"You are *not* going to eat that," Meg said.

"Not a chance."

"It's made of rotten fish." And, Meg thought, it *would* have been made of living people.

"Ain't sentrienza technology awesome?" Axel said, dropping the cylinder back into the basket.

"Monster chow," Meg said. But that made no sense, because why import a monster into Loch Ness, set it up with its own automated cafeteria, and then just ... leave it?

Axel shook his head. "The food's made from biowaste. But the TDP plant is also producing biodiesel for the generator. What does *that* do?"

No one knew. Meg lost interest and began to look for the way out. She tapped and thumped the walls until she found a metal plate set into the rock. She whacked it. A Nessie-sized section of wall swung back with a hiss of sentrienza hydraulics.

Dryjon and Diejen jumped. "We *tried* that …"

"Betcha the door only opens when the genny's running," Meg said. She stepped out cautiously into another corridor. Star fungi encrusted the roof. As before, she didn't even need her night vision.

The others came out after her. Axel examined the walls. "No Faraday cage."

The humans and the Ghosts regarded each other. No Faraday cage, and a working generator, meant the Ghosts could flit.

"You guys go on," Meg said, flapping a hand. "We'll be fine."

She could see that Dryjon and Diejen were at the end of their strength. Not surprising, after their ordeal. They needed to get out of here, get dry, get warm, get some food inside them. So did she, actually. But she couldn't leave Axel.

"You should come with us, Meg!" Dhjerga said.

"But she's not—" Axel started. Then he slumped slightly. "Oh."

Meg felt terrible. "I'm not really like them," she said. What use was a magical heritage when it couldn't even help her save Nicky?

"Exactly," Dhjerga said. "You don't know how to flit. Axel's got his battlesuit—"

"Yeah, I'll be fine," Axel said, standing there in his freaking underwear, with his arms not even working properly.

Meg took a deep breath. Her resolve was going to fail her any minute. "Would you guys just *go,* please? They need medical attention."

Dhjerga closed his eyes for a moment. He seemed to be communing with his conscience. "All right," he said at last.

"Come on, you two."

He put his arms around the twins. Axel silently pushed Meg towards them. She pushed him back. This was it, didn't he get it? He was never going to get out of here. She and Dhjerga had drained his battlesuit's fuel cell. He was stuck here, in the Loch Ness Monster's cave. So she was going to stay here and die with him. Without Nicky, what was the point of living, anyway?

"See you soon," Dhjerga said lightly, but there was nothing light in the glance he exchanged with her. She nodded fiercely.

The three Ghosts faded.

CHAPTER 52

Meg watched the three Ghosts fade, holding back her urge to shout at them: Wait, wait, take me …

Dryjon suddenly became solid again. "Actually, before we go, I'd like to see Scota's grave once more."

Dhjerga flashed back into solidity. "You *found* it?"

"Oh, didn't we say?" Diejen said, becoming solid in her turn.

"You're joking! Scota's grave really exists!? Where is it?"

"Right up there," Diejen said, pointing up the tunnel. "It's a bit underwhelming. Not really worth coming halfway across the galaxy for."

"I have to at least see it," Dhjerga said.

So now Meg had to hold onto her resolve for however long it took to do the freaking graveyard tour.

She trailed behind the Ghosts, digging her fingernails into her palms. After a few minutes the tunnel forked into two. Diejen and Dryjon led them down the wider fork. It ended in a tiny cave. They all crowded in to stare at a stone sarcophagus half-buried in phosphorescent fungi. Diejen was right, Meg thought: *underwhelming* summed it up.

Dryjon pointed out an inscription in chicken-scratchy characters, explaining that he had scraped the fungi off the inscription when they first found the grave, before the monster caught them. Diejen translated it: "'Here lies my mother, Scota of Caledonia, slain by my father.'"

"What does that mean?" Dhjerga said. His mood seemed to have darkened. He was scowling and shifting from foot to foot. Maybe, Meg thought, the tropo crash was hitting him.

"Don't know," Dryjon said. "Whoever carved this wasn't very good. Look, here and here, his chisel slipped."

Axel squeezed between the Ghosts and bent over the characters. "These look like runes, but they aren't Ogham or Viking runes ..." Of course, Axel had gone to top-flight schools where you learned that kind of thing. He had so many sides to him, and that was one reason she'd fallen in love with him. How could she have fucked everything up so badly?

She left the cave, deciding to investigate the other fork of the tunnel.

It was narrower, dank, and ended in iron bars, set into the ceiling and floor. The bars were set three feet apart, but that was still too narrow for an alien monster to squeeze through, suggesting that this was the Nessie equivalent of a safety gate. The sentrienza had not wanted the monster going beyond this point. Why not? Could there be another way out?

Despite that tantalizing possibility, Meg was oddly reluctant to explore any further. A bad smell wafted from between the bars. She wrinkled her nose. Not rotten fish this time; more like sewers. She trained her night vision on the darkness beyond the bars.

Nothing moved, and she was about to turn away when she heard a shuffling, dragging noise in the darkness.

A hideous night-green shape shambled towards her.

It screamed, and Meg screamed back.

*

Dhjerga heard screaming. He and Axel took off at a run, back up the tunnel. Dhjerga outdistanced Axel, because he had boots on while Axel was barefoot, but not by much. "Meg, Meg!" Axel bawled as he ran. He loves that woman more than is wise, Dhjerga thought.

He met Meg at the fork in the tunnel. In fact, she almost crashed into him. She caromed off the wall and stumbled against Axel.

"What the hell? Meg!"

"It's coming! It's coming after me!" She spun, grabbing her Gauss on its sling, setting it against her shoulder.

A heartbeat of silence. Then: *scrape, scrape, scrape.*

Dhjerga raised his own gun.

A grotesque form tottered out of the other fork of the tunnel.

Dhjerga had thought he'd already seen the worst that this hideaway had to offer. The Loch Ness Monster had been bad. But this was worse.

Short legs barely supported a pyramidical bulk of naked flesh. The lowest rolls of the body dragged on the floor, while the creature struggled to gather them up with weak little arms. In the bluish light from the star fungi, the monster's skin resembled the hide of a hog, rough and wrinkled, with bristly reddish hairs growing in a line up its stomach and around the fleshy flaps of its chest.

It stank like a hogpen, and left a smear of feces where its buttocks scraped along the floor.

Yet worst of all, the blunt head atop the mountainous body, resting on stacked jowls, had lips and a nose. A few puffs of red hair clung to its scalp. Its blue eyes brimmed with fear.

It was *human.*

Dhjerga slapped Meg's gun down. "Don't shoot!" He knew that he was on the verge of solving the mystery which had distorted his life and deformed his soul. Where did the taint of evil come from? What had warped his people? The answer stood in front of him, gibbering and wringing its hands.

"Stranger," Dhjerga said, consciously forming his words in the Teanga. "Who are you?"

The mountainous creature cringed against the wall. It whimpered. Perhaps it had forgotten how to talk.

"It thinks we're going to hurt it," Axel said.

Of course, Meg *had* been about to hurt it. She was hanging back now, wary.

"Please," the creature sobbed. "Food?"

So *this* was who ate those cylinders of compressed waste! The Loch Ness Monster had been its guardian, nurse, and captor. Faerie guards? The faeries had left, but their slave had stayed behind, to guard not just Scota's grave, but this wretched … man.

"I ask again, who are you?" Dhjerga said.

"Dragon?" the man said fearfully.

"The … dragon … is dead. You are free." Dhjerga smiled, although he wanted to vomit. By Scota's grave, there was *moss* growing in the man's skin folds.

Diejen and Dryjon emerged from the other tunnel.

"Oh," Dryjon said.

Dhjerga nodded. "I think we've found our inscription-carver."

Dryjon muttered, "'Here lies my mother, Scota of Caledonia, killed by my father …' Could it be?"

The three Lizps stared at the grotesque man-mountain in shared revulsion … and understanding.

Dhjerga spoke the thought that was on all their minds. "This is the Magus's son."

*

"Hang on," Axel interrupted. "That's not possible. It's just … nope. He'd have to be thousands of years old."

Dhjerga ignored him. He levelled his gun at the man-mountain. Hurt him? He'd do a damn sight more than that. For the sake of this ... this *creature,* the Magus had rebuilt their entire society into a war machine, had slaughtered millions, littered the galaxy with slaves, and warped his own mages into killers. Did Dhjerga bear a grudge? Yeah, you could say that. So he'd do what he was made to do. He'd kill—

Dryjon punched his gun arm. "Hold your damned fire, brother." He moved between Dhjerga and the Magus's son. With determined courtesy, he bowed. "Do you have a name?"

"I ... Drest." The man-mountain's voice was low, frightened. His eyes flicked from one to the other of them. How long had it been since he saw any other human beings? "Me ... Drest."

"Drest, I am honored to make your acquaintance. My name is Dryjon. This is my brother Dhjerga and this is my sister Diejen. We're, ah ..." Dryjon smirked nervously. "Your long-lost cousins?"

Drest pointed a trembling, broken-nailed finger at Axel and Meg. "Romans?"

"No," Dryjon said, "their names are Axel and Megumi. They are valiant humans of Earth."

Diejen broke in, "Drest, the Romans are no more! They wanted to enslave us, but instead we enslaved them." Her smile was as brittle as glass. "You need not fear them any longer."

"What the fuck? Romans, now?" Meg said.

Dhjerga knew that Diejen was simplifying it considerably. There had been intermarriage between mages and freemen, a little or a lot, depending on who you asked. That's why the Lizps were mages and not pure druids like the Magus. They were *also* descended from the Romans, those marauding, raping, plundering killers. The present echoed the past. And yet he still understood nothing.

"Oh, what a tragedy it has all been," Diejen said, in a thin voice that made Dhjerga remember their mother on her deathbed. She'd died of a wound taken in the Magus's war.

And Diejen was shivering in her wet clothes. Dhjerga forgot the big questions as concern for the twins filled his mind. "Diejen, you and Dryjon must leave here."

"What," said Dryjon, "when we've just met our long-lost cousin? There's so much I want to ask him!" He was shivering, too, but even the risk of death could not dim his curiosity. That was what he and Dhjerga had in common. Curiosity: their curse.

Drest squealed suddenly, "My father left us. My mother died but I did not." His eyes, mere flecks in his huge drooping face, filled with tears. "I cannot die."

"Oh boy," Meg said suddenly. "Emnl used to hint about the gift of eternal life. I thought she was just fucking with me."

"They gave you eternal life, Drest?" Dryjon said. "And *left you here?*"

Drest nodded. "My father said he would come back for me. But he never did. He never did."

A thought struck Dhjerga. A very good thought.

He smiled. "Drest, what would you do to him if you could meet him again, your father? What would you do, hmm?"

"Dead him." Drest's hands flexed. "Dead him, for leaving me and my mother! Dead, dead, dead!"

"Guess you're family, after all." Dhjerga stepped around his brother and sister . Repressing a shudder, he took Drest's pudgy, scaly hand in his own. "Dead him, huh?"

"Yes!"

"Sounds like a plan, coz."

CHAPTER 53

"Take me instead." Colm bowed his head and stretched his hands out, willing the Gray Emperor to accept his offer. *Me for the child. Me for my father. It's a good deal. Take it.*

The Walking Gun that crouched in front of the emperor, with a piece of parchment on its back, waiting for the emperor's signature, swivelled its head around and whined at him.

"No!" It was the Magus's voice. The lights dimmed. The shadow of the Magus surged between the trees and loomed over the man, the sentrienza emperor, and the child. The yellow grass under Colm's knees turned into nails, frozen stiff. "Your Imperial Majesty, he is lying to you! He's not a real mage!"

"Right. I'm a chemical mage," Colm said, looking up at the shadow. "Got a chip in my head and a Nessie mug full of nothing. As they say, what doesn't kill you makes you stronger. In fact, Mr. Gray—sorry, I'm Scottish, not awfully fond of imperial titles—I'm more a Ghost than the Ghosts are. Want a demonstration?"

The sentrienza emperor chittered laughter. He was tickled, Colm thought, by the spectacle of two magicians vying for his favor. "Perhaps a *small* one."

"Right," Colm said. For a terrible moment his mind was blank. Then he remembered the victory party on Atletis.

Such a small victory, in retrospect, and not even a final one. But it had felt plenty final at the time, and the Ghosts had expressed their joy in giddy demonstrations of magic, each taking a turn to strut his or her stuff while the others watched and ate and heckled and laughed themselves silly. "It is like the Games of old!" Diejen had said, delighted, before getting up to take her turn.

She had made the trees sing.

Colm had watched in awe. When she sat back down, amidst applause, she'd explained how she did it. Colm had never tried it for himself, as it seemed kind of pointless, but with Nicky's life at stake, nothing was pointless anymore.

He raised his Nessie mug into the air, leeched power from the multifarious electromechanical systems under the floor, and started to conduct the sentrienza trees.

"Oh come oh come Emmanuel," they sang in chorus, sweet and low, their withered leaves forming mouths. "And ransom captive Israel." It was autumn at home, Christmas was not far off: Colm had heard a syrupy instrumental version of this song playing at the Star Port Mall in Tokyo. "That mourns in lonely exile here, until the son of God appear!"

Nicky stopped crying, entranced by the eerie a capella music.

"Rejoice, rejoice," the trees sang, and the sentrienza prisoners hanging from the trees joined in the chorus, They had so many tubes and lines going into them that they were practically part of the system. They ripped their stitched lips open and sang through the blood: "Emmanuel! Shall come to thee, oh Israel!"

The Gray Emperor's face twitched. He stared in amazement at the spooky sight. Even Colm had not expected the prisoners to join in. He only knew the one verse so he repeated it.

"Rejoice, rejoice!" —yes, even here, he thought, even in the evil heart of the sentrienza empire, facing certain death, it was still possible and even necessary to rejoice. "Emmanuel shall come to thee, oh Israel."

The trees fell silent. The prisoners hung limp and bleeding. The emperor was yelping softly to himself.

Lloyd applauded. "You've come on, lad," he muttered. "You've definitely come on."

But Colm's gaze was fixed on the emperor. "How about that?" he said nervously.

The emperor stared at him, faceted eyes wide and wild. "That is *real* magic," he said in a voice thick with emotion. "Beautiful! Beautiful!"

He pushed Nicky away. "Grandpa," Nicky wailed. Ignoring Colm, he stumbled straight to Lloyd. Colm smiled ruefully. That was what he'd wanted, after all. Go, he thought at Lloyd. *Go!* What are you waiting for?"

"You will stay here with me," the emperor said to Colm, "and make the trees sing every day. There are no trees left on the surface of Elphame, you know. All of them died. These twisted underground specimens are all that remain. Yet you have given them new life!"

"I guess so," Colm said, quietly rejoicing. And he fetched the Emperor's Walking Gun onto his lap.

He had worked it out gradually, thinking about the Walking Guns that seemed to come with the *Shihoka* when he flitted. He hadn't wanted them along, far from it, so how had they stuck to him?

Answer: they hadn't.

Look at the way they'd rushed him when he finally emerged from hiding. Butting him and roughhousing like big metal dogs.

They were not mere machines. They were sentient enough

to be copied. And that's what he'd done, accidentally. They had not really been trying to demolish the *Shihoka*. Like slaves, according to their nature, they had just been trying to get close to him, so he could tell them what to do.

And now he had another one sitting in his lap. If it had a tongue it'd've been licking his face.

"Here's what you do," he muttered to it, while everyone else was still trying to work out where the heck an extra Walking Gun had come from, and why it was behaving so oddly. Colm pointed to the Emperor and *his* Walking Gun. "Sic 'em."

His Walking Gun leapt at the Emperor's Gun and slammed into it, razor claws slashing. While the two Guns rolled over and over, Colm calmly duplicated them both again. Two times two is four Walking Guns pouncing on the Gray Emperor.

They pinned the emperor and snapped his neck with the coil-powered, titanium-edged teeth.

"Heh, heh," Colm said. Then he turned to look for Lloyd, hoping his father would already have flitted with Nicky. What he saw chilled his blood. "Watch out!" he howled.

The sentrienza guards were rushing at Lloyd and Nicky as Lloyd struggled to peel his gloves off. Nicky, panicking, ran from the battlesuited figures. He was only two. He tripped and fell on the grass—

—in the Magus's shadow.

Colm hurled himself into the shadow as it drew back between the trees. He landed face-down in a mighty boot-print, still cold.

When he sat up, Lloyd had got his gloves off. He was grimly dealing with the guards, fetching lightning from the life-support equipment. Massive bolts of electricity jagged out from the medical units, and fused the guards' battlesuits into lumps of carbon, whilst putting the poor torture victims out of their misery. The deafening cracks left the air charged with ozone. Thank God the ground was dry, and the fake soil and fake grass did not conduct electricity.

Colm's Walking Guns won the fight with the Emperor's Gun and came prancing back to Colm for new orders.

The Gray Emperor crawled behind them.

Oh. Thought he was supposed to be dead.

The emperor's neck was clearly broken. He was holding his head straight with both hands, trying to joggle it back into place.

"That looks painful," Colm said.

"Yes. I am experiencing the state of consciousness called *pain*. However, I shall survive. I always survive. The pinnacle of sentrienza biotechnology is the gift of eternal life. I gave that gift to myself thousands of years ago—"

"And now you're paying for it," Colm said. He beckoned to the nearest of his Walking Guns. Stroking its steel neck, he copied it again and again. Elphame was riddled with power sources, near and far. There were power lines behind every wall, under every floor. The planet was a technological marvel: the sentrienza had destroyed their homeworld's original ecosystem, but recreated it underground. Wizened trees, fake skies, holo rivers. All of it powered by electricity.

Now, slaved to Colm's will, a growing army of Walking Guns embarked on a mission of destruction. They spat flechettes and slugs into sensitive machinery and howled their former masters' brains to jelly in their heads. Colm reckoned the emperor knew what was happening. "Told you I was pretty good at this," he said, although he was horrified at the scale of what he'd let loose. Each Walking Gun could destroy a planet, and now hundreds of them were rampaging through Elphame's subterranean habitats. In for a penny, in for a pound. He copied some more of them to the nearest heimdalls.

The Gray Emperor gave up trying to make his head stay on straight. It flopped over at an awful angle. The lustrous eyes stayed on Colm in their new position. "We tried so hard to civilize your species," he buzzed. "And this is how you repay us!"

"Yeah well; sorry about that." Colm had no energy left for conversation. Nicky was gone, again. Nothing could make up for that failure.

Lloyd, holding Mickle, stumbled over. He said to the Emperor, "How does it feel to have *your* planet wrecked? What goes around comes around. We'll do the heimdalls next, won't we? All of them."

"Already doing it," Colm said.

"I should have initiated the extinction protocol much earlier," the Gray Emperor buzzed. "But I had hopes for you! Such high hopes!"

"Expect nothing of people, and you won't be disappointed," Lloyd said.

"But there *are* certain expectations. There is no such thing as a free lunch, nor a free ride, nor free energy. Entropy always increases. As in the physical universe, so in sapient relations. What is given must be paid for; what is received must be paid forward. This is beauty, this is living in harmony with nature, this is the *law!* We have taught every other sapient species to obey the law. But then you humans came along, with your impossibly strong biofields, your impossible mass-energy conversions, your impossible states of consciousness—"

Colm glanced at his father. "I think he's saying we're ungrateful sods."

"No," Lloyd said. "He's saying that we're naturally religious. Other species aren't, as far as I can tell. Against all reason, we keep on believing in the impossible, and worse yet, *doing* the impossible. That's it, isn't it, you old devil?"

"I don't know," the Gray Emperor said. "I don't *know*." He lay down on the grass. "That is why I did not initiate the extinction protocol thousands of Earth years ago. I wanted to know how you did it."

"Same old story," Lloyd said. "The God-botherers from the middle of nowhere are interesting, until they're knocking your empire over."

"When the Ghosts appeared, it was agreed that your species had to be terminated. But it was already too late." The emperor smiled at the darkening ceiling. "Now I have the experience of unknowing everything I thought I once knew."

Lloyd chortled. "Turn about is fair play, you bastard." He seized Colm's wrist in one hand and curled his other hand through Mickle's collar.

The Gray Emperor's optical membranes retracted. His faceted eyes glittered. "I wonder," he mused, "what it would be like to experience the state of consciousness known as death?"

A rumble shook the grove. A flash of light blinded Colm, and then everything vanished.

CHAPTER 54

Where am I?

The nerve-shredding agony of the flit abated. Colm opened his eyes. He was sitting on a flat rock in a sort of Zen garden that seemed to stretch away to the horizon. His leathers were in shreds. Overhead, the sun of Elphame shone in a pale blue sky. It was chilly. He moved his arms and legs. He was in one piece.

"Your Walking Guns blew up the whole fucking planet," Lloyd said. He stood on the gravel near Colm's rock. Mickle clung to his shoulder, her tail a bottle-brush, her back fur hackling. "I think this heimdall's fairly far out from the star. Should be a while before the pieces of Elphame hit it."

"Don't you know where we are?"

"I just followed him."

Lloyd's duster hung in torn flaps. He pointed at some more rocks in the distance.

Colm heard a child crying. *Nicky.* He jogged towards the rocks, and the largest of them spoke. "Will you keep following me forever?"

Colm could still hear Nicky crying but he couldn't see him. Beyond the big rock, the rocky ground sloped down to a lake or sea. Little waves lapped on a pebbly shore.

"Earth is *mine*," the Magus said. "It is my home."

Lloyd caught up with Colm. "What've you done with Nicky, you bastard?"

The largest rock moved. For a mere instant, it took on the shape of an enormous man, his head hidden in shadows, holding Nicky on his knee. His fingers had far too many joints.

Some of them were wrapped around the boy's tummy and some around his neck.

"He is no use to me anymore. What will you give me for him?"

Colm had no authority, nothing to bargain with. He had used it all up. "Damn you," he sobbed.

The Magus chuckled coldly. "I am already damned."

The long fingers tightened on Nicky's neck. Nicky began to thrash. The Magus was going to kill him for sheer spite. Something snapped in Colm's mind. He threw himself at the rock. He would be the Magus's doom. He would hang onto him and flit with him wherever he fled until they both died of old age, just so long as the Magus died first.

He collided with tough, age-burnished leather. He kicked and punched and found flesh and bit. The Magus's skin tasted like dirt. Colm was fighting in the pitch dark. All he could see was the Magus's cold blue eyes. He shouted Nicky's name into the darkness, and suddenly the child's face brushed against his, sticky and cold. Colm frantically bent back the long fingers from around Nicky's neck and gathered the child into his arms.

An enormous fist knocked him sideways. He landed on his back, still in the dark, with Nicky on his chest. The blue eyes hovered above him.

"I lost my son!" the Magus thundered. "Why should you not lose yours?"

Winded, Colm could not reply. He rolled over to shield Nicky with his body from the blow that had to be coming.

"Here's your son, Magus," shouted a new voice.

A voice Colm knew.

Dhjerga.

The darkness drew back. Colm sat up with Nicky on his lap. Nicky began to sob. It was the best sound Colm had ever heard. Alive, *alive!*

The Magus towered over them, a sea stack of shadow.

Dhjerga was down on the desolate bach. He crunched up the incline towards them, carrying a gun in one hand. His other hand supported the elbow of a man-monster with a huge body and a small head. The creature looked around in fear and confusion.

The Magus stood up and doffed his glamor.

Like a cloak, the shadows fell to the ground, and like water they melted away. Revealed, the Magus was doughty in appearance, with Viking-style mustaches and a braided beard that reached his knees. His long hair glinted silver in the sun, but his mustaches and beard were still flecked with orange. His heavy jaw jutted like a shovel. He wore a vast leather coat, tight britches like the men of Kisperet favored, and those outsized leather boots that had given Colm nightmares as a child.

His feet really were that big. But so was the rest of him.

Holding Nicky, Colm stood up and backed away, anticipating a disastrous meeting between the two giants.

"Drest," the Magus whispered.

The smaller giant, guided by Dhjerga, tottered up to the Magus. He whimpered, "Daddy?"

"Drest!" The Magus wrapped him in his enormous arms, leather creaking. "Look at you, my lad. Ah, what have they done to you?"

Dhjerga stumbled up to Colm. He was in a crap state, wet and dirty, as if he'd been crawling through a sewer. He smelled like it, too. "I don't believe it," he muttered furiously.

"Is that really the Magus's son?"

"Yes. He was supposed to kill him, not *hug* him!"

"You could kill him yourself now he's distracted," Colm said, stroking Nicky's hair.

Dhjerga rubbed his face with his hands. "I'm not a monster," he said.

"Of course you're not. You're a goddamn hero. You just saved all of us."

Lloyd was talking to the giants. He looked very small and frail beside them, in his torn duster, with his cat in his arms.

"Drest's not a mage," Dhjerga said. "I mean, I knew that. If he was a mage, he'd have flitted a thousand years ago, wouldn't he?"

"So that's a copy?"

"Yes."

"So what?"

"The real Drest wanted to kill his dad. But the copy doesn't, does he? Look at him! He's *happy!*"

The smaller giant, Drest, snuggled against the Magus's bulk. Bliss radiated from his face.

"Well," Colm said, "I suppose even black magic can have good results, occasionally."

Lloyd beckoned them. "I've just heard the strangest tale in the universe," he said. "I think you should hear it, too."

CHAPTER 55

The Magus sat in the sunlight with Drest at his side. Everyone else sat around the giants, listening. Colm knew they should get out of here. They were all tired and hungry. Elphame was disintegrating into a cloud of lethal planetary fragments. His Walking Guns were chewing their way through the rest of the heimdalls in the system. But Nicky had gone to sleep on his knee. And he couldn't drag himself away just yet. Here, at last, were the answers they had sought so long. Here was the truth of the Ghosts.

"When I was young," the Magus said, "we were always fighting. When we were not fighting each other, we were fighting the Romans. They came from beyond the wall in the south. They were better trained, better equipped, they were better *fighters* than our folk. Our only advantage was magic. I was chief druid to Queen Scota of the Caledonii. I called the lightning upon them, I cursed their horses and their feet, and when the thunder was in the sky, I even fetched fighters into their rear and lions into their baggage trains. That was black magic, but we were desperate.

"Then one summer they came in greater numbers than ever before, marching behind their standard of the two-headed eagle. I took that standard later and made it my own, to spite them. They pursued us deeper and deeper into the north. We fled with our children and our animals, knowing the Romans would slaughter or enslave anyone left behind. The weather continued dry and clear; I was powerless. On the banks of the Long Loch, my dear Scota announced that we would stand and fight. The Ridge of the Bridge had always been a place of power for us. I and the other druids could work magic there, even when the sky was clear. On that holy ground, we might have a chance."

"The Ridge of the Bridge?" Colm could hear a familiar echo behind the words. "Drumnadrochit. Dad, he's talking about Drumnadrochit."

It was awe-inspiring to think that epochal battles had been fought, thousands of years ago, on the very same land where he had biked and played as a kid.

"The battle waxed bloody. They had dispatched scouts, unseen by us, to learn our position, so they were ready for us, and although I drew on the power of the ground and multiplied our fighters, sacrificing righteousness for the hope of victory, the Roman legionaries multiplied, too. Now I knew why we could not prevail against them: they had a druid or two in their ranks, as well! Our dead choked the bridge. The river ran red with blood. As sunset drew near, we lost the bridge, and retreated towards the loch.

"Then the miracle happened.

"The ground opened up. A door in the hillside, wide enough for ten men to walk abreast, spilled white light over us. A faerie stood there, radiant, with her eyes shining and her hair flowing like liquid gold. 'Men and women of Caledon,' she said, 'men of Rome, lay down your swords. Enough blood has been spilled. Follow me.'"

"Wonder-struck, we followed her into the hill. It was a maze of marvels: trees, grass, and sky, all underground. Dogs made of metal nosed around us. There was more metal in that place than our smiths could forge in a lifetime! The faeries offered us food and drink, and tended to our wounded. In our amazement we forgot our enmity, and I spoke to the

Roman mage, expressing my regret that our peoples were at war. He was a good man. His name was Rufus of Spain. He is long dead now.

"When we were fed and rested, the faeries came to talk to me and Scota. Our little son was with us."

"I remember that," Drest said, leaning against his father. His huge body wobbled beneath the cloak Dhjerga had fetched for him.

"They said they had been watching the battle, and they were very taken with the magic that Rufus and myself were working. They said they would like us to show them more magic. It was something they could not do, faeries though they were, and they wanted to learn how it was done. Scota told them that it was none of their business and that they should let us out of there immediately. She did not like or trust them, and I should have hearkened to her judgement. She was the queen. But I was tired and sick of fighting. And after talking to Rufus, I knew that we could not win. Magic was our only advantage and now I knew that the Romans had it, too. Sooner or later they would crush us entirely. I could not see any future for our people in Caledon."

Lloyd coughed. "The Romans never conquered Scotland," he said. "But they conquered England, and then the English conquered us. So you foretold it correctly. But we won back our independence a couple of hundred years ago."

Colm smiled bleakly. The druids of Caledon could've just held on until the 21st century. Right.

The Magus stared at Lloyd. "I have fought your people. I have seen your metal war cars and your flying machines and your legionaries in their metal armor, all organized by their tens and hundreds, serving your imperial dreams. And you say you were *not* conquered by the Romans?"

Dhjerga nudged Colm. "He's got you there …"

"So the faeries offered us a new place to live," the Magus resumed. "They said that they would take us all to Faerieland, a rich country where we could raise our children in peace. They would have to take the Romans, too, they said. They could not let them go now that they had seen the marvels of the faerie mound. There were about three hundred legionaries, but there were five hundred of us, counting the women and children, and many of us had druid's blood. I was content. But Scota balked. She said she would rather perish than leave Caledon.

"The Roman commanders had made the opposite decision. They and their men were eager to travel to Faerieland and live a life of ease. This, too, inclined Scota against the idea. And we argued fiercely, but neither of us could sway the other."

"I wanted to go," Drest whispered. Two big tears leaked out of his eyes.

"That night," the Magus said, "Scota assembled our people, in the grove where they had let us camp, beneath the ground. She told them that the faeries wanted to take us away to their own land, but that she would not go. She asked the people to remain with her. She was a great queen, but the promise of Faerieland was stronger than her words. The people stood up and said that they were going. She could stay behind if she liked. And she said, 'Then I will, and be damned to all of you!'

"Now the faeries were around us listening. And they said to me: 'Is this your decision, too? You will die with your queen, rather than accept our offer?' I could hardly speak for anger, but I told them yes. I had to stay with Scota, even to the death. She was my queen and the mother of my child.

"Then they said that this would not do. They wanted me in particular, as I was the chief druid of the Caledonii and the strongest magic-worker they had ever seen. I do not boast: this is what they said. And they said that the offer would be withdrawn. *All* our people should die, unless I agreed to come to Faerieland.

"Oh, then I grieved greatly. I was torn between Scota and our people. The faeries saw this and they sweetened their offer. They would give me the greatest gift in their possession: the gift of eternal life. I should live forever, if I would come to Faerieland.

"I accepted.

"But I set one condition on our bargain: they should give the gift of eternal life to my little boy, as well. They agreed, and they took us both into a metal room and made us go to sleep, and when we awoke we were immortal."

Colm tried not to stare at the two giants, with their hideously bloated bodies and long fingers. The Magus, he assumed, had kept a more human appearance by staying active. But he, too, had paid a high price for immortality.

"We did not look any different—at first," the Magus said. "This happened gradually, over the years."

Colm muttered, "I suppose they didn't know how it would work on humans, or even if it *would* work. It was just another of their experiments."

"They were not honest about anything. They do not lie, and yet they deceive," the Magus said. "The next day we all got onto the ship that would take us across the sea to Faerieland. They did not tell us it was really a sky ship that would take us across the stars. It was like a huge metal barge floating on the loch. I was busy all day, overseeing the loading of the animals and the seeds and the herbs and the tools. The Romans, as usual, had brought an entire city with them on the war trail. They were set on taking everything, and our people, not to be outdone, rounded up all our sheep and goats and horses ... it was complete chaos. When they finally closed the doors of the ship, the faeries told me Drest was safely on board.

"But he was not.

"I thought they had kept him on Earth as a hostage, and I was ready to jump off the ship and swim back, if I could only find the doors, but then my people told me the truth. Drest had decided to stay behind with his mother. He, alone, had remained loyal to her."

Drest said, "I was ready to die at my mother's side." He scrunched up his huge face, seemingly embarrassed by the memory. "I was only eleven."

"Jesus," Lloyd muttered. "They don't make eleven-year-olds like they used to."

"The faeries did not kill us. But, as they had threatened, they did not let us go. They kept us with them, like pets. After a while my mother died. We buried her at the bottom of the mound." His voice cracked. "Time passed and more time passed, and one day the faeries packed up all their machinery and went away. But they did not take me with them. I think I was an embarrassment to them. They left me there in the mound, with a dragon to guard me and bring me food."

"A dragon?!" Colm whispered to Dhjerga.

"The Loch Ness Monster," Dhjerga whispered back. "We killed it."

"Why do I always miss out on all the fun?"

The Magus took up the story again. "So we travelled to

Faerieland. It was a good land, as they had promised. It was covered in forest, and we felt light. We could jump higher and run further without getting tired. And there was power under the ground. So much power! I could have worked magic all day if I felt like it."

"It was a heimdall," Colm guessed. "Magus ... could you see the sun?"

"Yes, although it looked smaller than it had at home, and it did not seem to give as much heat. It was always winter in Faerieland."

"I bet they had a heimdall set up right in Sol system," Colm said. "An observation platform. The fuckers." But where was that heimdall now? he wondered.

"I did some magic for the people, fetching things we had forgotten, things we needed for our new farms. But I would not do any magic for the faeries. I was angry with them, and as time went on they got angrier and angrier with me.

"Rufus of Spain died at a ripe old age. By then most of our people could not remember Earth. There were many new druids and mages among us, for Rufus had many children, and I had other children, too. None of them were as dear to me as Drest had been, but all the same, I refused to let the faeries take any of them away for their experiments. I did not think we owed them anything. Yet they insisted that we must repay them for their generosity in finding us a new home.

"So I started to explore the stars. Living longer than any other mage, I had developed my art to a high degree. I learned how to search for new power sources among the stars, and flit to them. I learned that there were many, many worlds, and some of them were good for human habitation. And I made up my mind. We would flee. The faeries would never know where we had gone. I chose a world, a good world, and enlisted all the druids and mages in my secret plan."

Drest broke in. "Why didn't you come back to Earth? Why didn't you come back for me?"

The Magus said gruffly, "I did come back for you ... much later. I had to wait until I was strong enough to win. At that time there were only a few of us, and all we had was swords and spears."

Colm, breathless with curiosity, said, "How did you discover bolt-action rifles and mortars?"

"I am telling it," the Magus said. "We combined our strength and we *moved Faerieland.*"

"So that's where the heimdall went!"

"We flitted and we took the whole world with us. It was a heroic feat, but tinged with bitterness, because many of our friends and relatives were changed by the journey, and when they came back to themselves they were not quite the same."

Lloyd swore. "The corpsicles you left behind are probably still floating in the asteroid belt."

"We did what we had to do," the Magus said. "When we got to our new sun, we set upon the faeries, who were confused by the journey, and slew them all. Then we were the masters of Faerieland. We renamed it, after an old legend of Rome: Atletis. And we set out to colonize the new world I had found, which Atletis now orbits like a moon. I named that one: Kisperet."

Dhjerga rubbed his mouth with his knuckles. This had to be devastating for him, Colm thought. He was hearing the history of his own people, in all its glory and sadness. He said, "That's why Kisperet lost its water. You can't just put a moon in orbit around a planet and expect nothing to change. It must have disrupted everything."

"But for many centuries we lived well," the Magus said. "There was only one problem. We had fled so far, and hidden ourselves so well, that *I could not find my way back.* I spent those centuries searching the stars, looking for Earth. It was a weary time. At long last my quest came to an end. I found Earth … in the midst of a terrible war." He glanced at Colm. "That is how we discovered guns."

"First World War," Colm muttered. "Or maybe the Crimea?"

"I realized then that the Romans had won. Earth was now hostile to us. So I returned home, and I set about building my people into a war engine to match the Romans' might. That, too, took generations. By the time I was finally ready to strike, you had spread your empire to other worlds as well. We would have a fight on our hands."

Suddenly, the Magus laughed.

"But as it turned out, it was easy. Your faerie machines were no match for my Mage Corps. We rolled you up in just a few years."

Colm repressed a scowl. It was sadly true. He said, "But had you forgotten about the faeries? Did you think they would let you have Earth for the taking?"

"They *said* they would," the Magus answered. "I held talks with them on Ross 458c, after we conquered that world, and we signed a peace treaty. They promised that they would not help you oppose us."

"The bastards," Colm snarled. Nicky stirred on his knee. "Shush, shush." He had to get Nicky home. Meg and Daisy must be going out of their minds.

But Lloyd wasn't done with the Magus. "When they held

those so-called peace talks with you, the Gray Emperor had already initiated the extinction protocol. Their promise was meaningless."

"The emperor spoke of black holes," the Magus said. "What *is* a black hole, if you would be so kind?"

There was a moment of silence. Colm cleared his throat. He pointed up at the sky. "That's going to be one."

"That is a star," the Magus said.

"Yes … But I commanded all my Walking Guns to fly into it when they finished with the heimdalls. Each Gun has a black hole in its guts. So, er, long story short, that star's going to collapse."

"Poetic justice," Lloyd said, clapping him on the back.

Dhjerga said, "How long will it take?"

"I've got no idea, to be honest. Could be a few days, could be centuries …"

The Magus nodded. "Then Drest and I will remain here until it dies."

Colm met the huge druid's eyes, shocked.

"Drest cannot flit," the Magus rumbled. Colm caught his breath. The Magus *knew* Drest was a copy. Yet he was prepared to sacrifice for him as if he was his real son. "And I will not leave him behind. Not again."

He rose and gestured to the horizon.

"This is another Faerieland, I think: an unfinished one. They have not put in the plants and animals yet. So I will put in *our* plants and animals. I will make a world just for us."

"I thought it was impossible to fetch plants," Colm muttered.

"Not for me," the Magus said. "I am a *real* mage."

Colm smiled, acknowledging it.

Drest was paddling in the little waves, letting the water lift up the weight of his body. Suddenly a dolphin-like alien broke the surface. This heimdall was not completely uninhabited after all. The creater whistled and nosed up to Drest. It did not seem to be threatening, just curious. Delight radiated from Drest's face. "Dad!" he called out. "You realy have brought me to Faerieland!"

CHAPTER 56

"Welp, now it's just us," Meg said to Axel.

The Ghosts were gone. Only Meg and Axel remained in the clammy tunnel behind Nessie's lair. Oh, and the monster Drest. He was sitting on the floor, sucking his fingers and weeping.

Out of sheer habit, Meg tried to think about how they could survive. "We could eat the food Nessie made for Drest," she said. "Catch fish. Run the TDP plant. Drink water from the lake ..."

But that would only postpone their death, and frankly, she wasn't even sure she wanted to postpone it. Nicky was gone. There was no point to living any longer. She wrapped her arms around her legs and rested her cheek on her knee, detaching from her own body, from her pain, from everything, floating in an interior void of numbness.

Axel touched her arm. She looked up. He was kneeling in front of her. "There has to be another way out."

"Just shut up, Axel."

"The air's fresh. It has to be circulating."

"I said shut up."

"Drest got in here somehow, didn't he?"

"Leave me alone."

"No." He tried to pry her arms loose from around her knees.

She shouted into his face, "Nicky is dead!"

"We don't know that," he said feebly.

"People die." She was thinking of her mother and father now. "It's a fact of life. Pretending it didn't happen, pretending he might come back, pretending it might work out all right ... that's just weakness. Weakness!"

Axel said doggedly, "Even if he is ... gone ... we can't just lie down and give up."

"It's all right for you! He wasn't *your* son!"

Axel flinched as if she'd hit him. He stood up, turned away, and punched the wall. "Ow. Shit." He punched the wall again. It was freaking *granite*. Blood welled from his knuckles. "Oh damn it, dammit," he shouted, and hauled back to punch the wall again, because he couldn't punch her, because he wanted to punch *her,* he *must* want to, but he was better than that. He lived the virtues she had always admired—honor, justice, and all that good stuff. And she'd repaid him by hitting him where it hurt.

She jumped up and caught his arms.

"Leave me alone," he said, echoing her words.

"I'm sorry, Axel. I'm sorry."

"He *was* mine. I loved him as much as you did."

"I know." She remembered how Axel had been the one who looked after Nicky when he was a newborn, rocking him and feeding him and changing him and ... *loving* him. The memories cracked her detachment. Tears came.

"We have to keep going, Meg." He was crying too, holding her. "We owe it to him not to give up."

"I don't know how you figure that." She felt as limp as a soggy paper napkin. All the dead people she had carried around with her, a conga line of ghosts constantly urging her to fight, seemed to be washing away with her tears, leaving her empty.

"Ow. My damn hand. I'm so stupid ... There *must* be a way out. Dryjon and Diejen said they got in through a cave ..."

Drest spoke up, shyly. "I think ..." Both of them had forgotten about the man-mountain, sitting by himself, almost out of reach of the star fungi light. They whipped around to stare at him. "I think they came through my room."

"They did?" Axel said.

"I heard them come down the back stairs. I was frightened. I hid."

"Back stairs?" Meg yelped.

They hurried down the corridor together and stepped between the bars of the Nessie gate. It was a tight squeeze for Drest. Axel shone his headlamp around. Drest's room was completely barren, with only a pile of ancient blankets in one corner for a bed. A hole in one corner served as a toilet, but it seemed to have long since backed up. Drest had tidied his excrement into a neat mound and covered it with another blanket—a heartbreaking attempt at housekeeping. Meg's eyes overflowed again. Now that she had started crying, it felt like she would never stop.

"Here are the stairs," Drest said.

The back of the cave narrowed into a tunnel with a deeply corrugated floor, which led up at a steep angle. Drest had to squeeze through sideways.

"I have not come this way in a long time," he muttered.

The stairs led to a maze of echoing corridors and rooms, all empty. This had been a spacious sentrienza mound, no doubt housing dozens of aliens in its day. Drest said he had never explored any further than this—the sentrienza had not allowed him up here, and he had not challenged the prohibition after they left. Meg and Axel had to persuade him at gunpoint not to return to his wretched cave. Towing the poor immortal, they climbed up, and higher up, until they reached the mother of all tunnels, wide enough for ten men to walk abreast. By now Meg and Axel were about ready to pass out from exhaustion and thirst. They stumbled onward and upwards, stopping frequently to rest.

"Keep going," Axel muttered, when Meg felt like she could not get up again. "Keep going."

"Disable your damn implant," she said, "before I punch you for being so gung-ho." The rock was cold under her cheek. She saw Drest crawl past, the rolls of his torso dragging on the ground.

"It is disabled."

"It is?"

"Yup. I'm done with it for good this time."

"So this is who you really are," she said, mustering a smile. Nothing more needed to be said. She got up, and jerked her chin at Drest, who was now ahead of them. "Well, look at that. He's freaking *crawling,* and he's going to beat us to the finish line ..."

They covered the last yards of the tunnel in a walking-speed race, and wound up in a dead end. There had been a cave-in.

"Oh, hell," Axel sighed.

"No!" Meg said. "Look! I can see daylight!"

She scrambled up the rocks. There was a gap between two of the largest boulders. Wet, cold wind blew on her face. She thrust her head and shoulders out into the shelter of a craggy overhang. She was looking down through veils of rain, across neglected fields, to the roofs of Drumnadrochit.

She stayed there a moment, breathing the heady fresh air, and then jumped back down to the floor of the tunnel. "That must be how Dryjon and Diejen got in." The chink was wide enough for her, or the skinny-ass Dryjon, or even Axel at a squeeze. It was not by any stretch of the imagination wide enough for Drest.

"I will stay here," Drest muttered.

Meg took a deep breath. "No. You will not."

"I cannot die."

No, but what would happen to him without the Loch Ness Monster to look after him? She met Axel's eyes. He nodded. They had to take responsibility for the consequences of killing Nessie, and that meant *not* leaving Drest behind.

They both scrambled up and heaved on the car-sized rock that was blocking the gap. It did not move a fraction. Too heavy.

"OK," Meg said. "Get out of the way."

Bracing her feet, she inhaled.

Exhale.

Inhale.

She raised her right hand, her prosthetic one. That strange tingling feeling had never quite gone away. As she concentrated, it intensified.

With a piercing *ki-ai* shout, she let gravity drop the edge of her hand down on the rock.

It split down the middle. One half fell between Meg and Axel into the tunnel, and the other fell out and went thumping away, end over end, down the hillside.

Meg tumbled out after it, onto wet green grass.

CHAPTER 57

The sun was setting over the vineyard on the hill behind the Free Church Manse as Gilliam Tripsilion Nulth's guests rolled up in their cars and horse-drawn carts. It was perfectly safe to use electrically powered equipment these days, but the Ghosts preferred the technology they knew. And with the grid still down, four-legged transport was simply more practical. Gil perched on the roof of the old church, watching Morag Wilson and her boyfriend, Kalsp, unhitch the horses and lead them into the back field. Kalsp was a good lad. He'd won the approval of even the gimlet-eyed Bridget by teaching the islanders how to slaughter pigs and preserve the meat, in a world without refrigerators. Hard to believe that he, like all the Ghosts, had begun his existence on Earth by slaughtering human beings.

They were so *gentle*. Brothers Mark, Cassius, Julian, and Bertram—all of them Ghosts—greeted the guests warmly and guided them beneath Gil's perch, through the doors of the old church.

When everyone was inside, Gil scurried down the drainpipe, bringing a couple of broken tiles down with him. Brother Mark met him at the door. "Have you been climbing on the roof again, sir?" he smiled. "You're all mucky."

Gil glanced down at his official vest. The white "I Heart Skye" emblem—hand-embroidered, messily, by little Scarlett Wilson—was indeed stained green from the moss that grew through the tiles on the church roof.

"The roof needs mending," Gil informed the young monk haughtily. "You should take care of that before winter comes."

"On it, sir. We're already prototyping tiles at the kiln in Portree."

The Ghosts approached the mundane tasks of survival—everything from mending roofs to salting pork to breeding horses—with the same fanatical completism that they had once applied to mass murder. They had taught the islanders many crafts that the people of Earth had forgotten, providing guidance while humbly seeming to follow rather than lead. They may have come back to themselves, but in their hearts, Gil thought with a tinge of cynicism, they were still slaves.

That may be why they made such good monks.

One whole side of the church was occupied with Ghosts who had taken monastic orders, embracing Christianity and the promise of atonement that it offered, under the direction of a rather overwhelmed Roman Catholic priest from Glasgow. This fellow, Father Campbell, now appeared suddenly at the front of the church, vestments still wet from wherever he had been last. He twitched his chasuble straight and flung out his arms as if to embrace his whole Skye flock, who leapt to their feet, roaring a rather martial-sounding welcome.

"Did he manage it by himself this time?" Gil said to Diejen Lizp, who had appeared beside him at the same moment.

"No," she said. "I had to bring him. *None* of them can do it by themselves. They are worse than children."

Few human clerics had survived the invasion. Strangely enough, those that had almost all turned out to be mages. The genetic mutation for magic was more widespread than the CHEMICAL MAGE conspirators' data trawl had uncovered. But none of these 'mages' actually knew how to work magic.

Gil had brought a few of the esthesia implants designed

for CHEMICAL MAGE with him from the Betelgeuse system. He had offered them to the Priest Corps, but they'd all turned them down. Wisely, in Gil's opinion. They had all heard the story of what happened to Colm Mackenzie—his drug addiction, his slide down the slippery slope to black magic, and the way he'd disappeared over and over again, until he disappeared for the last time.

Lloyd Mackenzie had disappeared, too, even though he did *not* have an implant. That was an interesting mystery that Gil sometimes mulled in his private hours.

But it made him sad to think about Lloyd and Colm, and this was supposed to be a happy occasion.

He turned to Diejen Lizp. Her brother, Dhjerga, had disappeared, too. They had an unspoken pact not to mention it. Her hair and jacket were wet. "Where have you blown in from this time?"

"France. The weather was foul. There were too many ordinands to fit in the church, so what does this mad priest do? Postpone the ceremony until the weather improves? No, he holds it outside in the pouring rain."

"I wonder if holy orders would be so popular with the Ghosts," Gil muttered, "if there were enough girls to go around."

Diejen pretended to slap him. "Whatever works," she said. "Peace is better than war." Then she peered at him. *"You* are not thinking of taking holy orders, are you?"

"Absolutely not!" Gil said. "And now I must join the important people." He waved a foreleg at the raised sanctuary area, where the leading citizens of Skye were seated on handmade wooden benches. This was not a religious occasion; they were merely using the church. Father Campbell waved his arms, orchestrating the group of monks and locals who were rolling a large wooden cask up the aisle.

Diejen held him back by the scruff. "But you are lonely, Gilliam Tripsilion Nulth."

"Not at all. I am busy, busy, busy!" He swivelled his head around and nipped her wrist to make her let go.

"Ow." She rubbed her wrist with a rueful air. "I am busy, too, ferrying these bloody priests from one corner of Earth to another, and even to the colonies. I'm not complaining. It cannot be said too often: peace is better than war. Yet *I* am lonely." She admitted it with a simplicity that stunned Gil, to whom nothing was ever simple.

He cringed, said, "Perhaps you should get married," and fled before she could slap him in earnest.

Her brother Dryjon had married a girl from Kisperet. There he sat in the front row of the laity's side, with his wife and their two children. He winked at Gil and made a drinking gesture as the queazel undulated up the steps to the sanctuary. Pretending not to notice, Gil took the place of honor on the bench between Bridget Wilson and Axel Best.

The monks lifted the cask up the steps and placed it on a table. Father Campbell declared, "Here it is! The first cask of 2367 chardonnay from the Skye Wine Cooperative!"

Applause, and shouts of "Hope there's more where that came from."

Gil believed that life had to be about more than just survival. While the humans concentrated on staying alive, he—perversely, perhaps—had recruited a workforce of Ghosts to plant a vineyard. The climate of Skye was similar to the polar climate on Juradis, albeit wetter. He had never successfully grown grapes on Juradis. To his pleasure, they did better on their home planet.

"We have Gilliam Tripsilion Nulth to thank for this, so before we tap the cask, perhaps we could have a few words from you, Gil?"

"Certainly," said Gil, who had prepared extensive remarks on the challenges of winemaking. He rose, stood on his hindmost legs, and accepted the microphone from Father Campbell. He described the labor of breaking ground, the trial-and-error process of selecting the best grapes for the soil, and the factors he had considered when opting to store his vintage in wooden casks rather than clay jugs ("although we continue to experiment with amphorae, a technique the Ghosts inherit from their Roman forebears"). The journey, from first inspiration to imminent drinking, had taken ten years.

As he spoke, he focused on the familiar and beloved faces in the audience.

Dryjon Lizp, of course, with his wife Ansier and their four-year-old twins. Dryjon was rarely on Skye. Having taught himself electrical engineering, he was now helping to restore Earth's power grid.

Diejen sat on the other side of her sister-in-law Ansier. Even at forty-five she was still lovely, Gil understood, by human female standards, but her smile looked strained. He realized that it must actually have cost her rather a lot to admit to him that she was lonely.

He was not lonely. Oh, no. How could he be, with his workforce standing in the back of the church, and all his friends hanging eagerly on his words? There in the second row were six queazels, including three Nulths, who had travelled here on the third round-trip voyage of the

Unsinkable. They were inclined to treat Earth as an exotic tourist destination, but Gil planned to rope them into the effort to restore Earth's high-tech manufacturing capability.

It would be needed when the sentrienza attacked again.

FTL drones had recently brought news of a second assault on the Betelgeuse system. Admiral Hyland's much-expanded fleet had barely defeated the enemy force. Meanwhile, the Ghosts continued to report on Walking Guns harrying the colony worlds. One planet had been lost already. The human-queazel alliance remained vastly outnumbered and outgunned by the sentrienza empire. And the Gray Emperor's extinction protocol was still in effect, as far as they knew. The vast distances that the sentrienza fleets must cover to reach this tiny corner of space had given them time to regroup, but it would not last forever.

They ought to be focusing on ship-building. Not *wine-making.*

But only a few people had the expertise to build ships. And what was everyone else to do, while they waited for the blow to fall? Simply cower?

No, they must carry on living,

Gil had learned this lesson from one person above all: Megumi Smythe-Best. She sat in the third row, grinning at him and meaningfully tapping her watch. Beside her sat eight-year-old Phil and two-year-old Yuai. Meg had suffered the worst trauma imaginable: the loss of a child. One did not recover from something like that. But one could keep going, and Meg had shown them all how it was done.

Gil segued with renewed ardor into the section of his remarks that dealt with barrel-making. He was describing the pitfalls of forging metal bands—they had first had to build a forge! But it also came in handy for making horseshoes and pots and pans—when someone tapped his hindquarters. He glanced around. Axel whispered, through a solemn and attentive expression, "Maybe wrap it up? Not sure they need quite this much detail, and everyone's getting thirsty …"

Oh.

Realizing that Axel was probably right, Gil skipped the section about their first four, failed, vintages. Everyone knew about those, anyway.

He had wanted to conclude on a personal note, by telling them how his adventures in wine-making had cured his own dependency on alcohol and drugs. Strange but true: making wine substituted for drinking it. Nor did he any longer feel tempted to take pills or inject himself with stimulants, in search of some vaguely imagined peace. But actually, his cure owed more to the community on Skye than it did to his new hobby. By immersing himself in human life, he had outgrown his taste for human vices. And he did not really need to tell them about that. They could see it for themselves. He mentally shelved that section, too, for some future occasion.

"This concludes my remarks."

Heartfelt applause.

"I would now like to accord the honor of tapping the cask to a human we all hold in the highest regard …" Gil extended a forepaw to a silver-haired woman sitting behind him. "Daisy Mackenzie!"

Amidst cheers, Daisy rose. Still active at eighty-three, she was a universally beloved mother figure to the Skye community. She, too, had lost a child.

"Let's be having it," she said cheerfully.

After a ceremonial hammer-blow from Daisy, the cask was

tapped by a brawny Ghost, a spigot inserted. Gil poured the first glass of pale chardonnay and handed it to Daisy.

She sipped. Her mouth pursed up.

"Sakes, that's disgusting."

Father Campbell was next to sample the vintage. "Crisp," he said. "Light. Fine. It's got potential." He hurriedly handed the glass on to someone else.

After everyone had tasted the wine, Gil regretfully concurred with the consensus that it was undrinkable. This failure did not sadden him overmuch. They were getting closer to drinkability with every batch. And the Scots being Scots, and the Ghosts being Ghosts, the awful wine provided more fodder for merriment than a decent vintage would have.

"We can always use it for Communion wine," Father Campbell said.

They were milling around in the body of the church now, sharing mugs of hoppy ale made by a cooperative in Portree. Gil had foresightedly got in several barrels of ale just in case the wine turned out bad. The children had hot milk with honey.

"I wouldn't mind some of that," rasped a Scottish voice behind Gil.

The queazel turned. He found himself facing an elderly human male in a long black coat. The man held a tabby cat in his arms.

"Welcome," said Father Campbell, who clearly did not recognize the elderly man either. "Are you visiting the island?"

"This is my grandfather's house, ye upstart."

A cry pierced the hubbub of conversation. "Daddy!?"

Bridget Wilson hurtled through the crowd. Her face glowed.

"I don't believe it! Daddy!" She embraced the elderly man, cat and all.

A heartbeat behind her was Daisy Mackenzie. She faced the elderly man squarely. Her eyes glittered with tears. "You don't look a day older," she said.

He gently folded her in his arms and kissed the top of her silver head. "Neither do you, my love."

CHAPTER 58

Outside the church, Colm waited with Nicky in his arms, shivering in the twilight. The slanting light and the mildness of the air, tempered by an evening chill, felt like summer. Runner beans and redcurrants garlanded stakes in the back garden. Yet they had left in winter. It must have taken a full six months for them to travel to Elphame and back.

Oh well; he was just glad to see the Free Church Manse still standing. Looked like his family has made some improvements, too. Apart from the garden, which was coming on beautifully, they'd cut down those scruffy old pines and planted what appeared to be oak saplings. A new extension abutted the gable end of the house—an odd little lean-to with a child-sized door. The church had received a coat of paint, and a new cross surmounted its roof ridge. A diesel generator stood against the west wall of the church, rumbling quietly. That would be the power source they'd flitted to. He'd been a bit worried that there wouldn't be one. Had been braced to wind up in the back of some abandoned truck a hundred miles from home.

But here they were. "Here we are, Nicky. Home." He smelled clover, and manure. Horses. The smell took him back to Kisperet, and for a debilitating second he didn't know where was home and where was here.

Dhjerga came around the church. "Your father's gone in," he hissed excitedly. "Come on!" The doors stood open, and a happy buzz of conversation emerged. Colm felt reluctant to charge straight in, as Lloyd had done.

"Look at all those horse carts, Nicky," he said, stalling.

"And cars!" But Nicky was too tired to be interested in cars. He was riding on Colm's hip, floppy with sleepiness, sucking his thumb. "Let's go into the house," Colm said. He felt ridiculously nervous.

The back door was ajar, the kitchen bustling and warm. Strangers stood around chatting. They raised their eyebrows at Colm, Dhjerga, and Nicky, and conversation ceased.

Colm smiled weakly. This was *his* house. What were all these strangers doing here? A teenage boy was pouring hot milk from a pan on the stove into mugs. Colm said, gesturing with his free arm, "I was just wondering could I have a cup of milk for the child …"

The boy dropped his pan on the floor. His voice cracked. "Uncle Colm?!?"

Colm backed away as the penny dropped.

This was Bridget's son Ivor.

He was no longer a child.

He was almost grown up.

How long had they been away?

*

"Ten years," Meg said. She stood in the doorway of the kitchen, holding a little girl the same age as Nicky. Axel, behind her, rested his hands on her shoulders. Both of them looked older. Gray in their hair. Ten bloody years? "You left *ten years ago,* Colm. We thought you were never coming back."

"I've brought Nicky home," Colm said, idiotically, as if Meg might not have noticed.

Meg's face was stone. Then it cracked. Passing the little girl to Axel, she crossed the room and snatched Nicky from Colm. "Oh my sweetheart, my little love."

"Mommy," Nicky cooed, clinging to her. As far as he knew,

he had only been parted from his mother yesterday.

Meg rocked him, her face wet. Nicky struggled and stretched out his arms to Axel. "Daddy!"

Ouch. Well, as far as Nicky was concerned, Axel *was* his daddy.

Axel and Meg held up Nicky and the little girl, face to face, playfully introducing them. Meg laughed excitedly— "Look, would you look at this, everyone, they're the same age!"

"They are not," Lloyd said, swaying in with a mug of beer. "Nicky's ten years older."

"Oh, I know, but look! It's like we've got twins, honey." She was speaking to Axel.

Bridget came in with a small boy who had Meg's eyes and Axel's fabulous cheekbones. It was just dawning on Colm that Meg and Axel had had more children since he left. *Two* more, in fact. "This is Phil," Bridget said. "Named after Axel's dad."

"Hi, Phil," Colm said. He rubbed his eyes, which were smarting. "I can't wrap my head around this, Bridget." She had gray hairs, too. She must be fifty. She was older than him now. She was supposed to be his *little* sister.

Axel squeezed through the crowd and pulled Colm into a hug. "You're badass. Un-fucking-believable, man. So good to see you."

Axel's warm welcome seemed to be unfeigned. Colm had been braced for hostility. Thrown off-balance, he reminded himself that time heals all wounds. And Axel had had a lot longer to heal than he had. "Thanks for keeping the home fires burning. Any excitement while we were away?"

"Sure. You haven't lived until you've lived on a farm. It's not all wine-tasting and hymn-singing, you know. Try shearing sheep with a low-power laser!"

Colm smiled. His gaze travelled past Axel. Lloyd was sitting in his old place by the fire, recounting their adventures. His rapt audience included Meg, who was holding Nicky, rocking from foot to foot. Her face had filled out some, as well as acquiring new laughter lines and crow's-feet. She looked confident. Grounded. "Axel …" Colm started, and didn't know how to go on.

Lloyd said something that made everyone laugh. Meg, throwing back her head in mid-laugh, caught Colm's eye. She came over to them, carrying Nicky. "Thank you," she said to Colm. "You're officially my hero."

Then she passed Nicky off to Axel. She stepped closer to Colm and rose on tiptoe, so she could whisper into his ear.

"This is your home. But it's my home, now, too. And Axel's my husband." He saw the ring on her finger then. "We tied the knot last year; it was about time. So don't get any ideas about revisiting the past, 'kay?" She slyly pinched his cheek. "You'd be a sucky father, anyway. You're much better at wasting aliens than changing diapers."

Both shocked and relieved, Colm laughed out loud. "You're all right, Gunny."

"Just leave the diaper-changing thing to the Marines," Axel said with a grin.

"Spoken like a true hero," Colm said. He could not take his eyes off Nicky's little face on Axel's shoulder, sticky eyelashes sealed, rosebud lips open. He felt a wrenching pang of loss. But he couldn't make any noise about his paternal rights. This was justice. Nicky had been his son for only a day. He had been Axel's all his life.

"OK," Meg said. "Now here's what you need to know in terms of the overall security situation." Suddenly she was all soldier again. "We're doing pretty good here, but we're living on borrowed time. We are anticipating the arrival of a sentrienza fleet from the Orion Nebula in roughly nineteen months."

"The Gray Emperor's dead," Colm said in disbelief.

"Is he?"

"Yes! I killed him."

Over by the fire, Lloyd was recounting Colm's feat with the Walking Guns. "He turned them on their own masters …"

"Nice job," Meg said. "Problem is, the news hasn't reached the rest of the sentrienza empire yet."

Colm remembered that he'd come home at the speed of thought, which was much, much faster than any FTL drone. He wondered just how far away Elphame really was, and shivered. He might've been on the far side of the galaxy.

"And when they do find out you whacked the Gray Emperor," Meg continued, "how do you think they'll react? Think mayyybe they'll be even madder at us?"

"Oh Christ. I've screwed up again, haven't I?"

"Nah. Destroying Elphame was a big win. But we're going to have to *keep* winning … again … and again …. and again. We have to win every time. They only have to win once."

"Well, what's our operational status?"

"One ship. No, you didn't hear me wrong. We have *one* ship: the *Unsinkable*. Everything else is at Juradis, or the colony worlds. The Rat—who's pretty much the leader of humanity now, I have to warn you—already had to fight off one fleet at Betelgeuse, and that didn't go so well."

"We lost?"

"We survived. Barjoltan didn't."

Colm stiffened. "This is stupid, but … Gilliam Tripsilion

Nulth?" He had a horrible vision of the queazel dying at his post on Barjoltan. "Do you know if he survived?"

Axel laughed. "Gil? Colm, he's *here!*"

"He is?!"

"Yeah!" They all glanced around the kitchen. No furry Slinky was to be seen.

"He's probably drunk off his ass somewhere," Axel shrugged.

"Speaking of which, you deserve this." Meg put a mug of beer into Colm's hand. "So what it comes down to is, we're operationally on our own. I don't wanna make this sound like a guilt trip ... but we could seriously use your help."

"Right." Colm felt like slitting his wrists at the very thought of going back into action, *again.* "There isn't anyone else?"

"There isn't any other mage who can pilot a spaceship."

There was Dhjerga. But Dhjerga's idea of piloting a spaceship was a combination of flitting and suicidal button-mashing. He rubbed the left side of his head. "Where's Dhjerga gone, anyway?"

CHAPTER 59

Gil lay on the floor of his house, worrying the nails of his left forepaw with his teeth. His other legs were curled up and tucked inside the coil of his body. His house was the extension built onto the end of the Free Church Manse. It had two storeys of queazel height, and a door so low that human beings had to crawl to get through it, unless they were less than four feet high. Generally, the only people who visited Gil at home were children.

But now someone was knocking at his front door, and the children never knocked.

He uncoiled himself and scurried up the ladder to the second floor. He did not want to see anyone.

Colm was back, and with him had come the crushing weight of Gil's guilt. He was a coward, a hopeless coward. He hid under his bed.

The front door opened, and a voice that was not Colm's called, "Queazel, are you there?"

A mostly bald head poked up through the hatch from the first floor. It belonged to Lloyd Mackenzie.

"There you are," Lloyd said, catching sight of Gil underneath the bed. "Jesus, you're a funny-looking creature."

"It is an honor to meet you, too," Gil said. It was impossible to crawl out from under the bed with dignity. He brushed the dust bunnies off his fur and dipped his head to Colm's father.

Lloyd laughed. His breath smelt of booze. "Sorry I didn't introduce myself properly earlier. I'm Colm's dad."

"I know."

Lloyd extended a hand and shook one of Gil's foreclaws. At that moment a hissing noise came from below. A cat shot past Lloyd, ears flat, and hid under Gil's bed, where he had just been.

"Mickle! Mickle!" Lloyd said. He climbed up onto the second floor and reached under the bed, then gave up. His eyes gleamed as he regarded Gil. "You look a bit like a cat, don't you?"

"I most certainly do not," Gil said. "Cats are animals. Queazels are people. And if you do not remove your pet from my house, I shall eat it."

"Ah, come on," Lloyd said. "We're all animals. It's just some of us are animals with souls."

"Can I help you with anything, Mr. Mackenzie?"

"Colm's in the house. He was wondering why you didn't come and say hello."

"I—I—I ruined his life. The CHEMICAL MAGE project destroyed his health and his career. And now it has robbed him of ten years in his family's company. How should I face him?"

"He's not doing too badly, for all that," Lloyd said. "But you're right. You must atone for what you did."

He continued to speak, telling Gil what he must do.

"I cannot," Gil interrupted. "I cannot." He dived back under the bed, forgetting that Lloyd's cat was under there already. A hiss alerted him to her presence. Round black queazel eyes met slitty green cat eyes. After a moment, Gil realized that this cat was not like other cats. There was something … he could not put his claw on it … something *different* about her.

He slithered back out to where Lloyd was sitting on the

floor, calmly smoking a cigarette as he waited. "Your cat is not like other cats," he said grudgingly.

"Damn right," Lloyd said. "She's my familiar."

"Your what?"

"That's what I've been trying to explain to you." Suddenly a knock sounded on the door below.

"I shall be driven to distraction," Gil growled. "Yes? What is it?"

"It's just me," Diejen Lizp's voice came through the door. "Can I come in? Please?"

*

In the kitchen, the fuss was dying down. Lloyd had wandered outside for a smoke. Colm was sitting in his place by the fire, eating a slab of delicious meat pie and thinking drearily about sentrienza fleets. Nicky had gone to sleep in Axel's arms. "We'd better put him to bed," Meg murmured.

A little voice buzzed, "I have made up another bed in the children's room."

Colm jumped a mile, nearly dropping his piece of pie.

The speaker was a sentrienza.

In fact, it was Emnl ki-Sharongat, the former princess of Betelgeuse. She looked very odd indeed in a fleece and cargo pants. Her massive braid of lavender hair was looped twice around her head to keep it out of the way.

"You're an angel, Emmie," Meg said. "Did Phil go to sleep with his clothes on?"

"No, he is wearing his pyjamas. I also made him brush his teeth."

"Emnl's fantastic with the kids," Meg said to Colm. "We call her our faerie godmother."

Emnl reached up to Nicky and lightly stroked his cheek.

Her eyes glowed, the membranes sliding down over them.

Axel said, "Yup; here he is. Home at last."

"And you are home, too," Emnl said to Colm.

"I am." He wondered for how long.

"I wanted to be the one to unravel the mystery of magic," Emnl said. Her eyes glowed with something that he took for regret. He frankly could not believe Meg and Axel allowed her near their children. "I thought, naturally, that scientific experimentation would be the way to get to the bottom of it. But now I know there is a better way. I have learned so much just by living with magic." She spread her little four-fingered hands. "Just living!"

Axel whispered, "She's OK. She really is."

Colm was hearing echoes of the Gray Emperor's paeans to experience. Emnl was still a sentrienza. But maybe that wasn't necessarily a bad thing.

"I look forward to learning more about magic from you," Emnl said to Colm. "But the rest of my people do not understand the way of living that I have discovered, the Way of the Empty Hand."

"Karate," Meg translated. "We're still working together. Emnl's a black belt now."

"Yes. They must be taught the lessons I have learned. And I fear the only way to teach them will be by example."

"By example?" Colm said.

"By blowing up a great many of them, of course," Emnl said matter-of-factly. "They respect strength." She studied him. "Did you *really* kill the Gray Emperor? He was supposed to be immortal."

Com spread his hands. "The planet blew up. If he survived that, I've no doubt the Magus will sort him out."

"Even immortals cannot withstand magic," Emnl whispered ecstatically. "And you will do it again? Blowing up planets—yes, that is good. That will be a powerful demonstration. You should start with Harridulast, in the Orion Nebula—the King of the Nebula is revoltingly arrogant. Then I can make you a list of other targets, ranked by proximity and political importance."

Meg nudged her teasingly. "A.k.a. a list of your personal enemies?"

Emnl giggled. "We sentrienza know how to pick the winning side. I shall endeavor to convince them to pick the side of humanity."

"We've built a spaceport right here on Skye," Axel said to Colm. "Got a shuttle to go up and down to the *Unsinkable*."

"Sounds like you've got it all arranged," Colm said with a rictus grin. Then he murmured an excuse, stuffed the last bite of pie into his mouth, and went outside.

*

Dhjerga walked up the hill, away from the horses standing quietly in the back field. The beasts were well cared for, their coats brushed and their hooves shod. Everywhere he looked, he saw the signs of Ghost craftsmanship and animal husbandry. It wearied him a little—the attention to detail, the conservative adherence to formula. This narrow focus had doomed the Magus. They had exchanged a few words in private before Dhjerga and the others left the Elphame system. "Well, deserter," the Magus had said. "Are you happy with what you have wrought?"

Dhjerga had wanted to say yes, to rub his victory in the Magus's face. But something about his old commanding officer compelled him to honesty. "I am not happy," he had said. "I don't know if I will ever be happy."

The Magus had glanced at Drest, who was playing with the dolphin-like alien in the shallow water. "I am happy," he had said with the simplicity of that elder time he came from. "I have got what I warred for. What were you warring for?"

"Freedom," Dhjerga said.

The word had hung there in the air of that unfinished Faerieland, stale and inadequate.

Now Dhjerga was climbing in the evening between long straight rows of bushes. The sun had gone down, but there was still plenty of light to see by. Lemon washed the eastern sky, fading into violet in the west. He could hear the sea.

It was so peaceful here. And yet Dhjerga did not feel at peace.

At the top of the hill stood a square building that, he had been told, housed the wine press and crush pad. He looked west across rumpled fields. Ridges of rock pushed through the meager soil. Cows and sheep dotted the slopes. A pocket-sized loch reflected the twinkling lights of a spear-shaped tower that stood by the road around it.

A tower?

Dhjerga sucked power from the wine press, and flitted.

The Son of Saturn!

He laughed out loud to see it, and let out a glad shout when he saw Dryjon sitting on the bottom rung of the *SOS's* ladder. "I've been *looking* for you!"

The brothers embraced. Dryjon was older now, of course. "I've caught up with you," he said.

"By Scota's grave, you actually look like a grownup."

"Speaking of Scota's grave, I've had a proper tunnel made, with guide ropes and electric lights," Dryjon said cheerfully.

"It's quite the tourist attraction." Then his smile died. "Are you going, then?"

"I think so," Dhjerga said. He had not known it himself until that moment.

Dryjon gestured up at the *Son Of Saturn*. "I've had her fueled and checked over for you."

Dhjerga's mouth twitched ruefully. Dryjon had known he'd be going away again before he himself had. "What's *that?*" he said, indicating the new lettering on the fairing.

"Oh, she was sitting out on Juradis for five years, and then sitting out here for another five. She needed a paint job. So I thought I'd give her a new name while I was at it. Do you like it?" Dryjon said hopefully.

The five-foot letters read: *NUCLEAR DRUID.*

"I'm going to be the faeries' worst nightmare come to liffe," Dhjerga said, rubbing his hands.

"I hope Colm likes it."

Dhjerga grimaced. "I'm pretty sure he's not ..."

"Not what?"

"Not coming."

Before Dryjon could answer, an enormous form waddled around the spaceship, dragging a hose. "We can start LOX fueling anytime. Oh, hello, Dhjerga!" It was Drest—the original Drest. He wore a custom-sized mechanic's overall, and had grease on his huge hands. Dhjerga smiled, remembering the copy of Drest he had left in the Elphame system. His last copy ever had been a good one.

"You can't go by yourself," Dryjon said.

"Why not, brother? I've done everything by myself as long as I can remember."

"Is that really what you think?"

CHAPTER 60

Colm stumbled out of the house. He was sweaty and jittery. The meat pie he'd eaten sat like a rock in his stomach. He had come out to get some fresh air, but also to take a hit of tropodolfin without anyone noticing. He went around to the front of the manse, where the cars and horse carts were parked. They had left some of the pines standing here, and the trees were taller now. At the end of the track, numerous small boats were drawn up on the beach.

He dug in his pockets for his tropo, and found a stone from the beach where they had left the Magus and Drest. It was flat and round. He flipped it like a coin.   Heads I take the *Unsinkable* to the Orion Nebula and blow up some more planets. He pictured himself coming back in another ten years, when Meg and Axel's children, and Nicky, would be nearly grown. Don't worry, kids, it's just your junkie uncle come home for a bit of R&R. Tails I walk down to the beach and just keep walking. Both sides of the stone looked the same.

A soft voice said, "Colm?"

He startled. Whipped his hand out of his pocket.

Diejen Lizp walked out from behind the church. She was wearing Earth clothes: jeans and an anorak. Her hair fell to her shoulders in a wavy bob.

Colm cleared his throat nervously. "Thought you were avoiding me."

"I was hiding." She stopped in front of him. The extra ten years suited her. Her face looked more defined. Kinder.

"Why?"

She stared him in the eye. "Am I still too young for you?"

Colm reached out for her, and then came to his senses and dropped his arms. He turned away, jaw clenching. "Oh Jesus, Diejen. You don't want me. I'm a junkie. I came out here to pop a pill without anyone seeing. I'm so screwed up."

"You defeated the Magus."

"Not really. We just sort of talked it out. He did most of the talking."

"You slew the Gray Emperor."

"I blew up his entire fucking star system. Millions of sapient beings must've died. *Billions.* I can't stop thinking about it." But he would be able to stop thinking about it if he took tropo. Swallow enough of those little beauties and all he'd have to think about was where to get more.

Diejen bit her lip. Her face in the twilight brought back memories of that twilight party in Ilfenjium where he had pursued her and Gaethla Moro to the zoo, seething with jealousy. Twilight on Kisperet lasted for days, but this was Earth and the light would soon be gone.

"The old ways are dead," she said. "All that is left for us is to move back to Earth and place ourselves at the mercy of the Christian God. It is not easy for me."

Colm held up his pack of tropo in a crooked salute. "It's not easy for me, either. But I suppose I've got to try. To save everyone." He started back towards the house; hesitated. "Thank you. If you hadn't been here, I might have done something stupid."

"Might have?" she flashed. "You are *always* doing something stupid!"

"I've got to *go,*" Colm said desperately, and plunged away around the house. He strode through the people trickling out from the house towards the back field, brushing off everyone who wanted to offer him their best wishes. Halfway up the hill, he realized it was full dark and he couldn't see for shit. He barked his shin on a grape plant. Whose stupid idea had it been to plant a vineyard on Skye, anyway? "Ah, fuck it," he muttered. Mages don't have to walk. They travel at the speed of thought, and never mind if that means their thoughts come with them, like a ball and chain. He took the hit of tropo, and flitted.

He came to himself on a launch pad ringed by floodlights. Axel hadn't been kidding. They really had built a spaceport.

Just a flexible concrete pad, and a hangar, and some fuel tanks. Still, it was a spaceport, and Colm's heart lightened further when he saw the spaceship standing on the pad.

It was the freaking *Son of Saturn!*

Dhjerga came out of the hangar with Dryjon and—Jesus, that was Drest, wearing a mechanic's overall. Dhjerga came over to Colm, grinning. "I was just going to pop back and say goodbye."

"Goodbye?" Colm scoffed. "Did you figure you could leave me behind? Forgotten whose ship this is?"

"It's not really big enough for the both of us, *and* the smell of your feet," Dhjerga said.

"That's why we're not going to take *this* ship," Colm said. Seeing the incomprehension on Dhjerga's face, he grinned. "And this is why you need me along."

Dryjon offered cigarettes around. Colm took one and sat down on the bottom rung of the *SOS's* ladder, wanting to savor the summer air for just a few more minutes. He had been on leave, but now leave was over. The harsh lights at the edges of the pad buzzed, attracting moths. The breeze carried the scent of heather, a sweet topnote to the launch pad smells of machine oil and lightly toasted thermal tiling. Nicotine blended with tropo in his veins, making him feel that none of it very much mattered.

"Do you remember," Dhjerga said, "on Juradis, long ago, you said: *if we joined forces, no one could stop us?*"

Colm laughed at the memory. "Sure. Famous last words."

"It's true though, isn't it? We blew up the fucking faerie emperor. That felt like the end, but it wasn't. It was the beginning."

"Right," Colm said, gazing up into the sky, where the floodlights blacked out the first stars of the evening.

Dryjon took it up. "We humans are the rightful rulers of the galaxy. This is the beginning of the age of humanity. No other species has a hope of stopping us, if we're careful and don't over-extend ourselves."

"Fuck being careful," Dhjerga said. "We're going to conquer the entire fucking universe! The Magus will be sitting on Elphame eating his heart out with envy."

Colm studied Dhjerga. There was that glint of berserker craziness in his eyes, just the same as the first day Colm had ever seen him on Majriti IV. Colm had a little insight: Dhjerga had never really stopped fighting the Magus's war. He'd just differed with the Magus as to their aims. Despite his troublesome conscience, he was a warrior born, who'd never be happy unless he was blowing shit up.

You need friends like that.

Colm stubbed out his cigarette with his boot. "All right. Let's go."

There ensued a lot of cursing at the fuel gauges and temperature controls. Colm had to open several hatches on the engineering deck, visually check the wiring, and tighten up a couple of connections. An hour passed before he considered the *SOS* safe to launch.

He and Dhjerga climbed to the crew capsule, wearing their spacesuits—real spacesuits, brought from Juradis, with Fleet insignia. As he proceeded with the launch countdown, headlights bounced down the hill. A convoy of cars pulled up at the launch pad, and Colm's entire family jumped out, along with Meg and Axel and a whole gang of monks. They clustered at the distant edge of the launch pad.

Colm cued the PA system in the hangar, which could be remotely controlled from the ship. "Stand the hell back, everyone." His eyes watered as he gazed at the external feed screen. Meg. Axel. Nicky. His parents, arm in arm. All of them waving, their lips forming the word: *Godspeed, Colm.* He looked for Diejen, but she wasn't there.

"Put your helmet on," he said to Dhjerga, as he initiated the main drive. The ship began to vibrate.

"Why?" Dhjerga said, sprawled in the navigator's couch with his feet up.

"It's standard procedure."

"I flew the *Son of Saturn* from Kisperet to Juradis without one of these stupid suits," objected Dhjerga. He still didn't really get the difference between flying and flitting. Well, fair enough. For them, it was a continuum now.

"Yeah," Colm countered, "but one, you're crazy, and two, if we're going to conquer the galaxy, we're going to do it by Navy rules. And three, I'm going to be crying and cursing my fate all the way up to orbit, and I don't want you listening in."

"Cursing fate?" Dhjerga's smiling eyes darkened. "I'm good at that."

So they flew up to low Earth orbit shouting out the worst

curses they could think of, forcing the words out while clenching their muscles against the launch gees, in English and Teanga, until the words gave way to wordless battle yells. A few tears may have been shed, but absorbent helmet liners tell no tales.

The *Unsinkable* awaited them at 180 kilometers, looming out of the blackness in all her ungainly glory, like a skyscraper in orbit. Colm had not seen her for three years or thirteen years, depending on who was counting. It felt good to liaise with her remote systems and fly the *Son Of Saturn* into the familiar flight deck doors. Better not to think about what came next.

CHAPTER 61

There was a skeleton crew on board the *Unsinkable*, station-keeping. "Hi," Colm said. "I'm hijacking the ship."

"Son," said the veteran officer in charge, "I've been in the Navy since the year dot. Been fighting this war since the beginning. I've seen planets lost, planets regained. Seen Earth colonized by our long-lost cousins from Rho fucking Cassiopeiae. Seen alliances shift and flip on their heads. Now the sentrienza are the bad guys, and the Ghosts—" a nod to his own deputy, a Ghost— "are the good guys. Forty years ago I'd've laughed in your face if you told me how this was gonna end up. So you might say I've seen it all. But I have *never* seen a first lieutenant trying to hijack a carrier."

Colm laughed. "Better days are coming." His words were positive, his smile artificial. Fake it till you make it.

The crew got on the radio to Dryjon, who confirmed that Colm was to be given charge of the *Unsinkable*. Before they left on the supercarrier's single transfer shuttle, they fired up the textile printer on Deck 36 and made Colm a joke pair of admiral's shoulderboards. Dhjerga got the unofficial rank of captain. The veteran officer also presented them with joke t-shirts, which matched the *Son Of Saturn's* new name. Fluorescent letters on a Navy blue background spelt out NUCLEAR DRUID.

Colm and Dhjerga spent the next couple of days roaming the ship and double-checking the stores of water and Pink Slime. Colm had discovered during his travels with the *Shihoka* that Pink Slime could be fetched. He figured it counted as living, which did not make the prospect of eating nothing else for weeks or months any more pleasant. But hey, it came in three flavors!

They also test-fired the *Unsinkable's* guns at defunct satellites. The carrier had been extensively refitted at Barjoltan. She now had a keel-mounted railgun that fired projectiles fast enough that they could probably vaporize the moon if Colm pointed the gun the wrong way. The smaller coilguns he remembered were still operational, too, and a special ammo magazine held half a hundred nuclear rounds in vibration-proof, radiation-proof cradles. "Full marks to the Rat," Colm murmured.

The King of the Nebula was never going to know what hit him.

At last they were ready to leave. With a mage at the helm, the concept of the zero-gravity point was obsolete: the *Unsinkable* could go FTL from low Earth orbit.

Colm paced the bridge, moving from station to station, doing the job of thirty officers. Green lights across the board. All that remained was to juice up his own messy system. He'd been dialing back his tropo intake since they boarded, managing his tolerance downwards so that he wouldn't have to take so much when it was time to flit. He would be doing this for the rest of his life. It was important not to kill himself too quickly. Grit crunched under his bare feet; he was wearing nothing but his NUCLEAR DRUID t-shirt and a pair of shorts, his commitment to protocol having fallen by the wayside now that they were alone.

He paused to gaze at the sensor officer's screen, which showed Earth spinning past below.

"Cheer the fuck up," said Dhjerga, sitting crosslegged in the captain's couch, gobbling a last real meal of salt pork and turnip stew, which he was sopping up with flatbread, Ghost style. The turnips smelled extremely pungent.

"I wonder how many years it'll be before I murder you for making those noises when you eat," Colm said.

"I can smell your feet from here," Dhjerga said.

"No, that's those turnips you're smelling."

"Want some?"

"Stuff 'em up your arse," Colm smiled. He poured some orange juice into his Nessie mug and downed his pills. Contemplatively, he finished the orange juice. How many years would it be before he tasted that again? When the mug was empty, he made it fly over to Dhjerga and bonk him on the head. "Ready?"

"Ow! Let me just finish my—"

Colm flew the Nessie mug over the captain's couch, making it loop the loop like a swallow, and flitted.

"—lunch," Dhjerga said, one immeasurable interval of agony later. He gloomily set his bowl aside. It was now half full of disgusting smelly goop.

"Wow." Colm goggled at the optical feed on the big screen. The *Unsinkable* had popped out in a void so full of hot gas clouds that it hardly looked dark. So this was the Orion Nebula! He wished he could feel excited about it.

Something went *thump* outside the bridge.

Colm and Dhjerga leapt for their guns.

The pressure door rattled. Someone was banging on it.

They exchanged a puzzled look.

With a thought, Colm checked the internal camera feed for the corridor.

He had to be dreaming.

"There's a biometric recognition plate," he said, as if in a trance. "It doesn't recognize you." He went over and opened the door.

Diejen walked in.

"Hello," she said to her brother. Then she wrapped her arms around Colm, dragged his head down, and kissed him on the lips.

Colm surrendered to the kiss for an infinite, achingly sweet moment. Her body fitted against his so perfectly. She filled all the hollows in his body and his soul. Her mouth tasted of noak leaves, a bitter tang that brought Kisperet back to life in his mind.

Then he held her off, half laughing, half furious. "How did you get here?"

"We flitted to the *Unsinkable* while you were flitting here, of course. The void we travel through is only your zero-gravity field."

"Oh, Diejen." He heard the *we* but disregarded it, trapped by her gaze.

"If I had to wait another ten years," she said, "I would be dead of longing."

Colm clutched her close again with a sob of sheer gratitude. "Me too," he muttered.

Dhjerga cleared his throat. They broke apart. Dhjerga was smirking. "Doomed to conquer the galaxy with my little sister at my side? I can think of much worse fates."

"I must warn you, however," Diejen said. "I did not come alone."

Overwhelmed by her presence, Colm had not noticed the sound of scratching at the door. Now he did. He slapped it open.

Gilliam Tripsilion Nulth burst into the bridge and leapt into his arms. In the half-gravity of the bridge, the impact knocked Colm flat onto his back. Gil sprawled on his chest, their faces inches apart. His muzzle wrinkled in a queazel smile. His black eyes were luminous. "I have never experienced anything so horrible," he said. "Why was I not warned?"

"I did warn you," Diejen said, laughing.

"Gil—it's *you?* Not a copy?" Colm couldn't understand how that was even possible.

"I am *not* a pet," Gil said warningly.

"No one said you were," Colm said, puzzled.

"I am *not* an animal."

"I suppose we're all animals, in a sense …"

"That is what your father said." Gil scrambled off Colm, allowing him to sit up. "It is thanks to him I am here."

Now Colm understood. He crouched to look the queazel in the eye. "Gilliam Tripsilion Nulth, will you be my familiar?"

"I am here," Gil said. "And you are answered."

He undulated onto his hind feet and gazed at the big screen. "My heavens," he said. "Look at all those stars."

THIS CONCLUDES THE
EXTINCTION PROTOCOL
SERIES.

THANK YOU FOR READING!

DISCOVER THE ADVENTUROUS WORLDS OF FELIX R. SAVAGE

An exuberant storyteller with a demented imagination, Felix R. Savage specializes in creating worlds so exciting, you'll never want to leave.

Join the Savage Stories newsletter to get notified of new releases and opportunities to download free books:

www.felixrsavage.com/subscribe

EARTH'S LAST GAMBIT

A Quartet of Present-Day Science Fiction Technothrillers

Ripped from the headlines: an alien spaceship is orbiting Europa. Relying only on existing technology, a handful of elite astronauts must confront the threat to Earth's future, on their own, millions of miles from home.

Can the chosen few overcome technological limitations and their own weaknesses and flaws? Will Earth's Last Gambit win survival for the human race?

Freefall
Lifeboat
Shiplord
Killshot

THE SOL SYSTEM RENEGADES SERIES

Near-Future Hard Science Fiction

A genocidal AI is devouring our solar system. Can a few brave men and women save humanity?

In the year 2288, humanity stands at a crossroads between space colonization and extinction. Packed with excitement, heartbreak, and unforgettable characters, the Sol System Renegades series tells a sweeping tale of struggle and deliverance.

THE RELUCTANT ADVENTURES OF FLETCHER CONNOLLY ON THE INTERSTELLAR RAILROAD

Near-Future Non-Hard Science Fiction

An Irishman in space. Untold hoards of alien technological relics waiting to be discovered. What could possibly go wrong?

Skint Idjit
Intergalactic Bogtrotter
Banjaxed Ceili
Supermassive Blackguard

Made in the USA
Columbia, SC
30 December 2017